"A powerful and compelling novel about one family's dramatic resurrection after the devastation of the Chicago fire."

—Elizabeth Camden, author, *The Spice King*

"*Veiled in Smoke* offers a story line that draws the reader into the personal lives and historical events of nineteenth-century Chicago on the eve of the Great Fire. Jocelyn Green is a masterful storyteller who understands the power of the narrative tale and its impact on historical reality."

—Kevin Doerksen, CTG; owner, Wild Onion Walks Chicago; president, Chicago Tour Guide Professionals Association

"In *Veiled in Smoke*, Green frames a story of loss and redemption with sensory details, a nuanced historical backdrop, and an intelligent eye for flawed and utterly engaging characters. Shadows of the ongoing War Between the States as well as a deep literary resonance underscore what is, at its core, a study of the fallacies and strengths of the human heart. Green's eye for suspense is coupled with her passion for an American city on the rise. A thoroughly enriching and thoughtful reading experience by an absolute master of inspirational fiction."

—Rachel McMillan, author, *Murder in the City of Liberty*

Veiled in Smoke

Books by Jocelyn Green

THE WINDY CITY SAGA

Veiled in Smoke

The Mark of the King
A Refuge Assured
Between Two Shores

Veiled in Smoke

JOCELYN GREEN

Published by Bethany House Publishers
11400 Hampshire Avenue South
Bloomington, Minnesota 55438
www.bethanyhouse.com

Bethany House Publishers is a division of
Baker Publishing Group, Grand Rapids, Michigan

Printed in the United States of America

Library of Congress Control Number: 2019949898

ISBN 978-0-7642-3330-2 (trade paper)
ISBN 978-0-7642-3549-8 (cloth)

Scripture quotations are from the King James Version of the Bible.

This is a work of historical reconstruction; the appearances of certain historical figures are therefore inevitable. All other characters, however, are products of the author's imagination, and any resemblance to actual persons, living or dead, is coincidental.

Cover design by Dan Thornberg, Design Source Creative Services

Author is represented by Credo Communications, LLC

20 21 22 23 24 25 26 7 6 5 4 3 2 1

To all those who feel wounded
by loss and pain.
May God bring you beauty from ashes.

The strength, if strength we have, is certainly never in our own selves; it is given us.

—Charlotte Brontë

Chapter One

Chicago
Thursday, September 28, 1871

Meg's father was gone. Again.

She stood in his empty room for only a moment, summoning her wits. Crickets chirred outside the open windows, and moonlight spilled across the unrumpled bed. Surely he hadn't gotten very far.

A gust of wind swung the door closed behind her. Dread mounting, Meg pulled out the top drawer of Stephen's desk and found it empty. *Oh no.*

She hurried into the hallway of their second-floor apartment to find her sister, Sylvie, emerging from her room, her dark hair in a braid down her back. At twenty-one years of age, she was two years Meg's junior, but her brow wore the cares of someone much older.

"I heard a door slam. Did he leave?" Sylvie asked.

"He has his gun."

Meg rushed to the building's exterior stairwell. Cold metal met her skin as she climbed up the stairs barefoot, one pale hand on the railing, the other hoisting her nightdress as dew-heavy air flowed around her.

"Wait!" Sylvie cried from below, but Meg didn't slow until she gained the landing halfway between the third floor and the roof. The stairs shook as Sylvie chased after her. "Stop!" Wild-eyed and breathless, she caught up to Meg and grasped her arm.

"Shhh!" Meg pointed above them. Stephen was pacing the flat, block-long roof, patrolling to keep his property safe from dangers only he imagined. "Don't startle him. I need to talk him back inside before anyone else sees him."

"Please don't!" With uncharacteristic force, Sylvie jerked Meg down so they sat together on the landing, the bricks at their backs pressing through their cotton gowns. Coronas of light surrounded the lampposts on the street below.

"What are you doing?" Meg whispered. On the other side of the wall was the third-floor apartment they rented to James and Flora Spencer. Meg hoped the elderly tenants wouldn't stir.

"Listen to me." The end of Sylvie's braid swirled in the wind that moaned past the building. Her fingers dug into Meg's arm. "You remember him as he was before the war, before Andersonville changed him. I know him as he *is*. He's unpredictable, Meg. Stay away from him. I wish Mother had."

Meg's voice bunched into a hard lump at the base of her throat. Swallowing, she forced it back into service. "She was ill and never should have gotten out of bed."

Sylvie's jaw hardened, and her nostrils flared. "You make it sound as though it were her fault."

Meg's blond hair pulled from her braid and whipped across her face. "If I blame anyone, it's myself." Even in illness, Ruth's first concern was for her husband. Meg had fallen asleep when it was her turn to keep vigil through the night, or she could have stopped her mother and checked on her father herself. The drenching that Ruth endured in the storm that night while trying to coax Stephen down was too much for her weakened state. She never recovered. "With her last words, she begged me to take care of him. I promised. That's exactly what I'm trying to do."

Sylvie drew her knees up beneath her chin and looked toward the city's dark silhouette. Bats stitched their flight across the moon. Several blocks away, voices crescendoed, signaling a crowd's exit from a music hall, theater, or saloon. Hearing them, Stephen grew more agitated, muttering to himself as he paced.

Sylvie gripped Meg's hand. "I think he needs help."

"I agree. Before he hurts someone." A dim light flickered behind the window of James and Flora's apartment. Meg started to rise.

"No." Sylvie pulled her back down. "Not our help. Other help." She waited until Stephen's voice receded as he marched to the opposite end of the roof. "I think he needs more than we can give him."

"What are you saying?"

"It has been six years, and Father still isn't himself."

"He's not insane," Meg hissed.

"I didn't say he was. But he isn't well either. It's time to reconsider some kind of treatment."

"Treatment." Frustration licked through Meg. "That happens at the asylum. No. Mother never wanted that for him."

"Mother isn't here and hasn't been for two years."

"*I* don't want that for him."

Stephen's voice grew louder, hovering above them. He about-faced, and splinters of tar-coated wood from the roof rattled through the stairs and fell into Meg's lap. He was walking too close to the edge. Her heart banged within its cage. What if he slipped, with his foot or with the finger on the trigger?

Below, a dog barked and gave chase through the leaf-strewn alley, upsetting a crate of tin cans. Two gentlemen jumped out of the way, nearly falling over, then laughed drunkenly before weaving their way to the front door of the Sherman House hotel, which shared the building with the bookshop Meg's family owned on the ground level.

Sweat misted her skin, then chilled it as wind rushed by. "After being in a prison camp for so long, how do you think he would respond to being locked in an asylum?" A cloud passed over the moon. "He's not going." She stood without waiting for her sister's response.

"Who's there?" Stephen's pace increased as he neared. "Show yourself!"

Unmoving, Meg called out, "Father? It's me, Meg. It's all right."

"Meg?"

"Yes, it's Meg and Sylvie. We're on the stairwell. No one else is here."

Stiffly, he marched to the edge of the building and peered over. "What on earth are you doing? This is my watch, not yours." His Colt Army revolver glinted in his hand.

Meg steadied her voice. "Put the gun away. There's no need for it. Come on inside."

Moonlight gleamed in Stephen's eyes. "I can't go in. I must stand watch."

As Meg began to climb the stairs, Sylvie tugged her from behind with a whisper. "Don't you dare. Don't go up there."

Caught between her sister's fear and her father's paranoia, Meg felt her shoulders knot. How could she care for one without neglecting the other? Little wonder her mother had suffered chronic nosebleeds after Father came home.

Lifting her head, Meg tried to reason with him. "It's really windy up here. We're tired, and we'd like to go in. Let's all go in together. We'll lock the doors once we're inside, and we'll be fine."

Silence met her request. Long moments later, the stairs shook with his heavy tread. She knew better than to embrace him, for touch was no longer a comfort. It was just as well, considering she felt less affection than irritation right now. Compassion, she had discovered, was not a bottomless well.

"They took John." He glanced over his shoulder, then down below, scanning. Cares etched his face. "I received a letter today that said they took him right from his home and locked him up. They say it will keep him safe, but it won't, you know. It isn't right. They took John from his home."

"You need to rest," Sylvie told him. "Let's go inside."

A puff of air escaped his nose. "I don't feel restful." He hushed his voice. "There's devilment afoot, I know it. John must have stopped his lookout, or he'd never have let them take him. I won't be caught unawares. I won't be locked up again. Upon my life, I won't."

"That's right, you won't." Dust itched over Meg's skin with each gust of wind. "Now, let's go home."

He pulled at his beard, considering.

"Please, Father?" Sylvie whispered. She rubbed her arms.

Before he could form a response, the fire bell sounded from the cupola of the courthouse, jerking his attention that direction.

"It's all right," Meg said. "Look around, there's no blaze within sight. It's just a small fire somewhere else. You know the watchman in the tower is required to ring the bell whenever the firemen are called to action anywhere in the city."

She'd grown up hearing that bell and ignoring it, though lately it clanged more often than ever, thanks to the dry summer and strong winds sweeping in off the prairie. But the number of strokes indicated where in the city the fire was located, so she knew they were well out of harm's way.

Even so, each strike of the enormous bell heaped another layer of dismay upon Stephen's countenance. "Get inside, girls," he said at length. "There is devilment afoot. I know it. I won't be taken unawares."

Sylvie stomped down the stairs, Stephen marched back to the roof, and Meg stood in between, reaching out to both with empty hands.

Friday, September 29, 1871

Meg could barely admit to herself, let alone to Sylvie, that aside from keeping her father from being locked away, she was at a loss as to how to soothe his mind and spirit. That uncomfortable fact was far easier to ignore during business hours, when she could lose herself in what she did know how to do.

So in the southeast corner of her family's bookshop, framed by the display window, Meg squeezed paint from metal tubes onto her palette, then added a portion of medium to the center. She felt the tension in her shoulders slowly release as she began to mix the colors.

"Ten o'clock. Let's hope we're busier today than we've been so far this week." Sylvie unlocked the front door and flipped the sign to announce that Corner Books & More was open.

Meg glanced at the bustle outside. From their vantage point on the corner of Randolph and Clark Streets, she had a full view of Court House Square diagonally across from the store. Horse-drawn carriages, wagons, and drays clattered over the pine-block street. Ladies in smart jackets and skirts and men in sack suits streamed out of a streetcar and onto raised wooden sidewalks. Chicago held more than three hundred thousand souls. It did not seem too vain a hope that a small fraction of one percent might be persuaded to buy a book.

"We still have the rent coming in from our tenants," Meg reminded her sister. "And if Beth and Rosemary don't visit today, you'll have more time to devote to customers." Sylvie's two best friends from their school days were nice enough, but they ought to know better than to distract Sylvie from work. It should be enough that the trio saw each other at church, at Hoffman's Bakery down the block, and at Beth's and Rosemary's homes.

Sylvie stiffened. "If your friends stopped by to see you, I wouldn't turn them away."

But that was unlikely to happen, and they both knew it. The few friends Meg had were married now, tied by their apron strings to their households. They had husbands and babies to tend. Meg had the store and her father, and no girlish dreams of more. She'd accepted that the war had claimed many young men and that, regardless, her lot was to take care of Stephen. Not a husband, not a babe of her own.

Resolved, Meg turned back to her painting of Margaret Hale, the heroine of the novel *North and South* by Elizabeth Gaskell. Once completed, the portrait would join the dozen other beloved characters hanging on the shop's walls. Patrons came not just to purchase books, but to see which character Meg was painting next, which was why she so often painted here instead of in her art studio upstairs. A few paintings had even sold, but not nearly as many as she wished.

After mixing a little medium in with her paint, she scrubbed in the background on the canvas. She was so focused that she didn't notice anyone had entered the shop until she sensed someone at her elbow.

"Good morning, my dear!" Leaning on his walking stick, Hiram Sloane stood even with her height, his accumulated years stooping the shoulders beneath his brown herringbone frock coat. For years he'd played the part of benevolent uncle to her and Sylvie, and guardian of their family while her father was at war.

"Father will be so pleased to see you," Meg told him. The two men first met at an abolition rally a decade before the war began. They'd bonded quickly, meeting time and again to discuss shared convictions, the news, and literature. He was the only friend Stephen still had. "He's in the backyard, I believe."

"Fine day to be out in the sunshine. I would have walked if my carriage driver had let me."

"Then Eli has more sense than you." Meg laughed to take the sting out of her words. Hiram's home was two and a half miles south of the store. Not only was it too far for a man of Hiram's years to walk, but three times last summer he had set off and completely lost his way. Thank goodness he hadn't wandered into any of the vice-ridden patches along the river. Each time, a policeman had brought him home before he'd been in any danger.

"Yes. Eli." The way Hiram repeated the name, Meg could tell he was attempting to commit it to memory once more. "Well, then. I will visit with your father after I pay my respects to your sister." He moved toward the interior of the shop.

A few passersby paused outside the window, watching Meg blend the background with a large, flat bristle brush. Her thoughts, however, remained with her father, who ought to be bent over his worktable in the rear of the shop, repairing broken bindings on rare first edition books. Before the war, he had taken great pride and satisfaction in mending what was torn, restoring and renewing old treasures. These days he could not always muster the concentration required. She breathed in the smells of linseed oil and turpentine, then exhaled slowly. Her cares had finally faded to the corners of her mind when the door opened again.

Dried leaves somersaulted inside, crunching beneath a pair of shoes creased with use but polished to a shine. Their owner consulted his timepiece, then slipped it back into his vest pocket before removing his derby hat. Chestnut hair brushed the collar of his sable-colored suit.

Stepping away from Hiram, Sylvie approached the customer, her plaid pleated skirt rustling. "Mr. Pierce, what a pleasure to see you."

He gave a slight bow, then pushed his spectacles up the bridge of his nose. "Thank you again for the invitation to come."

"Yes, of course. This is my sister, Meg. Meg, this is Mr. Nathaniel Pierce with the *Chicago Tribune*. We met at the Soldiers' Home last Sunday."

Mr. Pierce looked at Meg. "How do you do?"

Meg sent him a smile while appraising him from an artist's perspective, noting the exact shade of blue in his eyes, the proportions of his lean frame, the sun's glints in his hair, and his tapered fingers, one stained with ink. "My sister can help you find whatever you want. Or whomever, as the case may be. David Copperfield, perhaps? Or the elusive Moby Dick?"

A corner of his mouth turned up. He smoothed a hand over the two cowlicks at the back of his head. "Stephen Townsend, if you please. If Miss Sylvie didn't mention it, I'm doing an article on Chicago's war heroes, and I'd love to record your father's experiences."

"An article." Swallowing the surprise edging her tone, Meg set down her brush. Her apple-green muslin skirt whispered as she stepped closer. "Now? Six years after the war's end?"

"Ten years after the war's beginning. A fine time for reflection, don't you think?"

What a luxury that some people might wait that long to consider the war's toll, when she and Sylvie could not get away from it. "It was ten years in April. You're a bit late, wouldn't you say?"

"I've been featuring our veterans on a regular basis since then." Mr. Pierce gave her a look as if to say she would know this if she read the newspaper. "I'm merely continuing the series."

Hiram joined them, wiry eyebrows drawn together. "Doing a story on the war, young man? Why, if I can be of service, I'd be most willing. I served as a prison guard at Camp Douglas in the south part of town. I remember it well."

That much was true. It was anything after the war that seemed to slip Hiram's recollection more and more of late.

While the two men chatted, Meg pulled Sylvie toward the counter. On it sat their mother's copy of *Little Women*, which Sylvie must have been reading. Not only did it contain their mother's notes in the margins, but it also held the photograph of their father when he enlisted. The precious image showed Stephen as he had been before the war had altered him. He didn't want to see it, but Meg and Sylvie wouldn't part with it for anything.

Meg glanced at the reporter before refocusing on her sister. "Exactly what have you arranged?"

"I see no harm in it. Mr. Pierce was gathering stories at the Soldiers' Home last week when I was there dropping off some books. When he learned about Father, he asked to interview him, and I agreed."

"For a newspaper article," Meg said. "He barely talks to *us* about the war. You suppose he'll talk to a stranger?"

"He might." Sylvie straightened the cameo at her collar. "I want Chicago to know of Father's sacrifices on their behalf. On the country's behalf. Look out there." She gestured to the window. "All those people going about their business like nothing ever happened. This city got rich off the war—filthy rich—while soldiers gave life or limb, or came home broken beyond repair."

Meg's throat cinched tight. "Father can heal. He just needs time and patience and love." This was her mother's conviction, bequeathed to Meg before she died. She only hoped her voice sounded as confident as her words.

Sylvie looked away. "He's had time and love and patience. But perhaps he could do with a bit more respect as well. And it could help the store. We need the business. We may draw new customers from other parts of the city who wish to patronize a veteran-owned shop. A newspaper article is our best chance to reach them."

"You want to exploit our father for gain?"

"Pardon me." Mr. Pierce inserted himself into their argument, Hiram still at his side. "I do not exploit."

"Our father—" Meg stopped before she could say that he was different from the average veteran. That he was easy to exploit, that children already taunted him. They threw bread crusts and apple cores over the Townsends' backyard fence just to laugh as Stephen scrambled to gather them up. Lifting her chin, she tried again. "Our father survived Andersonville."

"Exactly why his story should be shared."

Hiram pounded his walking stick on the floor. "Quite right! My dear girls, your father is a grown man. Let us leave the question to him, eh? Allow him the dignity of making his own decision."

The ridge between Sylvie's eyes smoothed away. "I'll mind the store."

Conceding, Meg turned her back on the unfinished painting and led the men to the work in progress she could not seem to improve.

It was a lie, Meg had realized years ago, that the end of the war meant the end of suffering. At the age of seventeen, she'd linked arms with Sylvie and their mother on the train platform, waiting for her father's return. Steam engines hissed, whistles blasted, crowds tramped across the soot-filmed floor. Nearly dizzy with anticipation, she had craned her neck, searching form and face. But the stranger who finally shuffled toward them had borne no resemblance to Stephen Townsend. Emaciated, covered with scabs, breath that reeked of illness. Even his voice was thin. Only the eyes belonged to the man they remembered, but those looked both haunted and hunted.

That night at home, rather than resuming his chair at the head of the table, he had left it empty, choosing to sit elsewhere. Pointing to the vacant spot Meg had waited four years for him to fill, he'd said, "The man who left is not the one who came home. I'm sorry. I am a shock to you. I'm a shock to myself."

Meg wondered if Stephen was a shock to Nathaniel Pierce as well. Though no longer stamped and scored by starvation, her father remained thin, his beard uncut, his eyes possessed of a fierce alertness. He squatted on the far side of the yard, the knees of his trousers threadbare to a shine though other pairs filled his closet. A canteen hung at his hip. He held up a hand to halt their approach, then pointed to the reason.

Beneath a naked linden tree, a stray dog devoured the blackberry pie Meg had brought home from the bakery last night. Scattered in a drift of dead leaves were the crumbs of what she could only guess had been a loaf of bread.

Meg watched helplessly, Hiram and Mr. Pierce flanking her. At last the floppy-eared stray finished his feast and scampered through the gap in the wooden fence. The air was warm as summer and dry as dust, for they'd had less than an inch of rain since July.

"Father." She made her way to him, carefully stepping over and around the marks he'd made on the ground, while Hiram stood back with Mr. Pierce. "The pie and bread were for us," she whispered.

"He was hungry. No man or beast should know hunger. If a creature comes asking for a bite to eat and it's in my power to give it, I'll do it. Every time."

She nodded, choosing to see the compassion and kindness in the act, though she wondered if the reporter would interpret it that way.

Stephen ran a hand down his brown beard, grizzled with coarse grey strands though he was only forty-five. "Who does Hiram have with him?"

"His name is Mr. Nathaniel Pierce, and he's with the *Tribune*. Sylvie met him at the Soldiers' Home. He'd like to hear about your experiences during the war for a series of articles he's writing on

Chicago's veterans. I'll introduce you, if you'd like." Her voice tilted up in question at the end.

"He wants information?" Stephen squinted across the grassless yard. At length, he said, "Let's see what he's about." With strides ungainly from perpetual ache in his joints, he led the way to the waiting men.

"Stephen!" Hiram shook her father's hand. "This young fellow wants to hear what you have to say about Andersonville. Whatever you want the city to know, he says he'll print it in that newspaper of his."

"It would be a privilege, sir." Mr. Pierce extended his hand.

Stephen turned away from it, pulling Hiram aside.

Mr. Pierce stepped back to allow them more privacy. Meg offered him an apologetic half smile. On the third floor, a window slid open, and she imagined the Spencers were watching and listening to everything.

"Who is this man, really?" Stephen whispered to Hiram. "What do we know about him?"

Hiram clasped Stephen's arm and held firm. "He's a reporter, friend. He merely wants to listen to you."

God bless Hiram Sloane. He could talk Stephen down from his suspicions in ways she couldn't, for her father considered her naïve. Perhaps if Meg had been born a son rather than a daughter, he would heed her insights. If she'd been a son, she would have gone to war herself and fought alongside him. Instead, she was the daughter who needed extra time and attention during her childhood, and he still deemed her *delicate*. If what he meant by that was *fragile*, he was wrong.

"It is up to you, of course," Hiram added. "But I trust him. He'd like to hear whatever you want to tell him. Some might consider that a gift indeed." Hiram didn't know that he was that gift to Stephen every time he came to visit, listening to the same stories over and over again with the same rapt attention, as though it were his first time hearing them. In Hiram's mind, it was.

Mr. Pierce shifted his weight, placed his hat over his heart. "I sincerely would be honored to hear and explain to our readers your sacrifices. We are all of us in your debt."

Stephen appraised him. "You served? Or were you not old enough to enlist?"

A bit of color rode the reporter's cheekbones. "I was twenty at the start of the war. Old enough to stay here and raise my three young stepsiblings."

Meg stifled her surprise. If he wasn't a veteran himself, how could he possibly understand and represent a man like her father? "Maybe this isn't a good idea after all. Thank you for your time." She touched Mr. Pierce's elbow, signaling that he should leave.

Stephen reached out to stay them, dirt beneath his fingernails. "Your parents?"

"Cholera, 'fifty-nine. Took my mother, stepfather, and many neighbors."

Hiram clucked his tongue. "And you were left to tend the children."

"The least I can do now," Mr. Pierce forged ahead, "is to record stories like yours. As you are a bookstore owner, surely we can agree on the importance of not letting history disappear. We have much to learn from you, sir."

Stephen hooked a thumb behind the strap of his canteen and angled toward the back of the house as though considering. "Far be it from me to fault a man for caring for his own." He cleared his throat. "I'll talk."

"Good. I'm grateful." A subdued smile warmed Mr. Pierce's face. Reseating his hat, he asked if there was some other place Stephen wanted to go to conduct the interview.

"Here's fine," Stephen replied. "Here's fitting."

He spread his arms and spun in a slow circle, dust clouding the tops of his boots. Meg followed Mr. Pierce's gaze and saw with his eyes what she had grown accustomed to during the last six years.

All the grass had been pulled up. In a large rectangle that encompassed nearly the entire yard, sticks whittled to pointed ends were driven into the ground. Inside that barrier was another perimeter made up of the same. Small pebbles spelled the words *Dead Line* inside the second rectangle. Three straight lines cut through the dirt, marked *Market Street*, *Water Street*, and *South Street*. Cutting across the width of the southern half of the rectangle was a deep groove Stephen had carved out with his knife. Seeing that it was dry, he crouched and poured water from his canteen into the cavity. *Stockade Creek* read the pebbles alongside its bank. Inside the Dead Line, uncounted scraps of fabric were nailed into the hard-packed ground to represent makeshift tents.

Rising again, Stephen took a drink from his canteen. "Welcome to Andersonville."

Sorrow clamped Meg's chest, screwing tighter with each breath. This model he'd made and faithfully maintained had been part of her landscape for so long that she had learned to bury its significance. After all these years, and in a city that had grown fat with profit from the war, her father still wasn't free of the prison that had shattered him.

Chapter Two

Sunday, October 1, 1871

Sylvie rarely won an argument with Meg. She didn't even like to disagree with her, preferring all the conflict in her life to be contained within the pages of books, where it was resolved by the last chapter, or in neat columns of numbers, which could be reconciled with a little careful figuring. So the fact that Meg had conceded to Mr. Pierce featuring Stephen in the newspaper was made sweeter still by the article in the Sunday morning issue of the *Tribune*. It was just as respectful as she'd prayed it would be.

If she was honest, however, the triumph she felt was tempered by the surprises the article contained. Sylvie knew Andersonville had held as many as twelve thousand prisoners in an open stockade. But she'd had no idea that to stave away mental decline, her father had organized an oratorical society among several inmates, wherein they debated all manner of lofty topics, starving though they were.

She'd had no idea that *"one man would kill another over a wash pail or a scrap of canvas for shade,"* as her father was quoted in the article. *"I reached out to stop such a rogue from taking a tin cup from a fevered man, and he broke my arm with his club. It was easy enough to do. We were all brittle. Bones like spun sugar."*

Sylvie was only thirteen when her father had been captured.

The two times he'd written home after that, he had said he was being treated well.

Lies.

She'd known so little about his experience. She knew so little about him now. When she'd asked him this morning before church if he wanted to read the article, he'd said he had no need to, since he had lived it once and then again in his dreams for good measure.

"You should know Mr. Pierce did right by you," she told him. "Even I learned some things. Things you might have told us yourself."

He'd dipped his chin, and that was that. A line from *Little Women* scrolled through Sylvie's mind. *"We haven't got Father, and shall not have him for a long time."*

Now Sylvie sat beside Meg in the landau carriage Hiram had sent to fetch the Townsends for dinner at his house, regarding the complicated man across from her.

Stephen's long fingers knotted together on his lap, then gripped the edge of the leather seat, knuckles brightening as he craned his neck to take in all he could as they trundled south on Clark Street, the river to the west and Lake Michigan to the east, yet neither close enough to glimpse. Always, always, he was watching.

Ironically, he didn't see Sylvie.

She shouldn't mind. He wasn't well. But even when he had been, he'd devoted far more time to Meg than he ever had to Sylvie.

Something like resentment had burrowed deep inside her, though it shamed her to admit that even to herself, especially after reading the *Tribune* article. But these days, Stephen might spend all day repairing the little fence he'd built around his replica of Andersonville, Meg might spend hours with her paints, and Sylvie spent herself studying ledgers and receipts and ways to stay afloat, though she was the youngest in the family.

An irrelevant point, and selfish. At twenty-one, she was old enough to manage a household and business. By this time, she had just hoped it would be her own.

She shook her head to loose the thought. Meg didn't complain about encroaching spinsterhood, so neither would she. There was more—far more—to life than courting and proposals. Which was well indeed, since no man had yet proven brave enough to seek Stephen's approval.

Sylvie had filled her head with too much Jane Austen, that was all. What she needed was more of the Brontë sisters, or nearly anything by Charles Dickens.

A sigh escaped her, and Meg sent her a smile. "You seem over-tired lately."

Sylvie couldn't deny it. "I hope there's coffee at Hiram's table."

"That and more." Meg brightened. "Did he tell you his nephew has come to stay with him? A fine young man, if even half of what Hiram says is true. He'll be dining with us today. He's in Chicago studying law."

"Then perhaps the conversation will be as stimulating as the coffee." At the very least, Sylvie hoped their topics of conversation would vary from the usual. Anything different would be welcome.

His toe tapping the carriage floor, Stephen snapped his pocket watch open and shut, barely looking at its face. He didn't handle new people well, but for a relative of Hiram's, surely he'd make an effort.

The wheels beneath her seat rumbled over the tarred seams between the pine blocks paving the street. Lampposts and public drinking fountains passed by at intervals, until Eli Washington steered the horses onto Prairie Avenue. From both sides, limbs arched to meet each other over the middle of the street. In early summer, it formed a ruffling green canopy of shade. Now, the bare branches fractured the sky.

Wrought-iron fences enclosed boxwood hedges and parched gardens where hydrangeas nodded their dried, bronze-colored blooms. Front porch steps were wide and tall, flanked by sculpted lions or topiary evergreens in stone pots. The stately houses in this neighborhood fairly bristled with chimneys, turrets, and cupolas.

The carriage slowed to a stop in a horseshoe drive. Hiram's

limestone residence boasted a tower to the left of a white-columned porch, ornamented hoods over the windows, double front doors, and a mansard roof as a dignified crown and functional third story over it all. Hiram had done well in the lumber trade before selling his half of the business to his partner upon retiring.

"Watch your step, Miss Margaret." With a large-knuckled hand, Eli helped Meg and then Sylvie from the carriage, while Stephen climbed out after them.

"Eli," Sylvie said, "do you suppose Hiram is . . . expecting us?"

It was a standing tradition to share the noon meal with Hiram on the first Sunday of the month, but he was losing his ability to keep track of the days. And last month they'd had to skip it, due to his having the grippe.

Eli smiled, pushing creases deep into his ebony face. "We all—Mr. Sloane's staff and I—been doing our best to see that he knows you're coming. Honest to goodness truth? We look forward to having you folks over as much as he does. It gives Cook and Miss Dressler all manner of purpose as they plan for it."

Sylvie smiled. Helene Dressler was a formidable force as the head housekeeper, but her heart was as stout as her waist. "I can only imagine the preparations for Hiram's nephew's visit."

"Well now, that would have been a sight, had they known he was fixing to come. Mr. Sloane must have arranged it and plumb forgot to let the staff know. Honest to goodness, I think he forgot about it himself until Mr. Jasper turned up on the doorstep a month ago. But we manage fine, just like always. Mr. Jasper spends most of his time at the university or studying."

Once inside, the Townsends were ushered past potted palm trees in the front hall and into the reception room to await their host. Stephen paced between the wainscoted walls. Meg pulled her gloves off by the fingertips and snapped them into her reticule before studying the Italianate mosaic above the fireplace, and Sylvie lowered herself to a leather chair, her fingertips grazing the brass rivets bordering the edge of the seat.

The walnut pocket doors slid open, and Hiram arrived on the

arm of a man with sharp, appraising green eyes and curly hair the shades of pine and oak.

"Fine time to come calling!" Hiram said, smiling. "I haven't seen you dear people in weeks!"

Sylvie's stomach sank as she rose, but she wouldn't correct him.

"This is my sister's grandson, God rest her, and my only living relation. My grandnephew." Hiram looked up at the young man, a struggle evident in his features.

"Jasper Davenport," the nephew supplied. Sharp cheekbones rode just beneath his skin, but a polite smile brought a dimple to his left cheek, warming his countenance.

"Jasper, I present to you . . ." Hiram cleared his throat and bravely tried again. "This remarkable family, all of whom I consider kin. I've known them since this fine man first opened his bookshop, when these young ladies were no more than yea high."

Stephen introduced himself. "And these are my daughters, Margaret and Sylvia."

"Yes." A mixture of disgust and relief passed over Hiram's face at hearing their names. It was the first time he was unable to bring them to mind, and it obviously rattled him. Valiantly, he lifted his chin. "Your dear wife could not join us today? Pity, that."

Sylvie feared to look at her father.

Meg blanched but quickly recovered. "Not today, Hiram."

"Ah. Do give her my best." Turning to Mr. Davenport, Hiram went on. "Stephen is a man of learning *and* a war hero. Meg is a promising artist, and Sylvie—" Just as he seemed to be gathering his recollections, he paused to look at her.

Sylvie shifted beside her golden-haired sister, feeling dull and mute and brown all over, from her hair and eyes to her skirt and boots. She tugged at the cuffs of her sleeves, wondering if it was evident she had turned them for more use. What could be said of her? That she was well-read? That aside from Rosemary and Beth, her best friends were fictional characters? That she was more comfortable in their world than in her own?

Hiram took her hand between his dry, papery palms. "Make

no mistake. Sylvie Townsend can run her family bookstore with her eyes closed. She is the engine that keeps it all moving. And important work it is too." His eyebrows arched as he released her. "Chicago has money and moneygrubbers aplenty, but if we were not also rich in culture, I would call it a very poor place to live indeed. The Townsends bring literature and art to a city that sorely needs both."

A flush warmed Sylvie's cheeks at his praise. Chicago had theaters, opera houses, art galleries, and cultural societies far grander than what the Townsends offered on the corner across from Court House Square. She smiled her thanks while Meg responded with actual words, a talent that had deserted Sylvie at the moment.

But when Mr. Davenport bowed and said, "Much obliged," with a curious lilt to his voice, it was Sylvie he held in his gaze. "Uncle has told me so much about your family already." A shaft of sunlight pierced between velvet draperies, shattered on the crystal chandelier, and landed in rainbows at his feet.

Stephen squinted at him. "Where did you say you're from again?"

"The accent throws you," Hiram guessed. "I understand. He comes from southern Indiana, close to the border of . . ." He dropped his gaze. Frustration screwed tight on his brow.

"Kentucky?" Sylvie offered, unable to bear his fruitless search for the word.

"Of course. I was about to say that. I did tell you he had come for a visit, didn't I? I thought I had. . . ."

"You did indeed," Meg assured him. "We're so pleased you have family in town. Will you be staying with Hiram for the duration of your courses?" she asked Mr. Davenport.

Hiram tapped his walking stick on the inlaid hardwood floor. "If I have any influence, he'll stay indefinitely."

It was the second time Hiram had answered for his nephew, Sylvie noticed, and she felt a kinship with him over that, for she had said but one word so far, herself. She wasn't miserably shy, as the Brontë sisters were said to have been. Sylvie was simply reserved until a topic was introduced to which she could contribute. Perhaps Mr. Davenport was the same.

"The house can surely accommodate," Hiram was saying. "But I won't pressure him. Not all young men want to lodge with an old man like me."

"I do hope you stay awhile," Sylvie blurted, surprising herself. "What I mean is, it is so nice to see Hiram so happy." Hiram had longed for family of his own ever since they'd known him. Now that his memory was so unreliable, his nephew's presence could help immeasurably.

Mr. Davenport's thin lips curved into agreement. "We get along fine, that's for sure."

"There's nothing more important than family," Hiram added. "Speaking of which, your dear wife could not join us today?"

Sylvie glanced at Stephen, whose face had the look of granite. His hand shook as he pulled at his beard. "Not today," he muttered.

"Pity, that. Do give her my best."

Sylvie stirred her steaming oyster stew, dreading the first bite. She could barely abide the smell. Her gaze drifted from the rams' heads carved into the floor-to-ceiling fireplace to the tiles covering the top half of the wall above walnut panels. A repeating pattern of passion flowers on the tiles brought a semblance of life to an otherwise dark room.

"Mr. Townsend, if you don't mind my asking, where was it you fought?" Mr. Davenport asked. "In the war?"

Stephen replied with the names of battles she'd heard a thousand times before saying he wound up in Andersonville.

Mr. Davenport caught a drip on his chin with a snow-white napkin. "You have a fascinating history."

"*Fascinating* is not the word that comes to mind when I think on those days." Stephen slurped another spoonful.

"A crime against humanity, that's what Andersonville was,"

Hiram muttered into his stew. "I know Camp . . . Camp David. No. Camp Douglas, that's what I meant to say. Camp Douglas here in Chicago was no Sunday picnic for the inmates either, but at least . . ."

Mr. Davenport looked at him intently. "So they had food enough here, Uncle? I suppose so, given the wealth of Chicago, especially when compared to the poverty of the entire Confederacy. The men here had enough clothing, I trust, to help them through the winters?"

There was something about the way he asked these questions, like they'd never discussed it in all the years that followed the war. Sylvie wondered how estranged they had been, and why, and what had brought Mr. Davenport back now. But it would be the height of rudeness to ask. She sipped at her stew, avoiding any rubbery bits of oyster.

The corners of Hiram's mouth plunged down. "Oh, no. I'd be lying if I agreed with that description. And I didn't run the camp, I just served as a guard with a regiment of other older men not fit for combat."

At the opposite end of the table, Stephen pulled a second roll from the basket and slathered it with butter. "Tell us, Mr. Davenport, how did you spend the war?"

"Fighting. From the start."

"The very beginning?" Sylvie calculated in her mind. "Were you old enough to fight ten years ago?"

"Fifteen was old enough for me and many others."

Sylvie smoothed her napkin in her lap. "I mean, did you need your parents' permission to enlist before you reached the minimum age?"

A chuckle sounded in Mr. Davenport's throat. "Permission? Where I come from, every man signed up to defend his country, whether he needed a razor in the morning yet or not. It was an honor to do it. It would have been shameful not to."

Stephen nodded, but Sylvie could tell it was reluctant.

"My nephew knew his duty," Hiram said. "Before he was old enough to vote, he fought. That's more than can be said for many here in Chicago, isn't that right, Stephen? You recall the weaselly fellow, Otto Schneider? Why, he was in his prime during the war and didn't volunteer."

"Who was Schneider?" Mr. Davenport asked, his tone more courteous than curious.

Hiram wiped his hands on a napkin and leaned forward. "I purchased stocks from him at a low price. He was only too grateful to have the cash, sure we were on the brink of another financial panic like that of '57. But we weren't." He shrugged. "I bought up everything Schneider offered, invested wisely, and enjoyed a healthy return. Would you believe he sued me for it? Claimed I swindled him and that the fortune really ought to be his. All through the war, when he could have been fighting for his country, he was fighting to get at my money instead. The waste of it all." Hiram shook his head.

Mr. Davenport's politeness had turned to true interest. "So what happened to him?"

"Oh, he's still around, but just scraping by. The legal fees bankrupted him. He blames me for that too, as he's told me in more than one angry letter. I pity his wife and children, with such a desperate man at the helm of their family."

Sylvie caught Meg's gaze across the table and shared a look that expressed their weariness with the familiar story. Surely they could talk about something else.

Apparently Stephen agreed. "You got through all four years unscathed?" he asked Mr. Davenport, effectively putting the subject of Schneider behind them.

The young man took a long drink of coffee and set it down before responding. "I wouldn't put it that way, quite."

"Wounded, then? Captured?" Stephen asked. "Or disease?"

A tight smile flicked over Mr. Davenport's countenance. "I wager there are more suitable topics for mixed company." He turned to Sylvie. "Have you read any good new books lately?"

Whether or not he held a genuine interest in reading, he must have known she'd have an answer to this, and she appreciated that he included her in this way. "As a matter of fact, I have. Louisa May Alcott published a brand new novel this year called *Little Men*. You've heard of *Little Women*, of course? In the new book, Jo and her professor husband open a home for little boys. It lacks the gravity of Dickens's work, but it's a delightful read, sure to appeal to—" She paused, noting the small smile on Mr. Davenport's face. "Perhaps I've said too much."

"Never heard of it," Hiram inserted. "But what about *Uncle Tom's Cabin*? Now, that's a book everyone's talking about."

"Well, they were," Meg said. "I believe the furor has died down quite a bit by now." Stowe's novel had released nineteen years ago.

"What do you mean?" Hiram leaned back as the footman removed his bowl. "It can't be more than a few months old. Our president himself gives it high praise." A plate of cucumber salad was set before him.

"That's not surprising for a man like Grant," Mr. Davenport said as his bowl was replaced with the next course.

"Ulysses Grant?" Hiram stared at his nephew. "The general? No, my dear boy, you're mistaken. Abraham Lincoln is our president."

It would do no good and cause much distress to tell Hiram Sloane that Abraham Lincoln was dead and that two more presidents had been sworn in since then.

Deftly, Meg changed the subject once again. While they spoke of the weather, Sylvie wondered how much Mr. Davenport knew about his uncle's condition and if the staff had divulged anything to help orient him. A headache swelled between her temples. Navigating conversation was proving to be more like winding through a field of hidden explosives, careful not to trigger anything that may upset the three men present. She glanced out the window at the garden, where rose vines withered on a trellis, crisp brown petals spinning off in the wind.

Hans, the footman, bent to remove her barely touched bowl. "Finished, miss?"

"I am, yes, thank you," she whispered.

"Very good." He nodded his white-blond head and took it away.

But not before Stephen noticed she hadn't eaten her stew. "Sylvia, that was wasteful of you." His voice held the low rumble of a coming storm. "Young man," he called to Hans, gesturing for him to return.

"Is there a problem?" Hiram asked.

Bread crumbs salting his beard, Stephen pointed at the bowl. "You didn't eat your food."

"I'm not hungry for it, nor overly fond," Sylvie whispered, before adding, "There will be more than enough food in the following courses. I'll have my fill and then some, I'm sure."

"How could you be so wasteful, when so many go hungry every day?" Stephen repeated as if he hadn't heard her. "Do you know how we survived down there? This stew you turn your nose up at could have saved a man's life. Three men. More."

"Sir?" Hans stood still, bowl on the platter he held.

"What will you do with that now, young man? Will you eat it?"

"Oh no, sir."

"Will you put it back in the pot and save it for Hiram to eat later?"

"That is not our custom, sir. To give Mr. Sloane food off other people's plates." The poor man seemed perplexed.

"It is perfectly good food!" Stephen exploded. "Barely touched!"

At his outburst, Hiram lifted a hand. "You're at odds with yourself, friend. Let me send for a doctor."

"No, thank you, Hiram," Meg was quick to say.

Stephen shook his head. "No, no doctors. But you must explain to me what you plan to do with that food. If you think it unfit for people now, at least put it outside for an animal to find."

When Mr. Davenport sent Sylvie a questioning look, she told him, "Our father is very concerned for the welfare of any living on the street."

"Is that right? Stray animals?" His voice betrayed his surprise.

"Animals, children, immigrants, the general poor," Stephen clarified. "The city is full of those in need. No living creature should go hungry. If you'd been hungry before, truly hungry, you would know what I mean. You'd agree."

Something shifted in the younger man's expression. "I do." Straightening his spine, he turned to Hans. "You'll do as Mr. Townsend requests?"

Hans looked to Hiram for confirmation.

The old man nodded. "Do as my nephew bids."

"As you wish."

But just as Hans turned to leave the room, another footman came in, carrying a platter of dome-covered plates. The two footmen collided, and Hans stumbled backward. The platter tipped, the bowl upended, and Sylvie's stew spilled all over the floor.

Crying out, Stephen took his spoon and flew toward the mess, trying in vain to scoop the stew back into the bowl. "What a waste!" With his bare fingers, he fished out the bits of oyster. Tears ran down his cheeks. "It could have helped a hungry creature!"

While Hans stuttered a stunned apology, Meg—predictably—pushed back from the table, ready to launch herself toward Stephen, but Sylvie stayed her with a look. This was Sylvie's doing, at least in part. It ought to be Sylvie at his side.

She joined her father on the floor, the fabric of her skirt drawing in the warm broth. Dismay spread from the center of her chest, edged with a searing shame. This was her fault. This wouldn't have happened if she had only eaten her food. But as quickly as the thought formed, another chased it: *The problem is not with me.* With her father, she felt forced to play child and parent both, when in truth she was neither.

Hiram stood. "It is nothing," he soothed. "We can still put out a bowl for the strays."

"But not this one." Stephen sat back on his heels, shoulders slumped. He buried his face in his hands. "Just that little bit could have helped them. It might have saved Pritchard and Jenkins and Smith. I see them still," he whispered. "Every time I eat, I see them."

Mr. Davenport rose into a beam of sunshine that cut across

the room and flared on his curls. Both footmen looked to him, and he dismissed them from the room, a gesture of respect for Stephen's privacy.

Not that Stephen noticed. How utterly alone he must feel. *I'm right here,* she wanted to say. *Look! You are here with us, we are here with you! Whatever burden you bear, let us share it! Wherever you go, take us along!* But words webbed in her throat. He had already traveled away from them in his mind.

Gently, she touched his back.

He flinched as though struck, then knocked her back with a force he could not have meant for his daughter.

"Oh! Sylvie, Sylvie, what are you doing there?" he asked. Had he really not noticed her until now?

"I say!" Hiram's voice sounded from somewhere above them. "You're at odds with yourself, friend. Let me send for a doctor."

Stephen thrust his fingers through his hair. "I . . . said . . . no!" He shuddered with silent tears.

Sylvie's eyes remained dry. The soiled patch of her dress, once warm with stew, was now cold and clinging through her petticoat to her skin, a thin layer of glue holding her to the mess.

It was Hiram's nephew who helped her up, a kind of knowing banked in his expression. Meg rushed to support Stephen as he pushed himself off the floor. But when he had gained his feet beneath him, he fled through the door and left them all behind.

Dust coated Stephen's skin as he dragged a stick across the ground, redrawing the Dead Line on his backyard map of Andersonville. Sweat itched across his scalp and trickled down the side of his face. That didn't trouble him.

All that concerned him right now was preserving the memory of that place in order to honor those who died there. He'd promised his friends they wouldn't be forgotten. That was a promise he aimed to keep.

Staring at the dirt, he blinked, and memory stained the soil the livid red of Georgia clay. He blinked again and saw the ground yawn wide, saw himself piling the bodies of his fellow Yankee prisoners into the pit. Stephen rubbed the heels of his hands against his eyes but could not stop seeing them. The bodies were ravaged by hunger and scurvy to the point that their mothers would not have known their sons. But Stephen knew them. He knew his friends. There was Jenkins, Pritchard, and Smith. He had fed them into foreign soil to be swallowed up. Another mass grave, unmarked, a grossly undignified end for any person, let alone a soldier in service to his country.

Most prisoners had considered burial duty a punishment, but Stephen had volunteered for it. He spoke psalms and prayed through the rag tied over his nose and mouth. "*We see you,*" he had said to each body as he hauled it from the dead wagon and into the pit. He refused to dump them like cord wood. "*We honor you and your sacrifice.*" He had spoken their names when he knew them.

"Boo!" a boy shouted from the other side of the fence, yanking Stephen back to the present. The boy's ruddy cheeks were as round as his eyes. Raw eggs sailed over the boards, one after another, smashing into the model of Andersonville. As the boy ran away with an accomplice, he launched a final missile with impeccable aim. It cracked on Stephen's temple. Rotten yolk ran down his face.

His pulse soared. White-hot anger vibrated through his frame. Why hadn't these eggs been eaten before they'd fermented? He swiped the slime from his skin and slung it onto the ground.

"It could have saved them!" he roared. "Just this much could have lengthened their lives! For shame, for shame, you wasteful people! Why don't you come back here and let me teach you a lesson! Ungrateful scoundrel! I dare you to set foot on my property again, and just you see what happens!" He shouted as loud as his lungs would allow, giving in to rage because that was easier than succumbing to sorrow.

His fury grew a blade inside him, and he held on to it as long as he could. But to his own shame, tears formed and fell. He felt completely unmanned and lower than a footprint. Could he not withstand a little schoolboy taunting?

Could he not keep from crying over spilled stew?

Stephen's pulse thrummed in his neck. His outburst at Hiram's house replayed in his mind. He knew his old friend had trouble with his memory, but part of Stephen suspected that Hiram just wasn't listening. Such questions, over and over! And Sylvie ought to have known better than to waste food like that. But had he struck her? Truly? His brow ached as he tried to recall the details. He could scarcely remember it, only the way she had looked at him, holding her arm, eyes shadowed with fear or accusation or judgment.

Stephen turned his hands over, inspecting them. Dirt lined his fingernails and the creases in his palms. Raw egg had made them shine. What had these hands done today?

He tried to calm his fearsome pulse. His breathing was too hard, too fast. It rattled through his chest, a reminder that he had never completely recovered from the debilitating diseases of prison camp. With a grunt, he stood, but too quickly. Feeling dizzy, he leaned against the fence, and flakes of chipped white paint loosened and fell to the ground. Everywhere he turned, things were in disrepair. Most of all, him.

Chapter Three

Wednesday, October 4, 1871

Meg's grip tightened around the two linen-wrapped canvases she carried. A policeman halted traffic on the corner, and she hustled to cross Clark Street. As she stepped back up onto the sidewalk, a streetcar clattered past her on Randolph, and she half wished she were on it herself, given the burden she carried. But then, her journey was a mere handful of blocks—two east on Randolph, three more south on State—and she ought to save cash whenever possible. After all, she hadn't sold these paintings yet.

She would, though. None other than Bertha Honoré Palmer had stepped into Corner Books & More yesterday morning in her fur and diamond earrings, *Tribune* folded to show the article Mr. Pierce had written about Stephen. She had come to shop from the remarkable veteran featured in Sunday's paper.

When Mrs. Palmer spied Meg painting, she announced she wanted not just rare books for her new library, but original art by a female Chicago artist. She selected two of her favorites to start: Margaret Hale of *North and South* and Helen of Troy from Homer's *Iliad*. Since the Margaret Hale required one more day of drying before it could be moved, Meg had offered to deliver both paintings this morning herself. Mrs. Palmer had agreed and purchased two volumes of early Chicago history on the spot. Witnessing this transaction, another new customer purchased portraits of Marianne and Elinor Dashwood, the sisters from *Sense and Sensibility*, along with a boxed collection of Jane Austen's work for his wife's upcoming birthday. At this rate, Sylvie wouldn't have to worry over the accounting books much longer.

Turning onto State Street, Meg's enthusiasm almost made up for her lack of sleep. The fire bell in the courthouse tower had continued to clang every day and night this week, each time sounding an alarm deep inside her father. Other than pacing the roof at night, he refused to leave their apartment. He must be ready, he'd said, for anything.

To Nathaniel Pierce's credit, nothing in his article had hinted that Stephen's state of mind ever faltered, and for this she was profoundly relieved. She knew what it was like to be misrepresented.

As a child, she'd been called an imbecile and had almost believed it was true. Written language and numbers, which had come so easily to Sylvie as a child, had exasperated Meg. Letters mashed together in jumbles of squirming shapes until she despaired of ever learning to read. She grew to despise both school and the bookshop for holding worlds within pages she could never unlock, worlds enjoyed by everyone in her family but her. She'd consoled herself by painting realms of her own and by eating too many sweets.

Meg's teachers had dismissed her as dim-witted, unteachable, and surly. Her father was the only one who saw past her temper to the frustration and heartbreak beneath. If he hadn't taken on her education at home, she never would have overcome her challenges.

Even now, numbers traded places in her vision when she was tired or stressed, but she'd long since learned how to manage, how to read. Still, the unflattering brushstrokes with which she had been painted had left their mark. She loathed the idea of Stephen being labeled insane. She would stay by him, in body and spirit, until he found his way again. Just as he had remained by her.

Shifting the paintings in her hands, Meg tucked her concerns about her father behind the opportunities broadening before her. On State Street, her steps quickly took her into the shadow of the six-story Marble Palace department store at the northeast corner of

State and Washington. The smell of roasting chestnuts drifted from a food cart as she passed the First National Bank and Booksellers' Row, a five-story building full of news companies and publishers.

At last she stood before the tallest building in Chicago and the only fireproof hotel in America, according to the papers. The Palmer House hotel was eight stories high and had opened to the public just last week. A thrill rushed through Meg as she stepped beneath Roman arches and through the massive double doors.

She was greeted by a smartly uniformed employee. "Mrs. Palmer is expecting me this morning," she told him, giving her name.

"Yes'm, Miss Townsend, she is." An approving smile flashed in his dark face as he welcomed her inside. His speech held a distinctive and pleasant drawl, hinting at Southern roots. At the sound of heels clicking briskly toward them, he turned. "Ah! There's Missus Palmer now."

"Meg! Thank you for coming." Rings dazzled on Mrs. Palmer's fingers. Her alabaster skin was radiant, her hair coiffed to perfection with diamond-studded combs, her corseted waist much smaller than Meg's. The socialite and philanthropist had been twenty-one when she married Potter Palmer last year. Which meant that at twenty-two years old now, she was one year Meg's junior and less than half her esteemed husband's age.

"I believe these belong to you now," Meg said. "That is, if they please you."

"Oh!" Mrs. Palmer exclaimed. "Zachary, would you?"

At her gesture, the man who'd greeted Meg removed the linen sheet from around the canvases and held the portraits while Mrs. Palmer tilted her head to regard them.

"Perfect." Mrs. Palmer smiled. "Even better than I remember them. Zachary, these are for my personal library in our private living suite. Would you take them there? I'll be along later to tell you where to hang them. Thank you." She waited until he walked away, then handed Meg a small purse. "Your payment, plus a little something extra for the trouble of bringing them here. I assume cash is all right?"

"Yes, of course. Thank you." Meg tucked the fee into her reticule. Businessmen eddied around them, their conversation a low drone.

"Not at all." Mrs. Palmer waved the matter aside with a flick of her elegant wrist. "Oh, what a madhouse this is! This was all supposed to be finished before the grand opening, of course. Mr. Palmer and I haven't moved into our suite quite yet, as there's too much to be done. It really is extraordinary, though. Two hundred twenty-five rooms, and each floor connected by an elevator, of course. It's Mr. Palmer's favorite ingenuity. I gravitate toward the imported luxuries: handwoven Axminster carpets, French chandeliers and candelabra, and genuine Carrara marble."

"Carrara? As in, Michelangelo's Carrara marble? The same marble from which he carved *David* and the *Pietà*?" Meg glanced at a grand marble fireplace in the lobby, longing to touch it, as if she could channel some of Michelangelo's artistic genius into her hand.

Truthfully, however, the painter of the Sistine Chapel was far too intimidating to be her role model. That honor went to Élisabeth Louise Vigée Le Brun, Queen Marie Antoinette's favorite portraitist. At a time when female artists faced nearly insurmountable odds, Le Brun not only survived the French Revolution but went on to add a long list of European royalty to her clientele.

Meg emulated Le Brun's blend of old master techniques and subjects in natural and inviting poses, even smiling, but she had no illusions of copying the Frenchwoman's success. She'd toyed with the idea of painting living subjects, but that would require spending large parts of her day too far from her father, who might need her. So Meg contented herself with painting from imagination.

"There is another matter I wish to discuss with you," Mrs. Palmer was saying. "I'm enchanted by the literary portraits you've done, and I'll want more. I would love paintings of Agnes Grey and Jane Eyre, but I saw neither of those in your shop yesterday. If I commissioned them, would you paint them for me? How much time do you need, do you suppose?"

Meg was already sketching the portraits in her mind. "I can get the first done inside of a week, since I have no other orders."

"That will be fine." Clearly distracted, Mrs. Palmer smiled at a lady gliding through the lobby.

"Then I best return to my studio straightaway," Meg said. "Would you care to see sketches before I paint?"

"Splendid idea. Let's make a luncheon of it. Say, next Monday, right here, at eleven o'clock? I'll see that Chef puts his famous chocolate pie on the menu." She walked Meg toward the door, leaning in to be heard above carpenters hammering finishing nails into the wainscoting. "Thanks again for delivering my Margaret and Helen to me. I shall cherish them always! I *must* write a note of thanks to that reporter for drawing my attention to your shop in the first place. By the way, I hope you aren't upset about the letter in today's issue. Pay it no mind. If the writer couldn't even bring himself to attach his name to it, then it's rubbish, pure and simple."

A loud crash sounded, and Meg startled, turning to see a man in coveralls righting a fallen ladder. Sarcastic applause surrounded him.

"As I said, a madhouse, yes? Until next time, my dear. Let us hope all our ladders will be put away by then." With that, Mrs. Palmer bid Meg farewell and sent her gently back onto State Street.

Looping her reticule over her wrist, Meg set her jaw and headed straight for the nearest newsie.

"Mr. Pierce!"

At the door to the *Tribune* building, Nate turned and blinked at the woman shouting for his attention from the other side of Dearborn Street. She marched across the road, the brim of her hat rippling in the wind. Blond ringlets fluttered over the shoulders of her fitted jacket. Upon reaching him, Meg Townsend held up a newspaper and rattled it.

He tipped his hat to her. "Miss Townsend. It's good to see you. Something the matter?"

"Is there somewhere we can talk?" Her tone clipped, she cast a glance at the four-story marble *Tribune* building behind him. "Not here."

"Shall I escort you home?"

"No, no, not there either." She pulled her hat a little lower on her brow. She was agitated. And she had come to him. Why?

Curiosity beat out his impatience to get on with his work, so he took her to the Wild Onion Café around the corner, where they both ordered coffee. Smells of sage, sausage, bacon, eggs, and onions wafted through the café, but she asked for blackberry pie a la mode. Her father had fed such a pie to a stray dog last week, but instead of mentioning that, Nate ordered a slice for himself as well.

Flipping over their mugs, the waitress filled them both with steaming coffee before whisking off to the pie counter, where several varieties waited beneath glass domes.

Lips in a tight line, Miss Townsend tucked her chin, obviously gathering her thoughts. She stared at the scallop-edged paper placemat, then at the single flower in the milk bottle vase, then at two college-aged young men scuffing across the black-and-white tiled floor toward a booth. Anywhere but at Nate. Odd, and slightly irritating, since she was the one who had come to him.

Not very subtly, he checked his pocket watch. "Is it a secret, what's on your mind?" He unrolled his silverware from the napkin.

Miss Townsend unpinned her hat from her hair and set it on the bench beside her. "I assumed you'd be able to guess." Sunlight slipped through the crocheted curtains and stippled her profile.

The clink of silverware on plates grew louder as other diners were served. Nate stirred cream into his coffee, and the aroma curled around him. "You mistrusted me from the beginning. I can only suspect my article proved your misgiving correct." Though for the life of him, he couldn't imagine how.

She shook her head. "If you only knew what your article meant to us! To me, to my family, to our business. Bertha Palmer read it and has become my most enthusiastic patron overnight. Sylvie is sure to be insufferable now, since it was all her idea." She poured cream, then sugar into her mug, turning her coffee the very caramel shade of her eyes.

"So the article brought your store business?" And from Bertha Palmer, no less. Someone might find a story in that—*Millionaire's Wife Prizes Hidden Gem in Local Artist*. He smiled.

So did she. "It did, and we have you to thank for it."

The waitress returned with two plates, then hurried away to take another table's order. Creamy mounds of vanilla ice cream dripped down the sides of their pie.

Miss Townsend took a bite and closed her eyes. "This is good."

Satisfaction filled him. She was much more agreeable now than when they'd first met. If he'd had a role in easing any part of the Townsend family's lives, he was grateful for that. "But then, what did you shake at me not ten minutes ago?"

Swallowing, she unfolded the newspaper and shoved it across the table at him. With two fingers, she thumped a column. A letter to the editor from today's paper. "Did you see this?"

He hadn't. Quickly, he parsed the text.

> People of Chicago, do not be fooled. Mr. Stephen Townsend, of the corner of Clark and Randolph Streets, may have fired a musket, he may have survived Southern captivity, but what is that to us today? Today he is no hero. He is a madman, given to violent tempers and abusive threats. Shame on reporter Nathaniel Pierce for associating such a man with honor. More investigation, Mr. Pierce, and less sentimentality would serve everyone far better.

Heat flashed across his face. He looked up to find Miss Townsend watching him, heartache sketched across her expression.

"Keep reading." She took a sip of coffee and pinned her gaze to the paper.

> Judge for yourself from his behavior, of which I am an eye and ear witness. He leaves the running of his store to his two daughters, both of whom are young and unmarried, while he plays in the dirt in his backyard, shouting obscenities to anyone who passes by his

> rickety fence. Not even children are safe from his abuses. He paces the roof of his building at night, shunning slumber for a chance to hunt ghosts. Who prefers darkness over light, except he who has darkness in his heart?
>
> Watch yourselves, fellow citizens. The city is not safe when lunatics are named heroes, unaccountable for their crimes. Watch him, fellow neighbors. What will it take before we insist he is locked up for his good and ours?

Anger coursed through Nate. He folded the paper, hiding the hateful slander.

"Well?" Miss Townsend asked him. She pushed her plate to the side of the table, the remains of the pie drowned in a vanilla puddle. "You talked to my father. He told you things he never told my mother or my sister or me. Do you think—that is, from what you know, do you believe he ought to be locked up? Be honest."

He could see that it cost her even to ask. "No." He held her gaze. "And you should know that I am honest whether told to be or not." To his shame, he'd learned at the start of his reporting career how easy it was to deceive the public through "embellished" reporting, and how damaging that could be. He'd devoted himself to the truth ever since.

A sigh slipped from her. "Then what on earth do I do about this? This is your newspaper, and the writer has slung mud at your name too. What are *you* going to do?"

Brow furrowed in thought, he ate the last few bites of his pie, swiped the napkin over his mouth, and wrapped his hands around his mug. "I'll discuss it with my editor, but I stand behind my article. The writer of this opinion piece is anonymous, which indicates a lack of confidence. He or she refutes no facts from my article. There is nothing in my feature story to correct, so there's no need to print any type of retraction."

She leaned forward, nodding at his every word. "Will you respond to the accusations at all, in a rebuttal of sorts?"

"Miss Townsend . . ."

"Call me Meg."

"Right. Thank you. Then you must call me Nate."

"You were saying?"

He watched the steam rise from his coffee, choosing his words with care. "The things this writer said about your father . . . some of them are true. It may be best to let the letter die a natural death. Let the next day's news eclipse it."

"But I can't imagine allowing it to go un—" She halted as the waitress approached and refilled their coffee, then carried their dirty plates away.

"Do you have a solution in mind?" Nate asked.

"If I did, I wouldn't be here asking you for one." Meg crossed her arms, clearly frustrated. A light sprinkling of freckles fanned across her slightly upturned nose, reminding him of his stepsister Edith.

Edith was Meg's age but had been married for four years now and had two children just outside Chicago. Edith's younger sister and brother had both remained with Nate until just this summer. Harriet taught school in a small town in Iowa now, and Andrew, only eighteen, had gone west to work on a railroad.

During the years he'd been their sole provider, Edith had often said they weren't related to Nate anymore since their parents weren't alive to make them a family. She'd been angry about how life had turned out for her. She missed her father and stepmom. He didn't blame her. But he did gently tell her that while it was true Nate was not a blood relative, if he took them to the orphanage, the three siblings would likely be split among separate homes. It had been Edith's freckles—an adorable spray she'd long since outgrown—that reminded Nate that underneath her surliness, she was just a little girl. One who had lost too much, too soon.

Freckles notwithstanding, the woman sitting across from him now was no little girl.

"Listen." He ran his hand over his stubborn cowlicks. "You asked me for my opinion, and I gave it to you. Let it go. Don't engage with an anonymous attack. I get the impression your father doesn't read the newspaper. Is he around people who might bring it to his attention?"

Meg shook her head. "He keeps to himself."

"So I've gathered. The people who know your family best will not believe what is untrue. If you're worried about business suffering from the slander—don't be. With Bertha Palmer as a patron, others will follow suit."

With a resolute nod, she pinned her hat back into place. When she stood, so did he. "Thank you, Nate." She shook his hand and smiled.

"You're welcome. Now, if you will allow me." He took the maligning newspaper from her. "I'll put this rubbish where it belongs."

Thankful the matter was so easily resolved, he bid her good-bye and wished her family well.

He meant it. The struggling Townsend family had touched a chord in him, more so than the other veterans he'd interviewed. In fact, he had half a mind to follow up with the Townsends later, to see how they were getting on.

But their welfare was not his responsibility. He'd had his share of that raising Edith, Harriet, and Andrew. At last, the only one he was truly responsible for was himself. Did he miss his stepsiblings? Sure. What he didn't miss was the burden of knowing three vulnerable souls depended upon him for provision and guidance. While he'd invested all his spare energy to their upbringing, his coworkers had snapped up stories he didn't have time to chase, and they still had time for leisure.

Now it was Nate's turn to focus on his career, to sleep at night without worrying how to make ends meet. Maybe he'd even pick up a hobby—or at the very least, a good book.

The Townsends were on their own.

Chapter Four

Sunday, October 8, 1871

The fire bell was ringing again.

Meg groaned. With this incessant clanging, her father wouldn't be able to rest tonight. Again. If only he could, he'd be more at ease, more himself. But it was wrong of her, that her first thought should be for this small comfort, when others might be in harm's way.

"How many strokes was that?" Sylvie asked when the last one fell away.

Meg hung her hat on the rack at the hall mirror. It was half past nine at night, and they had just returned from evening church services. "I don't know. Let's go to the roof to look."

When they reached the tar-covered roof, they found their father already there. He had long since given up attending church, unable to bear the crowds.

"What do you see?" Meg asked him. Her corset pinched as she inhaled deeply, alert for the smell of smoke.

Stephen pointed south to a patch of sky glowing orange. "Looks to be the same area that burned last night, or very near it. It could be that the ruins reignited themselves."

Meg squinted, trying to gauge both the distance and the intensity of the color, but it was a mere smudge of light scrubbed against the dark. It wasn't near enough to bother them here.

A strong wind freed wisps of Sylvie's hair from her snood, swirling them about her face. "I think it's farther away than last night's fire. Don't you?"

"Can't say." Stephen wiped a handkerchief across his brow and struggled to stuff it back into his pocket. Fire agitated him from any distance. "I'll stay here and keep a watch on it."

"Are you sure?" Meg asked, somewhat mollified when she noticed he was not carrying his gun. It had been four days since the anonymous letter had been printed in the *Tribune*, and as much as she wanted to put it from her mind, she couldn't. Whoever had seen her father on the rooftop—most likely their tenants—might be watching even now. "Won't you come to bed?"

"Please, Father," Sylvie added. She had seen the letter too, of course, and had been as upset as Meg. None of their customers had mentioned it, but more boys than usual had come by, spying through their fence. If Meg hadn't suspected it would humiliate Stephen further, she would have burst into the yard and scattered the rascals herself.

His eyes darting from one rooftop to another, Stephen ran his fingers through his beard. "I'm sure I'm not the only one outside fire-gazing tonight."

But the walk home from church had not shown a city concerned. It was a warm night, and the German beerhouses were full of merry singing. Promenaders, still in their Sunday apparel like Meg and Sylvie, strolled down sidewalks and through parks. If this evening was unusual, it was for its pleasantness.

Sylvie covered a yawn, then held her skirts to keep them from billowing indecently. "You can't believe that our safety depends on your vigil. If the danger increases, we'll hear of it."

Reluctantly, Stephen agreed. As they all headed back inside, Sylvie's shoulders relaxed.

Stephen's didn't. He went to the parlor and stared out the window across Court House Square. He did not sit, nor did he turn on any lamps. He mopped his brow again.

Meg approached him from the side, as she had learned long

ago that to come from behind would startle him. "Do you need anything before I retire?" She raised her hand to touch his back and then, thinking better of it, curled her fingers into a fist and lowered it into the folds of her skirt.

He opened the window, and the hiss of gas lamps on the street below floated into the shadow-cloaked room. It looked like a stage set, without light, without movement, save the wind that rippled the curtains. Stephen stood there, taut with suspense, like a player in some Shakespearean tragedy waiting for the curtain to rise.

He hadn't had another episode since his breakdown at Hiram's house a week ago, but a few times he'd teetered on the brink. If only these fires would stop and the fire bell with them! It was hard for anyone to function without enough rest. At some point, surely, his own exhaustion would overtake him.

As if he hadn't even heard her question, he finally noticed Meg with a start, then whirled to find Sylvie waiting for her in the curtained doorway. "Why are you watching me like that?" His breath pushed hard against the thin wall of his chest. Coughing, he turned back to the window.

Without a word, Sylvie brought him a pitcher of water, poured him a glass, and left both on the tea table beside him.

"Good night, Father," Meg whispered, then looped her arm through her little sister's. When they left him, his coughing had ceased, but he had begun tapping the side of his thigh. "He'll come around," she told Sylvie in the hallway between their chambers.

"Get some rest," Sylvie replied. "Tomorrow will be a big day for you."

Fatigue weighted Meg's limbs and eyelids as she slipped into her room. Since Wednesday morning, she had sketched and resketched the portraits for Bertha Palmer, her emotions swinging from jubilation over her new commissions and the opportunities before her, to lingering distress over the slanderous letter about her father. As she changed into her nightdress and collapsed into bed, her singular aim was to sleep long and soundly. Her luncheon with Mrs. Palmer was little more than twelve hours away.

Sylvie was right. Tomorrow would be a big day.

Smoke stung Nate's eyes and choked his throat as he made mental notes for his story. Before him, Chief Marshal Williams wrangled a thin circle of engines around the fire that had started on DeKoven Street an hour and a half ago. Horses harnessed to the engines stamped the ground and flicked their tails, nickering.

By Nate's count, there were five steamers, three hose carts, and a hook-and-ladder wagon, all pumping water into the fire from all sides. The streams hissed and boiled upon hitting the burning wood, sending up columns of white steam. Neighboring buildings were smoking, ready to ignite. The other firemen who had been called out had been sent to the wrong location.

"You there! All of you!" Williams shouted at Nate and the knot of spectators who had gathered. "If you don't want this blaze to spread, do something about it!" He gestured to the wooden fences and sidewalks, all fuel for the fire.

They sprang into action. Taking an ax from a fire engine, Nate rushed back to the sidewalk, heaved the tool over his head, and brought the blade down into the planks until he could rip the pieces out with his bare hands. A man named Richard took the ax while he did so, hacking away at the nearby fence, while others cleared the wood away to a place Nate did not see, nor did he have time to consider. No longer a mere spectator, he threw himself into his task. Shards of wood must have cut his palm, for he noticed a trickle of blood. He didn't feel it.

"Think they can hold it here?" Richard shouted over the roar of the flames. The fire had already eaten through five blocks.

Nate wanted to say yes but knew too much to believe that. Half of the one-hundred-eighty-five-man firefighting force had fought last night's seventeen-hour fire in the West Division well into today. Then, as was their custom, they had unwound by drinking. After only a few hours of sleep, they'd been called up again. Only now they had to work without equipment that had been damaged last night. There had simply been no time to repair it.

Sweat rolled into Nate's eyes, and with his wrist, he pushed up his spectacles before tearing at the wood again. It was warm in his hands and beneath his knees. Getting warmer. The fabric of his trousers ripped as he moved to a new section.

"The fire is getting out of control!"

Not slowing in his task, Nate looked up to find a former alderman by the name of James Hildreth shouting to Chief Marshal Williams what he surely already knew.

"What you need is a firebreak, a real one! Tearing up sidewalks and fences won't do it. Blow up those houses." Hildreth pointed to a row of them.

Williams's eyes were bright in his soot-streaked face. "Just blow up those people's homes? I don't have that kind of authority."

"This is an emergency," Hildreth persisted. "Take emergency measures, man! A few will suffer the consequences in order to save one hundred times as many, maybe more. If you don't blow up those houses yourself, the fire will devour them anyway."

"Even if I wanted to, I don't have powder."

"I know where to get it!" Hildreth yelled.

With a forceful thrust of his arm, Williams shouted back, "Then go!"

Nate stood, surveying the wreck he and the other men had created, and knew Hildreth was correct. Against such a blaze, with the winds blowing as hard as they were, their efforts had only succeeded in getting the bystanders out of the way. He predicted the fire would come this way in less than half an hour, either by lapping along the ground or by sending firebrands through the air, landing on the rooftops. Evidently of the same mind, Richard returned the ax to the fire engine and fled.

Nate stayed. This was tomorrow's front-page headline.

An updraft sucked pieces of burning cloth and wood into the air over the fire. A man's burning shirt sailed into the sky, its sleeves outstretched as though reaching for help. Sparks landed on the remnants of the sidewalk and flamed up. Nate stamped them out, one after another. Other spectators did the same.

Legs planted wide, exhausted firemen sprayed water on the flames in what appeared to be a futile exercise. One of them dropped his hose, ran beyond Nate's vision, and returned moments later carrying a wooden door, which he braced on the ground as a shield between himself and the heat of the fire. With the door leaning against his shoulder, he resumed hosing from behind it.

The door ignited. The firefighter leapt away when it burst into flame, jerking back as though burned.

"You're next!" Nate shouted in alarm, still stomping out small fires himself. The fireman's uniform had begun to smoke, and his leather hat twisted out of shape in the heat. "You're catching!"

"Come out of there!" Williams called to the men. "Wet the other side of the street or it will burn!"

Nate and another man sprang forward to help reposition a cart while the fireman held the hose. Before they reached their destination, however, the water pressure dropped to a trickle. Nate's nerves began to unravel. "What happened?"

Face grim and as slick as melting wax, the fireman pointed. "That steam engine just arrived and took my hose from the water plug so he could use it himself."

Though more powerful, the steam engine didn't get to their position fast enough. Nate watched as five houses across the street blazed up. Chief Marshal Williams bellowed in frustration.

The smoke made it difficult to breathe. The constant sparks landing around Nate, and on his clothing now, made it a feat to concentrate. Helplessly, he witnessed another steamer malfunction, rendering it without water as well. A quick repair recovered the stream, but not long afterward, an old section of hose burst, and the water stopped again, this time for good.

Williams scrambled to reposition the working engines that were left, but the wind had shoved the fire well past his men. It was pushing the flames northeast, racing across the wooden sidewalks

Nate and the others had given up on. As the tongues of fire spread, nothing stopped it. Everything in its path—fences, trees, chicken coops, outhouses, clapboard houses—was consumed.

By now the updraft was even stronger, lifting flames hundreds of feet in the air, turning the sky a lurid orange. Policemen arrived, and more citizen-volunteers, who frantically set about tearing down sheds and fences. This time, Nate didn't join them, convinced the fire was too far gone to be contained by such efforts.

Glowing embers fell like red snow on his hair, his shoulders, each one a stinging needle digging into his flesh. He slapped at the sparks as soon as they landed, all the while committing the scene to memory.

"The river will stop it, at least," said a man behind Nate. The south branch of the Chicago River flowed between the West Division and the business district.

But no sooner had the hope been uttered than the steeple of St. Paul's Church caught fire. Through clouds of smoke, Nate watched as showers of sparks blew through the sky, arcing directly into the heart of the city.

The fire was jumping the river.

Sylvie awoke to a pounding on her door, then listened as the noise echoed on Meg's down the hall.

"There is devilment afoot." Her father's voice registered a constrained alarm.

Stepping into the hall, Sylvie found him pacing. "What's wrong?"

The courthouse bell was ringing—without stopping. Church bells, too, sounded the alarm. An unnatural light spilled into the parlor. Sylvie ran to the window and peered out. The streets were full of people, all of them looking up, looking south to an orange sky as bright over that section of town as the morning sun.

"What is it?" Meg joined her, still rubbing her eyes.

"It's—it's the fire. Is it . . . ?" Sylvie leaned over the sill, as if that would help her get any closer to answers. Where exactly was it? How fast was it moving?

Stephen stood behind her. "It's coming," he said. "Mark me, it is coming this way."

"You're sure?" But her pulse was already galloping, telling her to run.

On the street below, a few fingers extended into the sky, pointing at something Sylvie couldn't see. Then more people joined the first to observe. It wasn't until she heard the screaming that she realized what it was. "Cinders."

Meg gasped. They were falling like giant grey snowflakes all over Court House Square.

"It's coming," Stephen repeated, almost as if in a trance.

Sylvie whirled to face him. "We are standing above a store full of paper!" If the fire reached them, they could lose it all. "There is still time to save some inventory. As much of it as we can."

Now it was Meg leaning out the window, calling to someone below. "Mr. Applebaum! Where are you taking that?"

"To the train station!" came the answer. "Take your valuables to the train station, and the cars will roll it out of the city until the danger has passed!"

Purpose surged through Sylvie. "That's it," she said. "Father, bring all the trunks and crates we own to the store. Meg and I will join you in a moment."

Footsteps trampled overhead as the Spencers rushed into action as well. For a fleeting moment, Sylvie's thoughts winged toward her friends, but she had to trust them and their families to God's care. Surely they were awake, packing, running. *God save us all.*

Without another word, the girls rushed back to their chambers and dressed in their simplest shirtwaists and skirts. Hair still in their sleeping braids, they flew down the stairs and met Stephen.

"Rare books first," Sylvie instructed, pointing to the shelf that held them.

When Stephen hesitated, Sylvie marched to stand before him and gripped just one of his hands in hers, holding fast even when he tried to withdraw. "Father, we need you now. Meg and I can't save the store—*our* store, *your* store—alone. You've got to help us. We need every bit of you, all right? We can't do this without you. Please help us."

Perhaps she only imagined it, but it seemed to her that her words brought a grounding to his restless spirit and a softening to the hard edges of his face. He looked directly into her eyes as if seeing her in truth for the first time in years. "I'm here for you, daughter. I'm here for both of you."

Sylvie's relief was palpable but short-lived. Outside, horses pounded the streets as they pulled towering loads of goods. The urgency to be among them was overpowering.

"I'll get the paintings." Meg fetched a ladder from the back room while Sylvie dragged another trunk to the counter.

The cash register, the accounting books, the records of inventory purchased and sold, the list of vendors and customers—all of this went into the bottom of the trunk. On top she piled novels by Austen and Alcott, Brontë and Brontë, Dickens and Defoe, Homer and Hugo, until the trunk was nearly overflowing.

Desperation flickered over her as she looked around the store. They had only three other trunks, one of which ought to hold Meg's paintings, and four wooden milk crates to fill. Forcing herself not to agonize over the titles, she blindly pulled them from the shelves.

Stephen lugged his burden of rare books to the front of the store. "I packed the repair tools too, as I'm sure we'll have more need of that than ever before. We'll need a wagon. . . ." His voice trailed off as he looked toward the window, and Sylvie could almost hear the protest sitting on his tongue. The people, the crowds, unnerved him. His reluctance was a tangible thing, a thickening of the air.

Meg climbed down the ladder and placed a portrait of Jo March in a crate. "If that would distress you too much, I suppose I could—"

"Don't you dare," Sylvie interrupted. All the times she had buried her disagreement in order to keep the peace seemed to gather with a building pressure in her chest. Anger burned through her, stunning her with its force.

Once again, Meg was making concessions for their father, and once again, it appeared that Stephen would let her. Deep down, there was a better person inside Sylvie, a woman of compassion and sympathy. But right now she was wearied to death of how Meg protected Stephen. Right now, there was a great deal more than his feelings at stake. It was time for him to protect and serve someone else. He'd done it for soldiers in his regiment. He'd done it for the sake of slaves and strangers. Could he not protect and serve his daughters too?

She swallowed the bitterness in her mouth before attempting to speak again. "Meg will be safer here with me, and more efficient too. While you're getting whatever conveyance you find, we can finish packing the store and choose some valuables from the apartment."

Seconds dropped away from the clock, every one of them precious. Stephen stood rooted in place, maddeningly motionless, when on the other side of the glass, the entire city had sprung into action, heads bowed, hair and skirts and nightdresses billowing behind them. Dogs plowed between people as they fled the danger, smart enough to do what her father refused to do.

"Go!" Sylvie shouted. "You said you would help us! Behave like a father for once this side of ten years!"

"Sylvie! You go too far!" The color draining from her face, Meg looked at Stephen, when she would be better served to look outside.

Guilt took aim at Sylvie, but she erected a barricade just as fast. "He will not go far enough, and you know it. He should go—not you, not me. He is stronger, and as a man, less likely to be taken advantage of."

At that moment, Karl Hoffman from the bakery down the block passed by the shop door. Still shocked at her own outburst—but not sorry for it—Sylvie rushed to unlock the door and burst outside.

"Mr. Hoffman! Wait! Are you going to find a wagon or dray?"

He turned but barely slowed his pace. "*Ja*, where else?"

Casting one furious glance over her shoulder at Stephen, she told Mr. Hoffman, "My father will go with you."

Stephen swallowed, then stepped forward, and Meg pressed money into his palm.

"*Schnell!* Hurry!" Mr. Hoffman called, his agitation evident in the use of his native tongue.

The bell above the door shook violently when Sylvie slammed it behind Stephen. Still steaming, she turned back to her sister. "It's only fitting he should go instead of one of us."

Meg moved between two shelves and out of view. "God will help us," she said.

"God will help Father too," Sylvie whispered so quietly she could not be heard. And yet tears of shame pricked her eyes over the words she'd used as weapons. As she hoped and prayed for his return, guilt dug in.

An explosion ripped through the night. Jumping, Sylvie covered her ears and stared in shock at Meg for a moment before running outside.

"Look!" someone shouted, pointing at an enormous ball of fire in the sky and columns of flame soaring straight up. "The gasworks have exploded."

All at once, the little flames in the gas lamps along the street guttered and died out. There would be no light for those fleeing now except for illumination by fire. Worse, the gas released into the air was now fuel for an already raging inferno. Sylvie stared around her in dismay. How would their father, who could not handle crowds or loud noises, navigate this?

Chapter Five

Stephen's heart felt near to bursting. Even after the explosion from the gasworks, his ears still rang. Bells pealed from every tower and cupola in the city, melding into a roar of indistinct clamor that made it nearly impossible to think. Even the wind was vicious, driving dust like needles into his face.

He had no concept of time or distance, so he could not say how long he'd been straining to drag the store's inventory in the handcart behind him. Nor could he judge how near the fire was, except that it was closer all the time. All he knew was that people had gone mad. In a vacant lot, fools drank liquor and fell to fisticuffs with each other. Looters broke into abandoned shops and businesses, piling wagons high with their goods. Thieves, families, and hotel guests with no sense of direction pressed from all sides, bogging him down in the road.

"Make way!" he shouted. No use. They wouldn't listen. More and more poured into the street, men and women in their nightclothes carrying baskets on their heads or lugging bulging tablecloths behind them. Several clutched birdcages the way their children clutched dolls. Rugs and mattresses rode on shoulders above the crowd.

How long until the last train left the station with the city's valuables? The question chewed at his mind, for his pace was horrifyingly slow. What would he do if he missed his chance? How would the girls react when they learned he'd failed them again?

Cinders peppered the orange sky. And then came something else.

Sparks.

Live embers, blown by the howling wind from the fire raging to the south. The only thing that moved faster was his pulse. He felt trapped. Stuck. Imprisoned in a sea of people who had no sense of an orderly retreat.

A sick feeling filled him for the people who truly were imprisoned. When he had passed the courthouse, he'd heard men screaming from the jail in the basement. What would become of those men? Would they be burned alive?

Stephen's nerves unraveled, his blood boiled. He was not so far removed from his own captivity that he could forget the overwhelming helplessness that came with it.

Palms slick with sweat, he adjusted his grip on the cart handles and glanced behind him. Noticing a milk crate about to slide off the heap, he pushed it back into position and tightened the rope around it.

"Keep moving!" Someone shouted at him from behind. "Move your blasted cart or get out of my way!"

"We're all in a hurry, mister!" Stephen yelled back. "I'll move as soon as there's somewhere to go!" A spark landed on his shoulder. He slapped it off before it had time to ignite.

Children were crying somewhere, grating his nerves even further. As he circled back to the front of the cart and picked up the handles again, he managed to move a few yards before lifting his head and shouting, "Will you please shut your children up!"

"You shut up, and leave my kid alone or I'll—"

The masculine voice faded beneath others, all angry, some threatening, each directed at him. More sparks fell, and people beat out small fires on each other's backs and hair. Stephen heard everything as though through a tunnel, and he felt himself moving backward through the halls of his memory until he was no longer in Chicago, no longer a veteran, but back in the war that had ravaged the South and wrecked the person he used to be.

He looked over his shoulder at the furious burning sky. Confusion shook him to the core. Was this a dream or a waking nightmare? Was he seeing things that were not really there? He shook his head to clear it. This was too elaborate to be a product of his imagination. He had known there was devilment afoot for months, hadn't he? And now here it was. But who was behind this blaze?

Boom!

Stephen threw himself to the ground and covered his head. His heartbeat raged. No fire could have made that sound. He was under attack. A buzzing filled his head and limbs. Someone stepped on his leg, and he grabbed the offending foot, yanked off the shoe, and hurled it away.

"Hey!" The man whirled on Stephen, pinned him down with his knee, and pummeled him in the nose.

Stephen fought back, fists flying until the man stood up, kicked him in the side, and went to fetch his shoe.

"Get up! Get up, you're blocking the way!"

Tasting blood, Stephen rose from the ground, gripped his cart handles, and moved.

Boom!

Stephen dropped to the street again, nerves afire, all senses on high alert. This time, he crawled beneath the cart and stayed there. Not five minutes had passed between explosions. The Rebels—it must be the Rebels—had brought artillery, and here he was, trapped.

There could be Rebels around him right now. There could be spies or agents or soldiers planted among the fleeing throng. The idea was diabolical but not impossible.

Devilment, indeed.

"Joe, give me a hand with this, will you?"

Two men began rolling and shoving the handcart of bookstore inventory to the side of the street. Stephen was too smart to come out from under it, but instead rolled his body to stay directly beneath it.

"Say, I could get a lot of money for this cart right now," came a voice from above him.

Clever. But Stephen wasn't about to let anyone steal his shelter.

Coming out from under the cart, he pulled his Colt from his belt and aimed. He cocked the hammer. "Move along, Johnny Rebs. This cart isn't yours to take."

"Take it easy!" Arms raised, the two men backed away, and Stephen lowered his gun.

Boom!

"Stay away from that crazy man!" a woman shouted. "He has a gun! He's shooting!"

Stephen looked at the revolver in his trembling hand. Had he fired it when that last burst of artillery fire startled him? He brought the barrel to his nose and smelled, then checked the rounds. One of the bullets was missing. He must have shot it into the ground.

Those Rebs had been lucky this time.

So had he. He didn't want to shoot someone today. All he wanted—all he *ever* wanted—was to be left in peace.

Knees weak, he tucked himself under the cart again, waiting for the next round of cannon fire.

The *Tribune* building, at least, was fireproof.

With enough information for a solid story about the early stage of the fire, Nate Pierce raced to the office, rattled out his article in the composing room, then passed it to editorial. The city might be burning around them tonight, but the *Chicago Tribune* would tell the tale tomorrow.

"There's no stopping the fire before it gets here," Nate told the copy editor. The fire department was divided over the city, attempting to save a few important structures with what exhausted resources they had. "You going to stay?"

The young man looked pointedly at the singed holes all over Nate's clothing. The wind had stolen his ruined hat an hour ago. "Why wouldn't I? This is probably the safest place to be."

Nate supposed he might be right. The exterior was granite, the interior ceilings were corrugated iron resting on wrought-iron I beams. Every wall inside was made of brick.

"But the roof," Nate said. "It's tar over wood."

"The subscription team is on it already. We'll be fine."

Nate took the stairs two at a time until he emerged onto the roof to see for himself. Several men from the subscription department were stomping out burning cinders, and one, a recent hire named Mike, was spraying the tar paper with a hose attached to their rooftop water tanks. Water evaporated dangerously fast off the roof's surface.

A spark landed near Nate's shoe, and he stamped it out. "You men all right up here?" he asked, keeping his eye to the south. The wind, by now, sounded like the lake in a storm.

One of them laughed. "It's a better show than any I've seen at the theater, I'll say that much." A flaming chunk of fabric landed two feet from him, and he leapt upon it.

Church and school bells rang endlessly over the collapse of brick buildings whose mortar had burned away. Timbers groaned, glass shattered. Then a new kind of explosion sounded from the south.

Mike flinched but kept his steady stream of water over the roof. "What was that?"

"Sounds like gunpowder to me," one suggested.

Nate agreed. "Enough to blow up a house." There was no way to see through the smoke to be sure, but he told the young men his guess. "Last I saw of Mr. Hildreth, he was dead set on getting enough powder to raze a row of residences and form a firebreak. Sounds to me like he found it."

"A firebreak. Like the river?" Mike dashed to another spark and ground it beneath his heel. Five other young men danced over the roof, doing the same.

Nate didn't respond. He was transfixed by the flames marching down the block toward them. The acrid smell of gas from the gasworks explosion came with them, stinging his throat and burning his lungs. He ran to the other side of the roof and looked north at the masses clogging the streets. His boardinghouse was down there somewhere, beneath the smoke blowing ahead of the fire.

With a final few words to the boys on the roof, Nate hurried back down to the street and fought his way to the boardinghouse on a side street off Clark. It was empty of people, thank goodness, and in a few minutes, his rented rooms were empty of his most valuable possessions too. All he took with him was what he could fit into his leather satchel: money, his parents' wedding rings, his mother's Bible, his father's pipe. These two rooms had held the last semblance of family he'd had.

But there was no time for nostalgia. Nate fled.

He'd never seen such disorder in the streets. Stoves, mattresses, and wagonloads of furniture had been abandoned, blocking the way for those trying to get around them. A riderless horse galloped by in a wild fury, its tail afire. One woman wore a fur coat and fox stole over her bedclothes, several necklaces glittering at her throat. Barefoot, she crushed her small dog to her chest.

Nate tripped over a crate of chickens left in the street, wincing at the strike to his shin. After wiping ashes and dust from his spectacles, he paused at a water fountain long enough to quench his dreadful thirst, but there was nothing he could do for the searing in his lungs.

A bright flare in a side street caught his attention. A handcart piled with wooden trunks and milk crates had caught fire from blowing embers. The man beside it swatted at orange sparks in his beard.

"Mr. Townsend?" After an instant's hesitation, Nate ran over to him. Whatever he was trying to carry would be ashes in minutes, if not sooner. "There's no saving it, Mr. Townsend. I'm sorry. You've got to come away from there and get to safety."

Stephen didn't acknowledge him, staring instead at the pages of books curling, crumbling, and scattering on the wind. Nate grabbed his arm, pulling him away from the flames.

"Unhand me!" Eyes shot through with red, Stephen rounded on Nate and punched him soundly across the jaw.

Nate staggered back a step, his lip split and swelling. A whisper of self-preservation urged him to keep running, to leave Stephen to his own fate. But his conscience wouldn't give in without another try.

"Mr. Townsend, it's me, Nathaniel Pierce. With the *Tribune*. Come on, now, let's go. Leave this and come with me. It's time to go."

Stephen rubbed his eyes and shook his head. No recognition registered on his face. Only terror, confusion, and barely restrained hostility. Nate could only imagine the havoc this fire, this flight, was wreaking on the veteran's battered psyche.

"What about your family?" Nate glanced around for some sign of Meg and Sylvie. "Are they here? Are they safe?" Surely his daughters could talk him into fleeing, and Nate could be on his way. The story of the century was unfolding all around him, and he aimed to cover it well.

Boom!

Stephen covered his ears and dropped to the ground. "Get down!" he yelled. "Take cover!"

Understanding stabbed through Nate. He crouched beside the veteran. "That's Mr. Hildreth creating a firebreak. He's blowing up houses, nothing more. Come on, we've got to get out of here!"

He reached to help Stephen up—and found himself on the wrong end of a revolver.

"I'm not going anywhere with you, and so help me, if you lay a hand on me again, I will blow it clean off."

Nate backed away, his pulse throbbing in his ears. Glancing around, he saw no sign of Meg or Sylvie and could only guess that if they weren't with their father, they were still packing at their home. He turned in the direction of Corner Books & More.

Then he stopped himself. Those young women weren't children. They were smart and had neighbors who could aid them if they needed it. He wasn't responsible for them. His duty was to document this disaster.

People fled all around him, some with such force they nearly knocked him down. He needed to move. Now.

The wind howled and threw dirt in Meg's face. A scarf about her hair, she scraped loose earth back over the valuables she and her sister had buried in the middle of their father's map of Andersonville. When Stephen had taken the cart to the train depot more than an hour ago, she'd decided not to wait for the cart's return before doing what they could to preserve more property. She and Sylvie had managed to dig shallow graves for more books, clothing, silverware, their mother's jewelry, the deed and title to their property and land, her paints and brushes, and bundles of old letters, including those their father had written during the war. Her back ached with the effort of breaking through the hard-packed soil, but when it was time to flee, they would do so with the clothes on their backs and nothing else.

The dissonant clanging of bells throughout the city echoed the alarm in every bit of Meg's body as the wall of fire crept ever closer. James and Flora Spencer had already fled, lugging a tablecloth full of goods behind them. "*Go!*" Flora had yelled to them while James hurried her along. Silver wisps of hair straggled from beneath her nightcap. "*What are you waiting for?*"

The question echoed Meg's own. Stephen should have been back by now. He should have returned for his daughters.

Sylvie tossed aside the shovel. "Maybe he's out front."

Sweat ran down Meg's sides beneath her arms as she followed her sister through the back door of the shop and out the front. People were escaping from the south through Court House Square, some of their clothes burnt nearly completely off their bodies. Dogs and cats raced with them. Guests from the Sherman House hotel streamed into the street. But there was still no sign of Stephen.

"We've got to go," Meg said, though she despised the idea of leaving without him.

At her side, Sylvie retied her scarf beneath her chin with trembling fingers. "I thought he could do it. I really thought Father would complete his mission and come back to us."

An enormous cheer rose up from across the street. Prisoners streamed out of the courthouse basement, running for all they were worth.

Their urgency fanned Meg's even hotter. With one backward

glance, she stepped into the current of fleeing people, Sylvie at her side.

Something hit the sidewalk, landing in a dark splay of beak and wings. Then another fell. And two more. "The birds," Sylvie said. "They're dying from the smoke."

Her pace quickening, Meg mentally recited the twenty-third psalm, for she could form no prayer of her own.

The courthouse bell stopped ringing. The cupola had caught fire from a flying ember. Faintly, Meg could hear the bright sound of shattering windows.

Turning, Sylvie looked across the distance they'd put behind them. "Meg, your studio! It's on fire already!"

Meg whirled to see for herself. "How—?"

But then she knew. The pile of rags she used to clean the brushes hadn't been washed lately. They were full of linseed oil, which could generate enough heat to combust.

Sylvie grasped Meg's hand. "Mother's book," she said. "I left her copy of *Little Women* in your studio the other night. Did you pack it in the crates Father took?"

Meg thought Sylvie had packed it. Her mouth turned to ash. She shook her head. Another bird dropped from the sky.

Sylvie's composure crumbled. "Father's photograph from the war is inside the book too! We're going to lose it! We'll lose them both!"

Desperately, Meg wanted to say they could get another copy of the book. But this one was irreplaceable, for it held Ruth's thoughts and musings recorded months before her death. Neither could they spare the *carte de visite* of their father.

Hoisting her skirts, Meg dashed the twenty yards back home, bounded up the stairs and into the studio. She choked on smoke and the smell of burning turpentine, linseed oil, and pigment. Flames ate through the pile of rags and up the curtains, which dissolved in heaps to the wooden floor, and puddles of fire began to spread.

Each breath seared her lungs. Meg felt struck dumb and slow with toxic fumes and with fear that plumed thick as smoke. Wind whipped through the room, bending and stretching the flames. Already, other canvases were blistering, then melting into pools of oil.

Timber creaked, snapping Meg from inaction. On the floor, the corner of the book poked out from beneath a sheet draped over a canvas. The sheet was already smoking. By the time she reached it, the paint-spattered cloth was in flames. Faster than thought, she ripped off the sheet, flinging it away. Her skirt caught fire, and she beat it out with her hands. When she looked up, the cover of the book was burning. So was the shelf of paint supplies behind it.

Time slowed, air thinned. Smoke and heat formed a jackhammer inside her skull and a vise about her lungs. Holding her skirts back, she kicked the book away from the burning canvas behind it. Sparks found her skirt again, and she slapped them out.

"Meg!" Sylvie's voice floated somewhere behind her. "Meg, leave it, it can't be saved now!"

But it could, and she was so close. She could scarcely breathe, let alone think straight. Flames danced over the hard cover of the book but hadn't yet eaten through to the pages inside. A fraction of a second could change that, however, and then it would be too late.

Lunging, she grabbed the burning book with both hands.

Chapter Six

Pain exploded in her flesh, consuming her mind. As Meg smothered the flames from the book, the shelf above collapsed, and a jar of linseed oil spilled over the right side of the cover and ignited, burning deep into her hand. The toppled shelf pinned her hand to the fire for too many moments, a timeless stretch of agony. She threw off the wood plank with her other hand, then tore away the book cover and cast it aside.

A hard yank pulled her backward. Encircling Meg's waist, Sylvie took the charred volume from her and propelled her out of the room.

Meg's skin was still burning, or felt that way. Without gaslight in the sconces on the wall, she could see nothing in the stairwell, could only grit the dust in her teeth and move blindly down, down, until she and Sylvie burst outside to a world painted in orange and grey.

"Meg! Oh no, your hands!" Sylvie cried.

Her palms and fingers felt as though they'd been branded and the hot irons had yet to leave her flesh. The right hand looked worse but now felt less pain than the left. For lack of water, Meg spit on her skin and heard it sizzle. A wave of nausea rolled through her.

"I'm sorry," Sylvie was crying. "I'm so sorry. This is my fault."

But there was no time for regrets, no time to wonder beyond the present moment. Meg clenched her teeth to trap the pain. Crows and sparrows continued to drop from the sky. The courthouse cupola kept burning, and a mountain of fire was bearing down on them.

"Meg! Sylvie!" Nate Pierce darted across the street and stood before them. "You should have left long before this! Are you hurt?"

Tears spilled over then, not just for the burns, but for their missing father, the burning city, the home she was about to lose. *Yes,* Meg thought, *I am hurt. We all are.*

But what she said was, "Just my hands. I can walk. Or run." With a glance at the pandemonium in the street and the glowing embers floating from the south, she added, "The book could be wrecked or lost. Or sparks could land on it and burn it altogether. We have to bury it."

Concern filled Nate's soot-smudged features, but urgency soon took its place. "I'll do it." Pulling his jacket from his satchel, he wrapped it around the book and disappeared.

Meanwhile, Sylvie ripped two long strips from her apron and wrapped a bandage around each of Meg's hands. By the time she was finished, Nate had returned.

"Come on." He offered his arms, and the sisters looped theirs through his.

White-hot pain pulsed in Meg's hands as they left the raised sidewalk for the street. But once they were embroiled in the moving crowd, her nerves focused on flight.

"We were waiting for our father." The wind snatched Sylvie's words away, muting her explanation to Nate. A piece of flaming tar paper traced a red spiral in the air before them.

"Thought you might be," he said. "I saw him."

"You did? At the train depot? Is he all right?"

"He didn't make it to the depot with the cart. It was burning when I found him beside it."

"What?" Meg slowed her steps, but Nate urged her along, Sylvie trotting on his other side. They swerved around a highboy and sofa.

"Don't worry, he'll take care of himself."

"But—"

A column of fire whipped up in a nearby alley, tearing through drifts of dried leaves and stacks of firewood prepared for the coming winter.

"I'll tell you more later," Nate panted. "Right now, I can't spare the breath."

Sparks rained down around them. One dropped onto Sylvie's scarf, and she hit it out in the same instant, but the singed smell frayed Meg's nerves even further.

No one mentioned Stephen after that. Meg looked for him in the faces of those they passed, but in vain. Shoved from behind, she stumbled.

Nate halted. A block ahead of them, a whirlwind picked up burning furniture left in the street, hurling it into the air. "Wrong way."

Everywhere they tried seemed designed to cut them off. A building collapsed on a corner, the rubble spreading over the street and sending up a cloud of limestone dust that layered their bodies, lined their nostrils, and scratched their throats. Another intersection was blocked by a fire engine trying heroically to save some grand building. The fire did not just tower over them from behind. It spread from firebrands and flying embers.

The crash of falling buildings increased, along with near-constant explosions. Barrels of oil in a general store burst into fire with the sound of rattling musketry. Then the fire itself was the only sound, drowning out all others. No more bells rang across the city, or those that did could not be heard. A hotel plunged inward with barely a noise.

"There's the bridge," Nate said at last.

The river was patched with fire from oil pooled on its surface. Ship masts burned before breaking off, collapsing and hissing into the water. A flying piece of burning sailcloth landed on the bridge and flared up.

"We'll have to run for it, but the steel frame will hold us even if the wood planks fall through," he yelled over the sound of horses and carts clambering toward the bridge. He was filmed in chalky powder from collapsing buildings, every inch of him a dull green-grey except for his blue eyes rimmed with red.

The ground shook, and a roar barreled after it from behind. The courthouse cupola must have collapsed, and the bell with it, Meg guessed, her thoughts gliding above her physical pain. Perhaps it was the instinct to survive, or simply God's grace in an extraordinary moment, but her mind was clearer than it had ever been. She knew that bridge would carry them and felt a magnetic pull to reach it. "Let's go."

They threaded themselves into the crowd and headed for the bridge.

Collisions happened every minute. When a wheel axle broke on one wagon, several men unloaded the coffins it held and carried them upright. When the bearers were swallowed from view, the coffins bobbed eerily above the throng.

Pain seared. Panic threatened. But there would be an end to this night, Meg told herself, an end to the ocean of flames surging toward them. There would be an after. This was not the end of the story, or at least, it didn't have to be, though it looked and felt and sounded like the Last Day on earth.

Crossing the bridge did not secure their safety. Just as the fire had jumped the south branch of the Chicago River, it leapt over the main branch as well. Just after three in the morning, word spread from behind Meg that the waterworks was burning.

A fresh wave of bedlam followed. People shoved and cried and prayed while stray horses and cows ran among them. Rats passed under Meg's skirts and around her ankles as the rodents sought safety too. They were surrounded by the river and the lake, but without the water pumps working, the water supply to the city stopped. What little restraint there had been on the fire was now gone.

"Keep moving," Nate called, as though the same urgency he felt did not burn within Meg as well.

Meg's scarf fell back on her head, and Sylvie pulled it forward to cover her hair again, then retied the ends of it beneath her chin.

"Thank you."

It hurt to speak or smile or frown. Her lips were cracked and blistered, her throat a desert, and now every fountain was dry.

The farther north they walked, the more it seemed that half the world walked with them, for the languages Meg heard besides English and the Irish brogue included German, Polish, Swedish, Czech, and Norwegian. All of them fleeing their homes. All of them homeless at once.

Small groups of people peeled away from the crowd, until scores and then hundreds of them sought refuge by climbing into Lake Michigan. The water would be frigid this time of year.

Nate, Meg, and Sylvie remained with the thousands heading north.

"I shouldn't have sent Father away." Sylvie craned her neck, searching, then gave up a moment later. Dust layered everyone, disguising who they were beneath. "If we find him—"

"*When* you find him." Sweat trailed from Nate's temples, cutting narrow paths through the grime. "He is nothing if not a survivor."

His confidence bolstered Meg, if not Sylvie. After all, Nate had been the last of them to see Stephen during the fire.

"But he didn't want to go." Sylvie's voice cracked. "He wasn't ready. I pushed him too hard, just like you said, Meg. I don't know if he'll be able to forgive me. If I'd had any idea what the night would hold for us, I wouldn't have done it. If anything happened to him . . ." She broke off, coughing on dust and soot.

Turning, Nate looked over their heads toward the fire. His jaw set, he caught Meg's eye and notched his head toward the north. "Keep moving." The roar of the fire behind them was a constant reminder of what threatened.

Meg put her arm around her sister's waist and kept pace with him, ignoring the throbbing beneath her bandages. "We can fix this," she said, her speech slightly altered by her thirst-thickened tongue. "Later. Soon."

Sylvie leaned her head on Meg's shoulder. "I pray you're right."

At last the sun rose on Monday morning. The fire was still burning at daylight, still too blinding in its brilliance to gaze upon, still a hound at their heels. Despite night's veil being lifted, the air was so thick and the wind such a tempest that Meg could not see to the end of the block. A steady storm of sand lashed her face like bits of glass.

The sunlight failed to filter through dust and powder, so the day remained shrouded and colorless. Hunger marked the passing of time as day melted into evening. Crossing through the old German and Catholic cemeteries, they came at last to Lincoln Park, a long stretch of land along the lakeshore. Thousands had come here before them, filling the park, and Meg supposed that hundreds, if not thousands, would arrive in their wake. Piles of furniture of every sort dotted the park: carpets, bureaus, deconstructed beds, tubs, clocks, chairs, and trunks.

The pervasive mood was that of terror spent, though fire teased them still, burning up the fence along Clark Street, which bordered the west side of the park. Embers fell on dead leaves and flared up. Great plate mirrors leaning against trees reflected the illumination. The park was lit with uncounted fire balloons sailing overhead. Flames consumed the cheap pine headboards at the old cemetery and sometimes even burrowed down into the bone-dry soil so that even the dead were not left in peace. But the living watched from the grassless bank of Lake Michigan, having already come through the crucible.

The fire had equalized them. Twenty-four hours after the flames broke out, Irish longshoremen, Swedish maids, and businessmen with clipped accents were covered in the same ash. A group of well-dressed people from a German saloon sang while a small congregation of Methodists held a quiet prayer meeting. All of them sat in the same dirt by the water's edge.

"Meg." Nate touched her shoulder, and she turned to face him. Dust filled the faint lines in his face, calling out every care that framed his eyes and mouth. He looked like one of her sketches, in dire need of color. "Come. You and Sylvie can sleep now." He gestured to a discarded piano box he had set on its side. "I'll keep watch."

She tilted her head and studied this man, so recently a stranger. "Why did you come for us?" Her voice strained to mask the agony in her hands.

He glanced at her bandages before lifting his gaze to meet hers. "Call it an overgrown sense of responsibility. Or a tendency to make other people's business my own? An occupational hazard." A smile cracked his lips.

Meg wasn't persuaded. "I doubt most reporters sought out their recent interview subjects last night."

He chuckled. "Perhaps not. But I wager I can still write a story to rival theirs." He tapped the satchel still hanging across his body, fingers twitching as though eager to begin transferring his mental notes to paper.

"We can't thank you enough." Sylvie let out a ragged breath. "But why didn't our father come himself?"

Nate rubbed his stubbled jaw, making an absolute mess of his face. But with some of the filth smeared away, Meg noticed for the first time the cut in his lip and a purplish bloom on his skin. "Let's just say he was fighting his own battles last night, and not just against the fire."

Meg winced.

Sylvie's nostrils flared. "And those were more important to him than we were."

"He wasn't himself. He didn't recognize me."

"What did he say?" Sylvie's words sounded dry and thick. "What did he do to you?"

Nate didn't respond right away. "The sounds, the smoke and fire. Part of him thought he was back in the war. As I said, he wasn't himself. I cast no blame."

So Nate had come for them of his own accord, without prodding from her father. Stephen had punched him in a blind fury, if Meg didn't miss her guess, and Nate chose to frame the story with compassion and understanding. She would bury the sting of rejection she felt from her father's choices and concentrate on that.

Sylvie drew her knees up and wrapped her arms around them,

looking away. "I don't know whether to be angry at him or angry at myself for insisting he go out into that chaos. All I know is that I'm angry that my father never came home. Not last night, not after the war. Our father just never came home."

It was excruciating, hearing her talk this way. Meg searched her exhausted mind for some kind of rebuttal that would mend her sister's broken heart—and her own, for she could not deny the truth of Sylvie's words. Stephen Townsend had never come home. But Meg's loyalty would not permit her to admit such a thing aloud. Since she couldn't make their trials go away, she would rather paint over them with a broad brushstroke of hope. But at a time like this, even that seemed a thin and garish varnish.

"I'm sorry," Nate said, placing his hand on Sylvie's shuddering back. "Please try to rest, both of you."

Nodding, Sylvie curled onto her side. The ridge between her eyes remained even as her breathing took on the slow, steady rhythm of sleep.

Meg lay down beside her, the pain in her hands competing with bone-numbing exhaustion. The last thing she saw before tumbling into a deep and unmoving slumber was Nate stomping out another small fire.

When she awoke, it was fully dark again and her legs felt cold. And damp.

With a start, she lurched upright and crawled out into the open air. Every muscle in her body protested the movement, especially her swollen and blistered feet. But she spread her arms wide and tipped her face to the heavens that had so recently been full of hell.

"Rain," she said. "It's raining!" Her boots sank into the softening ground.

"Thank God." Rumpled and tattered, Nate came and stood beside Meg, his warmth a comforting presence. "Thank you, God, for the rain."

Sylvie staggered out of the piano box, her hair wild and grey with ash, and rubbed the sleep from her eyes. "Is it really?" She held her hands up and watched moisture bead in her palms.

Nate captured her and Meg both in a brotherly embrace, then released them. Water streamed over their heads, making a paste of the ashes in their hair, rinsing their faces, soaking their spark-chewed clothing to their skin. All over the park, the sound of rejoicing lifted in half a dozen languages. They had survived the fire. After the drought that had turned the city into a tinderbox, God had seen fit to send rain. They were saved.

And yet Meg still felt lost. Rain mingled on her cheeks with tears of gratitude and sadness as both emotions tugged in equal measure.

Stooping, Nate pulled his satchel out of the piano box and slung it over his shoulder. "Ladies, it's time to get back to work." His smoke-roughened voice managed a businesslike tone. "Now that it's safe to go back, I've got to get to the *Tribune*. And I won't leave you here unchaperoned to spend the rest of the night in the rain."

Bracing herself, Meg pushed her hair back from her face with her forearm. "You're right. It's time to find our way home."

The words held more optimism than she felt. Her thoughts ricocheted from relief at their survival to concern for Stephen's fate and that of her hands, still thrumming with pain in their wrappings. But if she'd learned anything during the last several years, it was that the body repaired itself far easier than the spirit. Her flesh would recover from this ordeal. Could she say the same of her father?

She stood on the line between Before and After. She had crossed such boundaries before, or so it seemed, as she counted the other markers in her life: Before the war, and After. Before Father's imprisonment at Andersonville, and After. Before Mother died. After.

After was always worse.

"There won't be much to go home to," Sylvie said quietly. "But maybe Father will meet us there. I don't know what I'll do if he doesn't." She paused. "I don't know what we'll do, even if he does. Oh, Meg! What will we do now?"

Afraid to ponder the answer, all Meg could think was that it had been years since Sylvie had asked that question of her. When was the last time? Meg painted over the monochromatic scene of

Lincoln Park with watercolor memories instead. When had Sylvie stopped looking to her in a crisis? And why? Meg could not, would not look into the shadowy future just now, so she peered into the past.

She could see herself and her sister on the canvas of her mind's eye. Sylvie, fifteen or sixteen years old, was reaching for Meg. *What do I do? What do we do now?* Meg turned away from her to their weeping father, because he needed her more.

Regret stung her eyes. Meg hadn't known what to say then, and she didn't have an answer now.

This time, at least, she opened her arms to Sylvie and embraced her as best she could before falling in step with Nate.

The fire changed everything in ways she wasn't yet ready to imagine, and yet these two pillars remained: Meg had a sister beside her and a father beyond her reach.

Chapter Seven

Tuesday, October 10, 1871

Stephen didn't know where he was.

His brain told him this was Chicago, but he found no evidence of it, nor could he discern which street he was on or near. Everywhere he looked were heaps of bricks, fragments of tin roofs, telegraph wires, the occasional standing wall, or an arched entryway rising over its fallen building. Houses and hotels had sunk into their cellars. One ruined block looked like another. But if he could just find the courthouse or even its bell amid all the rubble, he could find his way home from there. He kept walking.

Some time ago, the streets had been raised between five and twelve feet above the original level of the city. Now they stood up like causeways, resembling the bones of a prisoner of war wasting away. It gave an eerie, gloomy impression.

A crumpled one-page newssheet cartwheeled across his path. Catching it, he smoothed the paper across his shirtfront before reading it. *Evening Journal—Extra*, the banner read. It was dated October 9, 1871.

The Great Calamity of the Age!
Chicago in Ashes!!
Hundreds of Millions of Dollars' Worth of Property Destroyed.

The South, the North and a Portion
of the West Divisions of the City in Ruins.
All the Hotels, Banks, Public Buildings, Newspaper Offices
and Great Business Blocks Swept Away.
The Conflagration Still in Progress.
Fury of the Flames.

Stephen scanned the rest of the sheet but didn't possess the focus to read it carefully. Giving up, he folded it and stuffed it inside his trouser pocket. Perhaps later he would try again to understand what had happened.

Several children skittered over piles of brick, pulling out silverware fused together, glass bottles flattened, candlesticks bent in half. One boy found a mound of marbles melted into one colorful misshapen blob. Curiosities, they called them. Fire relics.

Stephen felt like a relic too, a curiosity even to himself. A man whose spirit had been so flattened and misshapen, he had failed to care for his own children when they needed him most. His clothing still damp from last night's rain, he shivered with cold and something else, something that might have been shame.

He'd failed his girls. He'd lost everything they'd entrusted to him, and left them to fend for themselves. What would he say when he found them?

What if he wouldn't—*couldn't*—find them on this side of heaven? Curiosities weren't the only things people were unearthing today. Charred human remains were being carried away. His knees went soft at the realization that his own daughters might not have escaped the flames. What then?

Stephen sat on a still-warm pile of bricks and held his head, trying to order his thoughts. But they refused to fall in line. They were more like a train that constantly decoupled its cars and derailed.

He should have feared for Meg and Sylvie's well-being long before this, and it disturbed him that he hadn't. Even now, as he considered their possible fates, it was not with fatherly anguish but with a detachment, a numbness, that he felt sure would hurt his daughters if they knew.

As if they weren't already hurt by or angry about his absence.

Something was wrong with him. He should be able to feel more for them than he did. But feeling was easier before the war. Now when he felt anything, it was usually fear, suspicion, or rage. If he could feel sorrow, he would probably feel sad about this.

Gravel crunched beneath footsteps, and Stephen looked up to watch a pair of men carry another body from the rubble. This one hadn't been burned. Could have been crushed by a runaway horse or wagon, he supposed. Or killed by a falling building.

A snatch of memory flashed in his mind. During the fire, he had hurt people, or tried to. He remembered throwing his fists against flesh and bone. Someone—maybe more than one person—had bled beneath his hand. Then, just as quickly as he saw himself warding off his attackers, his recollections derailed from Chicago and took the track that always carried him back to Andersonville.

To the hurt he had inflicted there just to stay alive. But no, to be fair, it was more than self-defense then. When he beat a man to death with a club, that was only to mete out a terrible justice in order to preserve the weakest among them.

He closed his eyes, and he was there. He could feel the Georgia clay on his skin between the lice and scabs. The Raiders had gone too far. They were the ruthless band of prisoners who preyed upon unsuspecting fellow inmates, breaking bones, even killing men to get their rations or a place in the shade. The Raiders disgraced the Union uniform. They were the worst sort of men, and they thought they owned the whole camp. No one was brave enough to stand up to them until the prison guards secretly armed Stephen and several other men with clubs to beat the Raiders into submission. Stephen was a Regulator, that was all. He hadn't meant to kill that Raider with his club, but he had.

It was different from drawing a bead upon an enemy and pulling the trigger in a pitched battle. He'd killed a man—a fellow Yankee—in cold blood. And he'd been called a hero for it.

He'd been called a hero ever since.

But he wasn't.

"Hey, mister!" A boy about the age of twelve climbed over to where he sat, snapping Stephen back to the present. "Take a look at this fine specimen, why don'tcha? Wouldn't you like to have this as a souvenir from 'the Great Calamity of the Age'?"

Stephen frowned. "What is it?"

"Why, can't you see? It's a stack of ceramic coffee mugs welded together. Might even be from Wild Onion Café. Just imagine—there they were, all clean and shiny and ready to serve up some nice hot coffee to the next customers for Monday morning breakfast. Only those customers never came. The fire did. Now, what would you give me for such a token? Make me an offer, why don'tcha?"

"You're quite a salesman, aren't you?"

The boy grinned and shoved a hank of black hair from his eyes. "The name's Louis Garibaldi. You ever need anything, you ask around for me, and you can be sure I'll get it. I know everyone worth knowing. I got connections, mister."

Stephen was unimpressed. "No, thanks. I don't want your useless stack of cups."

"Okay then, how about this? Just what do you suppose this was in its previous life?"

Without bothering to look, Stephen pushed off the bricks to stand. "I have no idea."

"A revolver, of course!"

Stephen glanced to Louis, then down to the relic he held. "Where'd you find that?" He patted his waistband in search of his own Colt. It wasn't there.

"Why, what's it to you?"

Stephen grabbed the gun, turning it over to inspect it. The barrel veered off center. The cylinder holding the bullets turned only with brute strength, and the walnut handle had burned clean away. As a weapon, it was useless. But it was his, and he told the boy so.

"Not yet, it isn't." Louis snatched it out of Stephen's grip. "But we can make it yours for the right price. How much will you give me for it?"

"Kid, I don't have a penny in the world anymore. But that shouldn't matter because I'm telling you, that belongs to me."

"Prove it."

"Look closely at the side of the barrel. You'll see initials scratched there. SJT. That's me, Stephen James Townsend. That revolver and I have been through a lot together, and I'm not about to part with it just because it had a bad day. Hand it over."

Louis frowned, studying the initials Stephen knew were there. "*SJT* could mean a lot of things, mister. Could be Samson Jeffrey Talbot. Or Simeon Jason Thorndike. This here gun might be the precious property of one Surly . . . Jaw . . . T-bone."

"Surly Jaw T-bone?"

The kid shrugged. "Code name. Whoever this belongs to would pay a little reward for its return, don'tcha think?"

"Whoever steals property from its rightful owner will go to jail, how about that?" Frustration boiled beneath Stephen's skin. The boy meant to take from him the only thing that had made him feel safe.

A belly laugh erupted from Louis as he scrambled away from Stephen. "Oh, mister. You think the police care about something like this right now?" He shook his head, smiling gleefully. "You want it, you're going to have to give me something for it. Ain't nothing in this life for free, you know."

With that, the little street rat tore off, kicking up clouds of dust and limestone powder. After a few bounding strides after him, Stephen fell into a fit of coughing that crippled his pursuit. He'd never recover the revolver from that kid, and even if he did, he'd never use it again. A black mood possessed him.

A steam engine hissed as a locomotive pulled into the train station several barren blocks away. Trudging in the opposite direction, he found his way to Court House Square. The courthouse cupola was gone, along with the enormous bell that had rung so incessantly for the past week. Some outer walls still stood, but the building was gutted. Stephen stared for a very long time. He felt a kinship with those ruins that he didn't care to dwell upon.

Nor did he want to consider where all the criminals from the jail were now. He hadn't wanted them to be burned alive, but now . . . well, they were criminals, and they could be anywhere. Instinctively he reached for his gun, only to remember its fate.

Around him, men with spotless white collars and frock coats gave orders to men with shovels, pickaxes, and wagons. The ruins from buildings across the street clogged the road. His gaze drifted to where Corner Books & More should have been. In its place, a pile of bricks and more relic-pickers roving over them.

"Hey!" he shouted. "Get away from there, you scavengers! If anything there is worth finding, it belongs to me!"

One bedraggled gypsy woman gave a small cry at the sight of him, while the other covered her mouth with bandaged hands before lowering them. "Father!"

Stephen felt a twinge of something to see his daughters in rags, hair bound in filthy scarves, but alive. He was sure he should have felt more.

Sylvie hadn't sent her father to his death after all. Speechless with relief at the sight of him, she stood rooted in place as he scaled the mound of rubble where the sidewalk used to be. Early this morning, at the church Nate had taken her and Meg to for refuge and rest, Sylvie had desperately prayed this reunion would take place. But she hadn't rehearsed what to say.

Meg found her voice first. "Father! You're alive, and that's all that matters."

In the span of eight words, she had excused his loss of their inventory, his failure to come back for them.

All that matters? Sylvie twitched with irritation. Four solid miles of city had been decimated, miles which included their home, and Beth's and Rosemary's. State Street and Michigan Avenue were a barren wasteland studded with ruins to rival that of ancient Rome, not to mention the destroyed factories and lumberyards and ships that had been trapped by fallen bridges. The Palmer House hotel and *Chicago Tribune* buildings had only been fireproof until the water pumps stopped working and they could no longer keep their tar-paper roofs wet. Surely, all of that mattered too.

Evidently forgetting his aversion to touch, Meg reached to hug Stephen. He winced as she closed the distance between them, and she drew back. He would not hold his daughter even now. Instead he sidestepped her and walked over to view the bookshop's burned-out basement.

With stunning speed, Sylvie's relief at seeing him alive dissolved beneath her frustration. Meg was trying—far harder than Sylvie cared to. Could he not see how he pained Meg with such rejection?

"We were so worried about you," Sylvie began. "We thought we might have lost you."

He did not say he'd been worried for them. He did not ask about Meg's hands. Hurt fanned into anger for her own sake and her sister's.

"What happened, Father?" Meg asked him.

Stephen rubbed the back of his neck and kicked at a broken brick. "I lost it."

"We know," Meg said. "Nate told us. Nathaniel Pierce, the *Tribune* reporter, remember? Do you want to tell us about it?"

Their father's bloodshot gaze narrowed. "How would he know? I just now learned of it myself."

Impatience pricked Sylvie. "What are you talking about?"

"My revolver. I must have dropped it somewhere during the fire, and then just now some relic-hunter showed it to me but wouldn't let me have it because I couldn't pay."

Heat flamed into Sylvie's cheeks. "Your gun!" she cried. "Good riddance to it! You lost far more than that, and you know it. You lost our inventory and records. We lost everything except what we were able to bury in the yard and dig up again. Chicago is in ruins, and you pine for your gun!"

Meg might be too kind or too scared to say it, but someone had to. And Sylvie had nothing left to lose.

His eyelids flared. "What did you save? What do we have?" He lit upon the bulging pillowcases at her feet. "If I find that kid again, I can make a trade and get my Colt back. A man ought to have a gun, especially in times like these. The Rebels—"

"Not the Rebels," Sylvie hissed. "Enough about the Rebels." She wanted to scream. Fearing she very well might, she stalked away to cool her head.

"Father, what we saved is for us." Meg's voice trembled. "We need it all to begin again. We can rebuild and start a new life without your gun."

His expression darkened, but he dropped the point when he noticed Meg's bandages. Finally. "What happened to you?"

Meg swallowed. "I saved one of Mother's books from the studio at the last minute. It had your photograph from the war inside. My hands will heal."

A scowl slashed across Stephen's face. "Better to have let that burn, daughter."

Sylvie could almost hear her sister's heart breaking. "That's all you can say?" She paused, but he didn't respond. "We waited for you. We would like to know what kept you. Tell us what the night was like for you."

He took a step back from her. "You know as well as I do, don't you? Chaos in the streets, everyone rushing to get away but slowing their own progress at the same time. . . ."

Sylvie crossed her arms. "But what prevented you from getting to the depot? And if you could not get there, why didn't you come back for us as we arranged?" It felt almost sinful, the way she was pushing him for answers. But neither was he sinless, war trauma notwithstanding.

His brows knit together. He said nothing.

"Nate said the cart was already burning when he found you," Meg prompted.

Stephen's attention snapped to her. "That reporter was there? I don't recall that at all. I remember artillery fire, musketry, taking cover beneath the cart. But I don't clearly recall all the events of that night, so I can't begin to answer your questions, Sylvie. There are some memories my brain just rejects."

"We've heard that before," she said.

Stephen's expression hardened. "It's the truth. If the past is a book, some of the pages in my mind are either blotted out or ripped away completely."

"It's all right, Sylvie," Meg said, though her expression belied the statement. "He can't remember."

Or perhaps he didn't want to.

Stephen jumped down into the open basement and began rummaging for who knew what. If he'd wanted to preserve anything, he might have thought of that before.

"Sylvie!" Meg said quietly. "Let it go. Stop interrogating him. I'm just as upset as you are, but we can't argue about it now. Our house has fallen, in more ways than one. Now is the time to build it back up. Please. I can't forge our little family back together without you."

"And what makes you suppose you can do so *with* me?" Sylvie's words tasted as bitter as the sentiment behind them. She picked at the dirt beneath her fingernails, then abandoned the effort with a sigh. "I'm sorry. I just don't share your confidence."

A commotion drew their gaze to the street. A wagon had stopped, and people flocked to it with pails and buckets.

"Water!" the wagoner cried. "Get your water here, a shilling a pail! Water to drink, water!"

Sylvie dug through a pillowcase for cash and the pewter pitcher they'd saved. With both in hand, she hurried to the water cart, nearly as thirsty for news as she was for drink. After calling to their father to watch their belongings, Meg followed.

After a dozen others, it was their turn. "What can you tell us?" Meg asked the man who filled Sylvie's pitcher. "Surely there's more to report now than we read in the newssheet this morning."

"Aye," the man said. "The new estimate is one hundred thousand people homeless." The cart's horses twitched their tails.

"One hundred thousand!" cried a woman with a Polish accent. "Where on earth will we all go?"

Sylvie and Meg stepped aside after they had paid but stayed to hear the answer. Sylvie held the pitcher to her sister's lips before drinking herself. Never had water tasted so good.

The wagoner shoved his hat back on his head and mopped his brow before filling the Polish woman's pail. "The railroads are offering free tickets out of the city for those who've got someplace to go. General Sheridan and his troops are setting up fifty thousand army tents in Lincoln Park, or you can stay in any church or school you can find. Or you could do as them are, and build your own shanty with scraps of wood and cloth." He squinted at a scorched little lean-to being set up in a hollowed-out cellar.

Forlorn, Sylvie watched the lean-to go up. Such an arrangement would never do for her father. It looked too much like what he'd described of Andersonville. And she was sure he'd spent his share of time in army tents.

Then a familiar sight crossed her line of vision. "Meg! Isn't that Eli Washington?"

Meg watched a carriage driver painstakingly steer his horse and buggy through a cleared path on La Salle Street. "That's him! Eli!"

Leaving the water cart, she and Sylvie went to greet him.

Eli drew rein on his horse. "Well, praise be. At least all of you are safe, thank God for that." But he did not seem wholly relieved.

"I trust your neighborhood was spared," Meg said.

Before Eli could respond, the carriage door opened. Jasper Davenport unfolded his long limbs and stepped out. Sylvie barely knew him from Adam, yet his presence proved stabilizing.

"Our neighborhood was spared, yes," he said. "We're south of where the fire started, so we were not in danger at the house." His face was as grave as Eli's.

"What's this about? You have news?"

Sylvie looked up to find her father approaching, all their earthly belongings in tow. His beard was singed and powdered with limestone dust, his clothing full of holes, his face smeared with soot.

She was certain she looked no better, and it shamed her. In a futile effort to tidy herself, she stuffed stray strands of hair beneath the scarf around her head.

"It's my uncle," Mr. Davenport began, a faint drawl in his speech. He removed his hat from his curly bronze-colored hair. "Eli thought you would want to know."

All regard for her appearance vanished as dread twisted Sylvie's middle. "Something happened." Something terrible.

"Tell us," Meg pleaded.

Mr. Davenport matched Stephen's hard stare. "Well, you are aware he had a habit of wandering off. He went missing Sunday night, after he retired but before the general alarm began ringing."

"Oh no," Sylvie breathed. "How long was he missing this time? Where did he go?" She could only imagine how horrified and bewildered he would have been if he'd gone anywhere near the fire.

In the driver's seat, Eli's shoulders rounded forward, his composure sinking. He kneaded the reins.

"That's the trouble, I'm afraid." Mr. Davenport spun his hat by the brim. "We don't know where he went."

"You mean he's still missing?" Meg asked. "After all this time?"

Stephen circled a hand through the air. "Out with it, young man. Get to the point."

"We found him just now. At a stable on Milwaukee Avenue in the West Division." He said this as if they ought to understand.

"What on earth was he doing there?" Meg asked.

"The stable is being used as a temporary morgue for victims of the fire. When we couldn't find him among the living, the police suggested we look there."

Sylvie stared at him, waiting for more information. Anything that would make sense of what he'd just said. "But you cannot mean—he's dead?"

"It's worse than that." Mr. Davenport turned his sharp green eyes on Stephen. "Hiram Sloane was murdered. Bullet wound through the chest."

Chapter Eight

Wednesday, October 11, 1871

When Meg was a child and learning to read at home after her schoolmistress called her hopeless, she had pointed to each word as her father read it and memorized the shapes of entire words and phrases rather than individual letters. They practiced for so long during the day that after going to bed at night, words stamped themselves on her closed eyelids. *Once. Upon a time. There lived.* What a torture of concentration it had been to assign meaning to those shapes.

The words that marched across her consciousness now held meaning she struggled to grasp. *Home gone. Hiram dead. Murdered.* Beside her, Stephen mumbled the impossible phrases. Meg knew he was trying to make sense of them too.

She could not tell if sorrow—both his and hers—added to or overshadowed the pain in her hands.

Sitting on the floor of the ravaged church they now called home, Meg gazed at the gothic arches above where the altar had been, and imagined the stained-glass panes that used to gild the walls. In her mind's eye, she saw color and shapes, beauty and light, the story of redemption in a portrait of Christ on a heavenly throne, His scarred hands outstretched in victory over the grave. Just because the windows had been shattered in a fire that destroyed Chicago did not mean Christ was not still on His throne. Just because Hiram Sloane had been murdered . . .

Christ was still on the throne, she repeated to herself. Her own scarred hands aching, she squeezed her eyes shut, as shocked and grieved over the news as she had been yesterday when she'd learned it. There had been no good-bye, no warning. Had Hiram been afraid and confused? Did he suffer? Why would anyone kill the poor man?

Shifting on the stone floor beneath her, she opened her eyes, noticed Stephen had finally drifted into an uneasy doze, and looked past Sylvie, down the line of others waiting for the doctor's care. There were at least two hundred refugees in this church alone. Though most of them wore donated clothes distributed by the Chicago Relief and Aid Society, the smell of unwashed bodies was strong. Several people gripped rosaries or crucifixes as they waited, their dry lips moving in silent prayer. Others engaged in lively conversation around the fire.

"What else could it be but God's judgment on a sinful city rife with vice and crime?" one asked.

"No, no, you're looking at it all wrong. What you see as judgment, I see as mercy. It's a chance to rebuild this city even better than before." A ball rolled close to the speaker, and he sent it back to a dozen children playing in the open sanctuary, where wooden pews had burned away.

"Mercy?" A third man jumped in. "What you mean is opportunity. Leave it to Chicago to turn tragedy into a way to make money and show up New York at the same time."

Sylvie leaned over the bulging pillowcases wedged between her and Meg. "Let me roll up your sleeve. The doctor is almost here." Nimbly, she worked her fingers over the sleeve until Meg's upper arm was exposed.

Meg's nerves stood on tiptoe as the visiting physician introduced himself as Dr. Dennis Gilbert and administered a smallpox vaccine to her sister. His greyish-white hair signaled years of experience, and the gentleness of his manner was comforting. Then it was Meg's turn, and she watched the needle slide into her arm and back out again.

"Dr. Gilbert," she said, lifting her hands. Her bandages were rags by now, blackened and falling apart.

"So I see." The waxed tips of his mustache drooped as he frowned. The sweet smell of pipe tobacco lifted from his paisley vest. "The nature of the injury?"

Briefly, she told him.

"I don't suppose any unguent or oil or liniment was applied before the burns were wrapped?"

Sylvie's brow knotted. "There was no time, we had to—"

"I understand," he interrupted, producing a bottle and holding it to Meg's lips. "This will go easier if you have a drink of this. Two big swallows. I wish I had laudanum to offer you."

It must have been whiskey, for she'd never felt such a burning on her tongue or down her throat. She coughed and sputtered. Sweat beaded her hairline.

Meg hadn't even caught her breath before Dr. Gilbert unwound the bandage from her left hand until he reached the portion stuck to her wounds.

"You'll feel some discomfort." Then he peeled the linen away, taking pieces of burned flesh with it. A yellowish substance mixed with blood on hands that looked leathery, a blend of dark red and brown. "That's serous fluid. It's normal."

She shut her eyes and turned her head, gritting her teeth. She shouldn't have looked.

Beside her, Stephen awoke with a start. "What are you doing to her?" he fired at the doctor.

"Only what must be done, sir. If we had more time, and water at our disposal, I would take more care and bathe these burns properly."

Stephen bristled. "Do you mean you're treating her improperly? Do we have gangrene to look forward to now?"

Meg cringed at the mention but did not miss the sentiment behind it. That her father should express concern for her was an unlooked-for kindness. That it had grown rare enough to gain her notice, when before the war it had been as common as breath, was too tender a truth to dwell upon. She released the thought as one removed pressure from a bruise.

Dr. Gilbert began unbinding her right hand. "Be at peace, my good man. I am doing all I can."

"This one doesn't hurt nearly as much as my left," Meg told him. Still, she didn't watch as he exposed it. Neither did Sylvie, who caught and steadied Meg's gaze instead.

The pause that followed could not have been more than a few seconds. Yet it was enough to kindle uncertainty.

"Your left hand has sustained a deep second-degree burn. But your right hand . . ." The doctor's tone had shifted subtly yet distinctly.

Practiced in studying faces, she saw in the pull of his mouth and the sideways flick of his gaze that he was preparing what he would say next, and that she ought to prepare herself too. Dread vibrated through her.

"In your right hand, there is a section of third-degree burn that covers the underside of your thumb, index finger, and part of the palm beneath the middle finger before the third-degree burn fades to second-degree. That is why you don't feel pain there. The wound went so deep, the nerves have been damaged."

She heard him. But only as one heard a voice from the other side of a long tunnel. A flash of heat made her dizzy. Questions rose to the tip of her tongue, but she swallowed them, not ready to hear what level of functionality could or could not be recovered. She would nurse hope and determination instead. Had she not also been told that she would never learn to read or figure sums? Those dismal predictions proved wrong. Even so, a chill danced down her spine.

"What's next, doctor?" As gentle as her voice, Sylvie's arm came behind Meg's shoulders.

From his case, Dr. Gilbert pulled out a jar of ointment and began spreading it over her hands. Only the second-degree burns protested his touch. "We'll bind you up again. If you can come by any laudanum, you should take it for the next three days to help manage the pain, especially before you change your dressings, which you must do daily. Just unwrap your hands, soak them in water for a bit to wash them, and wrap them up again. I'm afraid I have no unguent to spare."

"But when will she be better?" Sylvie asked, a catch in her voice. "That is, when will her bandages no longer be needed?"

"For the left hand, in two or three weeks. The right hand will need them a few weeks longer. Follow up with me at the North Division free clinic in a week or ten days if I don't see you again here."

"And then? What about scarring?" Sylvie pressed. "It won't interfere with normal function, will it? At least in the left?"

The doctor finished applying the ointment, then wrapped her wounds with fresh linen. "Oh, certainly she'll be scarred even in the left hand. But the severity, and how it will affect daily life, remains to be seen."

The way they discussed her fate in front of her but not with her made Meg feel oddly, mercifully, detached from it.

Dr. Gilbert moved on to Stephen. "All right, sir, your turn. If you'll just roll up your sleeve."

Instead, Stephen stood and stepped away, sending a broken shard of slate skittering across the floor. The sound stirred Meg's attention, unfocused at the edges though it was.

"Sir?" the doctor said.

"All these people."

"Yes, and they are all waiting for my services. So if you'll just allow me to quickly administer the vaccine. . . ."

Stephen tugged the end of his beard, then tapped the side of his leg. "Too many people. I can hardly breathe in here." Wind swept through the open windows, ruffling his unkempt hair.

The men who had been debating the cause and benefits of the fire broke off their conversation to listen. One woman quietly tucked her rosary away and watched.

"Father, just let the doctor give you the shot, and then you can go for a walk," Sylvie told him. The curfew would start in a few hours and was strictly enforced, but he had plenty of time before then.

A storm was brewing inside Stephen, if Meg didn't miss her guess. She ought to soothe him, but just now she couldn't think how.

Dr. Gilbert's eyebrows pulled together. "I must insist. The mayor has mandated the vaccine to prevent an epidemic of smallpox. Such crowded, unsanitary conditions create an environment that breeds disease."

"I am familiar with crowded, unsanitary conditions," Stephen ground out. "I know full well how environment breeds disease. Ever heard of a place called Andersonville?"

Understanding softened the doctor's features. But before he could form a reply, a loud voice called out.

"Stephen Townsend? I'm looking for Stephen Townsend. Anybody seen him?" Two police officers stood in the church doorway. A pit expanded inside Meg's stomach.

Stephen wheeled around to address them. "Who wants to know?"

"That's him," someone in the line cried. "That's Stephen Townsend right there."

Both policemen marched toward them, faces implacable. Sylvie stood and helped Meg do the same. She swayed, the heat of the alcohol rushing to her head.

"What's this about?" She hated that her voice sounded weak.

They ignored her. The tall officer identified himself as McNab and the more robust officer as O'Hara. "Stephen Townsend, formerly of 133 Randolph Street?"

Stephen felt for the gun he'd lost. Sweat glistened on his face and neck. "So you've come for me at last. In a church, no less. I plead sanctuary."

"You're under arrest for the murder of Hiram Sloane."

Shock ripped through Meg. Sylvie clutched her about the waist.

"What?" Stephen shouted. "That's a lie! You've got the wrong man."

"And yet you seemed to know we would come for you. Interesting, you didn't seem much surprised."

Meg was going to be sick. Policemen now stood at every door, barring any escape. "What evidence do you have?" she asked.

"Hold him." Officer O'Hara drew handcuffs from his pocket.

Stephen lunged away, but there were too many people blocking his path. McNab struck his knee with a club.

"Stop!" If Meg's hands were not wrapped, she would claw at these men to *make* them stop. Meanwhile, Sylvie said nothing.

Her father was doubled over, coughing, unable to run away. In a heartbeat, his wrists were yanked behind him and cuffed.

"Don't do this! I demand to know what evidence you have to make such a ridiculous charge!" Meg tried to clench her fists, then gasped at the wave of pain that followed.

Stephen twisted violently against his captors and was rewarded with a blow to his temple that felled him to his knees.

"Stop! Stop, I beg you!" Meg cried.

Dr. Gilbert finally intervened. "Officers, you have your man in custody. Can't you show his daughters the courtesy of explaining why?"

O'Hara looked at Meg, his gaze directly on her level. "An eyewitness told us he saw Stephen Townsend kill Sloane in a rage the night of the fire, October 8."

"No, no," Meg said. "They were friends."

"Yeah, about that," McNab said, standing over her father. "We spoke to the deceased's nephew, Jasper Davenport. He says, and the household staff confirmed, that during a meal you all shared on Sunday, October 1, Townsend had some kind of outburst. Isn't that true?"

Meg's throat felt lined with fleece.

"Furthermore, the articles in the *Tribune* say this man became unhinged in Andersonville."

"That's not right." Anger eclipsed the pain in Meg's hands and clarified her thoughts. "The article by Nathaniel Pierce said absolutely nothing about him becoming unhinged. The letter to the editor that followed was hearsay and libel, nothing more." She looked to Sylvie for help. "Don't you have anything to say?"

But Sylvie's countenance was as pale and lined as a ledger sheet. "What can I possibly say that will make this better?" she hissed. "If I could offer some defense on his behalf, don't you think I would?"

One of the men waiting for his vaccination stood and pointed. "I saw him the night of the fire. He was hiding under his cart, and when I approached it, he came out and held his gun in my face. He called me a Rebel and threatened to shoot."

"Because you were about to steal my cart!" Stephen roared, then winced, tilting his head. "What has the world come to if a man can't even protect his own property from thieving Rebels?" Sweat poured from his temples. His shirt collar grew dark and damp. Even the children had stopped playing to gawk.

"Someone will take that witness's statement shortly. What do you think, doctor?" O'Hara asked. "Is this a clear case of another veteran who's lost his marbles? It wouldn't be the first time we locked one up for being a danger to society."

Unsteadiness washed over Meg. She wanted to protest, to shout that her father was no threat. But he'd just admitted to aiming a gun at one of the men in this room. There was something wrong with him, something mysterious and perpetual, something she hadn't been able to fix with love and time and willpower.

Dr. Gilbert twisted one end of his mustache. "It is my observation among my patients at the Soldiers' Home that veterans who were also prisoners of war suffer the greater percentage of mental breakdowns. They have trouble trusting people. Does that amount to lunacy? Not always. But their suspicions interfere with their relationships and daily life, as they are convinced someone is out to get them."

"And I was right." Stephen blinked excessively. "I was right."

"Many of these veterans are fearful and verbally combative," Dr. Gilbert continued, "but not all are prone to physical violence."

"This one is." O'Hara pulled from his pocket a Colt revolver with the handle burned off.

"That's mine!" Stephen cried, and Meg's knees threatened to give way. "Look at the side, it says SJT. Stephen James Townsend. I must have dropped it. I don't remember."

"Another common trait in this type of patient," Dr. Gilbert added. "They can experience or create a traumatic episode—as though a blinding fury overtakes their being—and then genuinely not have any recollection of it."

"Well, lucky for us, someone else remembered it." O'Hara tucked the evidence back in his pocket. "You didn't drop it, you buried it. Another witness told us where to find it."

"Wait, stop." Meg's thoughts whirled to keep up. "That can't be right. We buried our valuables, and they were saved from the fire. But that gun is warped, the handle burned away. It couldn't have been buried. Your so-called witnesses can't be believed."

"The witness clarified that your father did not bury it *well*." O'Hara smirked. "He was in a hurry to get rid of it and made a shallow hole with his hands. When the fire came, it wasn't enough to protect it. When we found it, it was buried in ashes at the location the witness told us."

"I tell you I have no recollection of doing that," Stephen insisted. "But if I'd wanted to get rid of the gun, I'd have thrown it to the flames or into the river, and we'd never have seen it again."

He was right. This was wrong.

"Enough chatting." McNab hauled Stephen to his feet. "We have more criminals to arrest, looters to catch, and convicts to find, since the jail was opened the other night." Shaking his head, he made a scuffing sound against his teeth.

With O'Hara gripping Stephen's other arm, the officers marched him out of the church.

"Where will you take him?" Sylvie called after them.

McNab paused, angling to look over his shoulder. "Where do we take all the criminally insane?"

"No." All hostility fled Stephen's voice, replaced by breathless terror. "Not there. Don't lock me up in that place. I swear I didn't kill Hiram Sloane."

Instinctively, Meg started after them, but Dr. Gilbert and Sylvie held her back.

"Stop, Meg." Tears coursed down Sylvie's cheeks. "There's nothing we can do. It's over."

"It isn't." And yet Meg's voice sounded as hollow as those empty words, for this moment was weighted with a finality like death. There had been a ripping in her soul the day Ruth was laid to rest, a searing knowledge that she'd never see her mother again, that the relationship of mother and child had been cruelly severed. There had also been guilt, for if Meg had known Ruth intended to climb to the roof in a storm, she would have stopped her. While she still ached over the loss, there was some comfort in the fact that Ruth was at peace now in heaven, a place free of tears, sickness, and sorrow.

How broad the chasm between heaven and earth. Stephen was not headed to a grave, but just as he'd lost part of himself in the war, he would be whittled down even further in the asylum.

Had this been inevitable? Was there ever a time after Stephen came home, some unseen crossroads, where they could have taken a different path that would have led anywhere but the asylum? Perhaps early treatment could have prevented all of this confusion and heartache. Guilt wrapped around Meg and squeezed until she struggled to draw breath.

Bracing herself, she waited for Sylvie to say she'd known it would come to this, that Meg had been mulishly blind and deaf to the signs. Sylvie could cut her to pieces with blame. By some measure of grace, she didn't.

"All the news Father received of old friends and their ends," Sylvie whispered, still holding Meg's arm. "Do you think he knew it foreshadowed the course his life would take?" Her voice broke.

Meg looked at her sister's reddened nose and tear-stained cheeks and grasped for an answer that would not crush them both. *Some paths turn around,* she wanted to say. *He could still come back to us.* The ache in her left hand pulsed in rhythm with the jerks of her heart. Her right hand hung dead and absent. *Wounds can yet heal in both body and soul.*

But all she could do was weep.

Chapter Nine

Thursday, October 12, 1871

Pain sliced through Stephen's bound wrists as two attendants dragged him by the elbows through an iron door and into a whitewashed room no bigger than seven by eight feet. His head still throbbed from where he'd been struck.

"I don't belong here," he growled. "I'm not insane."

"Judge says you are, and we generally trust his verdict over the patient's," the attendant named Linden said. "Now, settle in to your new accommodations. Rest. A doctor will see you soon."

When the other attendant, Slattery, released the bindings from Stephen's wrists, it took all his mental and physical strength not to lunge for the door. It was blocked by these burly men in white uniforms, and he knew from experience that they wouldn't hesitate to restrain him—by another blow if necessary—if he gave them reason. Besides, even if he did break past them, he wouldn't be able to escape. Every stairwell had a locked door, and the Cook County Insane Asylum was miles outside the city. He'd be caught and dragged back in no time.

"That's it." Linden smiled. "There's no point in fighting, 283."

Stephen's gaze shot to Linden's, heartbeat ratcheting. His breath sawed in and out. Had he spoken aloud? He covered his face with one hand and was startled by the smooth feel of skin beneath his palm. They must have dosed him with something to make him compliant, for they'd shaved his beard and hair as soon as they took his clothing and gave him a laundry number instead. 283. That was what they called him now, a number. As if searching for his missing beard, his hand tapered off his chin and stroked the air beneath it.

If he wasn't mad upon arrival, he would be in due course.

The door closed and locked. Alone, he looked up at the small square window at the top of his door and saw nothing but the bare wall of the corridor on the other side. It was white, like everything else here. But not the pure white of wind-driven snow. It was the white of painted tombs.

There was no doorknob or handle on the inside of the door. One window let in a patch of sunlight, but even that was fractured by steel rods barring the glass. A cot cowered against one wall, a chamber pot beneath it. A courtesy, he guessed, in case he wasn't escorted to the bathroom at the end of the ward in time.

A cot and a pot. That was all.

Stephen sank onto the thin mattress, feeling every spring beneath him. He clasped his knees but could not stop their quaking. The stiff asylum-issued garments itched. Behind him, someone pounded on the other side of the wall. Sweat slicked his skin, and his shirt clung to his sunken chest.

Summoning the soldier he once was, he shot to his feet and marched a few paces in the room before about-facing and marching again. "This can't be happening," he said to himself, his voice changed by the terror within. "Not now, not after everything I endured."

It was only a matter of time, a voice whispered to him. *And it is precisely because of what you endured*.

He chewed on this as he tracked a circuit in the cell. Enough of his friends from Andersonville had suffered a similar fate for him to realize this was no coincidence. "But is this the fate I must accept until the end of my days? Or is it a fate I can fight my way free of?"

Instantly, a vision burst upon his imagination of Scrooge and the Ghost of Christmas Yet To Come pointing to a grave. *"Are these the shadows of the things that Will be, or are they shadows of the things that May be, only?"*

Stephen shook his head. He didn't want to quote *A Christmas Carol* or give any space in his mind to fiction. He may have been a bookseller once, but that was a different life, one so charmed it might have been a fairy tale.

This place was no mere fancy, however. Neither was the unraveling he felt within himself. He needed to think.

"Why am I here? What reason did the judge have to deem me a lunatic? Feeding stray dogs is not so odd, nor is pacing my roof at night to guard my home."

Coward. You know the reason.

"I do not."

You do.

The knocking on the wall had not stopped. Stephen grasped again at a phantom beard until his fist came to rest over his frantic heart. "No. No. No." His denial matched the rhythm of his neighbor's wordless protest.

You murdered Hiram Sloane in a fit of insanity.

"I am not insane!" he roared.

The pounding stopped. So did the voice inside his head.

Spent, he dropped onto the cot, head spinning from the force of his shouting. He rocked back and forth to lull the beast inside.

So you murdered him aware of what you were doing.

He gasped at the brazen thought. "I'm not a murderer," he whispered. "I murdered no one."

Liar. How many women in the South are widows or fatherless or childless because of the Rebel lives you took?

"That was different." Stephen licked his lips. "That was war. Both sides kill their enemies in war."

And let us not forget the Union soldiers you killed in cold blood in Andersonville.

Stephen groaned and curled onto his side. "I had to do it. They weren't behaving like soldiers anymore. Those boys were preying on the weak. We had to inflict some justice. We had to make them stop before they killed any more sick and vulnerable prisoners, their own fellow Yankees."

There, now. You admit to killing both enemies and comrades. You have blood all over your hands. What makes you think that none of it could be Hiram's?

Stephen splayed his fingers. For a moment he saw red there and felt warmth trickling from his fingertips to his wrists. He blinked, then pinched the inside of his arm until the delusion disappeared. "I don't remember seeing Hiram the night of the fire, let alone killing him."

One of your friends hurt his own wife. He was a good man, like you, but after the war he saw ghosts where there were none and enemies in place of those who loved him. Can you honestly say you've not done the same? Perhaps during the fire?

Stephen's pulse pounded painfully, but he forced himself to revisit October 8. It was the night he failed to help his daughters when they needed him the most. This was a fact he considered with a detachment that kept him above the riptide of guilt and regret. His daughters' disappointment in him was not what landed him in the asylum. It was not the issue that needed solving in order for him to be free. He'd noticed how they looked at him. Somehow he'd gone from being their protector to being their biggest burden. Were they pleased now that he was out of their way?

He stepped around those thoughts as one sidestepped a puddle in the street, and moved on to what happened on his way to the train depot.

He'd been in danger. All those people, all the yelling, all the people yelling at him. He had used his gun to protect himself. It was his right, especially in the face of such lawlessness. Yes, he remembered that now—people were looting and stealing, and some were drinking away their cares as if it were the last night on earth. A man needed to defend himself against such rogues. How else but with a gun? It was the only thing some scoundrels understood.

Carefully, he scanned the faces of the people he saw that night. Hiram wasn't there.

Rebels were, however, along with their own weapons. They had artillery. They were firing at him, trying to kill him, even though the war was done. At least, that was what it had felt like, and that was what he'd believed at the time. Whatever the explanation for those explosions, he'd taken cover, and he'd aimed his gun. That much, he saw clearly.

But beyond that, deep shadows hid recollections spanning a few hours, he guessed, of that dreadful night. All the concentration he could summon would not illuminate it.

The pounding on the other side of the wall resumed, an echo to his thudding heartbeat. Hiram had grated on him lately, but he was never a threat. The bonds of their friendship had grown looser, but why would he kill an elderly man? Why had Hiram not been safe in his bed on Prairie Avenue when the fire broke out north of his neighborhood?

More written words sprang to mind, and these he clung to: "'Whatsoever things are true, whatsoever things are honest, whatsoever things are just.'" He recited the Scripture to beat the darkness from his soul. He'd been a man of God once, had even enrolled in seminary before deciding the pastorate was not for him. "'Whatsoever things are pure, whatsoever things are lovely . . . if there be any praise, think on these things.'" He would not dwell in those shadowy places of his past.

"No," he said aloud, fingers digging into his shaved scalp. "I don't believe I killed Hiram Sloane, by intention or by accident."

You don't want to believe you killed Hiram. There is a difference.

"No. Stop. Stop talking!" He raged against the whisper in his spirit, and the pain in his head swelled double. But he knew the whisper was his conscience, and silencing it might prove even worse a fate.

Keys jangled, then scraped the lock, and the door whined open. The two attendants had returned along with a psychiatrist Stephen had seen before. He had prominent brown eyes set into a fleshy face that suggested a fondness for food and drink. By the grooves carved between nose and chin and the hairline retreating from his brow, Stephen judged him to be at least a decade older than himself.

"Well, now." Dr. Franklin unwound his stethoscope from his neck. "Who were you shouting at? Hearing voices?"

Stephen stood. "What? No. I mean, yes, but it was only inside my head."

"So you didn't see anyone else in your room with you before the three of us arrived?"

"No, of course not." The delusion of blood on his hands had been easily managed.

The stethoscope pressed against his chest, metal cold even through his linen shirt. Holding his breath, he tried to slow his pulse.

Dr. Franklin frowned, gaze traveling over Stephen's head and down to his shaking hands tapping his legs. Stephen went to hide them in his pockets and found his trousers had none. The stethoscope moved to his back, a cold spot of pressure beside his spine. Light-headed, Stephen exhaled.

The psychiatrist draped his stethoscope around his neck again. "Your heart rate is dangerously fast."

He stood close enough for Stephen to count the pores on his nose. Feeling like he might suffocate, Stephen stepped back, stumbling against the cot before righting himself.

"Are you aware of how much you're perspiring? Have you exerted yourself in the last few minutes?"

"Exerted?" With the cuff of his sleeve, Stephen mopped his brow. "I paced some."

"We heard you shouting," Linden said.

"That too," Stephen admitted. "But I hardly think that qualifies as exercise."

Dr. Franklin held up a finger and told Stephen to follow its side-to-side movement with his eyes. That complete, he made a note in a file. "Pupils unevenly dilated," he murmured. "Your fevered mind has affected your entire body. The perspiration, the shaking, the voices in your head . . . we must treat it quickly."

"What kind of treatment?"

"Slattery and Linden will see to it. Cooperate with them for your own good. Gentlemen." Dr. Franklin nodded to the attendants and took his leave.

Flanking Stephen, the men gripped his arms and propelled him out of the cell, down the corridor, and into a room lined with tiles. Inside was a claw-foot tub full of water and ice.

"You're going to spend some time in the tub, enough to stop your shaking," Linden told him.

"That tub is full of ice!" Stephen protested. A chill came off the water and drifted toward him.

"Drink this. It will make it easier, trust me." Slattery squeezed Stephen's jaw open and poured a dose of laudanum into his mouth.

Swallowing and sputtering, Stephen was helpless to stop the men from stripping him of his clothing. Humiliated, he closed his eyes to his own nakedness. Almost before he'd had time to register that the attendants had picked him up, he was plunged into the bath and gasping at the shock of it.

Cold knifed through him and stole his breath. Frantic to escape, he pushed himself up only to be shoved down again by four strong hands. There they held him, by the shoulders and knees, to keep his body underwater. Stephen thrashed, desperate, and they cursed at being splashed.

"Stay down!" Slattery shouted.

Teeth chattering, Stephen shuddered violently, and his muscles cramped. Cold consumed him, replacing every fiber in his being until he could believe he was not just drowning in ice but made of it. Even his thoughts were slowing, freezing along with the rest of him.

"P-p-please," he managed to stutter. "L-let . . . m-me . . . out!"

"Doctor's orders," said Linden. "You'll be numb in a moment, and then it won't matter anyway. A little longer, and you may even feel warm."

He'd never had an ice bath in Georgia. But he knew what it was to be unmanned, and this was it. With Herculean effort, he struggled up, away from the needles that pinned him all over.

"I said, stay down!"

A force to his skull, an explosion of pain where his head hit the rim of the tub, and Stephen knew no more.

Nate Pierce stormed into his editor's office in their new three-story building at No. 15 Canal Street and slammed a newspaper on the desk, pointing to the headline. *Alleged War Hero Arrested for Murder of Fellow Veteran*.

"Has Stephen Townsend gone to trial and been convicted already? Because if he hasn't, the word *alleged* has been misplaced. It's the murder that is alleged, is it not?"

City Editor Joseph Medill leaned back in his chair and skewered Nate with his gaze. "A mistake by the copy editor, no doubt." He did not seem overly concerned.

On his blotter lay yesterday's paper. Personal notices bordered the pages, printed free of charge to all who sent them in. *Tommy Jackson, 10 years old, missing: information to be sent to Centenary Church. Henry Leary is at First Congregational Church. Mrs. Brown and four children missing. Information to be sent to First Congregational Church*. Within that frame of found and missing persons was a twelve-column story headlined *Destruction of Chicago!* But only a third of the city had been razed.

Nate mastered himself. "I've interviewed both the suspect and the victim. Why was this not given to me to cover?" He hadn't even heard about it until he saw the story in the newspaper that morning.

Outside the window, Canal Street teemed with wagons and men scrambling to secure temporary offices. Broadsides pinned to trees told the homeless where to find food and shelter. A train chugged parallel to the south branch of the Chicago River. When it had passed, the sound of digging and scraping could be heard from a few blocks away as work crews cleared away rubble.

"I'd think it obvious, Pierce." Medill clipped the end of a cigar and lit it. "According to that letter we received, your reporting on

Townsend was short-sighted and sentimental. That's not what this paper is about. Add to that the fact that you spent the night of the fire with the man's daughters when you could have been gathering news on the greatest calamity of the age—"

"I was gathering news at the same time, and my stories prove it," Nate seethed, pushing his glasses up his nose. "What other *Tribune* reporter made it as far as Lincoln Park to write about the masses huddled there?"

"Answer this." Medill put the cigar to his lips and inhaled before releasing curls of blue-grey smoke along with his words. "Why wasn't Stephen Townsend the one ushering his daughters to safety?"

The sweet tang of tobacco cloyed the room. Nate paced to the window and peered east, over the throng in the street and across the river, grasping for a response that would suit. Stuffing his fist into his trouser pocket, he fingered the embossed front and back of the dime that would pay for a loaf of bread after work. So, too, he held in his mind two sides of Stephen Townsend. One version fed stray dogs blackberry pie, and the other version had aimed his revolver at Nate, eyes wild and unseeing. Both pictures were true. It was unsettling.

And yet there had to be more to the story than this.

He spun to face his editor. "Who says the murder was not the doing of vandals taking advantage of the lawlessness created by the fire? Did the police consider that?"

"You forget yourself, Mr. Pierce. We are in the business of printing the news, not putting defendants on trial and judging for ourselves their guilt or innocence. But if it will give me peace from your incessant defiance—yes, the police considered it. The reporter didn't include that in the article because the possibility was quickly eliminated by the eyewitness accounts and the murder weapon bearing the initials of the accused. Paper is in short supply, if you hadn't noticed. We don't waste space writing about what didn't happen." He tapped the cigar over a glass dish, then puffed on it.

Nate couldn't deny that on the night of the fire, Stephen had been truly incapacitated by his affliction of mind and spirit. He'd pulled a gun on Nate, but would he have done the same to a friend he'd known for decades?

"I would like to read the full statements of the witnesses," he said. Perhaps even conduct fresh interviews himself.

"Pointless. The article's been published. There's nothing more to say on the matter." Tendrils of smoke scented the air between them.

"I disagree," Nate insisted. "A man's life is at stake, not to mention the fate of his daughters, who have been orphaned by Townsend's arrest." He had no idea how they were faring or where they'd landed. He'd found a two-room flat to rent near Canal Street at twenty-five dollars a month, a painful hike from the twelve he'd paid before the fire. He wasn't sure if Meg and Sylvie could afford such lodgings, or if they had sought refuge with relatives, or if they remained among the homeless.

Medill splayed his hands on his desk and stood. "We are newsmen living in a city the entire world wants to hear about. They want big stories of water shortages and the homeless, of destruction and reconstruction, of rebuilding bigger and better. They want stories of a phoenix rising from the ashes. We're learning more about other fires that occurred the same time as ours. The fire that wiped out Peshtigo, Wisconsin, took with it between eight hundred and twelve hundred souls. Holland and Manistee, Michigan, were destroyed too, but with a death toll much lower. What do you hope to gain by digging into the little story of one man?"

Nate tugged at his collar to loosen it. "I would not have a man smeared and ruined on account of careless reporting."

Mr. Medill stared at him for so long that Nate wondered if the editor was actually considering what he'd said. Then he rubbed the weariness from his face. "You've gone soft, Pierce. I've half a mind to put you on the society columns or the mail room. Everyone here knows you have a guilt complex over not fighting in the war. You deify those who served. Perhaps I erred in indulging you, allowing you to spend so much time on the puff series about Chicago's veterans."

Turning to hide the heat mounting in his face, Nate crossed to the table near the wall and poured himself a glass of water from the decanter. He stopped drinking when he tasted smoke and fish.

"Get over it!" Medill bellowed, pounding his fist on the desk. "Facts, man! We want facts, not fairy tales."

"Facts," Nate repeated coldly. "I wonder if the reporter who blamed Catherine O'Leary's cow for starting the fire is as zealous for facts as you are. You know as well as I do that Mrs. O'Leary hasn't allowed a single interview with the press. No one knows her side of the story."

"Seems to me you weren't always so keen to get both sides, yourself."

The arrow hit its mark. Suddenly Nate was the desperate eighteen-year-old who had cut corners investigating a story he'd written on speculation, a story he hoped would earn him a permanent position on staff. It had worked. He wasn't proud of it. Wearing a donated jacket today that was too long in the sleeves—his own wardrobe lost to the fire—made him feel even more like a youth pretending to be a professional.

But that was wrong thinking. He'd been young when he started in this business, but he'd clocked more than a decade since then. He was older and wiser. Disillusioned. Just now, he didn't mind if his countenance showed it.

Medill threw his arm wide to point with the end of his cigar toward the burned district. "There are a thousand other stories worth reporting out there without revisiting what's already been done. Leave O'Leary and Townsend alone and move on. If I so much as catch a whiff of you snooping around when you should be covering other beats, you'll be out of a job. And that's final. Do I make myself clear?"

Nate set his tumbler of grey-tinged liquid on his editor's desk. "Clear as water." Without waiting for Medill's reaction, he left.

Chapter Ten

With hands that still felt as though they were burning, Meg stood on the front porch of Hiram Sloane's house and waited while Sylvie gathered her nerve. "It's time," she said as gently as she could manage through her pain.

Twenty hours after their father's arrest, Sylvie had agreed to face Jasper Davenport, if he was still here, and whatever staff remained. Having no place to store their belongings, she and Sylvie had brought their tattered pillowcases. They had combed their hair but had few pins to hold it, and had had no chance to bathe since last Saturday.

Neither had they had much rest at the church last night, despite how much Meg had longed for sleep to dim her pain and carry her away. Damp stone had pressed her hip and ribs, her elbow had been her pillow, and a thin blanket brought little warmth. Babies wailed, children cried out with nightmares forged in flames. Sylvie gasped awake more than once, disoriented and trembling with cold or fear. Who among them, when they closed their eyes, did not see that terrible orange glow or smell the smoke or hear the bells of alarm? This morning Meg rose no less distraught over her father, and stiff and slow from lack of sleep besides.

Exhaling, Sylvie lifted the brass knocker and brought it down three times. Meg shifted her gaze to the movement of blue uniforms in the street. Two entire companies of General Sheridan's militiamen were stationed here to guard the few square blocks of the Prairie Avenue neighborhood. Compared to the five companies assigned to protect the below-ground safes throughout the business district, this street felt especially thick with soldiers.

A click sounded on the other side of the door. It opened slowly, then flung wide as Helene Dressler gathered Meg and Sylvie into an embrace that smelled of lilac talc.

"Girls!" she cried, releasing them. "You must forgive such an emotional display, but I've been so worried. Oh! Your hands, Miss Margaret—will you fully recover?"

It was so different from the reception Meg had expected that her throat stung with relief and gratitude. "I fully intend to."

With a flutter, Helene pulled them into the vestibule and locked the door behind them before drawing them into the main hall.

"Helene." Sylvie twisted her fingers together, her complexion a match for the alabaster statues of Greek goddesses flanking the grand staircase. "We're terribly sorry about Hiram. We cannot tell you how much. We're still so shocked by the news, it hardly seems possible that it's true."

Helene's eyes misted as she smoothed the black apron over her black skirt. "I never heard him leave. I don't know what happened."

Meg swallowed a knot of unshed tears. "We don't know what happened either. The police arrested our father. . . ." She trailed off. Of course Helene already knew this. All of Chicago knew it, at least those who read the *Tribune*. "But I don't believe for a moment he did this. Do you know of anyone else who would have wanted to harm Hiram?"

Helene spread her hands in a gesture of helplessness. "He's kept to himself for the most part since his mind began failing him. The only person I've ever known to wish Master Hiram ill was Otto Schneider, but that was years ago."

Meg nodded. It did not seem likely that a grievance as old as the war would resurface now without some kind of provocation.

"Will there be a funeral?" Sylvie asked. "Or have we missed it?"

"Mr. Davenport held a private burial service." Helene's voice contained her sorrow. "I suppose he hadn't the means for more. But please come in, you poor souls. You've been through hell and back again."

They followed her into the parlor, where polished woodwork bordered settees and chairs upholstered in ocher and crimson. Thick velvet draperies puddled on the floor. From an alcove between the windows, a bust of Robert Burns, Hiram's favorite poet, stared out at them.

Helene eyed the bundles Sylvie carried. "This is what remains?"

Meg said it was and eased into an armchair for the first time since before the fire. It would have been easier to leave everything buried in the ground, but looters were digging, searching for valuables and vaults. She wouldn't risk losing what little they had left.

"What will you do now?" Sylvie asked. Black crepe covered the mirror above the mantelpiece, but it was obvious that Helene was keeping the house clean. Equally obvious was the fact that she, and not the butler, had answered the door.

"Unlike most of the staff, I will stay at my post until things have settled. They've all left to find employment elsewhere, everyone except Kirstin, Eli, and me. All three of us plan to take on side jobs for other households for our income, but this remains our home, at least for now." She lowered her voice and leaned in. "Mr. Davenport is still here too. I expect he'll stay until the will is found, at the very least. Naturally he wants to finish his semester at the university, so if he does leave the house, he'll find other lodging in town."

Surprise pierced through Meg's fog of pain. "You have no copy of the will?" The official document would have been filed at the courthouse, a casualty of the fire. But . . . "Surely Hiram stored one here."

"That's what we all assumed. It wouldn't be right for us staff to search, but Mr. Davenport has looked all over, to no avail. It must turn up sometime, though. And if the property goes to him, as I imagine it must, as Hiram's only living relative, perhaps he'll keep me on. I have no desire to leave."

"And I don't want you to leave, for I cannot manage without you, Miss Dressler." With a smile that brought a flush to Sylvie's cheeks, Jasper Davenport strode into the parlor and lowered himself into a chair. "I wasn't aware we had company. How do you do."

Helene rose and bowed to him, though he was not her master yet.

"Mr. Davenport," Meg began, "we are so sorry for your loss." She stopped short of insisting her father had been framed for the murder. Whoever had killed Hiram, it was obvious his nephew was grieving. It would be crude to make her visit about shifting blame.

"We wish with all our hearts that Hiram was still with us," Sylvie added.

"I appreciate that, I do. Miss Margaret, it seems you've been tended. I'm glad." He did not comment on the charge brought against their father.

"May I offer the three of you tea and jam tarts?" Helene asked.

Mr. Davenport glanced outside at the lowering sun. "Let's be respectful of their time, Miss Dressler. They have a walk ahead of them, and the curfew is quite strict." He turned to Sylvie. "Eli would drive you, but he's renting his services to others at present. I'll walk with you."

Taking his cue, Sylvie and Meg stood to leave.

"Surely that's not necessary," Helene said quietly, her tone and posture more submissive than her remark. "We have plenty of space here, do we not? Mr. Sloane would have welcomed them with open arms."

The suggestion surprised Meg as much as it touched her.

Mr. Davenport jingled some coins in his pocket, his expression thoughtful. "Well, these are special circumstances."

"We would never wish to impose," Sylvie said. "Come, Meg."

"Oh, yes, excellent point, Mr. Davenport," Helene said, perfectly composed. "These are special circumstances indeed. In light of what is being circulated about their father and your uncle, it is especially Christian of you to open your house to these two orphaned girls. Oh, forgive me, I misspoke. The house doesn't belong to you, at least not yet. Yet if it did, you'd prove as benevolent as your uncle. Truly, it is an honor and privilege to keep house and cook for you, even as we wait for the will to be found."

Meg held her breath, marveling at Helene's outspokenness.

The clock on the mantel ticked away a full minute that felt like ten before Jasper turned and gave a little bow to her and Sylvie. "Miss Dressler will see you settled."

Meg felt a pang of guilt as Kirstin stoked the fire in the hearth of the bedroom where she and Sylvie would stay. The chamber was draped and carpeted in hues of Prussian blue and mustard, with vases of peacock feathers flanking the fireplace. The mahogany furniture included a canopied four-poster bed big enough for two surrounded by velvet curtains. Adjoining the bedchamber was a white-tiled room with a toilet, sink, and claw-foot tub behind a folding Japanese silk screen. With the water pumps still being repaired, however, there was no water coming through the tap yet. The water they had in the house Eli had hauled from the lake.

"We will pay for the wood," Meg told the maid, aware that much of Chicago's cordwood had been consumed in the Great Fire, as the papers were calling it. She stared at the embers and flames Kirstin coaxed to life, then at the glowing tips of the tapers in candlesticks on the nightstands. She would never look at fire the same way again. The same source of warmth and comfort had brought death and destruction beyond description.

"And the food we eat," Sylvie added, pulling Meg from her dark musings. "Keep a running tab of the expenses we add to the household. In fact, as the cooks have found employment elsewhere, I'd be happy to help in the kitchen. We don't want to burden you, Kirstin. We intend to pay for any work done on our behalf."

Kirstin straightened and set the fire poker in the stand with the other tools. "That's right decent of you, Miss Sylvie, Miss Margaret."

"I assume Mr. Davenport pays for your services as well, given that your income from Hiram has been cut off?" Meg asked.

"He lets me stay in the house, and that's no small thing. He's a decent enough gentleman and lets me take in laundry and sewing from other houses. He's not a bad fellow to look at either." She covered her mouth. "Oh, for heaven above. I shouldn't have said that."

Sylvie ducked her chin and smiled, an uncharacteristic flash of girlishness. "What can you tell us about him?"

Kirstin screwed her mouth to one side and straightened the cap on her hair. "He came to attend university. Or did he decide to attend after he'd already arrived? As I recall, there was a bit of a rush to get him admitted, since it was so close to when classes began this fall."

"Anything else?" Sylvie prompted.

"I know he's five and twenty, with no other family, but little else. Even in his conversations with Mr. Sloane, God rest him, he never said much about himself."

Meg frowned. "But you had no notice of his arrival? He came unannounced?"

Her sister crossed to the window and drew the drapes. "You know Hiram could have received word and then forgotten."

"True enough. But you must admit, it's all rather mysterious. And then Hiram's death, and the missing will . . ."

"For shame, Meg!" Sylvie flew to the door and locked it, then marched back to Meg, eyes ablaze. "He opens the house to us, after our own father was arrested for Hiram's murder—" She sputtered and went silent.

Truly, Meg wasn't ungrateful. "I'm as thankful as you are for the hospitality. But he was prompted by Helene. Could you believe she was so bold on our behalf?"

Sylvie couldn't.

Kirstin could, after Meg told her what had happened. "That sounds like the way she guided Mr. Sloane—God rest him—for quite some time. Poor Mr. Sloane needed it, but she's mistaken if she thinks the young sir will appreciate her 'help' the way his uncle did."

Meg agreed. She tilted her head to one side, then the other to stretch out the tension that had been gathering there since Sunday. It was no use. Until her father was acquitted for Hiram's murder and released from the asylum, she couldn't relax.

Stephen hadn't killed Hiram. So who had?

What motive could there be? Who would be better off with Hiram dead? Who was with him that night?

By degrees, a possibility emerged from her exhausted, overtaxed mind. She didn't like it. It was far-fetched, likely the result of too little sleep and too much stress. Yet if she didn't at least acknowledge the idea, it would hound her.

"Kirstin." Meg sat at the writing desk and scraped the inside of her wrist on its edge to relieve an itch. "Does Mr. Davenport believe that once the will is found, it will name him as the primary beneficiary? Do you?"

"I believe so, miss."

Helene had already said as much, so this was no surprise. The question remained, was this a motive for murder? But the question Meg asked instead was simply, "Where was he the night of the fire?"

The maid looked over her shoulder at the closed door. "Mr. Davenport was studying with classmates Sunday evening at the university, and by the time he arrived home, Mr. Sloane had gone to bed. Mr. Davenport retired shortly after that. When I went to tend the fire in Mr. Sloane's room, I saw he was gone and went directly to wake his nephew. After that, Mr. Davenport was always with at least one of the servants, trying to find Mr. Sloane."

Squinting, Meg imagined the course of events. "But was there a stretch of time when no one saw him? Between the time he was studying elsewhere and the time he showed himself here to the staff?"

"Meg!" Sylvie put a fist to her hip and looked down at her. "Listen to yourself. Are you so desperate to shift the blame from our father that you'd place it on our benefactor instead?"

Meg's temper flared, as it always did when she faced a problem she didn't know how to solve. "Are you so convinced of our father's guilt that you refuse to entertain the possibility of his innocence?"

Fire popped in the grate. Light and shadow danced over Sylvie's face. "You've been blind to the truth about Father ever since he came home. If you hadn't refused to take him to a doctor, he might have been helped, or at least placed where he could do no harm. Hiram might still be alive right now."

The words were a blow to Meg's gut, for they echoed the self-condemnation she'd already been wrestling. "That's not fair." But her rebuttal sounded weak and childish even to herself.

Kirstin rolled her lips between her teeth and let herself out of the room.

"The will," Meg said. "Can we agree to suspend judgment until we find the will?"

"Mr. Davenport has an alibi." Sylvie's voice trembled. "He cannot have done this, even if the will does favor him. Besides, who else would Hiram leave his fortune to other than his great-nephew if no other kin is left? It would be logical, not an indictment."

Was Sylvie right? Was Meg truly grasping for anything to clear Stephen's name? "But no harm can come from us helping Jasper search for the will."

She wished they could talk to Stephen. The trial for Hiram's murder would be weeks or months away, but the judge had already declared him insane and committed him indefinitely to the Cook County Insane Asylum, where no personal visitors were allowed. They'd been cut off from one another, an amputation of the family.

Sylvie sank onto the edge of the bed and leaned against the curtain gathered at the carved post. "We need to begin planning for our future. No one else will do it for us. We're on our own, more now than ever before."

Meg left the desk to sit beside her. While her thoughts realigned themselves, her gaze traced the budding vines in the mosaic tiles surrounding the fireplace. If her hands were free, she would unpin her sister's hair and take the silver brush from the vanity to untangle Sylvie's long brown tresses and soothe her nerves.

She tried to flex and curl her hands inside her bandages, but her palms and fingers resisted movement, unyielding in their shrouds. Meg frowned and tried again, until the pain of stretching her ravaged skin begged her to stop.

What a mercy that God was not limited by that which limited her. What grace that His power and presence remained, regardless of whether she felt close to them. She must trust Him for what she could not see. Wasn't that the essence of faith? Her hands were bound. His were not.

Tomorrow would be better than this.

"All right." It was determination, more than confidence, that lifted Meg's voice. She wondered if Sylvie could tell the difference. "Here's what we'll do. First thing, we write the insurance company and file a claim for our losses. I still have the money from Bertha Palmer for the two portraits she purchased last week. We have the deed and title to our property. Once the ruins have been cleared away, we will hire a contractor to rebuild." Meg had enough money to get them started, and by the time more was needed, they'd have it. Somehow.

Sylvie took a deep breath. "Tomorrow we will properly sort through what we have in the way of inventory and make a list of who may want to buy what." Leaving the bed, she unwrapped the rescued novel from Nate's jacket and set it on the tea table.

"Most of it is still readable," Meg told her, rising to stand beside her. The middle of the book still held the photograph of Stephen in his uniform. "We saved what matters most."

Sylvie ran her thumb over her broken fingernails. "I don't know if we did."

A lump wedged in Meg's throat at the difference between the family they'd once been and the remnant that remained. "We have to keep trying," she whispered. "*I* have to try."

"I know you do. It's who you are, to hope and pray and love and try. You will call me dreadfully pessimistic, but our futures have never been more fragile than they are right now. I would say that our best chance for security is to marry, but who would marry the daughter of . . . Even if he didn't murder Hiram, any potential prospects have been killed. Our family name is ruined. No one will have us now."

Rarely did Meg dwell on the fact that all her peers had married and begun filling their nurseries with children. At seventeen and fifteen when the war ended, she and Sylvie had barely come of age. But as the depth of their father's wounds became apparent, would-be callers stayed away. So absorbed was Meg in the health of her own family that she did not mourn their absence. What good was a Sunday stroll or a stiff visit in the parlor when her father teetered between life and death, and when her mother wasted away with the stress of it?

Besides, Jane Austen and her sister, Cassandra, had never married. Louisa May Alcott remained unwed. Charlotte Brontë, who hadn't married until she was thirty-eight, wrote that *"there is no more respectable character on this earth than an unmarried woman, who makes her own way through life quietly, perseveringly."*

But Sylvie's statement could not be ignored. Tentatively, Meg approached it. "Is there, or has there been, a certain young man you pined for?"

Guilt weighted her, that she'd been blind to her sister's longing for love or security or both. If Meg had noticed, could she have done anything to promote a match? Or would she have selfishly swept the idea away in order to keep her sister as a companion for herself?

Dropping her gaze, Sylvie pushed a greasy strand of hair from her face. "It would not matter if there were."

A denial formed on Meg's tongue, but she couldn't truthfully say otherwise. Instead, she pulled her sister into an embrace, the responsibility she felt toward her younger sibling pouring steel into her spine. "I'll take care of you," she told her.

"My dear sister." Sylvie pulled back and cradled Meg's bandaged hands, a bruised look on her face. "You cannot take care of yourself."

Chapter Eleven

Saturday, October 14, 1871

Sitting idle was out of the question.

Determined to ignore the injuries she could do nothing about, Meg set a course to do whatever she could to clear her father's name. There was only one logical place to start.

Helene Dressler, bless her, had agreed to chaperone her to the temporary headquarters of the police while Sylvie stayed at the house to reconstruct a list of their patrons and vendors. It was just as well. There didn't seem to be room for one more person in this choked building. The air was thick with the smells of scorched coffee and smoking piles of rubble along the nearby river. Embers continued to smolder and re-ignite, doused by vigilant citizens keeping guard.

Her face florid from the suffocating warmth of the cramped space, Helene fanned herself and Meg. Uniformed officers plowed through the lobby to the closed-off rooms behind it and barreled out again with nary a glance at those waiting on chairs and benches. A harried clerk sat with mounds of paper on his desk and stacks of cardboard boxes behind him.

"Next." He signaled with a flick of his wrist. Rings of sweat beneath his arms proved he was as uncomfortable as the rest of them.

Meg stepped over mud and leaves to approach the clerk, Helene standing staunchly beside her. "Hello. I'm here to see the police report about the murder of Hiram Sloane," she began, her hands hidden in the folds of the navy blue cloak she wore.

The clerk peered up at her. "And why is that?"

Meg lowered her voice. "Hiram was my good friend. And my father was accused of the murder. I have a right to see the report."

"Because you want to contest it, is that right?" The blond young man brushed crumbs from his shirtfront. A brown ring stained his desk near a mug lined with coffee grounds.

Meg disliked him, a reaction that was evidently mutual. Forcing a smile, she tried again. "I can see you're very busy. My name is Margaret Townsend, and I only want a moment of your time, Mr. . . ."

"Gruber."

"Mr. Gruber. I would like to see the police report, the medical examiner's report, the witness statements, and any photographs you have associated with this case."

Helene nodded for emphasis, standing up even taller.

The clerk's eyebrows rose. "I can't give that permission. I just started this week. The police force is so overworked, you see."

"Certainly." Meg willed herself to be patient and convincing. "Please ask whoever has the authority for this type of thing, then, won't you? We'll wait right here."

"Hey," called the man directly behind her. "How long is this going to take? I've been here for two hours already!" Others lifted their voices in complaint as well.

Helene cast a sympathizing look over her shoulder. "As have we, sir. As to how long this will take, that depends on Mr. Gruber, here. Mr. Gruber, how long do you need to find out?"

Straightening his necktie, the clerk pushed back from the desk and disappeared for a quarter of an hour before returning with a file. An extremely *thin* file. "This is all we can show you. And it doesn't move from this counter." He slid it to the end to make room for the next man in line.

Helene opened the folder while Meg looked on. The brief police report had been written so quickly that there were typographical errors no one had bothered to correct. Most of the information Meg had already heard from Officers O'Hara and McNab when they arrested her father.

"Does it say where the body was found?" Helene murmured, scanning the lines with her fingertip.

"There." Meg gestured to the margin with her bandaged hand. "It says the body was collected with all the others after the fire and brought to a stable on Milwaukee Avenue. Only there did anyone notice he'd been shot." He must have been so covered with dust and ashes, the wound and blood were not apparent.

It was another dead end. There was no record of who had brought in the body or where it had originally been found. Meg still had no idea where the crime had taken place.

She kept reading.

"Do you see this, Helene?" Meg whispered. "It says Hiram was shot in the back! Who would do such a thing?"

Helene pushed her slipping hat back from her brow and frowned. "Mr. Davenport said he'd been shot in the chest. Maybe that's what the police thought too, until the medical examiner learned otherwise." She slid the document to the side, revealing two photographs of Hiram's body.

Flinching, Meg turned away from the elderly gentleman's naked torso and face. There was no life there at all. It wasn't Hiram anymore, just a body. His soul had broken its bonds and winged to heaven, where his mind was whole again, his body renewed. This was what she clung to as she steeled herself to examine the sepia-toned images. It was a mercy they weren't made from a palette of nature's true colors.

Still, it felt disrespectful to look upon his undressed form. Helene, she noticed, had closed her eyes, pressing a fist to her mouth. Meg held her breath and looked again. The bullet wound on Hiram's back was smaller and more symmetrical than the hole on his chest, which was ragged and lopsided.

"Only a coward would shoot an unarmed old man in the back.

It couldn't possibly be my father." She was more convinced of that now than ever. "Is there nothing else in the file?"

Helene spread out the paper and two images, then shuffled them back into the folder. "Nothing." She pulled her gloves on, as if ready to be done with the affair. Perhaps it was too much for her, to see her former master that way.

But it wasn't enough for Meg's purposes.

As soon as Mr. Gruber was finished with the man who'd come after her, she caught his attention. "I need to see the witness statements and the medical examiner's report."

"Miss Townsend." His condescending tone galled her. He looked no older than she was. "You're taking up time we don't have. Those other documents you seek are filed away in Evidence, but our new filing system is imperfect, as you can imagine. There is plenty of confusion here since our headquarters burned down, and we're piecing together loose documents that were saved but are in total disarray. We have more work now than we've ever had before and not enough people to do it. This case is closed, and nothing can be gained from you digging through it. Good day to you."

"Can you at least tell me the names of the witnesses?" She hated that she sounded like she was begging. Then again, if that was what it took, she was not above it.

Mr. Gruber made a show of leaning to one side and looking at the long line behind her. Newspapers rattled above voices that thrummed in her ears. "No. I don't know where the files are, and I never read them myself. Move along."

Meg held her ground. "I want to talk to an officer."

"No can do. At least not right now. But I'll take your message, and someone will get back to you when he has time."

Which would be never. The mayor had invited Sheridan's troops to help protect the city, and the police were still overtaxed. No officer would have time—or make time—for her with all that was required of them in the wake of this catastrophe.

Her hands burned, shooting pain up to her left elbow. It made her irritable, sharp, and focused. "Would you at least have a detective find and question an Otto Schneider as a potential suspect for Hiram Sloane's murder? He has a motive. Stephen Townsend did not."

"Potential suspect? In a closed case?" Mr. Gruber's laugh was disbelieving. "Not on your—" He frowned, gaze darting to one side. "Hang on, I know that name." He shuffled papers on his desk until at last he plucked up a list of names.

"Here he is." He pointed to Schneider's name halfway down the page. "Already in prison, ladies, since October 1. Looks like your suspect has an alibi. And if you don't leave now, I'll call an officer to escort you from the premises."

Blood rushed to Meg's cheeks, while the image of McNab and O'Hara dragging her father away filled her mind. "That won't be necessary."

Helene thanked Mr. Gruber for his time while Meg struggled to regain her composure. She'd come here for answers and was leaving with more questions instead. The police weren't going to help her, that much was clear. If she wanted to get to the bottom of this, she was on her own.

Chapter Twelve

Sunday, October 15, 1871

Everything had changed since last Sunday. And yet here, inside Nate's stepsister's home just west of Chicago, it seemed like nothing had. The parlor still smelled faintly of lemon oil, Edith still served pot roast on the same mismatched china, and her two sons still napped peacefully, as if all was right with the world. It was an oasis of normalcy.

"Eat," Edith urged him, though he'd already had some of everything. "You look as though you haven't in a week." She wasn't too far from the truth.

Sundays had always been a relief to Nate. As a reporter, his hours were irregular, invading evenings and Saturdays, since news was no respecter of clock or calendar. Sundays were the one day of the week with a routine he could count on. Church in the morning and then time with family. For the last four years, that meant sharing a meal with Edith and Frank. Their home was modest but clean and without frills, since the wedding had been small and Edith had not had a mother to pass down the usual trappings of keeping house. The only difference was that now that Harriet and Andrew were gone, there were two fewer place settings than before.

"I still don't understand why you won't stay with us for a while," Edith said. "At least until the cost of rent sinks back to pre-fire rates. We've talked about it, haven't we, Frank?" She looked to her husband, but having just taken a bite, he wasn't ready to speak.

Just as well. "I appreciate the offer, but I need to stay in the city, close to the news and the *Tribune*." Nate had already explained this on Tuesday, when he'd paid a brief visit to tell them he was safe.

"Of course." Frank Novak helped himself to another slice of roast. A pharmacist by trade, he cut his meat with the precision required by his job. The starched white collar, meticulously trimmed mustache, pomaded black hair, and perfectly tied cravat added to the impression of one who valued neatness, even if his frock coat had worn a little thin at the elbows. "I don't blame you, Nate. You've earned the right to live as a bachelor for the first time in, well, the first time ever. No one to answer to, come and go as you please . . ."

"Well, listen to you! If I didn't know any better, I'd say you were jealous," Edith teased.

"Some days more than others." Frank winked at her and squeezed her shoulder, and she swatted him away with good humor. He turned back to Nate. "I'll bet you're grateful to be shed of family responsibilities, eh? Especially now. You could really make a name for yourself with the stories out there waiting to be written."

Nate swallowed a bite of clove- and cinnamon-spiced sweet potatoes. "I do feel more at ease about working long or odd hours." During the last several years, he'd been resigned to but not comfortable with the time he was away from his stepsiblings. Andrew, in particular, had been prone to trouble.

"By the way, I wrote to Harriet about your experience with the fire to let her know you're safe, but I'm sure she'd appreciate hearing from you personally." Edith sipped her coffee. "I don't have an address for Andrew, or I'd ask you to write him too."

"I've written to Harriet." Nate removed his spectacles, rubbed them clean with a corner of his linen napkin, and replaced them. "Andrew knows where to reach both of us."

Frank leaned back in his chair and narrowed his gaze across the table at Nate. "Don't be too hard on yourself where Andrew is concerned. You did your best with your family, which was far more than most young men would have done. Edith and Harriet turned out well enough. Andrew just . . ."

"Needed a father," Nate finished for him. "And I wasn't it." In fact, Andrew liked to point to their differing surnames—he was a Gibson, Nate was a Pierce—and say Nate wasn't even his brother. No shared blood at all.

"Who knows what Andrew needed, or what he needs still?" Edith said quietly. Sighing, she looked out the window, her face pale. "Whatever it is, maybe he'll find it out west. He was always so independent."

True enough. Probably because he didn't trust Nate would really look out for them. When Andrew was six years old, he'd stolen food, not believing Nate would return from work in time for dinner to feed them all himself. Shocked and embarrassed, Nate had marched Andrew back to the grocer to confess and perform a few tasks until the grocer was satisfied the debt had been paid. *"I said I would take care of you,"* Nate had scolded him. *"Why didn't you believe me?"*

The irony of it all dawned on him too late, for that was the week he'd submitted his story on the carriages that were breaking down all over the city. Nate had traced all the faulty carriages back to Martin Sullivan's shop. He'd quoted people who claimed the Irishman had sabotaged the axles in order to hurt upper-class patrons. Nate also quoted those who claimed it wasn't sabotage but the incompetence inherent among the Irish. His characterization of Sullivan made him seem both slow and menacing to match his accusers' descriptions, knowing full well this was what the public expected. What they wanted.

By the time Nate learned that Sullivan's competitor had altered the carriages after they'd been sold in order to run him out of business, it was too late. Thanks to Nate's story, the devious plan had worked. After Sullivan's business failed, he worked at the docks until a back injury made that impossible too.

Little Andrew had stolen bread and apples because he didn't

believe Nate would meet his needs, but Nate had stolen a man's reputation because he hadn't trusted God would provide a job without him resorting to dishonesty. A sin he'd vowed never to repeat. This was why he was so adamant with his editor about facts, enough facts, and only the facts.

He drained the last of his coffee. "I wasn't always the best example for Andrew."

Edith covered a yawn and shook her head. "Don't tell me this is about Martin Sullivan again. Do you still keep tabs on him?"

A rueful smile on his face, Nate spun sideways on his chair and stretched out a leg, exposing an old but shining shoe beneath his trousers. The fifty-something-year-old Sullivan spent his days bent over other men's feet, polishing shoes for a pittance.

She arched an eyebrow. "And do you still go without lunch so you can tip him a wildly generous amount?"

As often as he could. Two years, maybe three, had passed between the publication of Nate's story and the day he found Sullivan polishing shoes the first time. Martin hadn't recognized Nate, and Nate hadn't reintroduced himself.

"Business is booming for him at the edge of the burned district. Folks go in to satisfy their curiosity, and by the time they're done, their shoes are covered in dust."

The sun shifted, casting a ray into Edith's brown eyes. She squinted, and Frank moved to the window to pull the shade. "And do you also keep tabs on the young women with whom you fled the fire?" he asked. "Townsend, correct? We saw the article about the father's arrest."

Nate rubbed the back of his neck. "Ah. Count that as another article without all the facts," he muttered. "But no, I haven't seen her." Meg's face came to mind, and he wondered how she fared with her injuries. "I mean, them. I haven't seen the Townsend sisters since early Tuesday morning."

He had seen them to safety, and that was that. Especially since his editor had forbidden him to pursue the sad story of Stephen Townsend. He sympathized, but he wasn't ready to lose his job.

"Quite right." Frank took off his frock coat now that the meal was over. "You've done your part."

The sounds of the baby waking from his nap carried from the hallway. Edith excused herself and returned moments later with Henry on her hip, his face flushed and creased from sleep. He thrust a dimpled hand into her pecan brown hair, the very shade of his own, and pulled a strand free to rub between his fingers and his thumb. Tommy straggled behind her, rubbing a chubby fist to his eyes, his black hair and lashes a reflection of his father's.

"Hey there, Tiger." Nate scooped up the drowsy two-year-old and pushed the hair back from Tommy's brow, then thought of his own unwieldy cowlicks. Nate looked nothing like Edith or her children. He bore no resemblance to anyone. What would it be like to look into someone's face—a parent, a sibling, a child—and see a reflection of one's own?

Frank took Henry and lifted him high in the air, much to the baby's laughing delight, and Edith's. Nate wondered how it would feel to hang the lights behind someone's eyes the way Frank did for Edith. He was thirty years old and still didn't know.

Tommy squirmed and reached for his mother. Nate passed the boy to Edith, then folded his empty arms. Belonging and responsibility were two sides of the same coin. He could not have one without the other. And the only person he was responsible for now was himself.

Chapter Thirteen

Monday, October 16, 1871

Another door slammed in Meg's face. She remained on Hiram's neighbor's front porch until the brass knocker stilled and she could see her reflection in its polished plate. She didn't look like a murderer's daughter, but that was exactly what the lady of the house had seen.

Thunder groaned in the distance. Her nose and toes tingling from the cold, she turned and headed down the stone stairway, acknowledging a statue of a lion on her way. "Good kitty," she murmured.

A patrolling soldier lifted a quizzical eyebrow at her as she let herself through the iron gate to return to the sidewalk.

"Good afternoon," he said, and she merely nodded, unwilling to engage him in conversation.

The soldiers' presence in the neighborhood allowed her to feel perfectly safe going up and down the block alone. But she had no desire to explain herself to him. Or to anyone else today, for that matter.

All she had wanted was to find out if any neighbors had seen anything unusual around Hiram's house the night of the fire, and if they knew who might have wished him ill. She'd knocked on about a dozen doors today after lunch and had no new information to show for it. No, they couldn't think who would want to hurt Mr.

Sloane. No, they didn't see him leave the night of October 8, and they didn't see anyone suspicious come to the house. Then there were those, like the neighbor whose house she had just left, who realized she was the daughter of the alleged murderer—a lunatic, no less—and couldn't get rid of her fast enough.

It was time to be done questioning neighbors for now. She had spoken with Eli today too, checking on Mr. Davenport's alibi. But there'd been nothing in what he told her to cast doubt on the young man. According to Eli, Jasper Davenport had been vigilant and dogged about finding Hiram as they searched the city together for hours on end.

Her footsteps fell almost silently on mats of slick wet leaves. She tried flexing her hands in their bindings, hidden in the pockets of her cloak. The pain had gradually receded from its original excruciating intensity, but she required assistance to dress, to wash her hair in boiled and cooled lake water, and to change her bandages, a task Sylvie faithfully performed.

A light rain pattered the branches overhead, then dripped onto her hat and shoulders, yet her thoughts remained with her injuries. Meg tried to avoid drawing conclusions based on what she saw during her daily dressing changes. Even Dr. Gilbert, whom she had seen at the free clinic on Saturday after her errand to the police station, had not pronounced a definitive judgment. If she listened to her own fears, she would think her hands would never serve her again the way they once had. She would think that the right hand, her dominant hand, felt like a dead thing because it *was* a dead thing, curling in on itself like a drying leaf. One could not paint with a dead and deformed hand. One could barely do anything with it.

At least her left hand had healed enough that the wrappings covered only her thumb and palm, leaving the tops of her fingers free. That was something. All she could do was wait for further healing and do what she could in the meantime for the family she'd promised to take care of.

That was precious little.

Sylvie had been the one to inventory their possessions. There had been no need to write the insurance company, however, since it was reported in the *Tribune* that it was one of many bankrupted by the fire. The Townsends, along with tens of thousands of others, would get nothing for their losses.

It did not take any skill to stand in line, however, so that was how Meg had spent the morning. As soon as she'd read that the Relief and Aid Society was offering a limited number of free temporary houses, she'd gone to apply for one. At least she hadn't been rained on then.

Rounding the corner, Meg quickened her pace until she reached Hiram's house, climbed the steps, and let herself in. After Kirstin came to help her take off her cloak and hat, the young maid returned to the kitchen and Meg made her way to the library, ready to think about something other than herself and her own circumstances.

It was a masculine room with an ebonized cherry wood mantel for the fireplace, gold curtains at the windows, and brightly painted canvas panels on the ceiling. After perusing the floor-to-ceiling bookshelves, Meg selected a volume she'd sold to Hiram herself several years ago: *The Life of Charlotte Brontë*, written by Charlotte's friend Elizabeth Gaskell. The spine showed no evidence of use. The boxed set of Brontë novels appeared similarly untouched. Hiram must have purchased them as a kindness.

Meg took the familiar book about Charlotte's life to the study table and fumbled it open. She felt more of a kinship with Charlotte than with any of the characters she or her sisters had invented. Charlotte had spent years at home taking care of her ailing father, who slept with a loaded pistol beneath his pillow. She'd wanted to be an artist, but her eyesight was damaged. She only drew or wrote when she'd completed her daily duties at home and for her father, at least until she was required to nurse her dying sisters as well.

Duty had been Charlotte's byword, as it was Meg's. Charlotte published in order to support her family. Meg painted for the same reason. Everything came back to family. So while Meg admired

Madame LeBrun for painting Marie Antoinette when she was Meg's age, she modeled her priorities after Charlotte Brontë's: family above all else.

It stung that right now she could neither paint nor care for her father.

The fire cracked as it toasted the damp air. The rain grew from a purr to a roar outside, soaking the soldiers marching past the windows. Their fixed bayonets reminded Meg that while she was ensconced in comfort and waxing philosophical, Chicago still floundered for order, let alone reconstruction. Homeless still huddled in churches and schools. She'd lost so much, and still she was rich compared to them, thanks to the generosity bestowed upon her here.

Mr. Davenport entered the room and, with a nod to Meg, sat across the table from her before opening his law book. The warm glow of candles and fire highlighted his cheekbones and a white scar on his brow, while the dark corners of the library behind him provided contrast worthy of a Caravaggio painting. His face seemed to hold the same gravity.

It was this aspect of heaviness that had stopped her from sharing that Hiram had been shot in the back. It would do him no good to hear it.

Unable to bear his silence for long, she closed her book. "I was under the impression you preferred to study with classmates, Mr. Davenport."

Without hurry, he leaned back in his chair, hands clasped behind his head. The black armband of mourning about his sleeve melted into the shadows behind him. "Call me Jasper, since we are to be in such close company."

Thunder rolled outside. "Jasper, then."

"I studied with others, yes. But I've lost my taste for it, given that the last time I did so, my uncle was murdered."

Her mouth dried. The chair creaked beneath her shifting weight. "I read in the paper that students from the university enlisted in a regiment to help guard the city. You're not among them?"

"Ah, yes. Company L, First Regiment of Chicago Volunteers, raised by a private citizen to guard the city and shoot anyone they see outside after curfew. Upon whose authority? The mayor's? Sheridan's? I'm not convinced it's constitutional, and I have no inclination to cast my lot in with those young fellows. They're armed, scared, eager, and untested. A terrible combination. So no, I'm not part of Company L."

It was perhaps the longest speech she'd heard him give. Briefly, she wondered about his experience, and compassion stirred for the boy soldier he had been. Her gaze drifted from his angular face to the portrait of Hiram above the fireplace. It was a fair likeness of the beloved old man. He looked so proud and stately in his uniform, even though his service was only in the Invalid Corps here at home.

And here sat Jasper, between the image of the uncle he'd lost and the daughter of the man who allegedly killed him.

A discomforting mix of emotion cycled through her. "Be honest. On a scale of one to ten, how painful is our presence here for you? If we upset you by being here, you must tell me."

Appraising her, a smile slowly curled his lips. "And if I were to tell you that your presence is an aching reminder of tragedy, an absolute ten on your scale, would you go?"

"My sister and I both would. At least to the other side of the house whenever you're not in class."

To her great surprise, he laughed. And not a chuckle or affected snivel, but a great merry laugh that brought the dimple to his left cheek. "I appreciate a girl without guile. If you said you'd leave altogether, I wouldn't have believed you." He brought his arms to rest on the table, long fingers laced together.

"Oh, but we will leave," Meg asserted. "As soon as we have a place to go."

He cocked his head to the side, unruly curls falling over his brow. "And how soon will that be?"

She felt the color rise in her cheeks, for it might not be soon at all. "We'll rebuild, even without help from insurance," she said, and briefly explained her plan. "We have an application under review for one of the ready-to-build houses they're offering to those who were homeowners before the fire."

"I read something about that. But I heard they would only be shanties."

Meg swallowed her distaste for the term. "Each house is two rooms and measures sixteen by twenty-five feet total." It was small, but how else could the aid society hope to house the thousands of people applying for lodging? Besides, it would only be temporary. "It will have planed floors, good windows, and will be outfitted with a stove, mattresses, and some cookery. It's small enough that we can place it in the rear of our lot and live there while the store is being rebuilt on its existing foundation."

With the pad of his thumb, he spun a ring around his fourth finger. "So your application has been approved?"

"Not yet." Neither did she know when she'd hear the verdict. "But in any case, as soon as my bandages come off, I'll be more helpful to you here while we wait for the house to be built." She was certain her left hand would be better than the right. "I'll help you find your uncle's will. We could look for it methodically, attic to cellar. Sylvie could join us too."

He blinked languidly. "I wouldn't trouble my guests with that."

"What if we *want* to help?"

Wind moaned through trees outside. Small yellow flames on the tips of creamy tapers leaned away from the draft.

"I appreciate the offer, but I'm not sure he'd want anyone else besides family to comb through his every personal belonging."

Meg felt like she and Sylvie *had* been family to Hiram, more so than Jasper had been. She dropped her hands beneath the table and onto her lap where they lay dormant, as ever. Idleness did not suit her.

"Beg pardon." Helene entered the room with a bob, her complexion pale above her solid black mourning garb. "There's a caller waiting for you in the reception room."

Jasper stood, smoothing down the front of his shirt.

The housekeeper cleared her throat. "The caller is for Miss Margaret."

"By all means." Jasper gestured toward the door, his shoulders relaxing.

Grateful for a fresh distraction, Meg swept from the room and down the corridor. Helene opened the pocket doors to the reception room and took her leave.

"Nate!" she breathed as he turned to face her.

Rain puddled at his feet where he stood dripping before the fireplace, wiping droplets from his spectacle lenses. He slipped his glasses back on. "There you are." He smiled. The sleeves of his jacket were a shade too long for his arms, evidently a donation from another man's closet.

"You found us." She beamed, unaccountably relieved to see him and not quite sure what the proper greeting should be. It seemed an age since the calamity that had brought them together, though it had scarcely been more than a week. And it had been only two days since Sylvie had written to the *Tribune*, adding their whereabouts to the long columns that still bordered the front page.

"I believe you have something that belongs to me." With a little bow, he placed his hand over his heart, his finger stained blue with ink. "Or have you discarded it as worthless?"

"I have it. Wait here." Moments later, she returned with his jacket over her arm. "We laundered it, but I'm not sure you'll want to wear it again." She extended the garment, and he took it, unfolding it to reveal evidence of the fire that ravaged Chicago.

Nate poked his fingers through two holes. "It certainly wouldn't keep me dry today. And yet I'll keep it as a fire relic. Do I dare ask how the book fared? And your hands?"

She wiggled four fingers in answer. "Marginally better in the left hand," she said in a dismissive tone. "But that's not why I called you here."

He narrowed one blue eye, angling his head. "You called me?"

"I knew you'd come for your jacket as soon as you knew where to find us. That is, I hoped you would." Unwilling to abandon the privacy of this small room, she gestured to a leather chair. "Will you sit?"

Water dripped from the bowler he held. "It's enough that I'm creating a puddle on the floor without soaking the furniture too."

"Oh. Quite." She swallowed, her nerves flagging.

Moments stretched between them, filling the space with things unsaid. Nate had already done so much for her, and she hesitated to ask more of him. For all she knew, he might believe her father was a murderer, and she hadn't the courage to ask him.

"Meg, I had nothing to do with that article about your father's arrest in the *Tribune*," he said at last. "It's important to me that you know that."

"I need help." She blurted out the foreign words. "I don't know who else to ask."

"What is it?"

She firmed her resolve. "I want to go to the asylum. Sylvie doesn't think we should, and I know they won't let me see my father, but surely they'd let me see a doctor."

"You can't go to a place like that alone. It's out of the question."

She was hoping he'd feel that way. "I agree."

It wasn't just that she didn't want to face that horrid institution on her own. To do so would be improper to the highest degree, not to mention ineffective. In addition, Nate's job was getting information out of people. He would be a good man to have at her side on such a quest.

"I realize this is terribly presumptuous, especially after all you've done for my family. But you've earned my trust, Nate Pierce, and I don't know who else to ask. To come with me."

Don't get involved, Nate had told himself. *Don't call on those sisters, forget the jacket. Focus on work—there's plenty of it—and prove yourself to Medill*. But had he listened to his own reason? No.

He'd followed something else instead. Call it a nudge of conscience. Call it curiosity or a reporter's instinct to pry. Call it anything but a magnetic pull to see Meg again. He wished she'd really answered his question about her hands. Another day, perhaps.

Rain drummed on the hood of the small coupe carriage that bore Nate and Meg away from town, sharpening the scents of leather and axle grease. She seemed pensive on the seat beside him. She'd told Helene Dressler she was going with him on an outing, but as Helene helped her into a cloak and secured her hat to her hair, Meg hadn't specified the location. He had a feeling she didn't want to risk being talked out of it.

Nate could relate. If his editor learned of this errand, he stood to lose his job. But as long as Nate kept up with his other stories for the paper, what he did with his personal time should be his own affair.

Absently, he fingered the too-long cuffs of his jacket, willing them not to cover half of his thumbs. Of all the jackets he'd found in the relief piles for the fire victims, none were a true fit. Whether too short or too long, the resulting impression was that he was a boy still growing into manhood. Not exactly the image he wanted to project.

Not that Meg was looking.

He followed her gaze out the window. A sky of hammered pewter released its cargo into an atmosphere that smelled of wet metal. Nate was grateful Eli Washington had been available to hire for the trip. Meg had assured Nate that Eli wouldn't leak any gossip afterward. If Jasper were to learn of their visit to the asylum, it ought to come from Meg.

Bridles jangling, the two horses labored to pull the carriage over softened ground until, ten miles northwest of Chicago's business district, gravel roads offered relief. The Cook County Insane Asylum rose up like a fortress, bristling with towers and chimneys. A chill raced over Nate's damp skin as he regarded its immensity. He knew the complex occupied more than three hundred acres but hadn't recalled how dwarfed it made him feel.

Color drained from Meg's face, making her freckles stand out more. To gain a better view, she perched on the edge of the seat, and the soft folds of her skirts brushed his knees. She smelled faintly of rose oil. "What a perfect setting for an Edgar Allan Poe story. Especially with the dismal weather."

Nate couldn't deny it.

In the circular drive before the main entrance, Eli drew rein on the horses, then climbed down from his bench to see Meg out of the coupe.

Nate put his hat on his head and stepped out behind her. "Do you want to come in and get warm while you wait, Eli?"

The driver leaned back to take in the imposing structure, rain wetting his broad face. Bare vines kept a tenacious grip on the outside of the building. "No, sir. We just fine out here." He closed the carriage door and patted a horse's rump.

Thanking him, Nate offered Meg his arm, then climbed the stone stairs with her. She seemed smaller than usual beside him, though she straightened her spine in obvious determination. He sent her a small smile he hoped was reassuring.

Once past the first set of heavy wooden doors, Nate wiped his spectacle lenses dry, then pushed through one more pair of doors until they'd passed through the vestibule and into the hall. Thirty feet ahead of them was an arch, on the other side of which ran a corridor leading to wards on either side of the central building where they stood. To Nate's left were two offices with closed doors. To his right, a reception room connected to a doctor's office. It was into this reception room that he steered Meg.

Gaslight flickered in wall sconces above a row of straight-backed chairs. An elderly couple occupied two of them, the woman quietly knitting, From behind a counter, a receptionist looked up and smiled as Nate and Meg approached.

"How may I help you?" She peered at them over the rims of her reading glasses. Brown hair neatly secured in an ivory snood, she could not have been younger than forty-five. A cameo pin covered the top button of her dark blue dress.

Nate tipped his bowler, and water streamed onto the floor. "Nathaniel Pierce, *Chicago Tribune*. This is Margaret Townsend."

"And my name is Miss Dean." She laced her fingers together.

"How do you do." Meg was awkward with formality. "My father is a patient here. Stephen Townsend. I'd like to see his doctor."

"I see. Do you know the doctor's name?"

Nate glanced at Meg, who gave a slight shake of her head. "I'm sure your records indicate who Stephen Townsend's doctor is," he said. "And I'm sure you'll do your best to help us. If the doctor isn't in, I could look for him myself on a tour of your facility."

Miss Dean twisted the small gold ring on her pinky finger. "I wasn't aware of any scheduled tours." Yet it was an odd truth that while patients were not allowed personal visitors, asylum tourism was popular with people who had a taste for the macabre.

But Nate had come as neither. "I'm a reporter, Miss Dean. Unscheduled tours are more my style."

From somewhere unseen, a man's shrieking filtered through the walls. The steady clicking of the knitting needles stopped as the grey-haired woman closed her eyes, ridges grooving her brow. The man beside her patted her knee, his white mustache drooping. Meg squeezed Nate's arm. Another voice, more authoritative, responded to the shrieking patient, followed by an abrupt silence that only amplified a steady, rhythmic banging from some other unseen place.

"Please find the doctor, Miss Dean." Nate's tone bordered on congenial.

Miss Dean removed her glasses and let them hang on a beaded chain about her neck. "Wait here." She swished from the room with the sound of overstarched skirts.

Meg's tension radiated into Nate from her vice-like squeeze on his arm. She looked through the doorway that led into the hall. "Is there anything else we can see? Any windows that might lend a glimpse of . . . anything?"

A cold draft of air brushed the back of his neck and stirred the feather in Meg's hat. He shook his head. "The first floor is entirely offices and a storeroom. After patients enter the building, they don't spend time on this level because it would be too easy for them to escape. The stairwells are all locked, so unless we're escorted by staff, we can't go upstairs."

And he wasn't convinced she ought to see more, even if they could. She was under enough strain as it was.

Her hold on his arm loosened as she angled to look him square in the face. "You've been here before. Have you been upstairs to see where the residents live?"

He had. He'd covered the opening of this building last year and combined it with a story about methods for treating the mentally ill. Moral therapy was a regimen of rest and light labor on the asylum grounds, combined with opiates, stimulants, and "tonics" made of milk, sugar, eggs, and whiskey. But for patients who didn't respond appropriately, there were other methods. Containment in wooden cages called cribs. Straitjackets. Solitary confinement. For these cases, the only goal was to keep them separate from the rest of society until their lives ended.

"I have been upstairs," he admitted. "Each ward has its own dining room. A dumbwaiter brings up food from the kitchen in the basement. Patients share three water closets and two bathtubs on each floor."

She wrinkled her nose. "What else?"

Miss Dean returned to the reception room with a man who did not look well-pleased. Fading black hair lay in rows over the top of his balding head.

"This is most irregular," he said when he reached them. "You are aware you cannot see the patient, yes?"

The lack of common courtesy grated on Nate. If this was how the doctor treated them, how did he treat his patients? "Let's try this again, shall we?" He thrust out his hand, heedless of the cuff sagging past his wrist. "Nathaniel Pierce, *Chicago Tribune*, and this is Margaret Townsend. You are?"

Miss Dean excused herself and returned to the counter, head bowed.

Begrudgingly, it seemed, the man shook Nate's hand and cast a cursory glance at Meg. "I am Dr. Edmund Franklin. The patient in question is under my care."

"His name is Captain Stephen Townsend," Meg said quietly. "The 'patient in question' has a name, and he is my father."

Creases fanned from the psychiatrist's eyes as he regarded her. "To me, he is a patient. Emotional detachment from my patients is the way I can serve them best."

"Explain that to me, doctor," she said. "Explain to me how you are serving my father right now." Her voice trembled. Nate surmised it was not from fear but from the depth of the responsibility she felt.

Dr. Franklin exhaled a sharp sigh. Nonetheless, he led Nate and Meg into the adjoining office. Framed diplomas hung on the wall behind a desk that was clear of everything but blotter, inkwell, and a tray piled high with correspondence. Besides the door from the reception room, another led to the hall.

"Sit." He circled the desk and did the same, the smell of medicine lifting from his white coat.

Nate removed his hat, placing it on his knee while they settled into the hard chairs. Meg sat ramrod straight.

"You understand this is a public institution," Dr. Franklin began. "As a veteran, the patient receives free care. As you are not paying for it, we are not beholden or obligated to answer to you in any way."

Meg's cheeks flamed the color of poppies.

"You're beholden to the public," Nate inserted. "We are the public too, are we not? The readers of the *Chicago Tribune* are your public. They would be very interested to learn if a psychiatrist here is deliberately withholding information about a family member."

"I doubt that, with the fire and rebuilding efforts foremost on everyone's mind."

"Shall we test the theory?" Nate smiled, but he knew he was walking a tightrope between motivating and antagonizing Dr. Franklin.

"Please," Meg interrupted. "Tell me what you can. What are

you doing for my father, and how long do you expect the treatment to take?"

At length, the doctor responded. "283 suffers from a condition—"

"Excuse me," she interjected. "283?"

"Patients are assigned numbers upon their arrival. His number is 283. I'm a busy man, so if you insist on interrupting, I'll have to end our interview."

The slight lift of her chin was defiant.

"As I was saying. Patient 283 suffers from a condition called soldier's heart. In my experience, it is a chronic illness without cure. The heart was overly strained during the war and most specifically during his time at Andersonville prison camp. So the erratic and rapid heartbeat and other symptoms often associated with anxiety lead to other manifestations. Insomnia. Paranoia. Irrational thinking and behavior. There are many documented cases across the country."

Meg allowed a few beats of quiet to pass. "What happens next?"

"If you're asking me to predict the future of 283, I won't do it."

"The other cases, then," Nate said, struggling to mask his growing irritation at the doctor's blunt retorts. "What happened to other men who have had soldier's heart?"

Dr. Franklin opened a drawer in his desk, located a file, and slapped the manila folder on the blotter just as a knock sounded at the door from the hall. "Yes?"

An attendant in a white uniform stepped one foot inside. "Doctor, we have a—an issue we need to consult you on. A matter of some urgency."

Dr. Franklin left the office and closed the door behind him. Nate could tell the two men had moved a few paces away by the sound of their voices.

"Look!" Meg whispered, jerking her head toward the file.

Nate slid the folder toward him and opened it. These weren't confidential patient records, they were newspaper clippings and some typewritten notes. He parsed the text.

A soldier from the 16th Connecticut had come home from the

war so broken in body and mind that he didn't know his own name. He flailed in his sleep, dreaming that he was still searching for food at Andersonville. He perished at age twenty-two.

Nate flipped to the next page, this one with a heading of *Indiana Hospital for the Insane*. A bulleted list identified a veteran inmate who sobbed and cried and imagined that the Rebels were after him. Others were committed because they had barricaded themselves in their rooms.

His dismay deepened the more he read. Neither these veterans nor their families had had any idea they would sacrifice their sanity in service to their country.

In Utica, New York, a patient could not be soothed by his wooden cage but beat his limbs against it until he was bruised, shouting at invisible soldiers and driving phantom horses all the while. He died at the age of twenty-three.

But it was the next clipping that chilled Nate's bones. A veteran had killed a man with no recollection of having done it. He later killed himself in Sing Sing Prison.

"What does it say?" Meg leaned toward him, her arm brushing his.

Nate realigned the papers and closed the folder, sliding it back onto the desk. "I'll tell you later."

He couldn't bring himself to look at her wide hazel eyes for more than a moment. He wouldn't lie to Meg, but how could he tell her the entire truth? Was it right to tell her just part of it? That didn't sit well either.

The door opened again, and Dr. Franklin leaned into the office. "Our time together has come to an end."

Her chair scraped the floor as Meg stood. "But what about my father? Can't you tell me anything about the prognosis at all?"

"I can tell you that most cases like his stay at the asylum for the rest of their lives, however short or long that may be."

Meg looked as though she'd been struck. Tears filled her eyes, and she looked away.

"Do not come back, Miss Townsend. Should you need to say anything further, send it by post. Good day."

Bristling once more, Nate reseated his hat and brought Meg to the carriage outside. A miserly rain misted his face and clung in beads to the windows. He handed her up and followed her in. The pungent smell of moldering leaves and sodden earth permeated the air even inside the carriage.

A single tear ran down her face. "I'm sorry," she whispered, wiping it away with her wrist. "I promised my mother I'd take care of him, and—well, I'm not doing it. I don't know how to fix this. Tell me what you read in the file, at least."

He couldn't. At least not right now. "That information was collected about other people. Your father is an individual. It's best not to judge him based on other cases."

Did he know her well enough yet to tell her that fixing her father's situation was beyond her power, just as his stepbrother Andrew's character had proven to be beyond his?

He wished he did. For he saw in her the weight of responsibility for her family. He saw in her himself.

Chapter Fourteen

Tuesday, October 17, 1871

Dear Father,

This is Sylvie. I send you my greetings, but Meg is dictating this letter to me because she can't hold a pen yet.

Nathaniel Pierce and I came to the asylum today to learn what we could about your situation. Did they tell you? I didn't see the rooms, so I don't know if they are kept warm and clean enough, or if you get enough to eat. If there is any problem, find a way to let me know.

Sylvie and I are staying with Jasper Davenport in Hiram's house now, so you may address any mail to us here. Helene and Kirstin still live at the house too, and Eli lives in the carriage house.

We (Sylvie and I) went to church on Sunday, but not here in the Prairie Avenue neighborhood. It didn't seem right to worship in a place untouched by the fire, with a congregation we don't know. So we went to Unity Church, or what's left of it, where Reverend Collyer led a service inside the charred walls of his sanctuary, the open sky a canopy above our heads. He stood on a carved stone that had fallen from an arch as he addressed us. I wish you could have heard him.

Sylvie took notes so we could remember. We wanted to share a few lines with you. He said:

"Some men of a stronger heart are, perhaps, able to thank God for this great affliction. I, myself, have tried to find some altitude of soul, some height of moral sentiment, from which I might look down and thank God for overshadowing us with this great sorrow. . . . But I cannot get up to it this morning. . . . It is too near. We will thank God as soon as we can."

I hope that somehow, you might draw comfort from that, as we have. Our afflictions are too near. We will thank God as soon as we can.

And we'll get you out of there as soon as we can too.

Your loving,
Meg

P.S. This is Sylvie again. Meg says you have a condition called soldier's heart. Please do whatever the doctors say you must to get better.

Friday, October 20, 1871

The aroma of fresh-brewed coffee greeted Sylvie as she entered the kitchen. Last night's nightmare was no different than it had been every night since the fire, but at least she'd recognized she was only dreaming, that the city wasn't on fire all over again, no matter what she saw and felt in her mind. That was progress.

Sun slanted through the windows and flashed on copper pans hanging above the fireplace. Replacing a flour-dusted apron with a fresh one, Helene smiled as she tied the strings behind her waist. "Good morning," she said, "and good news. The water pumps are working again. We shall have as much coffee and tea as you wish now, not to mention enough for a proper bath. After nine days of drinking lake water, I expect you're ready for a cup of tea that doesn't taste like fish."

"I am. But a bracing cup of coffee will be just the thing this morning, if you've made enough. And if there is bread, one thick slice will do."

"Oh dear." Helene slid her gaze toward the stove, upon which sat a tray of blackened biscuits. "I'm not sure I'd call that bread, but it once aspired to be. You must forgive me, Miss Sylvie. This old housekeeper knows more about polish than baking."

"That's all right." Sylvie plucked up a roll, tossed it in the air, and caught it. "I haven't much practice at baking either, since we had a lovely bakery down the block from our bookshop. They made everything so well, our mother didn't bother teaching us."

Closing her eyes, she could almost smell the breads, milk rolls, soft pretzels, strudel, and the American-style pies Hoffman's Bakery had perfected. She missed it. She missed sharing a plate of Berliners there with Rosemary and Beth. She missed home and her friends with such a sudden stab that she found herself blinking back tears.

They'd called on her yesterday, having seen the notice in the paper about her whereabouts. They'd come to say good-bye. Their families had decided to start over somewhere else, where they had relatives they could live with until they got their feet under them again. Likely they were on the train even now. Sylvie did not make friends easily. To lose these two at once hurt more than she could say.

With a forced brightness, she smiled at Helene. "In any case, it's my turn to try baking for tomorrow."

"Very good, Miss Sylvie." Helene brushed some lint from her apron. "Will you be enjoying your rock-hard roll in the dining room this morning?"

"No." Sylvie giggled. "Right here is fine." She slid onto the bench at the broad worktable as Helene poured her coffee.

Jasper's tread announced him even before he entered the kitchen. Upon seeing Sylvie, he smiled. "Going somewhere?"

Her hands flew to the jacket she wore. "Oh. Yes, soon."

Accepting a cup of coffee from Helene, he eased onto the bench opposite her. "Not alone, though." The way his voice lifted at the end made the statement more of a question.

She stifled the urge to shrug. "I suppose I am," she said instead. She took a drink, and her brow wrinkled before she could stop herself.

"That bad?" he whispered.

"It isn't lake water anymore," she told him. "Perhaps I've grown unaccustomed to coffee made with water from the pipes."

He took a drink of his own. "I had worse during the war. Much worse. Is that hardtack you're feasting on there?" He picked up her roll and knocked it on the table.

"Oh, for goodness' sake." Helene threw up her hands in mock despair. "If you'll excuse me, I'm off to perform some tasks that actually do fall under my expertise."

Jasper chuckled as he watched her go. He seemed different here in the kitchen, like his hard edges had melted away. Sylvie snatched the roll back from him and tried breaking it apart.

"Try dipping it into the coffee," he suggested.

She did so. "A war trick?"

"Something like that. Don't bother trying to be dignified when you eat it either. Not on my account. Although I'd be entertained to see you try."

Leaning back, he grabbed his own roll from the stovetop, then dunked it into his mug. "Now, about you leaving the house alone. Where I come from, it isn't done. What business do you have, if you don't mind my asking?"

"I'm going to a church to sew or sort donated clothing—anything to be helpful when so many are in need."

"And anything to get out of this house?" There was no malice in his tone.

A fresh wave of homesickness rushed over her. "I don't really belong here. I'm grateful for it, but I . . ." She lifted the roll from her coffee and watched it drip back into the mug. Her appetite waned. "I'm restless."

"And homesick?"

"Desperately so." She found in his eyes an understanding that untied a knot between her shoulders. "My two best friends are moving away. I know better than to admit to Meg how much I ache for them. She's managed without close friends for so long that I don't expect her to sympathize. Especially since she has her own problems with her injuries." They had looked better during the dressing change this morning, but the right hand's prospect seemed bleak.

"That's a shame," he said. "But you're still allowed to feel homesick. You're allowed to miss your friends."

"Emily Brontë struggled dreadfully with homesickness. She tried going away to school where her older sister Charlotte was a teacher, but she became so physically ill from missing home that she returned after only three months. Isn't that interesting, that she had her sister with her, yet it wasn't enough?" In this, Sylvie felt some validation.

Jasper watched her intently. "Are these friends of yours? Emily and Charlotte?"

She smiled at him. "In a manner of speaking, yes. They wrote some of my favorite books. Women's novels," she quickly added, in case he felt embarrassed at not being familiar with them. "Do you miss your friends while you're here for school? Are you homesick too?"

He blinked in surprise at her query. "I didn't leave behind much that I ever loved. Just memories of the way things were in better times. We fell into hardship years ago and couldn't fight our way out of it, though not for lack of trying. I don't like talking about it. I don't belong here much more than you do, Sylvie."

The sound of her name in his voice rippled through her. Was this how Jane Eyre had felt with Mr. Rochester? Sylvie scolded herself for conjuring fiction when flesh and blood sat before her, taking her in.

No one else was in the room. But surely if Helene had thought the situation warranted a chaperone, she'd have found a reason to stay. Surely Sylvie was being ridiculous. This was breakfast by chance in the basement kitchen with scorched rolls and terrible coffee.

Nibbling at the bread sent a dribbling of liquid down her chin, and she wiped it away along with any girlish notions of a budding connection. Possessing herself, she sipped her coffee. "What do you mean, you don't belong here?"

"I'm not from a big city, for one. This is my first time in Chicago. The people here move a lot faster than I'm accustomed to. But it's more than that." He spun a ring on his finger and then took it off, rolling it between his forefinger and thumb. It had been Hiram's. "My grandmother had a falling out with Uncle Hiram long ago, and out of loyalty to her, I cut off communication with him too. My grandmother raised me, and when she passed away, I resolved to reconcile with my great-uncle. I wrote to him, and he replied with an invitation. I swallowed my pride and came."

"He was so glad you did." So was she.

Jasper took a drink of coffee. "He was, and it took the sting out of our arrangement. He paid for my tuition to law school. At least the first semester. As soon as I expressed an interest in it, he insisted on securing the education I hadn't been able to acquire on my own."

Sylvie exhaled slowly, tucking this information away to share with Meg later. "That sounds exactly like something he would do. He paid for Meg's membership at the Chicago Academy of Design so she could take painting classes there when it opened a few years ago."

If there had been a shred of doubt about Jasper's innocence, this dissolved it. No one would kill the man who was funding their education. But did this also cinch the guilt around her father? She hated to think so. For how could she ever face Jasper again, let alone be at ease with him, if her father had truly murdered Hiram?

"I'm an ordinary man pursuing a second chance at a future worth having," he said. "That's why I'm here and in law school."

"A second chance," Sylvie repeated. "I think we all want that, the entire city of Chicago. And I would like to do my part rather than sit and stew over my losses." Heat crawled under her collar. She'd been wearing her jacket indoors too long. "I really should be going."

Jasper downed the rest of his coffee and stood. "I'll take you. I don't have class until this afternoon."

Sylvie moved the dirty dishes to the sink. "Are you certain?"

"Regardless of how I view the mayor's methods of keeping order, he believes the dangers warrant martial law. Yes, I'm certain." He tipped his head to one side. "Your surprise is plain on your face. I'm almost insulted."

"I thought—after what happened with your uncle and what's being said—you would feel no obligation to take pains on our account," she stammered. "Especially since you've already opened your house to us."

He straightened the necktie at his collar. "It is not you and your sister who are on trial. And I'm no brute, Sylvie. It would bring me no pleasure to learn you've been accosted in the street when it's in my power to escort you safely."

Jasper Davenport might be poor in money, but he was rich in manners and Christian feeling. Meg was wrong to have ever doubted him.

"Shall we?" A tentative smile returned to his face.

Sylvie had no wish to refuse him.

Perhaps coming here was a mistake. But Sylvie climbed down from the carriage just the same, taking Jasper's arm to steady her steps. "Thank you, Eli," she called up to the driver. "I'll only be a moment."

"Take your time, Miss Sylvie." He tugged the brim of his cap lower on his head, shading his eyes. "I won't go anywhere."

Overcome by her longing for home, Sylvie had requested a detour to Court House Square before continuing on to the church. Along the way, they'd passed dozens of uniformed soldiers, bayonets flashing in the sun's brilliance. She had been shocked to see hundreds of temporary wooden structures thrown up in place of those that had burned down. They resembled little more than shanties of various sizes, but painted signs declared grocers and merchants open for business. Where larger buildings had collapsed or been burned out, other signs sprouted from what remained, listing the name of the establishment, along with a notice for customers.

Open for business at 23 Canal Street!

Rebuilding to begin December 1!

Bricklayers apply at 69 Canal St.

Gone east.

The overwhelming smell was that of charred earth. With one hand, Sylvie lifted her skirts above the ankle-deep dust that covered the ground. With the other, she clung tighter to Jasper, her steps faltering over hidden chunks of brick and stone. A blackened finial from the top of the courthouse lay on its side, half buried in a drift of debris that included tin and wire. At the corner of La Salle and Randolph, a woman sold chestnuts.

A flock of Canada geese soared overhead, but there were no other birds, for there were no more trees in the burned district to hold them. Some of the outer walls of the courthouse remained standing, but it was empty and barren inside. Crews of men with pickaxes and shovels were scattered over the square, bending and heaving rubble into wheelbarrows and wagons. Every turn of a wheel, every disturbance of the broken remains stirred up dust, and the air was so thick with it that Sylvie was obliged to drop her hem to cover her nose and mouth with her hand.

Slowly, she spun to face her old street. The wreckage of the Sherman House hotel was being moved, and so was that of City Coffee and the cigar shop. But the corner of the block that she'd called home looked much the same as she'd left it. Nothing had been cleared away save for a small patch upon which a table now stood, presided over by a boy of about twelve and a young man. They were related, judging by the resemblance in the eyes and cleft chin.

"That's our property," she choked out. "What are they doing there?"

Jasper frowned. "Let's find out."

Through a narrow path, they approached the table and found it full of small items that looked like rubbish.

"Fire relics!" the boy declared with a hint of an Italian accent. He twisted his newsboy cap to scratch beneath it, then tugged it back into place. "Get your fire relics here! Remember the desolation of Chicago! The name's Louis Garibaldi, ma'am and sir, and these are bona fide relics, curated and guaranteed by my brother Lorenzo and myself. Take a gander, why don'tcha? Carry a memento with you always!"

Smiling at the boy's theatrical style, Sylvie peered closer at the wares and distinguished a pile of washers welded together into one piece, a fragment of a marble statue that was just two clasped hands, a stack of charred invoices, and a prayer and hymn book from one of the churches, half burned away. Beneath those were rows of miniature firemen's hats and miniature bells, all of untarnished metal.

Jasper picked up a fireman's hat and balanced it on the tip of his finger. "These don't look like they've been through the fire."

"Ah." Louis spread his hands above them with the flair of a magician. Knitted fingerless gloves slouched beneath coat cuffs in need of laundering. "They have been through it and have been reborn, they have. All the miniatures were made from the courthouse bell, which was melted down and recast for the purpose."

Stunned, Sylvie placed a small bell in her palm and heard in her mind the great clanging from the night of the fire—not just the courthouse bell, but all the church and school bells ringing their alarm. The dust in the air became the dust borne on the vicious winds that rushed ahead of the flames. Her pulse leapt. *It's over*, she told herself, but sweat itched across her scalp beneath her hat and lined the inside of her chemise, the residue of fear not forgotten.

Shaken by the force of her body's response to the trinket, she dropped it as though it held the heat of that dreadful night.

Jasper's fingertips gave the lightest touch on her elbow. "Are you all right?"

Deflecting the soft-spoken question, she smoothed her jacket over her skirt and addressed the relic sellers. "This is my father's property," she told them. "We owned Corner Books & More."

"Is that right?" The young man, Lorenzo, stuck a toothpick between his teeth and chewed it. "You going to rebuild, relocate? It didn't seem like we were in anyone's way here."

"We'd like to rebuild, but . . ." Sylvie's voice trailed off as she looked at all the activity on the rest of the block. "It seems not a single brick has been moved from the lot. Do you know why?"

"Fire relics!" Louis shouted past her, waving his cap to beckon potential customers. "Come get your relics of the Great Conflagration!"

"Lady, it's up to the private property owners to clear their own land. Did you think the city would do it for you? I don't know where you or your father have been not to know this, but if you want to clean up, clean it up yourself. Otherwise folks assume you've gone east and the land is up for grabs."

She stepped sideways to look behind him. In the burned-out basement of what had been their bookshop, seven or eight people had set up lean-tos. A clothesline was strung from one to another on the opposite side, with diapers and breeches draped over it. With a toddler on one hip, a woman bent over a cookstove set up near the middle.

"Is that your family?" she dared to ask. "Are you living here?"

"Us? Nah." Lorenzo rolled the toothpick to the other corner of his mouth. "But you can see why they thought it was abandoned. My guess is they'll clear out as soon as the weather turns nasty. The Relief and Aid Society is erecting barracks, but I can't blame folks for wanting to stay out of those as long as possible."

Frustration swelled as Sylvie thanked him for his time and left him and his brother to sell their wares.

"What were we thinking?" she fumed, making her way back to the street. "Meg and I assumed the land would be magically cleared away. Such foolishness! Where did we come by such a notion?"

Jasper did not berate her. She did that well enough on her own.

"We've squandered time that could have been spent working. If we're approved for a house of our own, we need a place to put it. I'd rather not impose upon you any longer than we have to."

An eyebrow lifted beneath the brim of Jasper's hat, but he said nothing. Likely he completely agreed with her.

Clouds of dust turned her skirt a sepia tone below the waist, as if she were climbing out of a daguerreotype. After a backward glance at her corner lot, she continued forward, finding her footing one step at a time through the rubble. "We must hire a crew."

Jasper guided her toward Eli. "Can you pay them?"

"Some now, some later. Isn't that how business must be done all over the city?"

"It is." He handed her up into the carriage.

Eli spoke over his shoulder. "Everything all right, Miss Sylvie?"

She rubbed the chill from her arms and took a seat. "Meg and I have more work to do than we realized, if we have any hope of resurrecting Corner Books & More. I'm ready to go to the West Side First Congregational Church now, please."

The coupe lurched forward, and she pressed her hand against the side to steady herself. Settling into the rhythmic motion, she drew a handkerchief from her reticule and dabbed it discreetly over her face and neck to remove the dust that had settled there.

A soldier marched past them, rifle on his shoulder. Balling her handkerchief in her fist, Sylvie followed him with her gaze.

"Jasper, are there other young men at the university who might rather pick up a shovel than a weapon when they aren't studying or in class?"

He set his hat on the bench beside him and raked a hand through his curls. "I can find out. And if there are, I'm willing to lead them. Clearing the rubble is only a matter of strength, no real skill required. It's the construction afterward, materials and labor, that will prove the greater challenge by far."

"One step at a time," she told him, watching the ruins passing by. "If I must think of them all at once, I'll never take the first."

Jasper's small smile brought the hint of a dimple to his cheek. "You're braver than you think."

It was kind of him to say. But as she recalled her recurring nightmares, not to mention her reaction to a metal bell no bigger than her thumb, she knew it was a lie.

Chapter Fifteen

The morning was half gone by the time Meg finished her errand and returned to the house. Pinching the pearl heads of her hatpins between two fingertips, she managed to extract the long pins and remove her hat. The hall mirror showed shadow crescents hanging beneath her eyes. Her lips looked pale, her hair dull. Not a flattering portrait, but a true one.

With Sylvie volunteering at the church today, Meg was determined to be useful too. Helene had recalled the name of the attorney who officiated Hiram's will, so this morning Meg had gone to the *Tribune* to pick up a directory of relocated businesses, since the office of Thomas Grosvenor had been in the burned district. Nate was at the *Tribune* building when she stopped there, and after she told him about the missing will and her search for it, he had accompanied her to the attorney's office. Just as Meg feared, most records had been lost in the fire, Hiram's will among them. But the clerk thought Mr. Grosvenor might remember something helpful, so he arranged an appointment for Meg for next week. It was better than nothing, she told herself.

"Hello?" she called into the house. "Jasper? Kirstin? Helene?" Her voice bounced off the walls, bringing no response.

She couldn't remember the last time she'd been alone.

Facing the task of unbuttoning her cloak unaided, she used her teeth to pull down the bandage on one side of her left hand, exposing her thumb. When the top was free, she wiggled her thumb to loosen the wrappings. Scar tissue stretched. The movement felt unnatural and stiff. Frowning, she watched her fingers fumble at the buttons. The pressure she applied did not match the pressure she felt. The nerves seemed farther away from her skin than they had been before the fire. She'd expected nerve damage in her right hand, not this one. Even so, with effort, she managed to unfasten her cloak and hang it on the hall tree.

Meg stared at her left hand, pinching her index finger and thumb together despite the binding around her palm.

Could she hold a pencil without all the feeling in her fingers? Whatever marks she could make were bound to be inelegant, but she could try. She had to try.

Upstairs in the bedchamber, she found a pencil and writing paper in the desk. If she could write with her nondominant hand, didn't it stand to reason she could paint with it too? In time?

A sunbeam warmed the rug at her feet. Seated at the desk, she picked up the pencil, her grip awkward. It didn't feel right. When she put the lead point to paper, the pencil tipped out of her hand. She picked it up again, struggling to get it into the proper position and keep it there.

Slowly, she spelled her name, dropping the pencil three times in the process. The letters staring back at her looked like a child's attempt.

She tried again, noticing how her hand pulled the characters into a leftward slant. She tried compensating for this by adjusting where her wrist and elbow rested on the desk. Not only could she not sense the pressure in her grip, but the pressure between pencil and paper eluded her as well.

Apprehension gathered in her shoulders. When painting, the miniscule variations of pressure applied to a brush made a huge difference in the thickness of lines, the consistency of shading. It mattered more than she wanted to admit.

Head aching, she set that concern aside for another day, or tried to. As she studied her work, the letters began to wave and jostle in her vision. The harder she concentrated, the more fatigued she became, the more acutely her childhood affliction came back to her. Had she spelled her own name incorrectly? Now it appeared the words pushed together, letters out of order.

She closed her eyes, breathing deeply. She meant only to steady herself, but memories rushed at her, voices of teachers who'd called her lazy and stupid, of children laughing. Meg had not bowed to those taunts, though each one named her worst fear. *What if they're right about me?* she had secretly wondered. But on the outside, she was fiercely defiant.

Her parents had told her she was created in the image of a God who loved her no matter what. But if she had learned anything from her childhood, it had been that worth, as the world measured it, was not innate. It was defined by what she knew and did. Her gift for painting had been the evidence that she was valuable after all.

Opening her eyes, Meg turned the paper over, shutting out the wiggling words, and attempted to sketch a picture instead. She fumbled the pencil, and it rolled to the floor. After picking it up, she attempted a simple outline of a head and hair, a shape she had drawn countless times.

Even when she managed to keep the pencil in her hand, the lines veered off course, distorting the shape to a mockery. The disconnect between her brain and her fingers was maddening. A small whisper of reason suggested that she give herself some grace, for she was using a hand she'd never sketched with in her life. Louder was the fear that her skill had burned up in the fire, never to be recovered.

She held her breath and focused on another try. This time the pressure she poured into the task broke the pencil lead, marking her failure with an asterisk.

Meg threw the pencil across the room. She felt wrung-out and raw, every disappointment of the last couple of weeks collecting beneath the surface of her skin. Her soul craved beauty and hope, and what she found instead was disordered scratchings and a dread that time might not heal all wounds after all.

For herself or for her father. It galled her that she could control neither her own hand nor Stephen's fate. She must trust God for both. As Charlotte Brontë wrote, she must *"avoid looking forward or backward, and try to keep looking upward."*

Resolved to do better in that regard, Meg retrieved the pencil from where it had landed on the bureau. Her mother's *Little Women* lay next to it. It had lost its front cover, but that was all. The sight of her mother's name on the title page brought a hitch to Meg's breath. She could use a mother's comfort now.

After bringing the volume back to the desk, Meg carefully turned the pages, noting her mother's graceful handwriting. Ruth always wrote in her favorite books. She underlined passages and even talked back to the characters in the margins on occasion. Meg's exhaustion made reading challenging, since the letters refused to be still, but she managed to sort through a few lines. On the blank page opposite the start of the first chapter, Ruth had penned a quote from the character Amy March: *"I'm not afraid of storms, for I'm learning how to sail my ship."*

Meg had always felt an affinity for Amy's character because of their shared interest in art, even though the eldest March sister shared Meg's Christian name. But she had forgotten this quote. Written in Ruth's hand, it took on new layers of meaning. Beneath it in smaller letters, Ruth had added, *Yes, dear Amy, but I'm not afraid of storms, for the One who made the sea is in my boat with me.*

Turning to the window, Meg gave her eyes a rest from the text. A strengthening wind shook the trees outside. Bark stripped away and blew off the sycamore trunk.

Mothers weren't supposed to have favorites, but if Ruth had been forced, she would have picked Sylvie. It was Sylvie, after all, who knew to preserve this book. It was Sylvie who had excelled in school and who'd never distressed Ruth with tantrums or cluttered the home with drawings and paintings. Longing for a connection with her mother that had eluded her in life, Meg returned her attention to the book.

Near the middle of the novel, a folded sheet of paper covered with Ruth's script obscured the beginning of chapter thirty. Meg labored to unfold it. Dated 1865, it seemed to have been ripped from her diary.

Ruth had wanted to hide this.

The impulse to honor her mother's wishes guttered as soon as Meg spied the shape of her own name among the jumble of letters. Her mother had written about her. Such a small and simple thing, and yet it was enough for Meg to forsake the privacy of the dead for the chance to feel closer to her. She rubbed her eyes, then slowly untangled the letters.

Meg's hopes may prove false regarding Stephen. She insists he'll recover in time, but he'll never again be who he was. Forgive me, Lord, but at times I want to shake her for not accepting this.

Meg sat back in her chair and exhaled. This was not a diary but a prayer journal, a window into Ruth's soul. And Ruth had wanted "to shake her." Had Meg really grated on her mother so much? Tension coiled tighter inside her.

She paints only from imagination and not from life, but there is beauty in the imperfect too. You are a God who uses broken vessels. You are not afraid of human limitations or scars. I fear that if she doesn't accept this, she will one day weary of her father and cease to love him if he doesn't recover to her impossible standards. Hope can only carry her so far, so long.

The words wrapped around Meg like a vine, the phrase "impossible standards" a thorn that pierced her conscience. She railed against the idea that she would ever give up on her father. Yet did she persevere only for the chance that he would get better? Or would she still love him—truly and freely love him—if his current state never improved?

As for the scars her mother mentioned, Meg would live with her own for the rest of her life.

Clanging wind chimes competed with the clamor of Meg's thoughts. She leaned forward to examine the rest of the page. There was a change in the color of the ink in the next passage and a slightly looser script.

Lord, please comfort our dear friend Hiram.

Meg startled at the sight of his name. She squinted at the paper and kept reading.

He won't say why he changed his will to make Stephen, then me, then the girls his beneficiaries, only that he did it. He told us that it was something he'd done some time ago.

Meg's heart kicked in her chest. Her fingers and feet were as cold as the empty hearth. She reread the lines, not trusting her first translation of the jostling words. She willed the letters to rearrange themselves into a different statement, but in vain.

Jasper had nothing to gain from Hiram's death.

Stephen did.

Chapter Sixteen

Half exhausted and half exhilarated from a full day of sewing at the church, Sylvie climbed the stairs to the bedchamber she shared with Meg, preparing to tell her that they'd need to hire a crew to clear the rubble from their property. And that Jasper had offered to lead them.

A smile tipped her lips at the thought of him. Not only had he taken her to the church, he'd come back for her at the appointed time to see her safely home. It was unnecessary, she'd told him. He "*reckoned otherwise.*" It felt so good to be cared for, even in this small thing.

"Oh! Begging your pardon, Miss Sylvie." Kirstin met her at the top of the stairs. "I was just fixing the fire in your room. There's tea for you too, if you'd like it."

"Thank you, that sounds lovely." She nodded to the maid as she passed.

When Sylvie entered the bedchamber, however, her smile slipped. One glimpse of Meg's pallor, and Sylvie knew something was dreadfully wrong.

The room's blue and mustard tones that looked so cheerful in the daylight had taken on a duskiness to match the mood. Even the texture of the air was different. It was laced with scents of fire and peppermint tea, but there was something else as well, like the thickening before a change in the weather.

"Meg? What is it?" Sylvie glanced at the window and wondered if opening it would release whatever was building up and causing her head to ache.

"Did you know?" Meg whispered. "All this time you were so certain Jasper didn't kill his uncle, and now I want to know if this is why." She rested her hand on an open book. No, on a handwritten page atop the book. "Did you?"

Everything Sylvie had stored up to tell Meg about her day took flight from her mind. Unnerved by the accusation in her sister's question, she turned to remove her hat and set it on the bureau. Her mouth dried as she made her way to the desk and picked up the page Meg had been reading.

Ah, so she had found it. Sylvie's stomach churned.

"Answer me. Did you know Hiram had made Father—and us—his beneficiaries?"

With effort, Sylvie left the comfort of her mother's handwriting to face the judgment of her sister. She laid the page on the desk and sat on the edge of the bed, fingers tracing the stitching on the counterpane. "I knew."

Meg did not gasp or scold, but it seemed as though a curtain drew across her face, taking the light and leaving only shadow.

But Sylvie had done nothing wrong. "There are plenty of things you would have known if you had only bothered to look closely enough at Mother."

"What is that supposed to mean?"

Gathering her thoughts, Sylvie bent to unlace her boots. She pulled them off and folded her legs beneath her skirts. "Did you notice, during the war, Mother going into her room and smelling Father's clothes in the bureau, just to remind herself that he was real? Did you notice that cleaning became an obsession with her, until her knuckles were chapped and her aprons threadbare from kneeling on them?"

Meg's eyes shone. "I tried to help. But I could never clean well enough for her. She always came behind me and did it all over again. It got even worse after Father came home."

"It was the only way she could cope with everything, Meg. She couldn't make Father better, but she could wage war on dirt. It was a fight she could win."

"Yes, and she won it over and over every day. She made herself sick with work. Scrubbing, sweeping, and polishing were all she had time for."

"You could have helped more around the house. You could have lightened her burden, as I tried to do. You wearied too easily, choosing instead to paint and dote on the man who made her cry." Sylvie was the only one who seemed to see Ruth—really see her—before her death and after.

Meg closed her eyes for a moment, her mouth a tight stitch before she spoke again. "Right now we're talking about the will." She tapped the journal page once more. "You knew Hiram had changed it to benefit our family, and you didn't tell me."

"You would have known too if you loved her like I did." Ruth and Sylvie understood each other, in life and in ways that defied the grave.

Meg drew back. "What did you say?"

"After she died, I was *still* the only one paying attention to her. I combed through all her books and notebooks, especially the one that contained her prayers. I turned the pages so many times that the glue on the binding failed and they came loose, so I put them in the novel so they wouldn't get lost. I tried to read every word she read, every word she ever penned. Anything to imprint her on my mind. You didn't, and I always wondered why not. Why wouldn't you want to honor her by knowing more fully who she was? I would have welcomed you beside me. Instead, I mourned our mother alone, while you spent all your time fretting over Father."

Meg's nose pinked with emotion. "I did not give myself over to dwelling in the dark the way you did. Have you never considered that my 'fretting over Father' honored her in the way she wanted? She loved him, in spite of everything! Her dying wish was that I take care of him! He was reeling from her death, his despair so complete it was all I could do to tether him to this world when he might have followed her, willingly, into the next. I had no choice but to focus on his care and keeping."

Sylvie nodded, unable to squeeze a response past the lump in her throat. It should have been her in the room with Ruth when she died. But in a fit of restlessness, she had escaped to visit Beth, just for an hour. It was the wrong hour.

She had felt like she'd lost her entire family in the months following Ruth's death, and perhaps that was punishment for her lapse of vigilance.

"You were so busy with Father. Is it any wonder I looked for solace in books and my friends, since I could not find it elsewhere?" Sylvie had intended to sound angry and resentful. But all she heard in her voice was hurt, and that was worse by far.

Meg bowed her head for several long moments. She blinked rapidly, until finally catching a tear on her bandaged hand. "You left me to pick up the pieces of our father alone. I had no friend to turn to except you, but you were turning elsewhere. But if you felt neglected by me, as I did by you, I'm sorry."

The flames behind the grate bobbed lower, allowing a chill to creep into the chamber. Sylvie climbed down from the bed, resisting this new information—that she'd hurt her sister in the same way Sylvie had been hurt by her. The blame she'd cast on Meg circled back and settled into the hollow of her chest.

Careful to keep her skirts out of the way, she stoked the fire and added another log. "Mother's death is not what you wanted to talk about," she said at last, facing her. "I don't want to talk about it anymore either."

"Good," Meg agreed, her voice cool. She looked away, turning back again only when her expression had resettled into firmer lines. "Explain to me why you withheld a crucial piece of information about the will from me."

Sylvie crossed her arms. She shouldn't be surprised that she needed to spell this out for Meg. "You wanted to protect Father by finding the will. I wanted to protect him by leaving it alone."

"Because it's a motive."

"Yes. If he's not convicted on a plea of insanity, he could be for premeditated murder."

Meg lifted her teacup with her left hand, supporting it on the back of her right. "But given his state of mind the night of the fire, it would have been nearly impossible for him to pull off such a crime in the midst of chaos and catastrophe. He feared for his own life. He would not have traveled south through the flames to find Hiram when the only safety was fleeing north." She sipped the tea, then returned the cup to its saucer. "The question now is, what do we do with what Mother wrote about the will?"

Sylvie rubbed her arms as her back began to absorb heat from the fire. "They've already charged him with murder. If we keep this to ourselves—at least for now—he'll still be tried. I don't think an old journal entry would stand up in court. Unless the will itself is found, there's no conclusive evidence."

Meg stood and padded toward the hearth, her feet leaving imprints on the thick rug. She looked pale and fragile, even away from the shadows. "The will. I meant to tell you, today I visited the office of the lawyer who drew it up. He wasn't in, so I made an appointment to speak with him on Monday. But the clerk said he thought Hiram had made two different wills, or amended the first. He has no record, but I'll ask Mr. Grosvenor about it in person." A fine sheen of sweat filmed Meg's face and neck. She looked unwell.

Sylvie felt her sister's brow, then made her sit. The news must have overwrought her nerves. "That would be consistent with what Mother wrote in her prayer journal," she said. "At some point, Hiram changed his will. We just don't know why. Are you sure you want to keep digging, even if it could lead to evidence that Father is truly guilty?"

Meg slumped in the chair. "I don't think I could live with not knowing."

Firelight flickered over the silver tea service. But the thought of drinking anything only made Sylvie's stomach tilt uncomfortably. "Jasper needs to know too. None of us can afford to be in limbo forever."

The next afternoon, Meg still felt ill. But with the revelations of the night before, how could she be well?

She wanted to believe that Sylvie's secret-keeping was well intended, that it didn't signify a breach of trust. But something had shifted in the atmosphere between them. It wasn't hostility that cast a pall, but distance. Here was a new stone to add to the pile of burdens pressing down on her: when she had felt abandoned by her sister in the wake of their mother's death, Sylvie had felt just as neglected by Meg.

As far as it was in her power, Meg would not neglect her now.

Sylvie had said they would need to pay a crew to clear the rubble of their home. They could use the money Mrs. Palmer had paid for the two paintings for that purpose. There would be some left over, but it wouldn't go far. They needed a source of income.

Stomach still unsettled, Meg made her way to the servant's closet and plucked a dusting rag from a pail. Jasper was in class, Helene and Kirstin were out working for other clients, and Sylvie was sewing at the church, making new friends, while Meg was home alone. Again.

She could at least do some light housework. It took no dexterity to push a cloth along a surface. By its smell and feel, the fabric still retained some linseed oil.

Her right hand hung at her side, inert, while she dusted the library. It was all she could do.

This was how it had begun for her mother. As much as Meg hated that nothing was ever clean enough for Ruth, she understood that, at least at first, keeping the house clean when life was messy was her mother's way of loving her family. At the time, however, it hadn't felt loving. From Meg's perspective, her mother had cared more about the paint on the floor than the paint on the canvas, and more about symmetrical stacks of dishes in the cupboard than about the harmony of artistic composition.

She shoved that notion away and wiped down a bookshelf. Her

mother had loved her. Ruth had loved all of them the best way she knew how. It was a mercy she wasn't alive to see her husband locked in the asylum.

Head aching, Meg struggled to knit her thoughts in orderly rows. Her mother, her father, her sister, her hands. The bookstore, the murder, the will. But each line of thinking unraveled, and her mind bounced from one dropped stitch to another. She pushed the rag across the study table in long, smooth motions, then sat when the newspaper lying there caught her eye.

The paper crinkled as she slid it closer. There was a notice calling for portrait artists. The fire had destroyed so many paintings that the wealthy needed to have their likenesses recaptured.

A chord inside Meg thrummed in response to this call. Here was a need. Could she meet it?

Dusting rag forsaken, she picked up a pencil, dropped it a few times, then began sketching right there on the newsprint. Her lines were atrocious, as they had been yesterday. She concentrated harder, her right hand a lead weight in her lap.

A knock sounded at the front door. Expelling a sigh, Meg dropped the pencil and went to answer it. Nate stood on the porch, his hat in his hand.

"Why, Nate!" She'd seen him yesterday when he'd escorted her to Mr. Grosvenor's office. She hadn't expected him to visit again so soon.

He offered a tentative smile as he came in. "Are you well? You look tired."

After he hung his bowler on the hall stand, she brought him into the front parlor and opened one set of velvet draperies. Light poured in, reviving the colors in a stained-glass lampshade and gilding the pedestaled fern.

"Perhaps I am. I haven't felt quite myself since last evening, but I'm sure it will pass."

He sat beside her on the sofa, his fingers twisting through the fringe of a throw pillow. The callus on his third finger sparked a yearning in Meg to be similarly marked by long hours of creating. But other than his hands, he did not look his usual self either.

"How are you?" she asked.

"Fair enough."

Surely he could do better than that. "Perhaps you're more comfortable asking the questions than answering them, but we are friends, aren't we? Or we could be, if you would share with me even a fraction compared to all you know about me and my family."

She smiled to lighten her words, but mercy, she sounded desperate. Perhaps she was, but people were designed for connection and companionship, and it had been so long since she'd felt either.

He removed his glasses and rubbed the bridge of his nose. "Do you have any idea how long it's been since someone other than my stepsister asked me anything about myself?" A chuckle vibrated his chest. Spectacles still in hand, he leaned back and fixed his hooded gaze on the plaster rosettes and ornate moldings of the ceiling. His thoughts seemed to carry him away from her.

"Too long, apparently." Unwilling to rush him, she said nothing more.

What irony, she mused, that a man who bent his life to pumping the wells of information should be of unmined depths himself.

Birdsong was the only sound mingling with their silence. Though she wanted to hear whatever he would say next, it was not awkward to wait for it. There was comfort in being together. There was relief in thinking about someone other than herself and her family.

Nate finally stirred and said, "I seem to be out of practice at this. You asked how I am. I'm a little tired, though I've already had more than my share of coffee today."

Obviously. But it was a start. "Are you working too many hours? If I'm burdening you by asking for your help—"

He touched her wrist above the bandages. The pressure was light as a hummingbird and as fast, but enough to reassure. "You're not a burden to me. But I can see how burdened you are to help your family, and I understand what that's like." He told her about raising his stepsiblings Edith, Harriet, and Andrew, adding new layers to her understanding of who he was. His care for his family was evident.

Meg warmed to this tender side he'd revealed to her. "You loved them very much."

"With everything I had. If it was enough, that's only because God was more than enough and gracious to fill in where I lacked. We can only do so much, Meg. Ultimately, the outcomes are not up to us, but Him." His voice held a conviction and compassion that touched her.

For a moment, she could only return his earnest gaze. "And how do you feel, now that they've all left your nest?" she asked. "Lonely? Free?"

Faint lines fanned from his eyes as he replaced his glasses and straightened his posture. "You can be both, I've learned. But I didn't come here to talk about myself. I have news." His tone shifted. "Is Jasper about? This concerns him too."

She told him he wasn't. "He knows of the appointment with Grosvenor, and he'll go in my stead, since the attorney will likely only speak to family."

"No one is going to that meeting."

"What's wrong?" When he hesitated, Meg's gaze moved to the bust of Robert Burns sitting mutely across the room. *"The best laid plans of mice and men often go awry,"* he'd penned. Something was awry, indeed.

"I've come to tell you in person what the newspapers will be printing tonight for the morning edition. Thomas Grosvenor is dead."

Meg stared at him.

"Last night he was on his way home from a meeting that kept him out past curfew. A young man in the First Company of Chicago volunteers, a student named Theodore Treat, challenged him. When Grosvenor explained he was on his way home and kept walking, Treat shot him. He's dead."

Meg's pulse thudded between her ears. "Dead?" she whispered. She felt dull and childlike.

A muscle flexed in Nate's jaw. "I saw the body and wrote the story myself. Whatever information he might have had for you has gone to the grave along with him. I'm sorry. For Grosvenor and his family, for you, for Jasper, and even for that wild-eyed student from Wisconsin who thought he was doing his duty. I'm sorry for this city, which begged for protection and is harming itself instead."

Another man dead for no good reason. This was worth mourning on its own. It also meant they may never know who Hiram had left his property to.

"What happens now for Jasper?" Perhaps it was vulgar to think of the practical implications when Grosvenor's family was flung into sudden mourning, but Jasper would want to know. So did she. "If the will isn't found, will the property go to public auction?"

"It might," Nate responded. "Likely not anytime soon, but I can't think of a different plausible fate for it. For now, the government is preoccupied surveying and redrawing property lines, not to mention coming up with fireproofing ordinances to prevent such a disaster from happening again. You can be sure Jasper Davenport is the only one thinking about his uncle's property at the moment."

"Not quite." Fresh urgency brought Meg to her feet. "Hiram must have a copy of the will somewhere in this house. And I happen to have lots of time on my hands."

Nate stood and looked down at her, one eyebrow tented. "I thought Jasper said he didn't want you to look. That's why you asked me to go to the attorney's office with you instead."

"Jasper needs more help than he realizes." And so, perhaps, did Meg. "Come on. You have twice as many fingers at your disposal as I do."

Chapter Seventeen

With renewed energy, Meg followed the corridor until it brought her into Hiram's old study.

Nate halted in the doorway behind her. "I'm as curious as you are, but if I get involved in this, my job is on the line. Escorting you to Grosvenor's office was one thing, but actively searching like this—my editor wouldn't like it."

She turned to frown at him. "Since when is investigating outside the bounds of journalism?"

"He thinks I'm biased. He says I'm too close to the story." But his bearing looked willing to take another step. His lean frame made clean lines as he shifted his weight to his front foot. Even the cuffs of his sleeves now fit him, and she wondered if he had wielded needle and thread himself, or if Edith had done it for him.

She wondered what it would be like to paint him, to trace the contours of his cheek and jaw with her brush, and which colors she would mix for that particular blue of his eyes.

She shook the thought free. "And are you? Too close to the story?"

His lips pressed together as he considered his answer. He shook his head. "If you ask me, I'm not close enough."

"Your secret is safe with me." She smiled. "Let's get to work."

While Nate searched in the drawers and trays of the massive desk, Meg took quick measure of the rest of the room. The day shed scant light through the window, but it was enough to gleam on the silver candlesticks on the mantel. A cigar box inlaid with mother-of-pearl sat between them. She lifted its lid and felt inside. Empty.

She spent the next quarter of an hour pulling books from a low shelf and flipping through the pages for anything that might be hidden inside. Other than a few pressed leaves and flowers, she found nothing.

Until she looked inside a Chinese vase and saw an envelope. She reached inside to fish it out, then passed it to Nate. "If you please," she said. Pulling out the contents was too much for just one hand.

He removed a sheet of foolscap rather than a formal legal document.

"Not the will," she presumed.

He turned it toward her. "Take a look."

"Look at what?" Jasper entered the room, cheeks still ruddy from the cold outside. Sylvie could not have stood closer to him if her arm were looped through his. Meg wondered when Jasper had started escorting her home from the church. "You were searching for the will?"

"We've had a setback, Jasper," she replied. "The attorney, Mr. Grosvenor, was shot and killed for curfew violation last night. Your only hope to stay in this house lies in finding the will yourself."

"I see." Jasper removed his hat and tossed it on the desk, the white line of his scar stark on his brow. His gaze darted toward the paper in Nate's hand. "May I?"

Nate gave it to him.

Eyebrows knitting together, Jasper read it aloud. "It says, 'You ruined me. You ruined my name, my future, and my family. You're guilty as sin, Hiram Sloane. You'll pay for what you've done. Someday, when you least expect it, you'll pay your debt, and with interest.' It's signed, 'Otto Schneider.'"

The room was already cold without a fire in the hearth, but the chill Meg felt was something else.

Nate looked from one face to another. "The name is familiar, but I'm missing something here. What happened between Schneider and Sloane?"

Briefly, Meg relayed the story. "Years ago, Schneider sued Hiram, saying he'd been tricked into selling stocks to him, and that Hiram's fortune ought to be his. Legal fees bankrupted him, and his reputation was ruined. He had a wife and baby at the time. The child can't be more than eleven years old now. But he has an alibi for the night of the fire. He was already in prison."

"Schneider. Schneider. I know that name." Nate circled the desk and leaned his elbows on the back of the leather wingback chair, hands clasped. "He's been in and out of trouble with the law for some time now."

"And he seemed a likely suspect until I went to the police and found out he's already in prison," Meg repeated.

Nate straightened. "Now I remember where I've seen the name before. It was on the list of prisoners freed from the jail below the courthouse the night of the fire. They were all in for minor crimes like theft, drunkenness, or vagrancy. There was an Otto Schneider among them. He was in *jail*, not in prison. Whoever you spoke to at the police station was misinformed."

Meg replayed that day in her mind. Mr. Gruber hadn't been working there long, and the papers all over his desk were the picture of chaos. It would have been easy for him to mistake the list or simply use the wrong word. "This changes things," she breathed. "We have a new suspect."

Nate held up a hand. "Let's not rush to pin a murder on him because he wasn't behind bars that night after all. If he had done it—which would have been quite a feat on such a night—wouldn't he try to steal from Hiram too? There was no burglary in the house that night or any time after. Revenge is one thing, but this revenge was all about money."

"Maybe he didn't care about the money anymore," Sylvie guessed. "Maybe he saw an opportunity to kill Hiram and took it in a fit of passion."

Jasper framed himself in the window, staring out. Sunlight

dappled the wrought-iron fences and the soldiers patrolling the neighborhood. "No one stops caring about money, unless he has so much of it he can afford to think about other things. But a man like Schneider, if he really blames his financial ruin on my uncle, he wouldn't have stopped with murder. He'd have tried to get a piece of his riches too." Then, snapping his fingers, he spun around. "Schneider couldn't have robbed this house even if he tried. The night of the fire, Uncle Hiram wandered out of the safety of this neighborhood. When Schneider killed him—"

"Allegedly killed him." Nate nodded for him to continue.

"Allegedly, then. Schneider would have fled the scene of the crime, and the fire would have prevented him from coming here. He'd have had to preserve his own life and plan to come back later, assuming the house was empty except for the servants. But Prairie Avenue has been under armed guard around the clock ever since. He wouldn't have been able to get past the soldiers."

Meg caught Sylvie's gaze, gauging her reaction. She looked as weak as Meg felt.

Sylvie turned to Jasper and tilted her head. "But if he came straight from the jail, he wouldn't have had a weapon on him."

"True." Jasper crossed his arms. "But it wouldn't have been hard to find one, given the chaos and the thousands of people in the street."

Meg's heartbeat tapped against her chest. Stephen had dropped his gun, and someone else had found it. It would be too much of a coincidence to believe that someone was Otto Schneider. But the criminal could have found or taken anyone else's.

A few beats of silence passed, marked only by the muffled ticking of the timepiece in Nate's vest. "The police are already looking for the prisoners they set free," he said. "If they apprehend him, he can be questioned. I warn you against false hope, however. It may not turn up anything useful."

"Then again, it might," Meg whispered, and to her amazement, her sister nodded and smiled.

"If there's anything I can do to help, rest assured I will." Jasper touched Sylvie's shoulder, bringing an instant bloom to her cheeks.

Chapter Eighteen

Tuesday, October 24, 1871

Dust clouded Nate's steps as he sloughed through a southwest section of the burned district. He'd made a habit of touring it every day to mark its progress and keep tabs on any stories brewing there. Usually the hive of activity energized him. Today, however, he felt sluggish. Dull. In an hour he'd need to be sharp for the city aldermen's meeting, where they would be discussing the controversial ordinance to make downtown Chicago fireproof. But right now, all he wanted was to sit.

A loaded wagon crossed the road in front of him, the horses pulling it glistening with sweat. Wheelbarrows passed, and more wagons. Hoofbeats, scraping shovels, and voices amplified in Nate's ears, adding to the growing ache in his head. There must be something going around. When he'd called on Meg yesterday, Helene had turned him away, saying Meg and Sylvie were feeling poorly and didn't want him to catch anything. If he wasn't feeling better by the weekend, he'd skip visiting Edith and her family this Sunday rather than risk getting them sick.

Trudging to the western edge of the district, he made his way to a wooden chair set up as a shoeshine stand at the foot of the Randolph Street Bridge. He lowered himself into it, propping one shoe on the crate in front of him. The southern branch of the

Chicago River flowed under the bridge, the sound of its movement echoing off the steel girders.

"Afternoon." Martin Sullivan tugged his cap down, then set to work wiping the dust from Nate's shoes. Grey hair puffed over the tops of his large ears, the lobes sagging against his silver-stubbled jaw. "The weather's changing, it is. A chill in the air says winter's hard on our heels. Don't you think?" A trace of Irish accent lilted among his words.

Nate agreed but didn't say much else. He didn't need to, since Martin supplied a streaming monologue along with the polish. Nate didn't mind. His thoughts veered back to Meg.

He'd told her she wasn't a burden to him. More surprising, he'd meant it.

After all his resolutions not to get involved, not to care, not to tie himself to anything that might keep him from work, what was he doing? Endangering his job by doing the opposite.

Meg wasn't a burden, or at least not one he resented. That was the thing about people, wasn't it? If you were close enough to someone, if you were truly walking beside her, her yoke would fit over your shoulders too. Together, the weight would be borne, the load lightened.

This was different from the way it had been and how he'd felt with his stepsiblings.

Nate had had opportunities to back away from Meg. When she'd asked about long hours at work, he could have told her he didn't have time for her. He could have refused to help her search for the will. That would have been the more logical choice. But he found he didn't want to be released from whatever it was that tied them together. Friendship? Was that what they were calling it now?

Nate coughed into his handkerchief and turned his attention back to Martin, whose brown-spotted hands were thick and meaty yet, better suited to carriage-making than shoe-shining. Still, he rounded his back over his work to do an honest job.

"'Twill be a cold winter for many a folk this year," he was saying. "The barracks give us a roof, that's sure, but how warm we'll be in that flimsy, rushed construction, I can't say. We may have to huddle together like pups, which wouldn't be hard, given the number of us crammed together."

A raw wind from the northwest scraped Nate's face. He hunched his shoulders toward his ears. "Do you know your neighbors? Are they folks you knew before the fire?"

Martin rubbed behind Nate's heel. "Some yes, some no. But no matter. We'll all know each other well enough before long, won't we? You wouldn't believe how fast the gossip flies." His face pinching, he rocked off one hip, as though to relieve some discomfort.

Nate waited for Martin's grimace to fade. "Do you happen to know the Schneider family? Otto is the husband and father. I believe they have at least one child, about eleven years old." Nate didn't know where the Schneiders lived before the fire, since the city directories had been burned. But with the fire so widespread, and the Schneiders being poor after the bankruptcy, it wasn't such a leap to imagine they were one of the families who'd been burned out and who wouldn't qualify for their own shanty house.

Martin switched to the other shoe. "I know of the family, sure. Otto is no prize, I can tell you that, but for some reason his wife has stuck with him. They've got three kids now, if we're speaking of the same Otto Schneider. The oldest boy is eleven, then there's a set of twin girls. Six years old, maybe?" He shrugged. "Haven't seen Otto about the barracks, actually. But Martha and the kids, sure. They're struggling to get by, I can tell you that. They didn't have much before the fire. Now they have even less."

Three kids. Otto Schneider, who Meg hoped to prove a murderer, had a faithful wife and three kids.

On the opposite side of the river, a train chugged by, belching grey smoke into the fading sky. Nate watched Martin Sullivan finish shining his shoes, and he regretted all over again the story he had written a dozen years ago that ruined Martin's reputation and put him out of business. If he had slowed down, pursued all the leads, and questioned more people before drawing conclusions, Martin's life wouldn't have come off the rails.

Otto Schneider's reputation was already a wreck, it seemed, and that of his own doing. But the charge of murder was another thing altogether. Nate knew Meg and Sylvie were hanging their hopes on Schneider's guilt for the sake of their father. But as much as Nate wanted Stephen Townsend exonerated, he wouldn't be able to live with himself if he allowed another innocent man to take the blame for the crime instead.

All of this was assuming Schneider could even be found. Nate scanned the burned district to the east, noting how much emptier it was since martial law had ended yesterday, an action rooted in Thomas Grosvenor's untimely death. If Otto Schneider was still at large, still in Chicago, and if he did want to rob Hiram's house, he would know it was no longer protected.

That was a lot of *ifs*.

It was too late for Martin Sullivan. But perhaps this was a second chance for Nate to do things right. A chance to pursue the full truth instead of settling for halves.

Heaviness settled into his gut. His editor had told him not to get involved. He was not the police, he was not a detective. He was only a reporter—not even a famous one, at that—who wanted to see justice served.

Was that enough?

The polish complete, Martin snapped his blackened rag. "How do they look?"

Nate peered at his shining old shoes. "Perfect, as usual, Martin. Thank you."

He paid the fee along with a tip. It wasn't as much as he wanted to give, but it was all he had today. And Nate was the kind of man who gave all he had.

* * *

With a clang that woke Stephen from a nightmare, the metal slot at the bottom of the door opened, and a plate of food was shoved inside the cell, followed by a shallow dish of water. The slot closed and locked with a resounding click that reverberated through Stephen.

"Hey!" he shouted and lunged to bang on the door, a strait-jacket pinning his arms. "Hey!" he shouted again, ramming his shoulder into the iron slab. "What day is it? You have to let me out of here!" Desperate to be heard, he slammed his body against the walls of the cell until he felt bruised.

No wonder they locked you up in here. That voice again. It was his conscience, his tormentor, his sole companion while in solitary confinement. *You're volatile. You won't allow anyone near you without fighting, ever since the ice bath. They think you'll hurt others, not to mention yourself. Can you blame them?*

Stephen dropped to his knees, eating and drinking out of the dishes like a dog. Gruel smeared his cheek and chin, and water sloshed up his nose. He couldn't wipe his face. He felt food congealing on his skin, and he could not clean himself.

Tears of humiliation clotted his throat until he released them with a guttural howl of anger and despair. They had done this to him. They had taken a man and made him an animal.

You are not an animal. You are made in the image of God.

He lowered his head to his knees and wept. "*This* is not a reflection of Almighty God. I am closer to beast than man."

You are made in the image of God.

"The image of God," he repeated to himself. "I am made in the image of God. Oh my God, my God, how did I come to this?" Sitting on his heels, he rocked back and forth and called on the only One who could save him from himself.

Wearying, he leaned back against the cold tiles and stretched out his legs. Water that had spilled from the bowl soaked through his pants and chilled his skin. He coughed until his ribs ached, then shouted with frustration. His constitution had been completely broken at Andersonville, his lungs forever weakened. What further damage would he sustain in this place?

Be still. Just be still.

Squeezing his eyes shut, he moaned. He still didn't know if he had killed his friend, but it frightened him to think he might have. Whoever he was now, it wasn't who he wanted to be. A small part of him recognized that was worth grieving, as one would grieve a good friend who died. But if he mourned anyone right now, it was Hiram.

Like Stephen, the older man wasn't who he'd been a decade ago. Yet he'd always treated Stephen as though he were still the best version of himself. Hiram didn't deserve what had happened to him. He ought to have passed in his sleep, warm in his bed, when his time came, and even then Stephen would have lamented the loss of his loyal friend.

But the loss of himself? He would shed no tears for that. Stephen was still here, at least in part. So many good men weren't.

He opened his eyes. At last, he wasn't alone. There was Peter, who had died at Andersonville. Stephen had buried him, but here he was, a hallucination conjured up by his fevered mind. Normally Stephen would pinch his skin and watch the false image fade away.

"But given the circumstances"—he chuckled—"I don't mind keeping you around."

Peter was in his uniform, sitting on an overturned hardtack crate, warming his hands at the fire. "Hullo, Steve!" Light flashed on his polished brass buttons.

"Hello, old friend." Tears coursed through the stubble on Stephen's cheeks. He was talking to a figment of his imagination. Worse, he was enjoying it. "It sure is nice to see you again."

"You don't look too good, you know that?" Peter said.

"Well, that makes sense. I'm doing poorly, Pete."

Peter took off his foraging cap and buffed the emblems on the bill before resettling it on his head. "Spread that on the table for me. You made it out. You survived the war, that hell of prison camp, and returned to your family. You're lucky."

Stephen shook his head. "I'm not so sure. You—or the man you represent—are in heaven. You're in paradise. I'm trapped all over again." Even if he were free of the asylum, he'd be trapped within himself. "I'd be better off in your locale, and my family would be better off without me too."

Someone else might call the conversation ridiculous. On a different day, Stephen would agree. But right now, this was all he had, and he needed it. This wasn't a living picture of the men Stephen had killed in battle, or the comrades he'd had to dump into a pit outside Andersonville's stockade. This vision was not the mark of sainthood, nor was it a ghost who had come to haunt him. It was evidence of the sickness of his mind, and he accepted that.

The hallucinated version of Peter frowned. "Careful, now. Are you saying that after everything you've been through, you're ready to call it quits? You would take your own life? What about your family? What would the girls say?"

"Suicide is a dreadful sin, Pete. I have no plans at present for it. And as for my family, my wife has gone ahead to glory."

"I see. But your daughters. Are they not worth living for?"

Stephen's current state of existence could hardly be called *living*.

Peter tossed another log onto the imaginary fire, and Stephen's memory filled in the smell of smoke. "If I had my druthers," Peter said, "I'd watch my children grow up. I'd protect them until they were no longer mine to shepherd, and I would—"

"That's enough, Pete, thank you." Stephen had already missed his daughters' growing-up years. He'd failed to protect them and their interests, and didn't need to be reminded. "As I said, Meg and Sylvie are better off without me."

Peter mopped his perspiring brow. "Well, I don't know about that. It would seem a crying shame if you squandered the life you get to live, though, when so many of us boys are lyin' in an unmarked grave in Dixieland. Don't disappoint us by giving up."

"You don't understand what it's like here."

"Don't I?" The hallucination laughed. After all, this Peter was born from Stephen's mind.

"What I mean is, there's not much I can do while locked in an asylum, is there? I'm drugged by injection, force-fed pills I don't want, dunked into baths full of ice, bound up and shut away by myself. They've taken my clothes, my name, my dignity. I'm at their mercy, and they don't have much. What on earth can I possibly do here?"

Peter stood, brushing ash and bits of dried leaves from his trousers. "You can try."

"Try what?" Stephen asked almost frantically, for the hallucination was fading. He could see the other side of the cell through Peter's body.

"Try to get better."

Chapter Nineteen

The bedchamber had become a cave devoid of light, which was just as well, since any shard of sun sent darts of pain through Meg's head. Her sister was beside her in the bed, her feet like blocks of ice whenever they touched Meg beneath the sheets. And yet their pillowcases were sour with fever sweat. Greasy strands of hair stuck to her face. The hiss of the fire menaced beneath an incessant squeaking she realized only later was the mattress beneath her as she turned.

Whatever ailment had attacked had done so viciously and in equal measure between her and Sylvie. Half delirious, Meg sensed another presence in the room. The draperies around the bed must have parted, allowing a draft of cool air. The smell of lilac talc accompanied a soft murmuring and a damp cloth across her brow. In her mind's eye, she saw Helene bustling from one side of the bed to the other, caring for two patients.

Someone else was there too. A man's voice droned somewhere above Meg's head. Then it stopped, and a circle of cold pressure sank against her chest. She wanted to brush it away or roll to her side, but someone held her still until the spot was gone. Uninterested in what the stranger was saying, she groaned beneath unbearable heat.

Time ceased. Meg had no idea what day it was, for night and day stitched into one continuous thread that unspooled at an unknown and irregular pace. When she was not wracked by cramping or retching, she fell into a fitful slumber.

Dreams slipped over and around her like water until she felt she might drown in false images. A strange man's face appeared in the window, and though she'd never seen him before, she knew he was Otto Schneider bent on revenge. Encircling her bed, her mother, her father, and Sylvie stood together and recited in unison, *You didn't take care of me*. Then fire blazed up like a wall between her and them, leaping onto her hands and chewing through her flesh. She awoke gasping for breath and itching like mad beneath scar tissue tough as leather.

When at last she could tolerate sunshine and sitting upright, Helene assisted her into the bathtub and washed her hair before helping her into a fresh shirtwaist and merino wool skirt. Sylvie had recovered ahead of her, for she was sitting on the settee when Meg emerged.

She wasn't alone.

"Dr. Gilbert." Meg took a seat beside Sylvie.

The doctor smiled warmly, his mustache bending. He gripped the two ends of the stethoscope that draped around his neck. "Miss Dressler came to the clinic and requested I make a house call. Tell me, how are you feeling today?" His fingers felt flat and dry as he probed at the glands in her neck.

"Fatigued," she admitted. "My stomach has settled and my head doesn't ache as it did, but I have little appetite. Perhaps a cup of tea?"

"Perhaps not," Sylvie said, then nodded for Dr. Gilbert to explain. Helene stood off to the side, her face thatched with concern.

Tugging up his trousers, the doctor lowered himself to the armchair across from them. "Normally, a weak tea is just the thing for a convalescent. But in this case, the tea is the problem. That is, the water used to make the tea is the issue. It's been making people sick all over the city for more than a week."

"How are Kirstin, Eli, and Jasper?" Sylvie's weakened voice had a distant quality. Her dark hair smelled like rosewater but lacked its usual luster.

Helene pinched a loose thread from her apron. "Kirstin and Eli have already come through it, but Mr. Davenport fell ill three days ago and suffers still."

Dr. Gilbert laced his fingers. "You know that our water supply was cut off during the fire. The water pumps are working again now, but no one considered the effect of the dirt deposits in the pipes from the several days before water flowed through them again. That is, until now. Thousands are laid low, children most especially."

Helene clucked her tongue and shook her head. "How long do we need to boil the water to render it safe? Or do we need to bring it in from the lake until the water pipes have been properly flushed?"

The doctor twisted the end of his mustache. "Boil the water you get from your own tap for a good quarter hour before using it, and you should see marked improvement. In another week, the water will be safe to drink without that. Next order of business, young lady." He looked at Meg's hands.

Relief and dread filtered through her. "I thought we were going to wait until at least two weeks had passed."

"And so we have. You were ill for several days, Miss Townsend. It's time, at least for your left hand. The right will need a while yet."

Gently, he unwound the linen until her hand was free. Helene supplied a basin of water in which to bathe it, then toweled it dry.

Meg barely felt it.

The hand looked only slightly different from the last time she'd been awake for a dressing change. The color was more pink than red or brown, but scar tissue webbed over her palm. She wiggled her fingers, noting the restricted movement.

"Try making a fist," Dr. Gilbert said.

Meg did so.

"Good. Now try placing your palm against mine and pressing toward a flattened position. That's it. Press until you can feel the stretch. Then press a little more."

Sweat beaded Meg's upper lip. Her hand would not obey her orders, at least in this direction. "I'm pushing," she said when it wasn't obvious.

"I'm sure you are. You must keep at it, my dear, to recover your range of motion. That scar tissue is constricting, curling your hand inward. Your brain will find ways to work around the limitations, but you must use your hand, stretching multiple times a day. Like this."

Meg watched his demonstrations and mimicked them the best she could. The failed attempts mocked her.

"You can do this, Meg." No trace of pity tainted Sylvie's tone. "I have every confidence in you."

"Perhaps you would like to help?" Dr. Gilbert showed Sylvie how to help stretch Meg's fingers away from her palm, together and then one by one.

Meg flinched at the first touch of Sylvie's beautiful, perfect skin against her gnarled flesh. "Will the sense of pressure return?" she asked the doctor.

"You'll learn how to compensate for that and how to work with the sense that is left to you in that hand."

That was a no. This aspect would never get better. Her hand wouldn't straighten and could barely feel. When Sylvie stopped stretching, Meg's fingers returned to a claw shape in her lap. Her throat burned with unshed tears.

Dr. Gilbert begged leave to check on Jasper, and Helene accompanied him from the room.

The door clicked behind them. Closing her eyes, Meg sank against the back of the settee. She was already repulsed by the sight and feel of her own flesh, and exposing the right hand would be even worse.

"This is progress," Sylvie told her. "You must be content with that, at least for now."

Progress was scant consolation when what Meg wanted from herself was perfection.

Chapter Twenty

Friday, October 27, 1871

"Nate." Meg's eyes stung at the sight of him. His face was pale from his own recent waterborne sickness, but his eyes were bright as he stood on the front porch, arms full of angular objects draped in linen.

As she realized what he'd brought, her bare left hand went to the gathering tightness in her chest.

He smiled. "I figured you'd be ready for this. May I come in?"

"Of course." She led him into the reception room, bracing herself.

As she'd suspected, when he withdrew the linen, several blank canvases stared back at her.

He propped them up in a chair. "This size looked like what I remembered you using in your bookstore. Will these work?"

"Yes, of course, thank you. What a kind gesture." It was a thoughtful, extravagant gift, and equally intimidating. Since Dr. Gilbert had come on Wednesday, she'd spent hours trying to write and sketch. While the effect was better than when she'd first started, it was far from pleasing.

"So you have all you need now, don't you? To begin painting again?" He seemed so confident, so optimistic.

"A hand that obeys my direction is also helpful. Mine stumbles like a child's."

"And like a child, it will learn. You taught your right hand before. Now it's the left's turn." Gently, he took it in both of his.

The top of her hand registered the touch. Her palm did to a lesser degree, giving her a surreal sense of disconnection. But what she did feel spread a balm over her nerves. Like it or not, she lived in a society that judged a woman by three things: the clarity of her complexion, the smallness of her waist, and the beauty of her graceful hands. Meg was freckled. Her waist betrayed a penchant for sweets. And now her hands . . .

But Nate didn't recoil when he touched her.

"Besides," he continued, "didn't Michelangelo say that a man paints with his mind, not with his hands?"

"Easy for the most talented artistic genius of all time to say." But Meg couldn't help smiling in acknowledgment. Nate was trying, and she was more grateful than she could trust herself to express. "I'll paint again soon," she told him. "If I can manage anything acceptable, I'll take the portraits to Mr. VanDyke, the gallery owner and art agent who posted that notice in the newspaper. He's matching artists with wealthy patrons wishing to have their portraits remade after the fire."

Nate released her hand. "I was hoping you might."

But not yet. "Today I have other plans."

With a quiet tap on the doorframe, Sylvie stepped into the reception room, smiling when she saw Nate. "I thought I heard voices. It's good to see you, Nate. How are you feeling these days?" Glossy brown curls cascaded down her back from where her hair was gathered at the crown of her head. She'd been taking more care with her appearance since Jasper had recovered from the illness.

"Much better," Nate told her.

"Glad to hear it. Meg, what's this about you having plans for the day?"

Meg hadn't thought it would matter to her sister at all. "I'm going to visit the Soldiers' Home." She'd already hired Eli to convey her. "There may be some veterans there who knew Hiram. Maybe they know something that could help us."

The spark left Sylvie's eyes. "Help us do what?"

"Well, I won't know that until I learn what they know."

A sigh fraught with impatience blew from Sylvie's nose. "I don't know what you hope to accomplish. The police—"

"Aren't doing anything," Meg finished for her. "Maybe they're looking for Otto Schneider, but even if they catch him, they won't charge him with Hiram's murder with only that threatening note to go on."

"Nor should they," Nate added. "Visiting the Soldiers' Home is a good move. The more perspectives we gain, the better. As I said before, we don't know Schneider did it. We should talk to as many people who knew Hiram as possible."

"And the neighbors haven't been helpful." Meg had covered another block of them since recovering from her illness. It was time to pursue fresh sources.

"I see." Sylvie folded her porcelain hands in front of her green silk skirt. "I won't be going with you. And you cannot go on your own."

"She won't be." Nate straightened his hat. "I know several of the men there, since I wrote that series of articles on Chicago's veterans. I'm happy to make introductions."

"Of course you are." Sylvie's tone bordered on impolite. "Meanwhile, I'll stay home and do what I can to salvage the bookstore."

Meg blinked. "What are you doing?" She'd assumed that at this stage, without a building, very little could be done.

"I'm strengthening customer relations. While you've been chasing your investigation, I've been scouring the papers, making note of changes of address for our customers. Now I'm writing each of them a personal card, assuring them we will reopen when we can, that we appreciate their continued patronage, and that we'd love their input on which volumes they'd like to see in stock. I want to make them feel like they're part of it. Anything to prevent business from completely drying up before we have a physical presence again."

"That's brilliant." Nate rested one arm on the back of the wing chair and crossed his ankles.

"It is," Meg agreed. "I'd help you with all that writing—you know I would—if my script were legible. I appreciate what you're doing for us."

"I'm not the only one working toward reconstruction. Jasper and his crew of classmates will finish clearing the rubble from our lot today and will be coming here for some refreshment as a token of our gratitude. They did the work at such a reasonable rate that I fear they meant to spare us the true cost. I had hoped you'd be here too. I know you can't help me in the kitchen much, but you could at least convey your thanks to the men in person."

"I'll be sure to thank Jasper as soon as I see him next. Won't you tell the other men thanks on my behalf?"

Sylvie narrowed her eyes with a look that said she'd been doing quite a lot on Meg's behalf lately. "Did I tell you they found a small jewelry box under a pile of bricks yesterday? It's broken, but Flora Spencer's name is painted on the top. The jewelry is still inside it."

"I don't even know where the Spencers have gone." Meg hadn't seen their former tenants since the night of the fire.

"You could place a notice in the *Tribune* for her," Nate offered. "If they're still in the city, they can retrieve it. I'll make sure it gets printed, if you like."

Sylvie nodded, but her expression was stony, her throat taut.

"You have to believe that what I'm doing—talking to neighbors, visiting the Soldiers' Home—all of that is for us too," Meg tried. "Based on how Hiram's neighbors have treated me, how do you think our bookshop will fare if we never clear Father's name?"

Her sister's gaze traveled to the canvases Nate had brought. "You could paint again. Whatever sales you make would help us too. Tangibly and immediately. We need to be earning and saving for reconstruction costs."

In a hidden fold of her skirt, Meg grazed her thumb over the webbing at the base of her fingers. "I'll do what I can."

"But not now." Sylvie set her jaw, bade Nate good-bye, and marched from the room.

Heat prickled Meg's neck, from guilt or frustration or both. She looked at Nate for his reaction. "Am I being irresponsible?"

He shook his head. "If you don't keep digging, who will?"

Exactly.

This was the thought that comforted her during the thirteen-mile ride to the Soldiers' Home in South Evanston, on the shore of Lake Michigan. Well, that and Nate beside her.

Meg peered through the carriage windows at the limitless blue of the lake beyond. Seagulls squawked as they swooped over the pebbly beach. In the distance, the horizon melted water and sky together.

When she'd gone to the lakeshore as a child for a family picnic, she'd waded into the shocking cold while Sylvie and their mother stayed far enough away to keep dry. *"I can't see the end of it, Papa,"* she'd said while standing on the tips of her toes, water pulling at the hem of her dress. *"Pick me up, I want to see the end."*

He'd swung her up so she nestled into the crook of his arm, and her wet feet dripped onto his clothes.

Shading her eyes, she'd cried, *"The water goes on forever!"* She'd felt as though she stood at the edge of the world.

"Not so, little one! Just because we can't see the opposite shore doesn't mean it isn't there."

In a new way, Meg was still searching for the opposite shore, longing to reach the end of the unknown deep spreading before her. *Pick me up, Lord*, she prayed silently. *Let me see the end*. Then, thinking better of it, she added, *See me to the end*, instead.

"Meg? We're here." Nate looked at his pocket watch. "The men will be eating now."

Childhood memory faded as soon as she thanked Eli for the ride and entered the two-story brick building with Nate. A matron in a white uniform greeted them in the parlor before sending them to the dining hall in the basement below. Wide, short windows near the ceiling allowed a little daylight into the space.

Six long tables formed three rows, with benches of men sitting on either side. The air smelled of their lunch: pork chops, gravy, buttered squash, green beans, fresh bread, and coffee. Four women bustled among what looked to be four dozen veterans, rationing sugar into their coffee, pats of butter onto bread.

"Asa Jones!" Nate hailed a man whose ash-blond hair receded from his brow. He might have had the trim figure of a hardened soldier once, but he'd softened and grown thick about his middle. A crutch leaning against the wall drew Meg's attention to his legs. One of them was gone below the knee. An arm was cut short at the elbow.

With his cheek full of bread, Mr. Jones beckoned them over.

After the basic introductions, Nate added, "This is Stephen Townsend's daughter. Did you know him?"

Meg and Nate sat across from Mr. Jones, and she braced herself for another negative reaction.

But the veteran's face relaxed in understanding. "For the six weeks we both trained at Camp Douglas, yes. Then his regiment went a different way than mine. Seems to me he was a gentle soul with more smarts than most. He drew a raw deal, young lady. That ain't nothing to be ashamed of. That's just life dealing its cards. It's a gamble, you know. All a gamble."

It certainly felt that way at times. And yet what a hopeless philosophy, to think there was not a higher purpose, even if it defied human understanding. Meg had to believe God remained in control even when His children were not. No, especially then.

But all she said was, "It sounds like you've read about my father in the *Tribune*."

"Starting with the piece Nate here wrote. He wrote about me too." He wiped his napkin across his face. "But I'm sure you haven't come to get my autograph."

Meg rested her forearms on the smooth oak table, preparing her questions. Mr. Jones glanced at her scarred and bandaged hands, then held her gaze with his. He'd seen worse. Survived worse.

"What can I do for you two?" he asked. "Have you got more questions, Nate?"

"I believe Miss Townsend does." Nate nodded for her to continue.

"You knew my father," she began. "Did you also happen to know Hiram Sloane? He was a guard at Camp Douglas, part of the Invalid Corps."

Mr. Jones shook his head. "The prison camp was a separate section from where we trained. I had no call to be there, but I did take a gander at the Johnny Rebs a few times from the Union Observatory. It was a tower fifty feet high near the main gate on Cottage Grove. For five cents, anyone could climb it and see what was going on in the prison yard. Folks thought it great sport."

Meg bristled. Ruth had never allowed her or Sylvie to go near the camp, concerned about contagious disease spreading from soldiers of either side. So she hadn't known the prisoners in Chicago had been gawked at by the public, as Stephen had been in Andersonville.

"What did you see?" Nate prompted. Ever the reporter, he took out a pencil and pad of foolscap, ready to take notes.

"Oh." Mr. Jones grabbed a saltshaker and rolled it back and forth in his hand. "Those Southern boys were made to stand in snow and ice, facing an icy mist coming off the lake, for hours at a time with nary a bite to eat. But if they moved, they'd be shot by one of the guards."

"Not Hiram, though," Meg said. "I can't imagine him being so cruel."

"Like I said, I didn't know one guard from the other except by sight. There were other forms of punishment too, things so devious we'd cry foul if such things were done to Yankees down south. There were four guards most notorious for things like that. Big, burly fellows."

"That doesn't sound like Hiram Sloane," Nate said.

"Not at all." Meg inhaled deeply, ready to move on. "Mr. Jones, you didn't know which guard was Hiram Sloane, so you couldn't have known if he had particular enemies. Correct?"

Amusement played at the corner of his mouth. "Well, miss, he was a prison guard in time of war. Thousands of Johnnys were his enemies."

"Not his personal enemies," she insisted.

"Maybe from where he was standing. But if you'd asked those prisoners, they'd say it was plenty personal."

An older veteran shuffled up to the table with a half-filled cup of coffee. "Mind if I join you?" His joints creaked as he folded himself to fit on the bench beside Asa Jones.

Nate reached across the table to shake his hand, then introduced the man to Meg as Elton Burke. "He was a guard at Camp Douglas too. Perhaps you'd be willing to answer a few questions in a moment, Elton?"

He agreed.

Though eager to question Mr. Burke, Meg circled back to the fact that Mr. Jones had known her father. In a way, Stephen was a victim of Hiram's murder too, for his life had been taken hostage by the false charge.

"Mr. Jones, do you know if my father had any enemies?"

Mr. Jones set the saltshaker aside. "Stephen Townsend? No. I can't think of a single man who wasn't cheered by him being around. He ministered to me more than the chaplain did. You tell him that sometime. See if he remembers Asa Jones."

Meg smiled. "I will, thank you. I have just one more question for you. From what you knew of him, would my father ever shoot an unarmed man in the back?"

"What? Is that what they're saying your pa did? No, that's cowardice six ways from Sunday." Mr. Jones shook his head. "Don't you believe it."

"I don't. Thank you so much for your time, Mr. Jones."

"My turn?" Mr. Burke's voice had a distinctive gravelly tone. He set down his coffee with too much force—or too little control—and it sloshed over the rim.

Meg wiped up the spill with a napkin. "Thank you, Mr. Burke. You knew Hiram Sloane?"

He scratched his whiskered cheek. "I did. Not a bad fellow. I never knew him to shoot a prisoner for sport, nothing like that. And as for the more creative punishments that were common to all prison camps North and South, I never saw him direct those either."

Of course Hiram wouldn't have done those things. "Do you know of anyone who might have wished him harm? Other than all the prisoners who wanted to escape, that is." After pausing to allow him to think, she added, "Did he ever mention Otto Schneider?"

Nate nudged her with his elbow. "You're leading the witness," he teased.

"Otto Schneider?" Recognition lit Mr. Burke's watery eyes. "His legal sparring with Hiram was in all the papers. But nothing got Hiram so hot under the collar as the news that came out of Andersonville. He had a friend there, if I've got it right."

"My father," Meg said. "Stephen Townsend."

Mr. Burke looked at her as if seeing her for the first time. "Well, they must have been close. When word reached us about the starving Yankees in Georgia, Hiram zealously enforced the new policy to cut rations for our prisoners up here. Not that our prisoners were getting three squares a day. But if our men were suffering in Andersonville, the Rebs would suffer here too. That was the mindset."

"Retaliation," Nate confirmed.

"Exactly." Mr. Burke slurped from his mug.

Meg shifted on the bench and rearranged her skirt over her knees. "I never knew Hiram to be vengeful."

"You never knew him like I did, then. He did his duty and then some on account of the plight of his friend held down South. For instance, prisoners were searched upon entering Camp Douglas. Personal items were taken and recorded in a log, to be returned to the prisoner upon his release. But Hiram didn't stop there. He searched their persons at random in the square. He even searched their barracks, taking them by surprise. Rumor has it that what he found, he didn't always turn over to his superiors for safekeeping."

Meg couldn't believe that. "What are you insinuating, Mr. Burke?"

He smiled, his brow clear of concern. "I'm *saying* that Hiram Sloane didn't always play by the rules. The way he figured, our boys in Andersonville suffered far worse degradations. Just because he lacked the stomach for inflicting physical pain didn't mean he was averse to other methods, like taking personal effects and contraband items. Called it payback. Only the fellow he was paying might have been himself." He shrugged. "That's the rumor, anyway."

Nate put down his pencil. "We're more interested in facts, Elton. Did you ever see this take place? Did Hiram ever admit to you directly that he'd stolen from the prisoners?"

"We weren't that close."

Meg had heard enough. Swallowing her indignation, she thanked Mr. Burke for his time and rose to leave.

Chapter Twenty-One

October 31, 1871

Dear Father,

Meg wants to write you herself, but only her left hand is free of the bandages yet. She practices writing and drawing obsessively, losing all track of time, and I have to remind her to eat. She's made some studies with her paints to get used to the brushes again, but she seems embarrassed by the results even though I see progress. She dictates again:

We think of you often and wish we could see you in person. Did you get our last letter?

Nate and I visited the Soldiers' Home the other day. Asa Jones says to tell you hello. Do you remember him?

Jasper Davenport and some classmates cleared the rubble on our property so that when it's time to rebuild, we'll be ready. So much rubble from the fire has been dumped in the lake between the Illinois Central tracks and the shore that the man-made basin has virtually disappeared.

Many are rebuilding already, but the weather complicates construction, so we'll wait until spring. By then, I expect you'll be out of the asylum and can help oversee the building yourself, if you'd care to.

One of the stray cats you used to feed keeps coming back

to the corner where our shop was. He looks so pitiful with his whiskers singed off and bald patches where sparks burned away his fur. The day he followed Jasper all the way back to Hiram's house, he let him stay. Sylvie and I named him Oliver Twist. You'd love him, Father. We're taking good care of him.

If you're allowed to write to us, please do. We love you very much and pray for you every day.

Your Daughters

P.S. In case our father's mail is being read by asylum staff: if you refuse to give this to him, at least tell him we fare well and love him.

Friday, November 3, 1871

Stephen took the medicine because it was preferable to solitary confinement. But he hated what it did to him.

He'd supposed himself emotionally detached before, but that was nothing compared to this all-over numbing, inside and out. The medicine—some cocktail he couldn't identify—was meant to slow his heart and keep him from shaking. That it did. But it slowed his mind too and cast a veil of apathy over what was actually in front of him.

He sat on the floor in the corner of the day room, where patients passed the daylight hours when not in the dining room or in their cells. He had little interest in jockeying for one of the few chairs provided. There were never enough. It didn't matter anyway. Nothing mattered anymore. Head on his knees, he felt it altogether too much trouble to look around and connect with other men.

Vaguely, he registered the sound of buckles hitting wood. Without looking, he knew it was two patients in straitjackets, rocking back and forth at a table painted to look like a chessboard, though Stephen had never seen any playing pieces. They moaned and spoke unintelligibly. It didn't bother Stephen. He felt like moaning too.

A spot on his leg grew damp and cold. It took him a few minutes to realize he'd been drooling again. He drew the back of his hand across his mouth and then wiped it on his trousers. That made another wet spot. Next time he wouldn't bother.

"W-w-hat do you have th-there?"

The voice sounded Irish. It was loud. Stephen turned to find another patient sitting cross-legged beside him. His head was shorn like everyone else's, but the stubble growing in was like pepper, as were the whiskers shadowing his cheeks. His gums, when he spoke, showed signs of scurvy.

It wasn't surprising, considering the food they were served. The only full meal was the noon dinner. Meats were boiled, but they were never cooked thoroughly. Soup was the water in which the meats were boiled. There were no vegetables or fruit. The coffee was so weak it looked like tea, and the milk so repulsive only the most desperate among them threw it down their gullets.

Stephen ran his tongue over his teeth to see if they were loosening. Not bad. "How long have you been here?"

The man nodded toward Stephen. "B-bad news, is it?"

Stephen frowned. He'd completely forgotten he clutched letters from Meg and Sylvie. Stretching out his legs, he spread the papers over his lap and marshalled his focus to see what they had to say. Had he read them before? He must have. But recalling their contents was no easier than remembering a dream upon waking.

The first was dated October 16. It was Sylvie writing. Meg and Nate had come to visit the asylum. They had? The script was so fine, his head ached to follow its lines and loops. He'd never had trouble reading before. It should cause him a spike in heart rate to notice this deficiency, but it didn't. He felt strangely set apart from his own body and from his life, especially the life he had before the asylum.

"Who's it f-f-from?" the man beside him wanted to know. "I'm Hugh. Hugh B-Brodie."

Stephen looked at him sharply. "Are you really here and not some apparition?" He felt no fear. Just curiosity.

Hugh nodded soberly. "Hit me and s-s-see."

Stephen didn't want to hit him. But he did shake Hugh's hand and felt his bones within his grip. "I'm Stephen."

"You s-s-see other people too?" Hugh asked, eyes void of shame or surprise. "I do. I s-s-see people who aren't th-there, I mean. M-mostly dead ones. Doctor s-s-says I have s-soldier's heart. And I don't n-n-need him to tell me I've g-grown a s-s-stutter. S-since the war."

Soldier's heart. The term struggled to the surface of Stephen's mind. "Yes. I have that too."

Hugh pointed to the letters. "But you have people writing to you."

Stephen's ears adjusted to the man's stutter until it no longer registered in the flow of conversation. "My daughters."

Hugh blinked and scratched behind his ears. "My wife left me years ago. Took the children. I have two sons who pretend I'm dead. Maybe it's easier for them that way. Or easier for their mother." He picked dirt from his cuticles.

Light striped Stephen's legs. Dust particles suspended in the pale beams. Stephen watched them dance, transfixed.

But Hugh had said something. What was it? Bringing it to mind seemed too much effort.

"You're drooling." Hugh pointed, then rubbed his head again. "They're giving you that medicine to keep you quiet, eh?"

Only mildly embarrassed, Stephen wiped his chin. "They are. It's working."

With good humor, the Irishman slapped him on the back. "Yep. I can tell. I bet normally you wouldn't like me touching you."

Stephen didn't really like it now either, but his heart was beating so slowly, he couldn't muster much of a protest.

"You having trouble reading those letters? You want I should read them out loud to you? I could sing them to you, if you don't mind the tunes. I don't stutter when I sing." When Hugh reached for the first one, Stephen let him have it.

Squeezing his eyes shut, Stephen concentrated on the words and not the voice behind them. This was Sylvie talking to him now, and Meg. Not a singing inmate. It was surreal, hearing his daughters' words ring clear as a bell from Hugh's mouth in song. They told him they were safe in Hiram's house. They spoke of going to church. "*We will thank God as soon as we can,*" the reverend said. Meg thought that would bring him comfort.

She did not understand that right now, he felt no pain. Right now, he felt nothing at all.

Maybe it was better that way.

"Next letter," Hugh said. "Are you ready?"

Stephen pulled his knees up again and rested his head on their bony caps. "Yes."

Hugh sang it to a jaunty melody popular in saloons. This letter was longer. Meg's bandage was off one hand, and she was using it again. He ought to feel happy for that, and yet there was only a slight stirring in his gut that might have been indigestion. If that was what happiness felt like, he could do without it. No happiness, no disappointment, no pain, no sorrow. The pendulum of emotion no longer swung in either direction. It was locked into place in the neutral middle.

The rest of the letter droned on. Something about an Asa Jones, a name that only faintly rang a bell. Meg expected Stephen home by spring. Spring? Stephen stared at the iron bars holding the rest of the world away. It would be easy to lose track of the seasons in here. Of time itself. He could not even think beyond the hour, let alone to next spring. Ah, so they'd taken in a cat. He closed his eyes again. That was good. He wondered for a brief moment how the stray dogs of the neighborhood were doing without him there to feed them. But then he remembered that the fire would have driven them away. The fire . . . Hiram's murder . . . the reason he was here.

"Hey. Did you hear that? They love you very much and pray for you every day. You're lucky they remain devoted to you."

They shouldn't. They were getting along fine without him.

Hugh's family was better off without him too, or so he had said. Stephen's eyelids were so heavy. All he wanted to do was sleep and stay asleep.

With a jolt, the words of his hallucinated friend Peter rushed back to him. *Try to get better*, he'd said.

Stephen hugged his ankles. Drool puddled on his knee. *I can't.*

THURSDAY, NOVEMBER 9, 1871

Sunshine poured into the third-floor turret room, polishing the hardwood floor to a gleam. With windows on three sides, the space was cool even with a small fire frolicking behind its grate. The natural light, however, was perfect.

And that was where the perfection ended.

With her left hand wrapped around a piece of charcoal, Meg breathed in its earthy scent and looked from her reflection in the mirror to her sketch on the canvas beside it. Modest resemblance, indeed. Jasper had allowed her to use this storage room for a temporary studio, but she still didn't feel like an artist.

During the week she'd been working here, she'd hoped the space would become like a sanctuary, as her old studio above the bookshop had been. Instead, it felt more like a crucible, a place of testing skill and spirit. During the daily dressing changes for her right hand, she'd seen enough to know it would never serve her the way it had. If she was to paint again, it was up to her left hand to do it.

Rocking her head from one shoulder to the other, she expelled a sigh and adjusted her grip on the charcoal. This was her third attempt at sketching a self-portrait. If she didn't get it right, Mr. VanDyke would know it right away—and he was the one she must impress. If she did, he would match her with clients ready to pay for their own images. But so far, sketching without a perfect sense of touch was only slightly easier than forming letters.

Meg walked several paces away from the easel and tilted her head, studying it.

Rubbish. She saw in the sketch the mere impression of herself, not a copy.

A soft knock preceded Sylvie coming into the room. Tucking a book under her arm, she took Meg's hand in hers and stretched it until Meg cringed. The painful part over, Sylvie began massaging, breaking up the tough scar tissue that layered Meg's palm and fingers.

"That should do for now." With a sly smile, Sylvie dragged an armchair into a soft beam of light and sat before opening the book on her lap. "You need a change of scenery," she said. "I'm at your service."

Guessing her sister's purpose, Meg's stomach quavered. "You want me to paint you?"

"I want you to practice, yes. Look what I found in the library." She held up a copy of Charlotte Brontë's *Villette*. "It's a long book, and I can be quite still when I read. What else do you need in a model?"

Perhaps painting someone else would be better. At least this way, Mr. VanDyke wouldn't be able to see how far Meg had missed the mark. After moving the mirror and leaning her own portrait against the wall, she set a fresh canvas on the easel.

Oliver Twist meandered into the studio and jumped onto Sylvie. The buff-colored cat curled into a ball on her lap, his tail wrapping around his body as he purred. As long as the cat was content to sleep and not explore shelves of paint tubes and jars of oil and medium, Meg saw no reason he couldn't stay.

The soft sound of charcoal on canvas filled her ears. She mentally dissected the image of Sylvie's head and transcribed it one line, one shape at a time. Forcing her hand to obey her mind was a slow and deliberate process. At least she didn't drop the charcoal.

Shifting her gaze from the canvas, she regarded Sylvie with new perspective. There was a softness to her expression that hadn't been there three weeks ago. Even the manner in which she interacted with Meg had evolved. It had grown lighter but not superficial, deeper without being darker. She suspected the change had more to do with a certain gentleman than with the suffering cat that came home with him the other day.

A tread on the stair interrupted them. Setting her charcoal on the easel's ledge, Meg hurried to the door, unwilling to have an audience. If someone watched her work, they'd see not only her imperfect renderings, but they could stare at her scars as well. She wasn't ready for that.

Kirstin held a pinafore she was hemming for a client. "It's Mr. Pierce for you, miss. He's visiting with Mr. Davenport, but he's come to see both you and Miss Sylvie too."

"Thank you, Kirstin. We'll be along directly."

Meg and Sylvie descended from the turret and found the men in the parlor. Jasper's gaze searched out and settled on Sylvie. His illness had left him even thinner than before, but at least his color had improved.

Hat in hand, Nate turned as soon as Meg entered the room. "I don't mean to interrupt your work. You were painting, weren't you? How's it going? Are you satisfied with your progress?"

"Did anyone ever tell you that you ask too many questions?" Meg smiled, hoping to deflect the topic, even as she slipped her hands into her skirt pockets. But, knowing he wouldn't relent, she finally admitted that yes, she'd been working, and that no, she wasn't satisfied.

"You have news for us?" Sylvie looked from one man to the other. "Has Otto Schneider been found?"

Nate hooked his thumb behind the strap of his satchel. "Not yet, as far as I know. I'll swing by the police station after this and ask which jailbirds they've managed to recapture since the fire."

Meg tried to hide her disappointment.

Oliver ambled into the room. Jasper scooped up the cat and rubbed behind his ears. He slid a glance at Nate. "Are you going to tell them why you're here?"

"Right. I came to invite the three of you to join me for a benefit concert at Turner Hall this Sunday. Proceeds go to the Relief and Aid Society. Full disclosure: I'm covering the event for the paper, but I'd enjoy it much more with your company."

Sylvie sparkled with anticipation. "I think it's a fine idea. We haven't been out—socially, anyway—in such a long time. Besides, it's for a good cause."

Jasper lowered the cat to the floor, then brushed fur off his clothing. "All excellent reasons for you to go. I'm afraid I must decline, however. I have an exam Monday morning that I need to study for."

"Oh." A crestfallen look stole over Sylvie's face. "I can help you study, if you like."

"Thank you, but no. Despite your good intentions, you'd only distract me. You're far more interesting than municipal law." He smiled. "You should go, though. Have a good time."

"We will," Meg said, aware she was answering for Sylvie too.

"Good." Nate grinned.

Before he could say anything else, a pounding on the front door moved Jasper to answer it.

"Can I help you?" His voice carried into the parlor.

"I beg your pardon," came another man's voice. "We're looking for the Misses Townsend. This notice in the paper said they could be found here. They have something that belongs to us."

"You must be the Spencers," Jasper said. "Come in."

Meg and Sylvie stepped into the hallway, Nate behind them, in time to see their former tenants, James and Flora Spencer, entering the house while Jasper introduced himself. Beneath a somewhat battered felt hat, Flora's hair was far more silver than Meg remembered, her hands roped with veins.

"I'm so glad you're all right." Sylvie shook their hands, a formal gesture given the circumstance, but there had been no real affection between Townsends and Spencers.

Before James could reach to shake Meg's hand too, she let him see that it was bandaged and not up to the task. "This is our friend Nathaniel Pierce, a reporter for the *Tribune*," she said.

At the almost imperceptible shift in their expressions, she wondered again if one or both of them had penned the anonymous letter in the newspaper slandering her father.

She went to the hall stand and withdrew the small jewelry box from the drawer. "The lid is cracked and chipped, but we thought you'd still want to have it." She set it in Flora's open palm.

Tears rimmed Flora's eyes as she withdrew a locket from inside. "The box must have fallen off the back of my bureau, otherwise I wouldn't have left without it. I'm so glad to have it back, you've no idea."

James doffed the hat from his bald, brown-spotted head. His old-fashioned suit hung loosely on his bowed frame. "You could have kept the box and pawned the jewels, not bothering to find a curmudgeonly old couple like us. We're staying with Flo's sister now, by the way. It does seem you've landed on your feet." He waggled his eyebrows at his surroundings.

"Oh, this is temporary." Meg glanced at Jasper, wondering if they'd yet worn out his hospitality. "We're rebuilding the bookstore and apartment. We'll be starting over."

James crushed the brim of his hat. "A daunting prospect for two young ladies. It's a shame your father isn't here to help you."

Meg struggled to mask her surprise. Even Sylvie faltered, her eyebrows tenting before she schooled her expression once more. "It is," she said. "A shame indeed."

Flora slipped the jewelry box into her reticule. "We ought to tell them, James. Tell them what we saw the night of the fire."

Meg's heart leapt at the possibility of more information. "Won't you come sit down?" She invited them into the front parlor before realizing that was Jasper's place, not hers. This was not her home. "If that's quite all right?" she asked him.

He said it was.

They took their seats in the parlor, where the crimson draperies absorbed the natural light. The hearth was cold without a fire, so seldom was the room used. But at least the gaslights were working again. Jasper turned them on, a rare indulgence for a household without steady income.

His russet hair catching in the light, Nate took out his pencil and paper. "You don't mind, do you? I have a feeling I'll want to remember what you say."

Flora licked her papery, pleated lips. "Is this—are you going to put this in an article?"

James grunted. "Maybe he ought to. If they won't print it, we could send a letter to the editor ourselves." His gaze darted to Sylvie, then Meg. "This time we'd even sign our names."

Warmth flooding her face, Meg turned to the window while regaining her composure. Fog rolled over the ground, catching on trees and fences, blotting the distance from view.

"You knew already, didn't you?" James asked. "You must have suspected."

"We did." A pulse of anger throbbed beneath Meg's skin. But these people had information she wanted. At least, she hoped so.

Flora shook her head, a wilted feather bobbing with the movement. "It hasn't been easy living so near a man so unpredictable and knowing he was our landlord. But that letter—well, we took it too far. You thought so too, I daresay, and yet you returned my most precious belonging to me." She clutched the beaded reticule in her lap.

Meg wiped her left palm on her skirt. "I appreciate that, Mrs. Spencer. But there's something else you wish to tell us?"

Jasper leaned forward, his dark trousers a stark contrast to the ochre stripes of the settee.

"We saw Stephen the night of the fire." James cleared his throat and frowned. "We saw him lashing out at folks, yelling at babies to hush. He accused a man or two of being a Rebel. All of that is God's truth. But we also saw a fellow take particular offense to his ravings—understandable, given Stephen was pointing a gun at him. The man knocked it out of his hand, then knocked him out cold with a blow to his head."

So far, this wasn't what Meg wanted to hear. "And then? What happened next?"

"The man scooped up Stephen's gun, spun the chambers to check for bullets, and ran off with it. Both of us saw it, didn't we, Flo?" James scratched the side of his nose. "I have said a lot of things about your father, I own that. Now I'll say this. If his gun was the one that killed that man, like the papers said, he wasn't the man who pulled the trigger."

Meg felt her pulse at the base of her neck. "You're sure of what you saw?" she whispered.

"As sure as I am of you sitting before me now."

Flora grasped James's hand. "You ought to know. You ought to know your father didn't shoot that man."

Sylvie turned to Jasper. "He didn't kill your uncle. I hoped so desperately that he didn't, but now we know, Jasper. It wasn't my father who did it."

Tears of gratitude streamed down Meg's cheeks. Nate offered her his handkerchief, then squeezed her shoulder while she wiped her face. "Thank you," she said. She had never believed her father killed Hiram, but hearing this from the Spencers, of all people, brought relief she hadn't felt before.

"Will you tell the police what you've told us?" Nate asked. "They seem to put a great deal of stock in witness statements for this case, since the so-called evidence is circumstantial."

"You'll be directly contradicting previous statements," Meg warned, "but that's no reason not to offer your perspective. If you don't mind, could you send a letter to the Cook County Insane Asylum too? Address it to Dr. Franklin."

"We'll do it." Flora sniffed and gave a tremulous smile.

"We ought to have done it sooner," James added, "but we've been caught up in our own affairs. Losing everything will do that to you."

Jasper extended a hand to help him out of the armchair. "Thank you for coming. Thank you for sharing what you saw." He'd paled in the last few minutes. His uncle's murderer was still at large.

But for Meg, the case against her father was officially closed.

Chapter Twenty-Two

Sunday, November 12, 1871

Sylvie sat straighter in the folding chair in Turner Hall's gymnasium to relieve pressure from the stays digging into her ribs. It was such a pity it was only Meg and Nate with her and not Jasper, for it wasn't often she wore so fine a gown. Lavender silk with royal purple ribbon trim made her feel like she was dressed in twilight. Meg wore dark blue with a lighter shade brocade in a Grecian key pattern. She was the color of the lake bordered with sky, her upswept blond hair the sun. Sylvie had found both gowns this week in a giant pile of donated clothing in the basement of the First Congregational Church, where she continued to volunteer. But after tonight, she couldn't guess the next occasion that would warrant such gowns. She and her sister were simple women, better suited to sensible wool than to satin.

Especially once they moved.

Friday's mail had brought the news that they'd been approved for a shelter house and that materials would be delivered by eight o'clock Monday morning, along with a construction crew who were to be paid only for their time. By way of apology for the delay, the letter mentioned that the aid society had received 6,259 applications and that theirs was the 4,564th one to be approved. So their time in Hiram's house was drawing to an end. Her time with Jasper was too.

The heat from the tittering crowd defied the chill outdoors and cloyed with clashing scents of perfumes and pomades. Waving a fan to stir a breeze, Sylvie glanced at Meg, whose attention was focused solely on whatever Nate was saying. Just as well. Sylvie was lost in her own thoughts, all of which centered on Jasper.

Was she a fool to believe there was something growing between them? Something rippled through her middle at the thought of his kindness. She didn't think this was a mere fancy. At least, she hoped it wasn't.

After she'd recovered from the water sickness, but while Meg was still laid low and Kirstin was convalescing, Sylvie had slipped down the corridor and into the wing that held Jasper's bedchamber. Helene had fallen asleep keeping watch over Meg, and all Sylvie wanted to do was check on Jasper without rousing the dear housekeeper who had been acting as nursemaid for them all.

Jasper had been delirious with fever, and she'd bathed his brow with cool cloths. In his sleep he muttered words that made no sense. She had tried to calm him, but he wouldn't be still. Then he'd said, *"I'm cold. It's so very cold."* This, she'd understood. She stoked the fire and laid another wool blanket over him. He kicked it off.

Three toes were missing on one foot, and two from the other. Shock had stolen only a few moments before she'd tucked the blankets beneath the mattress to keep them in place.

When at last Jasper had opened his glassy eyes, he'd caught her wrist and said, *"Don't go. Angel of mercy, don't leave me."*

She'd stayed for hours that night. He asked her to sing to him, and she did. He requested a few songs she didn't know, then tried singing them himself.

> I'm just a poor wayfaring stranger
> A traveler through this world of woe
> But there's no sickness, toil nor danger
> In that fair land to which I go
> I'm going there to see my father

I'm going there no more to roam
I am just going over Jordan
I am just going over home

The lines had been broken with labored breath until Sylvie bade him stop altogether. Gently, she'd touched his lips to quiet him, and he'd kissed her fingertips.

Did he remember that? Because she did. The moment of his need and her meeting it was embroidered on her memory in shining thread. He'd been half out of his mind with fever and might not even have known who she was, but it was the first time a man had kissed her. Pity it didn't signify a thing. Did it?

Either way, she hadn't told Meg. Some secrets were too precious to reveal.

Gaslights dimmed in their sconces along the sides of the auditorium, casting shadow over the masses and a spotlight on the stage framed by scarlet velvet curtains.

Meg leaned over to Sylvie and whispered, "I'm glad you're here."

Sylvie smiled and nodded, resolving to enjoy herself.

After an announcer in a long-tailed tuxedo praised the Relief and Aid Society, thanked sponsors, and introduced the evening's program, a succession of musicians occupied the stage. Some performers were local, and some had traveled specifically for the occasion. Sylvie recognized most of the songs. At the conclusion of each, the gymnasium-turned-auditorium thundered with applause.

It was a shimmering, silvery evening. Sylvie felt restored not only by the entertainment, but by the coming together of so many people who cared.

She glanced at Meg, ready to comment on the last performance, but her sister was riveted by Nate whispering in her ear. Clearly forgetting to be ashamed of her scars, Meg rested her fingertips on his arm. He covered her hand with his.

What Sylvie wouldn't give for such a sign of affection from Jasper. With a wistful sigh, she looked away.

The master of ceremonies retook the stage, beaming in front of the lowered curtain. "And now, ladies and gentlemen, for the grand finale, a special treat. Two original songs written specifically for Chicago in her time of need, and performed by Boston soprano Constance Jacobs. The first is entitled, 'Pity the Homeless.'"

He stepped out of the spotlight, the curtain rose, and with quavering tones, the soprano sang:

> Pity the homeless, pity the poor,
> By the fierce Fire fiend forced to your door;
> List to their pleading, list to their cry,
> Pass them not heedlessly by,
> Roused from their slumbers, peaceful and sweet,
> Hastening in terror into the street,
> Leaving behind them treasure most dear,
> Flying in anguish and fear . . .

Sylvie shifted uncomfortably in her chair, longing for someone to crack open a door or window to permit a draft of cool air. She had not expected a song about the fire itself, nor did she want to relive it. She folded her hands. Her palms were slick with sweat.

At last the song was over, and she drew in as much breath as her corset would allow.

"Are you all right?" Meg asked during the clapping.

Was her unease that obvious? "Better now," Sylvie replied. "That song . . ."

Meg nodded. "Let's hope it garners large charitable contributions."

When the next song was announced as "Passing Through the Fire," Nate gave Sylvie and then Meg a reassuring smile. The three of them had endured that dreadful night of real flames together. Surely Sylvie could sit through mere words put to song.

> Flames! flames! terrible flames!
> How they rise, how they mount, how they fly.
> The heavens are spread with a fierce lurid glare,

Red heat is filling the earth with air,
While, mercy! mercy! We hear the despairing ones cry.

Eyes squeezed shut, Sylvie fought the urge to cover her ears as well. Really, must this woman put so fine a point on it? Her lungs constricted, and she felt like she was pulling air through a cheesecloth.

Passing thro' the fire! passing thro' the fire,
And it is our Father's hand,
Tho' we may not understand
Why we're passing thro' the fire,
passing thro' the fire!

Sylvie fished her handkerchief from her reticule and pressed it to her face and neck. Were they trying to re-create the heat of that night in here? Desperate for fresh air, she suppressed a groan and fanned herself instead.

Flames! flames! terrible flames!
How they sweep, how they rush, how they roar.
See the hideous tongues round the roof,
tree and spire,
As swells their wild carnival higher and higher,
Till falling! crashing! Our glorious
city's no more.

She could see it, then. By some trick of her mind's eye, the terrible flames rose before her and behind her, encircling the auditorium while all of them just sat there, unmoving. She felt the terror that had overwhelmed her the night the fire chased her—chased all of them—as it destroyed everything in its path. Her pulse pounded in her ears so resoundingly that it became the clang of the courthouse bell, and then all the other bells of churches and schools.

But this was madness. The courthouse bell was destroyed, melted down and molded into relics, one of which she had held in her palm.

She was shaking, crushing fistfuls of her skirt. An unaccountable anger consumed her. This soprano from Boston had no idea what she was singing, had no inkling what it was to lose everything. How dare she sing it, with melody and measures and mathematical beats that created order out of a night that wrought pure chaos? Sylvie was livid, even though she knew the audience needed to be emotionally moved in order to fill the offering plates that would soon be passed. But she could barely eke that small amount of logic from her agitated mind.

Something pulled at her, and she jerked away from it, startled, before looking down at Meg. Somehow Sylvie was standing, as if ready to run all over again.

"Sit down," Meg hissed. "Or do you need to leave?"

Sylvie nodded. She couldn't control her rapid breathing. She needed air, she needed to get away.

Meg whispered to Nate and gestured to the aisle on his other side. A glimmer of light from the stage reflected off his spectacles as he glanced at Sylvie, then quickly rose and slipped out of the row of chairs. Meg and Sylvie followed him as he moved toward the rear of the gymnasium. After helping the women into their cloaks, he threw on his frock coat and led the way outside.

A welcome November chill blasted over Sylvie as she escaped Turner Hall. Leaning on Nate's arm, she gulped cold air as if to quench a fire in her lungs. It had a bracing effect, and her pulse began to calm.

Meg wrapped her arm around Sylvie's waist. "What happened?"

She shook her head to clear it. "I don't know how to explain it except that those songs brought the fire too vividly back to life. I could *see* it again, right there in the building, even though I knew it wasn't there." She placed a hand to her chest. "My heart is beating as though we've been running from the flames all over again. And I was terrified and furious at that singer, completely beside myself with feelings that felt too big to contain." She paused to catch her breath. "That sounds crazy, doesn't it?"

"No." Nate's voice gentled. "It sounds familiar. For someone who has experienced trauma, that type of reaction can be triggered without warning. It's not uncommon."

"Did you feel it too? Either of you?" Sylvie looked to her sister for an answer.

"Not to the same degree that you did, perhaps," Meg began, "but of course I couldn't help but be transported to a place I'd rather forget."

Tears welled in Sylvie's eyes. Meg's mild description was nothing compared to what she had experienced. "That's not the same. That's not the same at all."

Gaslights hissed, spreading amber puddles over the sidewalks on both sides of Prairie Avenue. The lampposts made lonely sentinels now that soldiers no longer marched the street. Meg's arm was linked through Sylvie's as they approached Hiram's front porch, but her gaze flicked to Nate's profile beside her.

Perhaps it was the artist in her that admired the depth in his eyes and the way his finely drawn lips turned slightly up at one corner, even in repose, as if he were processing some fascinating information and almost ready to speak of it. Perhaps she looked at him, at everyone, differently now that she must learn to paint from life.

"Thank you for leaving the concert early," she said. "I know you were there for work."

He lifted an eyebrow in subtle challenge. "We only missed the last verse or so of the last song, and then the closing. I would have missed more for Sylvie's sake or for yours. However, after I see you safely inside and say hello to Jasper, I do need to go back to find out how much money they raised. I can't give my article to Medill without that sum."

Meg had wondered if Joseph Medill was still Nate's editor. He'd been elected mayor last Tuesday. "How much longer will he stay at the *Tribune*?" she asked.

"Not much longer." Nate climbed the stone steps beside her.

"He takes office December 4, so I'll have a new boss to impress soon."

"I have no doubt you will. But for now, come inside for a cup of tea while the donations are tabulated," she suggested while Sylvie unlocked the door and stepped inside. Helene and Kirstin were visiting friends and family tonight, but it would be no trouble to put a kettle on to boil and to serve a plate of shortbread cookies.

Nate crossed the threshold and moved to close the door behind him, but a gust of wind slammed it shut right out of his hand. "Is there a window open somewhere?"

Sylvie rubbed her arms. "I can't imagine there would be. Unless Jasper burned his dinner and needed to let out the smoke. . . ."

Meg doubted he'd cooked anything at all. Without pausing to remove her hat or cloak, she set off down the corridor, Sylvie and Nate right behind her. "Jasper?"

A plaintive moan came in reply.

Gasping, Sylvie hastened past Meg and into the library. "Jasper, you're hurt!"

Meg froze in the doorway long enough to see him holding the back of his head before she hurried to fetch a basin of water and clean cloths. On her way to the kitchen, a chill wind grazed her skin. The window by the rear door had been broken. Glass lay in shards all over the floor.

"Meg, stop." Nate pulled her back as if she were about to walk on the pieces. "There's been a break-in. Jasper was attacked."

His hands warmed her shoulders through her cloak. "Who was it?" she whispered. Was it wrong of her to hope it was Otto Schneider?

"Come talk to Jasper yourself. He doesn't need tending—the wound already stopped bleeding."

Questions galloped through her mind as she sat on the brocade sofa across from Sylvie and Jasper, who shared the other. Behind them, the study table was scattered with textbooks and a pad of foolscap paper. Nate added a few more logs to the guttering fire, then brushed loose bark from his palms. Unbuttoning his frock coat, he sat with Meg.

"Start over," Meg said. "Please. Tell us everything from the beginning."

Touching the back of his head, Jasper winced and licked his swollen bottom lip. "I was studying. I must have fallen asleep on my books, because I didn't hear the window break. I didn't hear him coming until too late. As soon as I startled awake, he struck the back of my head with that brass bookend." He pointed to where it still lay behind the table. "I wish I could say that I rallied and that we fought it out, but the truth is, the blow knocked me out. I must have split my lip on the edge of the table."

Sylvie's complexion turned waxen in the firelight. "He robbed the house, didn't he?"

"He made off with silver candlesticks and silverware, and I don't know what else. I haven't made a thorough inventory. Thank goodness you ladies weren't here when he came. If any harm had come to you, I—"

"But did you see him?" Meg interrupted. The clock on the mantel whirred as the minute hand advanced. Eleven chimes marked the hour.

Jasper sighed. "Average height, medium build. He had a stocking cap pulled low over his brow, so I don't know what color his hair is. The lines on his face marked him as older than myself, but younger than your father."

Meg's breath caught. It was ridiculous how much she wanted the attacker to be Otto Schneider. But if he was, it was all the more likely he'd shot Hiram, and her father had more of a chance to be acquitted. "Could you describe him to the police?"

"I only saw his reflection in the window, and just for the briefest instant. When I started to turn around, the bookend came down on my skull."

Nate took off his spectacles and rubbed the bridge of his nose. "Have you reported the burglary?" When he looked up, his eyes were blue chips of ice.

"In a way. The night watchman noticed the disturbance. I roused to the sound of him beating on the front door. He must have scared the attacker away. When I answered the door, I explained what happened."

"Fortunate timing, that," Nate said. "In any case, you'll need to see what else has been stolen and then make a full report at the police station, which is now at the corner of Union and West Madison."

"How hard was the blow?" Sylvie asked. She brought her fingertips to the back of his head and cringed. "There's already quite a lump. Are you dizzy?"

"Not if I don't move."

Nate replaced his glasses and leaned forward, elbows resting on his knees. "If no one else is going to state the obvious, I will. Meg, Sylvie, it isn't safe for you to stay here anymore. Pack up what you can now, and we'll come back for the rest tomorrow."

Sylvie opened her mouth, then closed it, bowing her head. "I thought we'd have a few more days here. Our shelter house hasn't been built yet." She pulled a pillow onto her lap and hugged it.

"He's right," Jasper said. "Whoever came here knows there is more to be taken than what he stole tonight. He may return. I'll board up the broken window, but who is to say he might not break another next time?"

"There doesn't have to be a next time," Sylvie protested. "If we tell the police and ask them to post a guard . . ." But her voice trailed away, as even she knew that wasn't realistic. Now that Sheridan's companies had disbanded, the police were spread thin and wouldn't waste a constable to patrol one house, especially one that might go to public auction anyway.

Resignation settled in Meg's middle. They had lived here for one month and had always known it would be temporary, but part of her had conveniently forgotten that they were homeless. They'd found refuge here and been grateful. But with a burglar—and possibly murderer—attacking this household, it was no longer a safe haven.

"What about Helene and Kirstin?" Sylvie asked. "Will they stay?"

Jasper leaned back, holding his head straight and still. "I'll advise against it as soon as I see them. I can't risk any harm coming to either of them. Eli may stay in the carriage house at his own risk."

Meg nodded. "It's time to go," she whispered. "But where?"

Nate hated to wake Edith at this late hour. But heaven knew he'd lost enough sleep over the years for her and Harriet and Andrew.

But it was Frank who let him in, eyes bleary with sleep, face shadowed with black whiskers. "Nate? Are you in trouble?" The lamp he held cast a glare into the night.

"Not me." Hands tingling with cold from the cab ride through the city to get here, he ushered Meg and Sylvie into the house before him and shut the door. "Frank, meet Margaret and Sylvia Townsend." He kept his voice low to avoid waking the babies.

Clearly bewildered, Frank tightened the belt around his robe and mumbled a how-do-you-do as Edith emerged from the hallway, her hair in a braid down her back.

"Sorry for the timing, Edith." Nate kissed her cheek. The house still smelled faintly of the roast she'd fed him after church earlier that day. "Remember when you told me if I ever needed a place to stay, I could come to you? I'm really hoping the offer might be transferable." Briefly, he related what had happened.

"Oh, how awful," Edith murmured, rubbing her arms. "Yes, of course, you may stay here as long as you need to, so long as you don't mind the accommodations. We have a bed in the spare room and this couch, which Frank insists is the most comfortable place to sleep in the house."

"Are you sure you don't mind?" Sylvie asked. "We would hate to impose."

"Not at all," Edith insisted.

Sylvie exhaled. "It won't be for long. Tomorrow morning, construction begins on our new home. The materials have been cut to size already, and the crew has already made thousands of them. It won't take long to put our own roof over our heads."

"Then we'll enjoy each other while we can. Nate has told us so much about you, and I welcome the chance to get to know you myself."

"Likewise," Meg said, plucking the pins from her hat and lifting it off her hair. "I understand you have two little boys. I can't wait to meet them."

She looked exhausted, and for good reason. Yet she still managed a smile that was warm and genuine. Nate would have offered her and Sylvie his own room in the boardinghouse while he camped out in his neighbor's rooms, but this arrangement was far more suitable.

Frank cleared his throat. "Nate?" Leaving the lamp in the parlor, he jerked his head toward the dining room.

Nate followed his brother-in-law past doily-topped tea tables and into the shadows.

"Is this what you call not getting involved?" Frank asked. "Whatever happened to you enjoying your bachelorhood? You've taken two more little chicks under your wing. Only these chicks are really, really complicated. Their problems don't have to be yours. Nate. Brother. How many times do I have to tell you? You are not a mother hen. Stop acting like one."

Nate kept his laughter to a low rumble in his chest. "I'm not."

Frank crossed his arms. Without his usual pomade, his hair flopped onto his brow. He smelled of the lavender sachets Edith used to scent her sheets.

"This is different," Nate said. "Especially with Meg. If she needs me, Frank—well, let's just say it's not in the way a girl needs a father. Do you mind the way Edith needs you?"

Frank's eyebrows arched. Looking over his shoulder, he watched his wife bring glasses of water to Meg and Sylvie, then disappear again before returning with linens for the couch. Facing Nate again,

Frank clapped his shoulder. “The truth is, I need her just as much. More, I think. Yes. Definitely more.”

Nate stole another glimpse of the women. “I know the feeling. Or I’m beginning to, at least.”

“Is that right?”

Nate smiled. “Yes, it is.” It was very right, indeed.

Chapter Twenty-Three

Monday, November 13, 1871

Dear Father,

It's me, Sylvie. It's one o'clock in the morning, but I can't sleep.

I don't even know if you're getting our mail. Somehow it's easier to write what I have to say thinking that you won't, that no one will ever see this. But part of me wants you to as well.

I'm having a difficult time adjusting, after the fire. Nate said what I'm experiencing sounded familiar. Now I wonder if he was referring to you.

My heart beats too fast sometimes, and I have episodes where I sweat far too much for a lady if I'm thinking about the fire. Sometimes even in the day, my memories overwhelm me and it's like I'm right there all over again. My nightmares are so vivid I'd rather suffer insomnia than willingly rest. I think I understand why you barely slept.

I wish I had asked you more questions about how you were doing when you were home. Maybe you wouldn't have wanted to answer them, anyway.

I wish I knew you better.

I want you to be well. Come home, and we'll try again.

Your daughter,
Sylvie

November 13, 1871

Dear Father,

I hope this letter finds you well. I hope it finds you at all. Did you get our letter about what the Spencers told us?

By this time next week, you can send mail to us at our old address. I don't want to upset you, but they are building our temporary shelter in the backyard, over your map of Andersonville. We plan to sell books out of the house on the back of the lot until the new shop can be built.

I'm trying to paint with my left hand, because my right will never cooperate. I've been working on a portrait of Sylvie for practice. Do you remember when I was very little and starting to paint? The flower I made on the paper was nothing like what I had in mind, and I wanted to quit. But you told me not to. You told me that if painting was what I loved, I shouldn't give it up, I should do it more. That's what I'm telling myself now.

Do you have enough books to read? I know the asylum has Bibles. I'd like to send or deliver something else too, but I wish I knew the package would reach you. Please write and let me know what you'd like to read. If you can. (Asylum staff, if you're reading this, the least you can do is reply to this question.)

We can't wait for you to come home. We still need our father.

Your loving daughter,
Meg

Tuesday, November 14, 1871

Stephen paced four steps in his cell and about-faced to march the other way. It was past time for the medicine, and they wouldn't let him out until he'd had it. He could tell by the vigorous beating of his heart that the previous dose had worn off almost completely.

Letters from Sylvie and Meg had arrived today, and what Sylvie had shared upset him. His little girl was suffering.

Hours ago, when the drugs were still dimming his mind and spirit, this discovery bobbed among his turbid thoughts, refusing to sink below the surface. Sylvie suffered in a way she didn't understand. Meg wouldn't fully understand it either. But he did.

He cared. He felt. He hurt, but he felt alive again. Perhaps it was by some miracle that his next dose had been delayed long enough for him to reawaken.

Stephen knew exactly what was happening to Sylvie. He didn't pretend to know why or how, but her descriptions were indeed familiar, just as that reporter had said. The young man ought to be thanked for mentioning it, for if he hadn't, Sylvie might not have brought this to him.

She was embarrassed. He understood that, of course he did, but she shouldn't be ashamed about this, not with him. Once upon a time he'd been able to soothe her cares by scooping her onto his lap and letting her stay there until she wanted to climb down of her own accord. Sometimes he'd read stories to her, other times he made them up, customized to fit her trouble and please her. He'd never pushed her away.

At least not before the war.

If asylum patients were allowed to communicate with the outside world, he would pick up a pencil and write to her now. He would tell her a story of a father who lost his way, and of the daughter who was the light that led him home.

He wanted to go home now. He needed to go home. Sylvie wasn't insane for her reactions, and if she wasn't insane, neither was he.

Stephen wasn't getting better here. He was disappearing.

In a sense, staying here was easier than leaving, but his girls had already lost their mother. They still needed their father. He bowed his head into his hands, fingertips grazing scabs left by vermin, and examined himself afresh. The Spencers had said they'd seen a man take his gun from him, which meant he hadn't killed Hiram.

But they'd also seen him pointing that gun at people. It was loaded. If he hadn't killed anyone that night, it was only by the grace of God. Were his daughters really better off with a father as volatile as he was?

Anguish dropped him to his knees on the hard floor. Stephen cried out, "Oh, Lord, I need you now. I need you to make me into the man my daughters deserve."

The iron door squealed on its hinges, and two attendants filled the room. Linden folded his arms across his white uniform while Slattery brought the glass vial forward. "Talking to someone who isn't here again? Good thing we've brought your next dose."

"I was praying to God." Stephen pushed himself up, his joints aching. "And He *is* here."

Linden smirked. "Remind me to add religious fanaticism to your list of mental diseases."

"I'm not taking that." Stephen planted his feet wide and clenched his fists to keep them from nervous tapping.

"This bottle has your name on it," Slattery said. "It's yours. It's time for you to take it."

"I told you, I won't do it." Sweat trickled from Stephen's temples.

Linden latched and locked the door behind him before angling toward Stephen again. "You're saying you want the jacket, then. And solitary confinement. Is that it?"

Nausea rolled through his middle. He swallowed hard and shook his head. To be alone with his thoughts and hallucinations made for poor company indeed. Last time he'd nearly gone mad with the isolation.

"You can't go without treatment."

His wits scattering, Stephen uncurled his fists and slapped his legs before he could stop himself. He rubbed his chin and felt only stubble, his former beard a phantom. He was weak. But God's strength was made perfect in weakness, wasn't it? The Bible's promise, long ago memorized, rattled through him now.

Slattery whistled. "Look at you. You're a mess. This is what happens when we're late with medicine, Linden. I told you we should have come earlier. Now 283 isn't in a temper to cooperate."

Were these really the only two options? Isolation or mind-numbing drugs? His knees softened. He needed to be sharp, to remember who he was and the daughters he could still father.

The attendants grabbed him by the arms and threw him to the cot, pinning him there. Stephen clenched his teeth and thrashed until a knee to his groin sent white-hot pain darting through his middle. He closed his eyes, and a hand squeezed his jaw, forcing it open.

He didn't want these vile drugs. But God help him, he could not face confinement again.

Chapter Twenty-Four

Tuesday, November 14, 1871

Dawn slipped in through scalloped curtains and landed in pink and grey curves, like oyster shells, across the quilted bed. Languidly, Meg listened as someone padded into the baby's room to answer his waking cries. The smell of coffee and hiss of bacon in a pan signaled a new day.

It all felt so ordinary. She could almost believe she'd only dreamed of the break-in at Hiram's house, and that she was here on holiday, visiting friends. But she couldn't forget that every day Hiram's murder went unsolved was another day her father endured the asylum. She still had no idea how he was.

Suppressing a groan, she pulled the blanket over her head as all her concerns rained down on her at once. The Bible said to cast her cares on Jesus, and she did. But every day, it seemed, she took them back into her own hands.

Her hands.

With a start, she sat up and wiggled her fingers. It had been five weeks since Dr. Gilbert had first wrapped her wounds. It was time for her right hand to be free again.

Pushing back the quilt, Meg swung her legs over the edge of the bed and stood on the braided rug. She didn't need the doctor for this. She didn't even need Sylvie. What she needed was God's courage to finally face what she'd been dreading since the fire.

Shivering in front of the cold hearth, she removed the pin from the end of the bandage and unspooled the linen strip.

There.

She stared. She'd seen this before, but today was different. It held a note of finality that hardened into a stone in her chest. Tears caught in her throat and burned her eyes.

Her thumb and first two fingers had been fused together, the pink scars contracting them into a permanent position. The fourth and fifth fingers could move stiffly, like the fingers on her left hand, but she had lost the ability to hold anything unless she could pin it between her last two fingers and her palm.

No glove could cover this.

In a fall of watery light, Meg stretched her hands and fingers the way Dr. Gilbert had shown her. She'd had more than a month to prepare herself for this moment and ordered her thoughts to fall in line with the truth. She was limited, but God was not. She had to trust that He would find a way to make something beautiful through her. She thought of Asa Jones at the Soldiers' Home, who'd lost both leg and arm, and of so many others who also bore injuries. She was not the only one who suffered a loss of function.

Meg knew all this in her mind. But as she washed her face, brushed her hair, and painstakingly pinned half her locks in coils on top of her head, the ache she felt persisted.

As Meg finished dressing, Sylvie knocked on the door and came in, her face still puffy from sleep. Her gaze fell first on the linen strip in a pile on the washstand table, then moved to Meg. "No more bandages?"

Meg shook her head. "This is as good as it gets, or near it."

With a determined smile, Sylvie embraced her. "It's a new chapter, then," she said. "'As good as it gets' may be better than you expect."

After making quick work of their morning routines, Meg and Sylvie joined Edith in the kitchen, where Edith held baby Henry on one hip while scrambling some eggs. She was still in her dressing gown, her light brown hair pinned at the sides of her head but otherwise falling in waves down her back. Meg almost reached to take the baby from her, wishing to lighten her load. But with only one hand that could grip a squirming ten-month-old, she backed away. Sylvie took Henry instead, with an ease that made Meg's heart sting.

That wouldn't do. "Is there something I can do for you?" she asked Edith. She could have entertained Tommy, but apparently the toddler still slept.

Frank clomped unevenly into the kitchen, his hair slicked back and a bit of shaving soap still visible above his collar. With a wink, Edith pointed to the spot on her own neck, and he wiped it away. "Help me find my other shoe, Meg? Tommy loves to walk around in them but doesn't love putting them back. I've got an early meeting today, so I'm in a bit of a rush."

She smiled at his stockinged foot and agreed.

When she found the missing shoe in a laundry basket, she brought it to Frank as he was eating eggs and bacon.

"Thank you!" He took it from her, saw her hands, then met her gaze with steady eyes. As a pharmacist, he had likely seen much worse. "Nate says you're an artist."

She hadn't been expecting that. "Yes, I was." She glanced at Sylvie feeding Henry shallow spoonfuls of mush.

He took a drink of coffee. "No, he says you *are*. Present tense. You're doing the stretches? How is it going, training your left hand?"

"Frank," Edith said, warning in her tone. "Are you hungry, Meg? There's plenty of food. And you'll have to forgive Frank. He can be so inquisitive. But I suppose you're used to that if you've spent much time with Nate."

"It's all right." Meg sat at the table and helped herself to a crisp slice of perfectly fried bacon. "To answer your questions, yes, I'm doing the stretches. As for training my left hand to substitute for my right, I'm making progress, just not as quickly as I'd hoped."

Frank nodded without a trace of surprise in his expression. "That's typical. If I could bottle patience and sell it along with pills, I'd be a rich man." He shoveled the last of the eggs on his plate into his mouth and glanced at the clock. "Wish I could give my boss a double dose of it," he muttered as he shoved back from the table and straightened his tie. "I'm off." With a kiss to Edith and another for Henry, he grabbed his cloak and valise and left.

Edith poured a cup of coffee for each of them. "Frank can be direct and abrupt. I'm sorry if it's jarring to you. Especially today. It's a big milestone, isn't it?" She laid the question down as delicately as if she had been dressing a wound. In a way, she was.

Even fully dressed in her mauve jacket and skirt, Meg felt raw and exposed. But Edith's gentle manner soothed her. "It is."

"Well," Edith said, stirring cream into her coffee, "don't hesitate to tell us how we can make you more comfortable. What our home lacks in crystal and damask, we make up for in ointments and tonics. Do you have pain? Physical pain?"

A discerning distinction. Meg glanced to her lap at the hand half-dead to sensation. "It only hurts when I stretch the scar tissue, and I need to feel that so I know how far to push."

Edith pushed a strand of hair behind her ear. "Ah. If only we all knew that. Some pushing is necessary for growth and healing, but too much, and we may snap something that isn't meant to be severed."

Sylvie looked up. "Something tells me we aren't just talking about the human body anymore." Henry leaned forward, mouth wide open, for more food.

A thoughtful smile warmed Edith's tired face as she watched Sylvie feed her son. "There are parallels to be drawn, yes? Take Nate, for example. He pushed himself to become a guardian, providing for my siblings and me when he was eighteen, and he pushed us to certain standards of responsibility and morality too. In the case of my sister Harriet and I, I'd say it worked. But when he pushed my brother, Andrew, Andrew pushed back. It became a match of wills, and eventually something snapped between them that hasn't yet been repaired."

A low, comforting purr came from the fire still burning in the stove. "Are you saying Nate was too hard on Andrew?" Meg hadn't observed a stern disciplinarian side of Nate, but she could well imagine it.

Edith passed Sylvie a napkin for the baby's face. "He was no harder on him than he was on himself. That's the trick of it, isn't it? Everyone's different. You have to know how hard to push and when to give a little grace." She wrapped her hands around her mug and smiled at Meg. "The same goes for yourself. I realize we haven't known each other long, but I feel like I know you through Nate. So if I come across as too straightforward, blame it on that, or on my husband's influence. But what I want to say to you is this: push yourself, but don't set an impossible goal."

Meg would push herself, indeed. But her goals remained the same.

Thursday, November 16, 1871

As soon as Jasper opened the door, Meg knew something had changed.

"Come in." He stepped aside, allowing her and Sylvie to enter. The vestibule no longer smelled of lemon or linseed oil, now that Helene and Kirstin had taken work elsewhere.

"What's going on?" Sylvie unpinned her hat and hung it on the hall stand along with her cloak. "You seem different."

"Everything's different." He looped his thumb on his belt. "I found it."

"The will," Meg whispered. Steadying her breathing, she unfastened the buttons of her cloak and hung it beside Sylvie's. The suspense coiling inside her was so strong she nearly forgot to be embarrassed by her right hand, which Jasper had seen yesterday. There had been pity in his eyes, which she supposed was better than disgust. Today she saw neither.

"Yes, the will," he confirmed.

"And?" Sylvie dared to ask. "Is it—did he leave the property to you?"

The slightest smile betrayed him. "He did. Come see for yourself."

Relief flooded Meg as she followed him into the library, where a legal document lay on the study table beside a stack of textbooks and a candlestick. It was creased where it had been folded. Quickly she scanned the date—December 30, 1869—and type until she found what she was searching for. Just as he'd said, Jasper Davenport was named the sole beneficiary of Hiram's estate. At the bottom were the signatures of Hiram Sloane and his attorney, Thomas Grosvenor.

So it wasn't left to her father. Stephen had no motive, none whatsoever, to kill his friend. She'd already known that, especially since the Spencers had shared what they'd seen, but seeing the will made her breathe easier.

Oliver darted into the room and onto the table, skidding dangerously close to the document. Sylvie scooped up the purring cat. "I'm so happy for you," she said. "This means you can stay and finish your law degree!" The cat squirmed, and she lowered him to the carpet.

"This means a lot of things. I just need to find another attorney to execute the will, now that Grosvenor has passed." Jasper shook his head, a muscle clenching in his jaw. "And I would really like the police to find Otto Schneider, or whoever it was that broke in on Sunday. Otherwise I have a hunch he'll be back. Eli has taken permanent employment elsewhere, by the way, and I don't blame him. But that means I'm alone here now."

Meg nodded. She was sorry she hadn't said good-bye to the faithful carriage driver but was glad to hear he'd found a stable position. "Where did you find it?" The cat rubbed against her ankles, then wandered off in favor of a spot on the warm hearth.

"It was in this room the entire time. Folded and tucked into a book about Roman history, of all things. Little wonder I didn't find it until now."

"Yes, quite." Meg scanned the shelves upon shelves of books. She had been on the right track when she searched some volumes in Hiram's study. If she'd only brought her method to the library instead, she would have found the will far sooner.

Knowing all of this belonged to Jasper now brought a finality to Hiram's death that hadn't locked into place before this moment. Bringing her gaze back to him, she pasted on a smile. This was the resolution everyone needed, after all. "I'll finish Sylvie's portrait today, and then we'll be out of your way."

Jasper cocked an eyebrow. "Until you come back to paint again, you mean."

Sylvie fiddled with the trim on her sleeve. "We received word this morning that our new home is ready for us to move into. We don't need to come back after today." But there was a pleading in her eyes for him or Meg to say otherwise.

Cupping an elbow in his palm, he tapped a long finger on his cheek. "You still need to practice portraits, don't you?"

Meg told him she did. One sample was certainly not enough to impress Mr. VanDyke at the art gallery.

"Paint me," Jasper said. "Your supplies are already arranged upstairs. This will give you time and space to get settled into your new quarters before designating part of it as a studio. Consider it a commission, Meg. I'll pay you for it when it's done."

"What a grand idea." Sylvie's response was so swift, Meg nearly laughed.

But in this case, she had to agree. "After I finish Sylvie's portrait, I'd like it to stay here and dry before we move it. If you have time tomorrow, I can begin to sketch you. But first, I must ask—have you seen the portrait upstairs?" If he wasn't satisfied, she couldn't accept him paying for his own.

"Don't be cross with me, Meg, but yes, I looked. Rest assured, I liked what I saw." He glanced at Sylvie, who colored to the shade of poppies as she returned his smile. She seemed very pleased by his approval.

That settled, the Townsend sisters ascended to the studio in the turret. Inhaling the smells of turpentine and linseed oil, Meg donned an apron, since she was liable to drop the paintbrush, then squeezed a portion of ivory black onto her palette.

"What a relief to finally have the will found." Sylvie opened the drapes, then sat and arranged her skirt. "I didn't know what to think, after what Mother wrote in her journal. But the date on the will was after she died, so it must be the most recent version."

"I noticed that too," Meg murmured and then immersed herself in her task. A low fire smoldered behind the grate, barely taking the chill off the room. She fed wood to it and watched the flames revive.

Returning to the palette, she mixed the black paint with enough medium to create a thin glaze, then layered it over the background.

Sylvie looked up from *Villette* and let her gaze wander over the molded plaster ceiling. "I wonder if Jasper will keep the house or sell it," she mused.

"Ask him." With a large dry brush, Meg blended the background, letting the underpaint show through. She then painted over the rest of the figure and head with a coat of medium and a touch of ivory black, then blended that with a dry brush too. Studying her sister's face, Meg backed up from the portrait to gain perspective, then approached again. With a dry, clean cloth, she wiped out the highlights on the face on the canvas.

Keeping her posture immobile, Sylvie slid her a sideways glance. "Are you erasing me now?"

"It's Rembrandt's technique," Meg told her. "When you wipe out the highlights, the thin black glaze is forced down into the crevices of the brush strokes. It gives the appearance of even more relief than it already has. That's what makes it lifelike." At least, that was the goal. Cloth in hand, she put a fist to her hip and stood back.

Marking her place in the book with her finger, Sylvie rose and circled around to face the portrait.

"It's no Rembrandt," Meg said.

Sylvie cocked her head to one side. "You're right. This is a Meg Townsend original."

"Very clever."

"I mean it, Meg. It's not the same style you used to have, but it's beautiful in its own way. It's softer. And the farther away you stand from it . . ." She backed up several paces.

"The better it looks?" Meg laughed, but the comment stung, for there was truth in it. The lines were not as precise, nor the details as fine. If time and money were not issues, she would spend months practicing before showing anything to Mr. VanDyke. But she couldn't afford to take that long. She'd have to expose her art, and herself, for what she was and wasn't. "Maybe I can get Mr. VanDyke to view it from across the street before he makes his decision."

While Sylvie tried to rephrase what she was trying to say, Meg accidentally dropped the cloth she'd been holding. Kneeling, she quickly rubbed away the black smudge it left on the wooden floor.

The sun glinted on a sliver wedged between two floorboards. She traced the spot with her fingertip but couldn't sense from the touch what it was. "Sylvie, look at this. Can you get it out?"

Sylvie knelt. When she failed to dislodge the shining item with her fingernail, she pulled a pin from her hair and used it as a lever. A coin popped out of the crevice and rolled across the floor. She held it up, rubbing its embossed surface with her thumb. "It's gold. But—read this."

Meg squinted at the curving text on the back of the coin. *Confederate States of America*. She felt the color drain from her face as the story Elton Burke had told her at the Soldiers' Home came rushing back to her. Had Hiram's patriotism, and his friendship with her father, truly pushed him to cross a moral line?

"Why would Hiram have Confederate gold?" Sylvie asked.

"I don't know," Meg whispered. "All I can tell you is what his fellow prison guard told me. It was only a rumor, with no proof at all, so I didn't believe it then. I don't know if I can bring myself to believe it even now. But Mr. Burke said Hiram stole from the prisoners at Camp Douglas."

Ridges pleated Sylvie's brow. "That doesn't make sense. Besides the fact that Hiram wouldn't do something that low, he had no need for more wealth. Jasper might know how to interpret this."

Meg considered it. "Do you really think we should tell him? How would it help for him to hear the slander against his uncle?"

"You don't need to tell him anything. Just give him what we found. It all belongs to him now, anyway."

Jasper was in the library when they found him, going through more books on the shelves.

It was Sylvie who approached him. "We found this between two floorboards in the turret room." She dropped the gold into his palm.

His face blanched as he examined it, but when he spoke, his voice was steady. "Confederate gold. It must have come from someone at Camp Douglas. I suppose it belongs in a museum now." He rubbed it between his fingers and looked from Meg to Sylvie. "I don't know how my uncle came by it. Was it a bribe paid for extra wood, or medicine, or food? Was it given freely as a token of gratitude for some secret kindness? Or did he steal it?"

Sylvie shook her head. "We'll never know. But it's all right, Jasper. We don't need to. We remember Hiram for the good man he was."

Slowly, Jasper nodded. "I'll see that this gets to the Chicago Historical Society, so long as I can be sure my uncle's name won't be attached to it. But as we have nothing but speculation as to its origin, the less said about this, the better."

Meg fully agreed.

Chapter Twenty-Five

Friday, November 17, 1871

Clouds moved in off the lake and hovered over Chicago, blotting the blue from the sky. In the burned district, wind stirred dust into the air and whipped the skirts around Meg's legs. Nearly six weeks had passed since the fire, and there was still a brisk trade in fire relics, judging by the customers at a table where the sidewalk used to be. Smiling, she and Sylvie waved at the enterprising brothers Louis and Lorenzo Garibaldi while winding around the cellar of their old bookshop. Those who had once camped here were gone, presumably finding shelter in the barracks in the North Division for the winter. Behind the little house, close to the alley no longer fenced, an outhouse leaned slightly in the wind. Stifling a shudder, Meg fit the key into the lock of the small house and entered the dwelling she and Sylvie would learn to call home.

Nate came in behind them and set down their belongings before closing the door. Already a fine layer of dust and sand had crept beneath it and coated the planed wood floor. Natural light struggled through bare windows, illuminating the hard corners of the space. Meg had known the building would have two rooms, the first measuring twelve by sixteen feet, and the second, eight by sixteen. But somehow she wasn't prepared for how close it would feel, especially when considering adding paints and books.

Sylvie's boots clicked across the floor as she went to peer out the window. "We can track the progress on rebuilding the courthouse from here," she said.

"Yes, and you'll hear it too." Nate rapped two knuckles on the wall. "I wager you'll hear most everything."

Meg smiled. "Then at least we'll know we're not alone." As if on cue, Louis shouted about his fire relics with a volume barely muted by the walls that stood between them.

Crossing her arms, Sylvie rubbed her hands over her sleeves and surveyed the two rooms from the doorway between them, her lips a thin hard line. There was one stove in the main room, along with a table and two crude benches tucked beneath it. A shelf held crockery, a skillet, one pan for the oven, a teakettle, and an earthenware pitcher. The bedroom in the back had a mattress layered with sheets, two army blankets, and a quilt. No doubt they would drag all of that into the main room to sleep near the fire at night. Still, they were dry and protected from the wind. There was no gas lighting and no indoor plumbing, of course. They'd need to carry water from the artesian well on Court House Square across the street. Everything smelled of new wood and sawdust. Though Meg wouldn't admit it aloud, now she understood why some people called these shanty houses.

"At least we know we're safe. No one will break in to steal anything here." She removed her hat and cloak, draping them over a chair. Though it was cold enough to leave both on, she meant to show that she would stay and settle in here. This would be her home. For now.

With a light squeeze to her shoulder, Nate brushed past her and built a fire in the stove. Then he moved to the table and ran a flat palm across the surface. He winced. "Watch out for splinters," he said. "I'll come back tomorrow with sandpaper."

"You don't have to do that." Meg held her hands close to the stove. They tingled as they warmed. "I'm sure I can borrow some from any number of folks around here."

Nate pushed up his glasses. "I know I don't have to. But you wouldn't turn me away if I showed up with the right tool in the evening, would you? Possibly some pegs to hold your coats?"

"No." She smiled at him. "I wouldn't turn you away."

A bench scraped the floor as Sylvie pulled it out from beneath the table. Still in her cloak, she sat. "This is temporary," she said. "But do we have any idea *how* temporary? How soon can we start building our permanent residence?"

Rubbing a hand over his jaw, Nate sat across from her. "You have a few things to consider, and I advise you to think carefully about each option. Assuming you have the funds to begin construction at any time, you could do so. But—"

A sharp knock on the door cut him short.

"Miss Townsend? Miss Townsend?" a familiar voice called from the other side.

Meg left the warmth of the stove to open the door. A gust of wind blew sand over the threshold. "Mr. and Mrs. Hoffman!" she cried.

A smile wreathed the baker's face as he held out a plate of huge soft pretzels studded with coarse salt. Beside him, his wife, Anna, held a basket whose twisted handle resembled the braid of pale blond hair crowning her head. Meg didn't know them very well, but when Anna reached for her with one arm, she gladly sank into an embrace that smelled of yeast and sugar.

"Won't you come in?" Meg stood aside, and they entered, followed by a quick round of introductions with Nate. Anna wrapped an arm around Sylvie too, kissing her cheek. The warm aroma of the pretzels quickly filled the small space.

After Meg took their hats, Anna gave her a knowing look, one that said she'd seen Meg's scars. "Are you all right?" she asked in a low voice thick with concern.

Eyes misting, Meg swallowed. "I will be."

Karl quietly watched this exchange, then nodded as if to put an end to it. "For you and your sister." He laid the plate on the table. "Mrs. Hoffman and I, we see your house being built, we knew you two were coming back. We want to say it will be nice to have you for neighbors again."

"Look, here, you will need these things." Her cheeks flushed red with the cold, Anna peeled away a linen towel and withdrew items from her basket. "Candles, matches, wool stockings. Towels and soap. Curtains to cover your windows. And you must have coffee. It cannot be a home without coffee, *ja*?" She opened a small tin canister, releasing the scent of pre-ground coffee beans.

Sylvie inhaled appreciatively. "It grows more like a home the longer you're here."

Unfurling the yellow-and-white plaid curtains, Anna beamed. "These will add some cheer. See the loops at the top? Fit them over the rods already built above the windows. You girls need anything, you come find us. Just watch your step along the way!"

"We were on the same block before." Karl pinched the lapels of his coat. "Now we will be true neighbors. Ja? Your *vater*, Stephen. How is he?" Furrows grooved his brow.

Surprised by the sudden shift in conversation, Meg stumbled to find a response. The truth was, she had no idea how her father was.

"He's in a doctor's care," Sylvie replied. "That's all we really know."

Karl's chin bobbed. "He did his best, the night of the fire. You should know that. He did his best. I was sorry I lost track of him after we finally found wheels to carry our things."

"Were you able to secure some of your property on the trains, sir?" Nate asked.

Gravely, Karl nodded. "The equipment I could move, I did. The aid society has replaced my ovens to help me get back in the trade. And you? What did you save?"

"Very little." Sylvie unbuttoned her coat now that the room was heating, and hung two curtain panels on the window in the front room. Her expression softened as she arranged the sunshine-colored fabric. "But we intend to open to our customers soon, all the same. We'll purchase some titles to carry in stock, but people can place orders with us, and we'll get them what they want."

"We couldn't save our books." Wide-eyed, Anna turned a pointed look to Karl. "I would very much like to have something to read."

"And so you shall," Karl boomed, his voice brimming with good humor. "You need to settle in tonight, but soon, very soon, we would be honored to count ourselves among your first customers after the fire."

Meg smiled as she watched Sylvie light up.

Nate clapped Karl on the back and shook his hand. "The Townsends are fortunate indeed to have neighbors like you."

"Come, husband," Anna said, "let us leave before we overstay ourselves."

They walked the Hoffmans back outside, where Meg thanked Anna again for all the gifts. As Nate asked Karl what his rebuilding strategy was, movement caught Meg's eye from down the street.

A newly built two-story brick building teetered in a strong gust of wind. Meg covered her mouth as she watched it tip, then lean, and finally collapse with a crash. Clouds of dust billowed up from the impact.

Meg hoped it wouldn't trigger another episode similar to what Sylvie had experienced during the concert. "Are you all right?" she asked her sister.

A hand pressed to her bodice, Sylvie nodded.

"Ach," Karl said. "You must get used to the sound of falling buildings, and remember to steer clear of new construction." With that, the Hoffmans bade them goodnight.

Back inside the little house, Meg struck a match on the stovetop and lit one of the tapers the Hoffmans had brought. "You didn't seem at all surprised by that collapse, Nate. Tell me why, and I'll let you share a pretzel with me." She twisted the candle onto the candlestick's spike and moved it to the center of the table, then slid the Hoffmans' basket to the end.

Grinning, he sat beside her and tore a pretzel in half, and steam spiraled upward. Sylvie passed out three small plates of plain white crockery and sat across from Meg, helping herself to a pretzel with a contented sigh.

"Bricks need to be kept dry for a while after they've been formed," Nate began. "Without summer's hot and steady sun, they aren't. Even when they aren't being rained on, they aren't drying out all the way. Not only that, but brick walls set over time in the warmer months, becoming more stable as the mortar hardens. But now, the mortar is in danger of freezing when the temperatures dip low overnight. That building that just collapsed? I wager it was held together by little more than gravity and balance. I've seen four- and five-story buildings suffer the same fate from ordinary winds." He tore off a piece of pretzel and popped it into his mouth.

"So we wait," Sylvie said after swallowing her bite.

Nate shifted, and the bench creaked. "I won't tell you what to do, but I will tell you what I know. I've just come from the Common Council's special committee meeting, where they were considering fire safety regulations. They're proposing a virtual ban on wooden houses and very high standards for those made of brick."

"But people are already building wooden structures in the burned district," Sylvie said.

"Yes, and they're rushing to get them completed before the Council formalizes a ban. The regulations would be for new construction only. They wouldn't force anyone to tear down what's already built."

Meg savored the soft pretzel as she considered this. "Our shop was built of brick before. How high, exactly, would the new standards be?"

"By the terms of the proposal," he answered, "walls of one-story brick houses must be at least twelve inches thick, and taller homes must have even thicker walls in their lower stories. All roofs are to be made of metal, slate, terracotta, or another fireproof material."

"No more tarpaper roofs," Meg said.

"Exactly. And any cornices, coping, bay windows, or other projections must be similarly nonflammable."

Before the fire, most buildings had carved wood cornices and ornamentation painted to look like marble or stone. Banning wood like this would drive up the cost exponentially. But if it would be safer for the common good, perhaps it was worth the cost.

Still . . . "In that case, we would need all winter to save up for the new shop. Do you think the ordinance will pass?"

Finished with his share of the pretzel, Nate angled toward her. "It's already facing criticism. Working-class residents can't afford such buildings, and people in the real estate business say it will drive up prices. Believe me, strong opinions reigned during that committee meeting."

"I do believe you. But the question is, what are *we* going to do?" Sylvie crossed her arms on the table and stared at Meg.

"It's a big decision," Meg started. "One with lasting impact on the family and our business. If Father would only answer a single letter, I would write him and ask his opinion."

"Meg." Sylvie gave a dark laugh. "Even if he could respond, would you trust him to make the choice?"

Tucking her hands in her lap, Meg chafed beneath her sister's scrutiny. "Are you saying he shouldn't even be consulted?"

"He hasn't been the head of our household for years. He can scarcely handle his own future right now, let alone ours. We're on our own, Meg."

"If you ask me, I think she's right," Nate said quietly.

"Well, I didn't." Meg rubbed at the scars on her palms, instantly regretting her quick retort.

"All right," he replied. "Then let me do the asking. When your father went to war, what did you and your sister and mother do while he was gone?"

"We waited for him to return with hope and expectation and many, many prayers."

"And we carried on with our lives," Sylvie added. "We waited for his return while still making our own decisions. Father trusted us to do that."

"This is different," Meg countered.

With a frustrated huff, Sylvie slid off the bench and lit another taper. Scooping up the other set of Anna's curtains, she retreated to the back room with a book.

Meg braced herself for Nate to tell her that she was wrong and foolish. That Sylvie was the sensible one.

Instead, he swung one leg over the bench to straddle it and

face her. When he reached for her right hand under the table, she flinched. He didn't. He hadn't the first time she'd let him see it either. She'd been more anxious about his reaction than anyone else's, for she couldn't bear the idea of Nate recoiling. Butterflies had filled her stomach until he came to Edith's house for a visit, and with a look, a smile, a touch, had calmed her clamoring nerves. *"Do I repulse you?"* she had asked. *"On the contrary,"* was all he'd said before his nephew began climbing up his leg.

Now, cradling the back of her right hand in both of his, he used his thumbs to massage her palm in circles, using more pressure than she would have. She winced at the darts of pain as the scar tissue yielded and broke under his touch.

Outside the thin walls of the house, they could hear people leaving the work site across the street in Court House Square, voices volleying over crunching, heavy footsteps. Somewhere on the block, a woman scolded someone for smelling of liquor.

Nate lifted his gaze to meet Meg's. The reflection of candlelight bobbed on his glasses. "What are you afraid of?" he asked.

"I forget you ask questions for a living," she said, hoping to lighten the solemnity in his expression.

"Don't do that. Don't pretend I'm asking because it's what I do. I'm asking because I care, and because you need to hear your own answer."

She looked away, and he shifted to massage her other hand, probing the toughness to soften it. "I'm afraid we're learning how to live without Father, not just because we must, but because it's easier. A relief, even. I'm afraid we're moving on without him." She paused, collecting her thoughts into a pattern she could understand. "It feels like we're betraying him—the man he used to be, the man he is now, and the man he can become. That's what I'm afraid of. I'm afraid we're getting so comfortable living without him that we won't want to bring him back. We could leave him there in the asylum for the rest of his life. But would that be for his sake, or for ours?"

Slowly, Nate nodded. He was touching bruises and scars inside and out as he massaged her fingers one by one, pinching and rolling the webbed tissue between them. The rhythm and motion would have been hypnotic if it didn't hurt. He was pushing her in more ways than one, and it wasn't comfortable. But then, it wasn't meant to be.

"What else?" he asked.

She shook her head. "Isn't that enough? It's everything."

He clasped her hands, shaping his to fit hers. "Talk to Sylvie about it. Your father would want you to make decisions based on the information you have. That's not a betrayal, Meg. You're doing the best you can."

She wasn't convinced. "I'm writing to him, but I'm not getting any replies. I don't even know if he's getting the letters. I don't want him to think we've forgotten him or given up on him. I still believe he can get better and come home to us."

"He may get better, and he may come home. But if you're hoping for the father he used to be, you'll forever be disappointed. He's marked by his scars as surely as you are by yours."

She tried to jerk away, but he held her fast.

"Meg, you are lovelier now than you ever were. Your refinement comes not from charm school or polite society, but from coming through the fire. You and your father and Sylvie—all of us—we can never be who we once were, because we keep changing and growing. We're not defined by our hurts, but by God's grace we can overcome them. We are transformed. So if I were you, I would not pray for the father you knew, but for your father *made* new, not in spite of the scars but because of them."

He turned over her hands and pressed a kiss to each palm.

Heat flashed through her as she closed her fingers over the faint trace of warmth left by his lips. Her skin didn't feel sensation as keenly as it had before the fire, but what she felt now wasn't limited by her scars. It was a crossing over a threshold, from the world she knew to one unknown to her. She felt as unsteady in her footing as if she were wading through the ruins to reach the other side.

Perhaps she was. Perhaps they both were.

A lump shifted in Nate's throat. With a tentative smile, he cupped the side of Meg's face in his hand for the briefest of moments. "I should go." A hint of color tinged his cheekbones. Rising, he tapped the basket from the Hoffmans. "It appears you have everything you need to get settled. I'm glad you and Sylvie won't be alone here."

Tugging on his cap, he called good-bye to Sylvie before nodding to Meg and leaving. A gust of cold air took his place.

Sleep did not come swiftly for Meg, huddled beneath army blankets on the mattress on the floor. The fire in the stove hummed beneath the wind that wrapped around the house. Without trees and with far fewer buildings to break the currents of air, gusts swept through the neighborhood as they might on the prairie. The sound was forceful and moaning, an echo of Meg's wrestling with unnamed longings.

She was homesick for the life she'd lived on this corner before the fire. It wasn't just things that she missed, but the security and peace she'd taken for granted. When they'd stayed at Jasper's house and with Edith's family, it was far easier to ignore the devastation in the city. Now she was right in the heart of it. And she had literally made her bed above her father's rendering of the place that had broken his spirit. Sleeping here would take some getting used to.

Meg ached for her father, but she missed her mother tonight. She would have loved for her to meet Nate, the story-hunter who became a friend and might become something more. Pulling the blanket beneath her chin, she wondered if he was awake and if he was thinking of her too.

Dust blew in through a chink between the wooden planks, spraying across Meg's face and igniting all her senses. Heart pounding, she forsook the warmth of the bedding to rummage for a stocking or towel to wedge in the crack, and wondered if the feel of dust on her skin would forever remind her of that terrible night when she had been nearly blinded by dust and chased by fire. Brushing a hand over her face and hair, she crawled back under the covers.

"Thank you," Sylvie whispered.

"You're welcome." Such small words to fill the distance between them. Meg hated that the gap had widened since Nate had come and gone. "Can't sleep either?"

Before retiring to bed, Meg had conceded that they would make their decisions about rebuilding without consulting Stephen, and Sylvie had agreed to the courtesy of informing him of their rationale along the way. But there was more to say tonight than that.

Sylvie rolled onto her side and exhaled. "Nate's a good man."

Meg turned, eyeing her silhouette. Her form was a darker shade of the rest of the room, her expression fully cloaked in shadow. "Yes, he is."

"I overheard what he said to you. I didn't mean to, but I did. He was right, you know."

"About what?"

"About you, about Father. About being refined and praying for Father to be made new. I think we might pray that all of us are made new. I understand Father so much more now that I don't understand myself." She chuckled. "Do you know what I mean?"

Meg stared at the faint orange glow cast by the stove. "You're referring to your reaction at the concert?"

"And more. You know about the nightmares, but sometimes my daydreams seem even more real than my hand in front of my face. I can't stop my heart from pounding so hard that I feel it will bruise my chest. And I was angry, so angry with that soprano from Boston. I scarcely recognized myself." She paused and steadied her breathing. Wind lashed at the house, and wood creaked in protest. "But, Meg, I don't think I'm insane."

"Of course you're not. I never would have suggested such a thing."

"But I did. Don't you see? I didn't understand what I saw in Father, and I called it insanity."

Meg held her tongue, afraid to interrupt. When the silence stretched out too long, she quietly asked, "And now?"

"Now I think about how long we were in danger—it was less than two days—and I consider how difficult it is for me to get past it. Then I consider how long Father was at war, first fighting, and then at Andersonville for two years. No wonder he was so affected!" Sylvie's voice grew brittle. "I judged him for it. My pity and compassion ran out long ago, but my supply of resentment and shame seems limitless."

"I've had my share of resentment too, Sylvie," Meg whispered. "Perhaps the difference is that I haven't been as honest about it, turning instead to art to make me feel better."

Sylvie sniffed and drew a deep breath. "You could have turned to me."

Meg reached beneath the covers and grasped her sister's hand. "I'm sorry. You're right."

"And now you will turn to Nate. Not that I blame you, Meg, for he really is a good man."

Meg squeezed her hand. "He is. But you make it sound as though he's declared some intention with me, and he hasn't."

"Not with words, perhaps."

"Oh, fiddlesticks." Meg rolled onto her side, laughing.

But after she and Sylvie prayed together for Stephen and themselves to be made new, she closed her eyes and felt Nate's hand warm against her face.

Chapter Twenty-Six

Saturday, November 18, 1871

There was no reason for Sylvie to stay in the shanty alone all day while Meg was sketching and painting Jasper. So she curled up in a wingback chair in the turret room with them, Oliver on her lap. She peered at Jasper over the top of *Villette*, whose pages she hadn't turned in quite some time.

He didn't look at her.

He certainly didn't look at her the way Nate had looked at Meg last night. The shanty was too small for Sylvie to miss it. What he'd said to Meg was both wise and compassionate. But paired with his kiss to her hands, the moment was utterly romantic.

And jarring, at least to Sylvie. She'd slept little last night, realizing that perhaps Meg would not be a spinster all her life. For years they had foregone courtship, and they had done it together. But now Meg and Nate were forging an attachment that went beyond friendship.

Swallowing a sigh, Sylvie stroked the cat's fur, mindful of his sensitive bald spots, and was rewarded with a contented purring in sharp contrast to her state of mind. Someday Meg very well might marry, even if it wasn't to Nate. She would leave Sylvie—as Ruth had, as Stephen had. Would it be so awful a life to be surrounded by books and readers all day, and to have the evenings for her own leisure, to escape into the literature of her choosing?

She stole another glance at Jasper. Then, chasing her longings away, she turned a page and stared at words without reading them.

"Right now I'm roughing in the outline of your head and hair and your shoulders." Meg stood behind the easel, sketching charcoal lines on the canvas. "So it's fine for us to talk. I've never asked you what made you want to pursue a law degree. What was it?"

Jasper licked his lips and cleared his throat, prompting Sylvie to set aside her book and the cat and pour him a cup of tea. Her skirts swished as she brought it to him. He thanked her without meeting her gaze. He must be concentrating.

Sylvie returned to the wingback chair and moved Oliver to reclaim her space.

"Well, I told Sylvie that I grew up without many educational opportunities. I read as much as I could, but that wasn't much," he said.

"Ah. Like Lincoln," Meg suggested.

"Not like Lincoln." Jasper responded sharply, then sipped the bergamot tea. "I'm far less like Lincoln than you might want to believe."

"Oh?" Meg glided to the window, adjusting the shade to control the light before returning to the easel.

He stared into his cup. "I've no taste for politics. But I do have a taste for justice. That's why I want to practice law. To be a voice for those who cannot defend themselves." His tone was edged with conviction.

Sylvie tilted her head, considering this. "Were you once in need of such a voice, Jasper? Or was there someone you loved who couldn't defend himself?"

He snapped his attention to her as if only now realizing she was in the room. He set the teacup back on its saucer and balanced it on his knee.

"You were wronged somehow," Meg said quietly. "It marked you. It changed your path. Am I right?"

He blinked and forced a stiff smile. "I was wronged. I needed a voice and didn't have one. I couldn't defend myself."

Sylvie's heartbeat tripped over itself in sympathy. She wanted to hear more. She wanted to know everything about him.

"I don't like to talk about that, though," he admitted. "If you don't mind."

"Of course." Meg rubbed out a line and redrew it. A few quiet moments passed before she spoke again. "Did you take the gold coin to the historical society yet?"

Shifting on his chair, Jasper sat a little straighter. "I haven't made the time to hunt down their new location. Nate could probably tell me where they've set up quarters since the fire." He sipped his tea, but not much of it. Sylvie ought to have brought him coffee instead.

Meg smiled, then squinted at his ear as she drew it. "I bet he could. Otherwise, you could talk to the staff at the Soldiers' Home. They moved into a new building in Evanston in February, but until then they were right on the edge of the old Camp Douglas property, so they might have a collection of things related to it. Most of it would pertain to the training section, I'd imagine, but you never know. They might be interested in the prison camp part of it too."

His teacup clinked on its saucer. "Perhaps."

An almost imperceptible change flickered over his expression. If Sylvie hadn't been watching him so closely, she would have missed it. He didn't like talking about this either. Thankfully, Meg seemed to have dropped the subject.

Sylvie crossed her legs, shifting the book, and something fell out from between the pages. She picked it up from the floor and laid it in the book. It was a carte de visite, a small photograph of a soldier in Union uniform. The sides had been trimmed a little, as though to fit into a frame. Written on the back in Hiram's hand were the words, *The likeness of Jasper. Taken March 1865.* She turned it again and studied the face, looking up at Jasper in wonder. Yes, it was him. He must have been nineteen years old at the time, two years younger than Sylvie was now. He was much thinner then, his cheekbones sharp blades beneath his skin. But his curly hair and the thin scar on his brow were clearly recognizable.

She wondered why his photograph had been taken so late in the war, when most soldiers had theirs taken upon enlistment. Perhaps, given his humble roots, he hadn't been willing to pay for it until later. He was likely the type who sent home every dollar he could. She slid the photograph back into the novel and closed the book, setting it aside.

"Tell us about where you grew up," Sylvie suggested, thinking to move away from the subject of war.

Stuck in Meg's pose for him, Jasper replied without turning to address her. "It was no place you've heard of, I'm sure. It was a hardworking community, though, where neighbors helped in time of need, and family was more important than anything. Kids worked alongside their parents as soon as they were old enough to begin learning."

"Was your family musical? Did you sing while you worked, or when you went to bed at night?" Sylvie prompted. "What about this one? 'I'm just a poor wayfaring stranger,'" she sang to the tune he'd sung when he was sick. "'A traveler through this world of woe—'"

Jasper stood, upsetting his teacup and spilling it all over the floor as he spun to face her. "What are you doing?" His eyes pierced hers. "Why are you singing that song?"

Sylvie's heart plummeted to her stomach, aware she had done something wrong but not sure what. She reached for Oliver, wedged beside her, and buried her fingers in his fur.

"Tell me," he demanded.

"It—it's the song you asked me to sing to you when you were sick," she told him, refusing to be afraid of his mercurial mood. "You taught it to me, or tried to. The first verse and chorus, I think. I thought you liked it."

Making no move to clean up the spill, Meg's gaze swiveled between Sylvie and Jasper.

"When I was sick? With the water illness?" He blinked rapidly. "You were there?"

"Just one night. I'd recovered, and you were so ill. Helene had fallen asleep at Meg's bedside, and Kirstin was still recovering herself. You needed help, and I gladly gave it." She was furious at the emotion thickening her voice.

"And I sang that song?"

Sylvie nodded. "Yes."

"I don't remember that. I don't remember you being there at all."

Disappointment splashed over her. "But you—" She recovered before making an even bigger fool of herself. When he'd kissed her fingertips, he'd thought her someone else. His mother, perhaps. Or a lost love he'd never forgotten. Tears bit the backs of her eyes. "You needed help."

"What else did I say that night?" He approached her.

Meg hastened to his side, clearly at a loss for what to do or say. "Does it matter, Jasper? We were all so ill."

"It matters to me. What else?" He knelt before Sylvie.

She could barely think with him so near, staring at her that way. There was no love or compassion in his eyes. Instead she saw fear, hurt, and anger.

"I let you live in my house, Sylvie, for four weeks. The least you can do is answer a question when I ask it."

"You said you were cold!" she spat. "You said you were cold, and I piled blankets on top of you and stoked the fire through the night to keep you warm." If he was this agitated already, she knew better than to mention that she'd seen that he was missing toes as well.

"Nothing else?"

"You don't remember. Why should I? And why are you so angry with me?" Inwardly, she chided herself for sounding so childish.

Jasper bowed his head, and his curls brushed her knee. "I'm sorry. Forgive me, Sylvie. Meg." He rose. "I think that's enough for one day. Shall we try again tomorrow?" He stalked out without waiting for an answer.

Meg lowered her voice. "I didn't know you tended Jasper when I was still sick."

"It didn't seem important to tell you."

"Well. You certainly touched a raw nerve. I'd love to know why and how, but I suppose it's none of our business." After a brief squeeze to Sylvie's shoulder, Meg went to mop up the spilled tea.

Composing herself, Sylvie picked up the china and took it down to the kitchen.

But when they left the house that afternoon, she took the book. And the cat.

MONDAY, NOVEMBER 20, 1871

"Come on, Gruber. You're new, but not that new." Nate handed the wrong file folder back to the police station clerk and asked again for the correct one. The stale-smelling lobby behind him was thick with bodies and complaints, as usual. Nate loosened his tie while he waited.

At last Gruber returned with the police reports Nate was after for his current assignment. He was covering the influx of men from out east, all allegedly looking for construction jobs, and the effect the extra population was having on public safety when the police were already overtaxed. The story was all but finished, but Nate needed to double-check the statistics he'd used from the police reports. One wrong digit would paint a completely different picture.

"Thanks." Satisfied, Nate slid the folder of reports back across the counter while Gruber brushed a crumb from his chin. He was ready to file the story and move on to something new.

Turning, he threaded between officers and citizens waiting in the lobby until a familiar voice stopped him.

He frowned. "Jasper?" Adjusting his satchel's strap on his shoulder, Nate approached him.

"Nate!" Jasper paused his conversation with an officer to shake his hand. "What brings you here?"

Nate told him and asked him the same question.

"I came as soon as O'Hara arrived at my house to tell me the good news. They've apprehended Otto Schneider. I had to come down and see him for myself before I could believe it."

Nate's eyebrows vaulted as he swung his gaze to Officer O'Hara. From what Meg had told him, this was one of the policemen who'd arrested Stephen. "Really? Where did you find him?"

O'Hara rocked back on his heels. "Hiding out in one of the barracks in the North Division. Well, no. At the time of the arrest, he wasn't hiding. He was drunk and disturbing the peace outside a German beer hall. Gave himself away by causing such a commotion, he did."

"So he's in holding now," Nate prompted. "Here?"

"Not only that," Jasper answered. "They found the silver candlesticks and my uncle's gold cuff links under his bunk. He's given a full confession. At least he had the sense to recognize it was futile to do anything else." His last words were all but lost to the clamor of a train on the nearby tracks.

Nate leaned in to be heard. "When you say a full confession, are you referring to the break-in of your house and the theft? Or . . ."

Jasper clapped him on the back. "To everything. To murder. He signed a confession saying that he murdered Uncle Hiram after he was released from jail the night of the fire."

Breath stalled in Nate's lungs as he took this in. "Which means you can now exonerate Stephen Townsend." He turned a sharp gaze on O'Hara.

Shrugging, the officer took a sip from a mug, then wiped his mouth with the back of his hand. "The murder charge will be thrown out, sure. But this doesn't mean he's exonerated from insanity."

Running a finger along the inside of his collar, Nate chafed at the implication that mental instability was a crime one could be found guilty of, like any willful wrongdoing. Or perhaps the discomfort came from the truth behind O'Hara's statement. One didn't have to be a murderer to be held at the asylum.

Still, congratulations for Jasper were in order.

"I know it doesn't bring your uncle back, but it must feel good to have some closure on the matter," Nate told him quietly, now that the train had passed.

"I'll feel better once Schneider's in prison and not just in holding, but yes. It's a major victory." Jasper glanced at the clock on the wall. "I'd best be off. Meg is coming to the house at two. Glad to see you, Nate. Take care of yourself." He tipped his hat and left, allowing a cold draft to sweep into the station.

Nate watched his retreating form, wishing he was the one meeting Meg in half an hour. He'd gone back to her shanty house with sandpaper, as he'd said he would, but other than grinding off the splinters and rough edges of the furniture, he hadn't known how to behave. Had he gone too far when he'd kissed her hands? She'd blushed scarlet to her hairline. Perhaps he'd broken a boundary she'd never meant for him to cross. But the way she looked at him was not like a woman who'd been offended.

"You're blocking the way. Do you mind?"

Stepping toward the wall, Nate set thoughts of Meg aside to revisit the conversation he'd had with Jasper. *Full confession. A full confession. Schneider signed a confession to everything.*

That hadn't taken long.

He looked around. O'Hara had gone while Nate was woolgathering, but another officer stood at the counter, filling out a form. Nate recognized him.

"McNab," he called. "You done with your paperwork yet?"

It took only a little persuasion on Nate's part before McNab agreed to his request. It was straightforward, really, and hardly uncommon for a reporter. He simply wanted to talk to Schneider before they moved him anywhere else. He would get a quote from the accused, from the officers in charge, and write a story from there. Medill had told Nate not to spend time investigating a closed case, but now that Schneider had confessed, he might as well be the one to break the news. He was in the right place at the right time, after all.

The holding cell had no bars in this temporary location. It was simply a room on the other side of a locked door. A small window cut out of the door was insufficient for Nate's purpose. "Let me in," he told McNab.

The officer frowned. "You sure about that? He's a confessed murderer."

"Without a weapon or a reason to kill me. Put me in. I can't talk to him through a door."

Uncertainty slanted across the young officer's features, but he unlocked the door. "Five minutes."

Nate stepped through. The door clicked back into place behind him, echoing in the bare chamber. He waited until his eyes adjusted to the shadows. The room had but one small window to the outside, and it was streaked with grime.

A cot squeaked as Otto Schneider sat up. Whiskers stubbled his jawline. His thin shoulders failed to fill the breadth of his garment, but his rounded stomach strained the fabric. "Who are you?" His voice sounded garbled.

"Nathaniel Pierce, *Chicago Tribune*." Nate plucked the pencil from behind his ear and pulled a pad of foolscap from his satchel. "I'm here to ask you a few questions."

Schneider made no response. A bruise purpled one eye, but his gaze was dull, not defiant. It was the look of a broken man, one who had nothing left to lose.

Spying a three-legged stool in the corner, Nate pulled it closer to the cot and sat. The bedding—or the man upon it—smelled stale and unwashed. "I hear you signed a confession. Care to tell me what was in it?"

"Can't you read it?" Schneider stared at the broken seam around his shoe where the leather peeled away from the sole.

"I'd much rather hear what happened from your own lips. Your own voice."

A throaty chuckle gurgled within Schneider. "You think I have a voice? Not a chance."

Nate's pencil hovered over the pad. "You mean you haven't seen a lawyer yet? You have a right to one. He'll be your voice, if that's what you mean."

The slight curl of Schneider's lips suggested it wasn't. "Sure, that's what I mean. You want to hear me talk? All right. I did it all. I killed the old man. I hid and waited for the house to not be guarded, then I broke into it and I stole what I could before the watchman scared me off. Oh, there was a man I knocked on the head too, wasn't there? Yes, I beat a man unconscious so I could get to stealin'. After that I waited for things to cool down a bit, but I was planning to go back again. There's a lot in Hiram's house worth having, that's for sure. There, now." He cocked his head. "Happy?"

Odd. There was no justification, no veiled attempt to garner pity. "But why did you kill Hiram Sloane the night of the fire when you could have been running for your life?" Nate asked.

"Revenge. It was a golden opportunity."

Nate waited to see if Schneider would elaborate. Seconds ticked by, and still he didn't. "What did you steal, and what would you have taken if you'd gotten back inside?"

"Silver candlesticks, silverware, gold cuff links." He recited these items as if he were reading from a market list. "You want to know what I would take if I went back? What kind of question is that? Have you not enough charges against me for the crimes I've actually committed?" He shook his head. "'Spose it doesn't matter anyway. I'm going to be in prison for the rest of my days as it is. But then, that's no big surprise. I've been in and out of jail for years."

"For petty theft," Nate remarked. "Vagrancy and public drunkenness." Never before for violent crimes or murder.

"I did what I had to do for my family." A fire lit behind Schneider's eyes where only embers had been before. "You think it's been easy for my wife and children? I lost everything in the bankruptcy. Couldn't keep a steady job, had to slug it out at the docks in the morning to see if I could get hired on for a day at a time. That's no way to raise a family. My wife and kids deserved more than that. More than me. And who did Hiram Sloane have to provide for, other than himself? No one. Not a single soul that I could tell." The cords of his neck stood out.

"No one?"

"Well. Except the nephew." Schneider gestured toward the door, then slapped his knee. "That's not the same."

"You've met him?"

A nod. "He wanted to meet me, same as you. Which is ironic, since my own son doesn't care to be seen with me. The girls are more forgiving, but my boy says he's known me too long for that. Can you believe that kind of talk coming from a kid of eleven years? But he's got more sense than I do, and a heap more luck. There may be hope for him yet."

"Did you write a threatening note to Hiram?" Nate asked, aware of the time slipping by.

"I wrote a lot of angry letters," Otto scoffed. "He cheated me."

Nate had figured as much. But then his thoughts followed a circuit back to Stephen's arrest. "Mr. Schneider, there were two witnesses in this case. One said he saw Stephen Townsend shoot Hiram Sloane, and the other said he saw Townsend bury the weapon. He was framed. Does your confession explain how you did that?"

Schneider scratched his belly. "People will say just about anything for money," he muttered.

But Schneider had just been released from jail the night of the murder. He couldn't have had much to offer. "You paid them first?"

He shrugged. "Told them I'd make it worth their while."

"So you didn't pay them on the spot. They agreed to lie to the police based on your promise to find them and pay them later?"

"That's what I said. Can I help it how desperate some folks are for easy money?"

Nate decided to try a different tack. "How were you acquainted with Stephen Townsend?" He'd been a perfect scapegoat for the murder. But how did Schneider know it? Even if he'd read Nate's article about Stephen in the *Tribune*, he wouldn't have known Stephen was friends with Hiram or how intense his paranoia could be.

"Time's up!" McNab opened the door. "That's it, Pierce, let's go."

Schneider glanced at the officer, then turned back to the wall as he lay down on the cot once more. Nate tucked his foolscap and pencil into the satchel and moved the stool back to its corner. As he left the room, Schneider mumbled to himself.

"I did what I had to do. For my family. Golden opportunity."

Chapter Twenty-Seven

Tuesday, November 21, 1871

Dear Father, we're coming to get you.

The thought had echoed through Meg's mind ever since Jasper had told her that Schneider confessed to Hiram's murder. But there had been no point in writing to Stephen when she could just as quickly deliver the message herself. This time, when Meg prepared to visit the asylum, Sylvie was ready to go with her. So was Nate.

After climbing out of the cab they'd hired, Nate handed Sylvie down and then Meg, whose hand he tucked firmly into the crook of his arm. Then he asked the driver to wait.

"Thank you for coming with us," Meg whispered as they approached the stone steps. Fog wreathed the brick fortress today.

Nate smiled. "I'd hate to think of you two coming here alone. As capable and intelligent as you are, you might not have a warm welcome. I'm happy to be your buffer."

Hugging the package she'd wrapped for Stephen with one arm, Sylvie lifted her skirts above her ankles and climbed the steps beside them. "Is that what you are? A buffer?"

Meg looked into Nate's blue eyes. "You're more than that, Nate."

His eyebrows lifted above the rims of his glasses. "Am I?" He winked and opened the massive wooden door, waiting for Meg and Sylvie to enter ahead of him.

Her heels clicking across the floor, Meg entered the reception room on the right and approached the counter.

Miss Dean looked over the top of her reading glasses and greeted Meg with a smile. Her mouse-brown hair was still bound in an ivory snood that matched her crocheted collar. "Miss Townsend. Mr. Pierce. I was wondering when I would see you again."

Briefly introducing Sylvie, Meg unwound the muffler from her neck. "We'd like to see Dr. Franklin, or whoever is in charge of discharging the patients. But first, we've brought something for our father, Stephen Townsend." In the likely scenario that their father would not come home today, they at least wanted him to have some things from home, including a copy of the *Tribune* with the story about Otto Schneider's confession to Hiram's murder. "Would you see that this gets to him?"

A troubled look creased Miss Dean's forehead. "Oh, I don't know. That's against regulation."

Sylvie placed the small bundle on the counter. "Please. There's nothing harmful here, only things that would surely help him. Wool socks, a newspaper, a book of poetry." Inside the book, they'd written notes to him between the sonnets. "Our father owned a bookstore. Surely you would allow us to give him something to read. Surely it isn't healthy for his mind to be unoccupied."

Miss Dean twisted a finger in the beaded chain attached to her glasses. "I'll see what I can do. Now, as for your appointment with Dr. Franklin, I wasn't aware of anything on his schedule today."

Nate rapped his knuckles on the counter. "Excellent. Then he can make time to see us. We'll wait if necessary, but we won't leave without speaking to a doctor. Thank you."

The receptionist sighed. "The three of you will need to find some seats and be patient."

"Of course." Nate smiled, and Meg watched it produce the desired disarming effect on Miss Dean. She plucked off her glasses, slid Sylvie's package into a drawer, and excused herself from the room.

Seated against the wall was the same elderly couple Meg had seen the last time she was here. The grey-haired woman knitted while the man beside her stared vacantly at the tops of his shoes. Meg ached with sympathy for them. When the woman met Meg's gaze and smiled warmly, Meg couldn't help but return it.

Meg sat down beside her. "Excuse me," she began. "You were here last time I came to visit my father's doctor, weren't you?"

"Why, yes, I'm sure I was. I'm here every day, you see. My daughter is somewhere up there." She lifted her gaze toward some hidden place.

"Do you get to see her?" Meg asked.

"Oh no. No, not unless it's warm enough for the patients to work outside. In that case, they sometimes let me see her through a window. But I find comfort in being beneath the same roof as her. I can't let her go, you see, even though she's fifty and I'm seventy-one. I'll never stop being her mother. At least this way we're not really apart, even though we aren't together." With a gentle nod, she resumed her knitting. "And if you don't mind my saying so, your father will never stop being your father either. That bond is for life, and beyond."

Though age and hardship had touched this woman, her kindness and love made her so beautiful to Meg that it nearly took her breath away. She wanted to paint her seamed face, to capture the bright flame of generous spirit in the midst of such a place.

"So where is he?" Sylvie murmured. She wandered from the reception room into the hall, looking toward the arch that divided the public rooms from the corridor that led to hidden places.

Meg excused herself and followed her sister. "Up there somewhere." She pointed to the ceiling. "That's the floor that holds the men. Women are on the upper floors."

The buttons of his frock coat unfastened, Nate hooked his thumbs into his trouser pockets and joined them.

"Do they ever go outside?" Sylvie asked.

"Sometimes." Nate cleared his throat. "There is a farm on the grounds behind the building. They use the patients to work it. But during the winter, no, they don't get out much."

Pounding sounded on the floor above them. A man screamed, and another shouted to drown him out, his chanted nursery rhyme growing frantic to cover the sound of another's despair.

A ridge between her eyes, Sylvie glided closer to the arch, staring up at the noise. A dull thump and a cry of pain silenced the screaming. The patient shouting "Humpty Dumpty" continued. "'*All the king's horses and all the king's men couldn't put Humpty together again!*' He sat on a wall! He had a great fall! They couldn't put him back together!"

Meg shuddered. "All things made new," she whispered in spontaneous prayer. "Dear Lord, make all of us new."

"Ah, Mr. Pierce? Misses Townsend?" Miss Dean's meek voice was soon overshadowed by a heavy tread.

Meg wheeled around to see Dr. Franklin approaching and Miss Dean ducking back into the reception room.

"You stay away from there." The doctor beckoned them away from the arch.

"Dr. Franklin. Good to see you again." Nate's voice bounced off the walls.

"I doubt that, but let's not waste time quibbling, shall we?" He jerked his head to indicate they should follow him into his office.

The room felt even smaller now that there were four of them. Even before the doctor claimed his chair, Meg began.

"My father, Stephen Townsend, is innocent of the crime charged to him, the murder of Hiram Sloane, that prompted his arrest and committal to the asylum. Another man confessed to it. You can read about it in this morning's *Tribune*."

A copy of the paper lay folded on his desk. He must have already seen it, for his expression bore no surprise. With a hooded gaze, Dr. Franklin stared at her. "And?"

"And so he doesn't need to be here," Sylvie replied. "The cause of his arrest is obsolete. We want to take him home."

"Just like that." The doctor snapped his fingers. "Without even asking about his treatments and progress."

"Would you tell us if we asked?" Meg gripped the ends of her muffler, burying her fists in the wool. Nate's presence was a quiet source of strength beside her. As he let her and Sylvie steer the conversation, she knew he was observing it all, digesting and dissecting, ready to step in.

A slow smile parted Dr. Franklin's chapped lips, revealing small, straight teeth. "I would tell you that he has responded to treatments the way we expected him to. I would also say that even if we were sure he was no longer a danger to society, removing him from our care makes him more of a danger to himself. He's at peace here. He's happy."

Meg scoffed. "Happy?"

"The pressures of the outside world are so many, and especially heavy for one burdened with soldier's heart. Here, there are no expectations upon him. We do not require him to do anything except eat and sleep and take his medications. He is free from the fear of failure, because there is nothing he can fail at."

"You mean there is nothing for him to do," Nate said. "He eats and sleeps and takes medicine? What kind of life is that?"

"A safe one, Mr. Pierce. And for a patient with soldier's heart, safety is a luxury he's rather fond of."

Memories reeled before Meg of her father pacing, patrolling, up at nights, completely convinced that Rebels were coming to kill him. "You mean he doesn't suffer paranoia about lurking danger anymore?"

The doctor spread his hands wide. "Even he can recognize the security of our facility. Not even his family can get in to see him."

"But we're no threat," Sylvie said.

He cocked his head. "Aren't you? Have you never demanded that he perform a task of which he was incapable? Have you never made him feel the weight of your disappointment in him? Your shame?"

Pink blotches crept up Sylvie's neck. Meg's fingers went cold even though they were wrapped in fabric.

"As I thought." Dr. Franklin smiled. "He is free from all of that here. He poses no threat, for he feels no threat."

Nate frowned. "You mean he feels nothing at all. How much opiates do you give him?"

Dr. Franklin stood. "Enough to do the job. He's learned to prefer them over the alternative."

A picture of her father filled Meg's mind. But he was neither the bookish, affectionate father of her childhood, nor the suspicious insomniac who could not let a stray animal go hungry. The vision she conjured instead was of a man slumped in a chair, unresponsive, a string of drool swaying from his mouth. Looking at Sylvie, she saw her horror reflected in her sister's dark eyes.

"The alternative," Nate repeated, a fire kindling in his voice. "An alternative method of keeping him subdued. Which is it, Franklin? A wooden crib or isolation?"

"The crib proved ineffective. Isolation, however . . . We learned to add a straitjacket to keep him from injuring himself. But like I said, 283 now takes his medicine."

Meg winced at the idea of a crib for a grown man. How wretched. How dehumanizing.

"What?" Sylvie whispered. "Stop this. Stop what you're doing. He's not a number, he's a person. He's my father." She was shaking.

"What you're telling us is that our father would rather feel nothing at all than feel alone." Meg's eyelids grew hot and sticky, and her voice faltered. Nate gently put his hand on the small of her back. Meg knew it was not a gesture to quiet her but to infuse her with strength she sorely needed. She drew a fortifying breath. "But he's never been more alone than he is here, even without solitary confinement. Discharge him."

"I can't do that. It isn't up to me alone."

Sylvie folded her arms. "Does he even get the letters we send?"

"Calm yourself, young lady. If I say he gets your letters, he gets them."

But Meg suspected her father was in no condition to read them. Not if he was drugged into oblivion. Hurt and frustration combusted into anger. She clenched her teeth, completely at a loss for a reply.

"This isn't a prison, Dr. Franklin, or at least it shouldn't be," Nate said. "Ironically, if it were, he'd be released. He's innocent of the crime that brought him here. You keep him at taxpayer expense against the wishes of his family. Might make for an interesting story on the use of public funds."

Dr. Franklin threw back his shoulders. "I told you, the decision isn't mine alone to make."

"Then whose is it?" Meg asked. "I want to talk to them."

"The committee includes several doctors and psychologists, and they are not available to you. Now, if you'll excuse me, there's nothing more I can do for you today."

"You can tell him we were here." Meg wrapped her muffler around her neck. "Tell him we want to bring him home and will do whatever it takes to make that happen. He needs to be with his family."

"Sometimes family doesn't know best." The doctor's tone was clipped and clinical.

She looked him square in the face, refusing to be cowed. "Sometimes family is the only thing worth living for. And what he's doing here isn't any kind of living at all."

Wednesday, November 22, 1871

Two slices of bread sagged on a tin plate black with filth. Poorly cooked hominy pooled beside it, soaking into the crust. But paired with the recent news that Otto Schneider had confessed to the murder of Hiram Sloane, Stephen felt like he could stomach it.

He hadn't done it. He hadn't killed his friend. It was right there in the newspaper for all to read: charges against Stephen Townsend had been dropped. Schneider remained in custody. Inwardly, Stephen celebrated this, even though the authorities still called him crazy. Not every battle was won—or even fought—at once.

Hugh elbowed Stephen in the ribs. "Look at that slop and tell me it doesn't take you back to a nobler time, eh?" His stutter hadn't faded, but it no longer fazed Stephen at all.

He watched the gruel's sickly spread and knew exactly what Hugh meant.

A tremor shook the Irishman, either from too much medicine or from being without it. It was hard to tell the difference. "At least during the war we were fighting for something. We were taking a stand." Hugh spooned the food into his mouth, just the same.

The windows were locked shut, and without a breath of fresh air, a foul smell permeated the room. It might have been the food. Or the men.

Sipping cold tea from a rusty tin cup, Stephen scanned the dining room. Fifty men hunched over their plates in rows on long narrow benches. A few of the men looked up at him, their expressions lucid. A man named Charlie, prone to seizures, sang to himself in the corner of the room. Henrik rocked back and forth on the floor, arms wrapped around his knees. In straitjackets, Patrick and Amos ate off their plates like dogs. Learning who they were had been an act of defiance and humanity for Stephen. If he didn't want to be known as a number, he ought to know their names too.

At Andersonville, he had organized an oratorical society among the prisoners to keep their minds sharp. In the last couple of weeks, he'd tried to rouse interest in such a group here too. Hugh wouldn't join, on account of the stutter, but a few other patients did. The mental exercise helped a little. It would have been better if more participated, but most were too mellowed out with medicine.

Perhaps that was how they preferred it.

Stifling a sigh, Stephen folded a piece of bread in half and sopped up the repulsive liquid in case there might be any nutrients hiding inside. As he muscled it down with a hard swallow, he fought the current of memory threatening to sweep him back to the war. "'Make not your thoughts your prison,'" he muttered to himself.

"What's that?" Hugh blinked at him. "Your thoughts a prison?"

"It's a line from Shakespeare's play *Antony and Cleopatra*. Caesar is speaking to Cleopatra, but I find the words a relevant reminder to myself."

Hugh scratched behind his ear. "'Tis a fancy line of thinking for a man supposed to be taking the drugs."

Instinctively, Stephen scanned the room for attendants, but none were present. They didn't eat here, but in a separate room, probably with better food. "I don't take the opiates. I tuck the pills in my cheek when I swallow, but I don't wash them down. I'll never go back to that drooling slow-witted version of myself again. But I do take the tincture at night that helps me sleep." He still had hallucinations, but not when he was sleeping.

A slow grin split Hugh's weathered face, revealing the loss of two more teeth to scurvy. "You mean the whiskey. You drink the whiskey they give you at night."

Stephen frowned. "It doesn't taste like whiskey."

"No, not like the good stuff. They've added powders to it. But the effect is the same, isn't it? It makes you feel better. Whiskey'll do that. Bet you'll never go without it again."

Cold expanded from the pit of Stephen's stomach. He didn't want to drink whiskey every night. He didn't want to form a dependence on it, or soon he'd be drinking more than a man should. But neither did he want to return to insomnia. Years of sleep deprivation had whittled away at him physically, mentally, emotionally. Now that he knew what solid sleep did for him, he couldn't bear the future without it.

"Me," Hugh was saying, "I'll never give up the whiskey or the opiates. I've gotten to where I can't stand to be without either one, you know?"

"You mean you're addicted?"

An exaggerated shrug yanked one shoulder toward Hugh's ear. "Don't mind if I am. As long as I stay here, they give me what I want."

"But that stuff changes us. You can't possibly feel like yourself that way."

Hugh's checkered smile turned wan. "My friend, that is entirely the point. You think I like who I am? You think anyone here likes who they are?"

Stephen dropped his spoon onto his plate. "I think you've forgotten who that is. How long have you been in the asylum, anyway?"

"I came right after Lincoln was shot."

That was more than six years ago. Six years! Stephen couldn't imagine passing such a vast amount of time in this place. Especially since Meg and Sylvie had delivered a taste of the outside world.

"You done eating yet, Hugh?"

The Irishman slanted his gaze. "Why do you ask?"

"Because I have something for you, and believe me, you won't want to put anything else in your mouth after this."

Hugh's eyebrows lifted. "I'm ready now, I am."

Stephen smiled as he pressed a peppermint candy into his friend's palm, then unwrapped one for himself and popped it into his mouth. Sylvie had added them to the package with a note: *Hope you still like these.* Of course he did. He'd forgotten how much.

The vibrant flavor sprang to life, refreshing his palate and clearing his mind. He used to keep peppermints in the pocket of his waistcoat when he ran the bookstore with Ruth. Whenever he'd held Sylvie on his lap, she'd sneak one out for herself. Any time he needed to approach a customer, he made sure to freshen his breath with a peppermint first. So the taste wasn't merely a pleasure for its own sake. It brought forth recollections from the happiest years of his life, when Ruth was still beside him. The girls paged through storybooks by the hearth. The smells of coffee and pastries from the neighboring merchants mingled with the smell of books. Oh, how he had loved those books, before the war stole his ability to concentrate.

Hugh groaned with pleasure. "Where on earth did you get it?"

"My daughters brought a package for me yesterday. Miss Dean snuck it in to me, but don't say anything about it. I'd hate for her to get in trouble."

"What else was in it?"

Stephen tucked the peppermint into his cheek. The most significant item was the newspaper with news of Schneider's confession, but he didn't want to talk about that right now. "Socks," he said instead, pulling up his trouser leg to show the thick grey wool on his feet. "And a volume of poetry by John Donne. He was—is—my favorite poet." When Hugh gave no sign of recognition, Stephen continued. "He was the dean of St. Paul's Cathedral in London in the 1600s. It was a tumultuous time for religion, and he was passionate about his faith." In fact, Donne's passion had both inspired Stephen when he was considering a future in theology and reminded him that faith was profoundly personal.

Hugh puckered his lips, sucking on the candy. "Did he write anything I might have heard? Give us a line."

This was unexpected. But the first stanza of one of the holy sonnets easily rolled off his tongue:

> "Batter my heart, three-person'd God, for you
> As yet but knock, breathe, shine, and seek to mend;
> That I may rise and stand, o'erthrow me, and bend
> Your force to break, blow, burn, and make me new."

He watched Hugh for his reaction.

Hugh's face was blank. "'Tis a pleasin' rhyme. I've no idea what it means."

Smiling, Stephen slipped into an older version of himself to explain the meaning of the written words. "The poet is asking God—the Trinity—to make him new using whatever force He needs to. He says that up until now, God's methods have been too gentle, but the transformation he needs is so complete, he needs more than that. 'Bend your force to break, blow, burn, and make me new.'"

That was exactly what Stephen needed. Perhaps it was what God was doing in him now, and he was only now seeing it.

"Do you believe that?" Hugh asked. "You believe that God could make you new?"

Stephen examined himself, for the question deserved an honest answer. "I do."

"Do you not blame Him for the ill that has befallen you, then? He could have prevented your trials. If He is all-powerful, and if He is good, He could have healed you before it ever came to this."

Hugh's remarks stayed with Stephen far longer than the bread and gruel did. That night, as his stomach growled and coils from the thin mattress pressed into his hip, he rolled the challenge in his mind. Yes, God could have intervened and prevented his arrest and subsequent captivity in this wretched place.

But this place had been the breaking of him. It was here that he'd remembered his utter need for God and the potential relationships that still awaited him with his daughters. Here he had begged for new life. This was the battering of his heart of which John Donne had written. On the other side of his need, there was the One who could meet it.

The image of Hugh materialized in the shadows. Another hallucination, but a mild one, as these things went. "You took it again, didn't you? The whiskey tincture. Is God meeting your need by using that? Or can He make you new without it?"

Chapter Twenty-Eight

Wednesday, November 22, 1871

Meg had thought she was ready for this.

She was wrong.

The art that hung in Mr. VanDyke's gallery seemed to mock her. The gaslights had seemed to hiss *Imposter* as she entered the shadowy room. In one corner, she and Nate held the portraits of Sylvie and Jasper to show Mr. VanDyke.

The gallery owner's reaction to her work was written plainly on his face.

"I'm sorry, Miss Townsend." Mr. VanDyke's gentle tone did nothing to soften the rejection. He looked pointedly at her hands. "I can see your resources have been compromised in the fire, and you have my deepest sympathy. But my clients want portraits they can be proud of for generations to come. It's a business arrangement, not a charity offer."

Whatever humiliation she'd felt burned away in the ire now licking through her. Nate's jaw hardened before he opened his mouth to speak. She touched his sleeve to stop him. She could speak for herself.

"I have not come for sympathy or charity." Meg lifted her chin, glad her voice was steady. "If that's all you see here, I won't waste any more of your time. Or mine."

And it was over. Just like that.

She didn't look at Nate as they walked down the stairs and out into the late afternoon light that leaked from an ash grey sky. The door slammed shut behind her. She felt the blessed cold on her hot face, but no tears, as Nate hailed a cab. Likely she appeared composed. But on the inside she fought to keep herself from fragmenting into pieces.

After Nate loaded the portraits into the carriage and handed her up, he sat beside her, his knee touching hers. They trundled along without speaking, for what was there to say? Meg stared at Sylvie's likeness across from her and wondered how she would tell her sister that their hopes of her gaining clients had come to naught. Coming on the heels of her failure to get her father released from the asylum, it was another blow to her already bruised spirit.

Nate took off his glasses and rubbed his eyes. "Mr. VanDyke was out of line in what he said, you know."

Outside the cab, long shadows of lampposts leaned down the street. "I agree. But he does know his clients. If he says they wouldn't like my style, I believe him. I barely like my style myself."

"Meg." Nate wrapped his arm around her shoulders, and she allowed her head to rest against him as she inhaled his scent of sandalwood soap and newsprint. When he kissed her temple, the gentle pressure released the tears that had been banking inside her. "All I've wanted to do, almost since the moment I met you, is protect you. I hate that your heartaches keep coming. If I could take them from you, I would. I'm no art critic, but I'll tell you what *I* think of your style. Do you remember when you asked me why I look at the city without my glasses on sometimes?"

She did. "You said it was a relief. It was a respite for eyes and mind not to see every single detail, and that there was beauty in the blend and blur."

He twirled a lock of her hair around his finger. "That's right. There is a certain charm in the softening of the world's hard edges. My vision isn't much without my spectacles, but the change in perspective has become a gift to me. That's how I see your painting,

Meg. I know you admire the realism of the old masters. But what you've done since the fire carries even more emotion. What you call imprecise, I call gentle. You've painted with your whole heart, and it shows. Did you ever consider that this"—he gestured to the portraits across from them—"is more reflective of yourself as an artist than what you've ever done before?"

She leaned back and turned to face him. "No." A smile lifted her lips at one corner as she looked into his eyes. She saw kindness there but not flattery. He believed what he'd said, and that alone took the chill from the air.

"Well, maybe you should." With the pad of his thumb, he swept a tear from her cheek. After his touch lingered for a moment, he withdrew his arm from around her and replaced his glasses.

Slightly unsettled by the abrupt change in the atmosphere, Meg looked out the window. "This isn't the way home. Or to Jasper's home." She needed to return his portrait to him. At least he'd said he was pleased with it, no matter Mr. VanDyke's opinion.

Nate glanced at a passing carriage before facing her again. "I told the driver to take us to Edith's house. I'll take you home right after."

"That's fine, Nate, but why?"

"Frank should be there. I want to talk to him about your father's situation."

By the time they arrived at the Novak home, Meg's hopes had risen and deflated several times as she tried to manage her expectations. Edith welcomed them warmly, then hugged Meg with a little extra force after hearing about Mr. VanDyke's rejection.

"Can I get you anything?" Edith wiped her hands on her apron before brushing a strand of hair off her brow. She was obviously making use of Henry's nap to work on dinner.

"You can get me this guy, how about that?" Nate scooped up Tommy and held him upside down by his ankles. "Have you got anything in your pockets for me today?"

Belly laughter tumbled out of the little boy. "Try again! Try more!" he cried, and Nate lifted him up and down in the air in a game Meg suspected had become a common ritual. She laughed along with him.

"Ah, well." Nate feigned disappointment as he gently put his nephew down. "Maybe next time."

As Edith returned to the kitchen, Frank entered the parlor, his necktie loosened about his collar, and tickled Tommy mercilessly until the boy took off running.

"Have a seat." Frank took an armchair, while Meg and Nate sat on the sofa where Sylvie had slept last week. "Special occasion?"

"You might say that," Nate replied. He tossed his hat to the end of the sofa.

"I saw the article about Otto Schneider's confession and your father's name being cleared of the charge," Frank said. "Congratulations to both of you. After all your editor's warnings to stay away from anything related to the Townsends, Nate, you must have felt vindicated writing this article."

"I did. But Stephen still hasn't been released. That's why I wanted to talk to you." Briefly, he laid out what had happened with Meg's father at the asylum.

"What can we do?" Meg rested her left hand over her right in her lap, a habit she'd quickly formed. "I've written letters, but I doubt that will be effective on its own. Do you have any ideas?"

Comforting smells of potatoes, sausage, and onions wafted from the kitchen. Tommy toddled back into the room and climbed onto Nate's knee with a wooden truck in his fist. Nate held him on his lap and let him run the truck up his arms and across his chest.

"Soldier's heart," Frank repeated. "One of the doctors I work with prescribes medicine for that condition for some patients at the Soldiers' Home."

Meg leaned forward, spirals of her hair falling over one shoulder. "You mean, they have what my father has, and they're not committed as lunatics?" This was news she could use.

Crossing an ankle over one knee, Frank pulled his necktie from his collar and laid it across the arm of the chair. "I suppose it depends on which doctor you ask. But do talk to the doctors there.

At least one of them says there are varying degrees of the condition and that not all require institutionalization. I'm inclined to agree."

Dr. Gilbert came to mind. If she recalled correctly, he split his time between the free clinic in the North Division and the Soldiers' Home. Surely he'd speak to her about this.

The last sunrays of the day filled the room with the rosy glow of a goblet just emptied of its wine. With one hand on Tommy's back, Nate said, "We ought to talk to some of the asylum trustees, as well. I interviewed a few of them when I wrote the story on the asylum's new building last year. I'll track them down again and see if they're on the committee in charge of discharging patients. If they aren't, they can tell me who is, and we'll go from there."

Meg exhaled, grateful they had a plan and that she wasn't alone in her quest.

Friday, November 24, 1871

Jane Eyre didn't need anyone's permission to return to Mr. Rochester. Neither did Sylvie need approval to visit Jasper at his house. Even so, she felt the flutter of moth wings in her stomach as she waited for someone to answer the door. When Kirstin opened it, the maid's bright smile put her immediately at ease.

"Miss Sylvie! We've missed you so. Do come in!" Kirstin pushed her ruffled cap back into place over her auburn hair.

Sylvie stepped inside and removed her hat, drinking in the familiar smell of this place. When only Hiram lived here, the atmosphere was old and stately. Now its essence was balsam shaving soap and black coffee. Masculine. It was Jasper.

"You and Helene are back for good, I take it?" Sylvie asked.

"We are indeed, heaven be praised, now that Mr. Schneider is in prison and the will has been properly executed. I saw Eli on the street the other day and asked if he'd return, but he decided to stay where he is."

"He must be happy in his new situation, then. In any case, it sounds like everything's official now. All has been transferred into Jasper's name?"

"That's what I understand, miss. We're drawing wages and he's looking for a cook, so it must be true."

Jasper entered the hallway, a shaft of sunlight glancing off his hair. The smile he gave Sylvie could not have been manufactured. He was happy to see her, and his happiness was her own.

"Sylvie," he said. "Have you and Meg come to see how the portrait looks hanging in the library?"

Kirstin took Sylvie's cloak and hung it on the stand before bobbing and scurrying away.

"Not exactly." Sylvie smoothed the sides of her skirted jacket. "I mean yes, of course I want to see it. But I came without Meg. I came to see you, not just your likeness." She watched a hint of pleasure filter over his finely chiseled features.

"Ah." A dimple starred his cheek. "Well, do come see it so you can tell Meg about its place of honor. When she returned it, she told me what Mr. VanDyke said."

"Yes. She took it rather hard, at first." Truth be told, they both had. Without income from portrait painting to bolster their meager book sales, they'd need to pawn some of their mother's jewelry. But she wouldn't tell Jasper that. She would hate for him to think she'd come asking for money now that he'd inherited Hiram's.

"And now that it's been a couple of days? Has her mood altered?" he asked.

"Her disappointment doesn't seem quite as bitter. At least she's painting again. She could no more stop doing that than I could stop reading books. It's part of who she is."

Jasper's shoulders squared. "Let's send you back to your sister with news that her portrait of me fits the library—my library—perfectly."

Sylvie followed him into her favorite room and gazed at his image above the fireplace mantel. As she'd tried to explain to Meg, from a distance, the portrait was even more striking. She smiled. "I'll tell her. She'll be so glad to hear it." She turned from the canvas to the flesh and blood man it represented. "I'm so happy for you, that all your legal questions have been settled."

"I'm happy for me too." He chuckled. "I didn't realize how much it weighed on me until I could put the matter behind me. Now I can move on."

"Yes." Sylvie turned her bracelet on her wrist to hide the clasp. She could no longer put off the chief purpose of her visit. She didn't like asking him for favors. How much better would it be if she could bestow a kindness upon him instead. Still, she pressed forward. "Now that you've put the matter behind you, I have a request to make."

He gestured toward the settee and sat beside her. "Name it."

Firelight burnished the walls, warming the room. "Now that Otto Schneider is where he belongs, Meg and I have been trying to get our father out of the asylum. They know he didn't kill your uncle, but for some reason they still say he's dangerous. He isn't. He was paranoid and suspicious before the fire, but he wasn't a danger."

He held her gaze. "Go on."

She fingered the velvet buttons on her cuff. "Meg spoke to a doctor who thinks our father might be treated without being institutionalized. Then she and Nate talked to a member of the asylum's board about securing Father's release. We heard yesterday that the rest of the board is concerned about public opinion in their handling of the case. Our former tenants, the Spencers, sent the asylum a letter, asking them to discharge him too, but it didn't move them. It feels like we're trying to reason with a brick wall."

Jasper shifted on the settee, sitting so close to her that the toe of his shoe disappeared beneath the hem of her skirt. "I know what it's like to have a loved one in need and not be able to do a thing about it."

His nearness emboldened her. "I haven't always gotten along with my father, but he isn't insane. I want him back. Please—" Her voice cracked with the weight of her conviction. "Please help me get him back."

His green eyes widened before understanding registered there. "You want me to write the board too."

"It would mean so much coming from you. Considering the false charge that our father killed your uncle, your willingness to see him released would carry far more significance than ours."

He leaned forward, elbows on his knees, and spun Hiram's ring about his finger. "What you need isn't a letter from me personally so much as the letter of the law. Keeping a patient without his family's permission cannot be legal if he's no threat to public safety."

Sylvie ought to have known the law would be on their side. "But I—we can't afford an attorney."

"Then isn't it fortunate you happen to be friends with one in the making?" He smiled. "I'll draft the letter myself, outlining the laws the asylum violates by keeping your father. Then I'll take it to my professor this afternoon to make sure I've got it right. He's a kind man. He might even let me use his letterhead to type it up and sign his own name to it. Either way, I'll deliver the letter myself before this day is through."

Wonder filled her. In all her mental rehearsals of how this meeting would go, the law, and Jasper's love of it, had not factored in at all. "Your professor will want payment for his time," she guessed. She twisted a ring off her finger and held it out to him. "We're short on cash. Do you suppose this will suffice?" It was only a simple pearl set in gold.

Jasper took the ring and slid it back on her finger. "Keep your ring. If I incur any costs for his services, I find myself in a position to pay them myself now. It will be no hardship, believe me."

"Are you certain? This is so generous of you, I hardly know what to say."

He enfolded her hands in his. "There are things you don't know about me, Sylvie. The things I've seen and done . . ." His voice trailed away, buried, she suspected, beneath memories of war. "But you make me want to be the best version of myself I can possibly be."

Her breath caught. For one shining moment, fiction and reality blended. Jasper's words were an echo of Mr. Rochester's, who'd told Jane Eyre, *"I wish to be a better man than I have been."* And Sylvie, like Jane, felt her *"thin crescent-destiny"* begin to enlarge.

Tears brimmed in her eyes. "I can't thank you enough. Your help is so much more than I imagined you would do for my family."

He circled his thumbs over the backs of her hands. "I like Meg. I have sympathy for your father. But, Sylvie, I'm doing this for you."

Any doubt she'd had about coming here shattered with the force of her joy. There was no mistaking his affection now, not with those words, not when he looked at her like that. Whatever he'd done before she knew him, she forgave him. Whatever ghosts of war still haunted him, she could understand those too, at least in part. Did he know he held not only her hands, but her heart as well?

A log crumbled behind the grate, releasing a shower of sparks. Jasper's gaze dropped to Sylvie's lips, launching her pulse to a painful speed.

But just as quickly, he released her and stood, for Kirstin bustled into the room to stoke the fire.

Her face flushed with the heat of a summer's day, Sylvie stood and thanked Jasper once more while the maid knelt at the hearth. "By the way, Nate's family has invited us to join them for Thanksgiving dinner on Thursday."

"Have you agreed?" A shadow flitted over his expression. "I should have asked you to come here sooner. It won't be the same without you."

"The invitation extends to you as well, Jasper. I wouldn't think of leaving you to dine here alone. Besides, I hear you don't yet have a cook."

"In that case, I accept." He gave a charming bow before gazing at her in a look that stretched overlong.

Suddenly flustered by the attention, Sylvie told him the time to arrive and hastened to go, nearly tripping over a cardboard box in the hall.

He steadied her. "My apologies. Helene must have brought this down from my uncle's room. She cleaned out his clothing. I've no use for it, and I reckoned it might fill a need for someone else. I need to take it to one of the relief depots to donate it."

"Oh, I'll do that. It's no trouble, since I'm already going that way." She bent to lift the box, but he stopped her.

"I appreciate that. But allow me to load it into the cab for you, at least."

Sylvie smiled. "I'm sure I can manage one box. You've no idea the crates of books I've handled for the shop."

"Your capability isn't in question." He hoisted the box of clothing and straightened. "You're a lady, Sylvie. Allow me to treat you like one."

When was the last time she'd been taken care of like this? Sylvie couldn't recall.

From the hallway, she turned to gaze at his portrait once more and imagined hers on the wall beside it. Same artist, same background, a matched set. It was as though it was meant to be.

Saturday, November 25, 1871

"You're not too cold, are you, Louis?" Meg turned from the easel she'd set up among the ruins of Court House Square. Woolly clouds drifted across an ice-blue sky. The air, damp and sharp, still held the smell of burned things and of the coming winter.

"Ah, this is nothing, Miss Townsend." Newsboy cap worn backward on his head, Louis's cheeks rounded with a grin. A knobby scarf wound about his neck, the tail of which dangled over his shoulder. "Don't you know I spend every day outside anyway? How else do you think I make a livin'? I reckon I can outlast you by a mile."

"I reckon you can." Laughing, she turned back to the portrait unfolding on her canvas.

After Mr. VanDyke's rejection, she hadn't been in the mood to paint again right away. But she'd found such a fascinating subject in Louis Garibaldi, the child relic seller of Court House Square, she couldn't help but try to capture him. His older brother, Lorenzo, handled most of the transactions today while Louis sat gamely at their table, a mound of fused washers in his gloved hand.

Painting was also a refreshing distraction from her failure to bring her father home. In addition to her own efforts, Sylvie had talked to Jasper, who had also addressed the board by letter. What the result of all this talking was, Meg had yet to learn.

"You're good for business," Louis said, scattering thoughts of the asylum. "People come to see what you're up to, and Lorenzo makes them an offer they can't refuse."

"Happy to oblige. Now hold still." With her palette knife firm in her grip, she mixed colors until satisfied she had a perfect match for his olive skin tone, then began adding it to the sketch she'd completed yesterday. Later she would fill in the background of the skeletal structures behind him, and only then would the portrait make sense. Then it would showcase the beauty of this child, so full of life, right here among the ruins. He had a long future ahead of him, just like Chicago did.

Louis and his family were survivors, he'd told her. His parents weren't as fluent in English as he and Lorenzo were, but they'd found work where that didn't matter—his father at the docks, and his mother in a garment factory. Selling relics was great fun for Louis, far better than shining shoes or getting up before dawn to sell papers. His mother was going to have another baby, so selling relics was a job he took seriously. There would be another mouth to feed soon.

"That is going to be simply marvelous, I can already tell." Bertha Palmer's voice rang bell-like beside Meg.

"Mrs. Palmer!" Meg nearly dropped her paintbrush but caught it in time and set it on the easel. "It's so good to see you. How have you been?"

"Better than many." Mrs. Palmer reached for Meg's hands, then hesitated and offered a smile instead. Too well-bred to inquire about the scars, she glided gracefully into her next sentence. "We lost the hotel in the fire, your lovely paintings included. I'm so pleased to see you painting again."

The sight of Mrs. Palmer's long, elegant fingers brought a twinge to Meg's chest as embarrassment flared and died. The wind kicked up, and she tucked a strand of hair behind her ear while searching for something to say. Would Mrs. Palmer consider any further talk of paintings a bid for charity? Mr. VanDyke's words still shadowed her.

"Fire relics!" called Louis. "Get your memento of the conflagration right here, and remember the event of the century for all your living days!"

A genuine smile unfurled over Mrs. Palmer's countenance. "Excuse me for one moment."

She crossed to Louis's table and bent to peruse the merchandise. Her perfectly bustled silhouette in emerald green was a striking contrast to the child's mismatched and threadbare attire and to the ruins behind her. Engaging in amiable conversation with him, she selected an item and handed him his price. Beaming, Louis presented her with the charred remnant of a statue.

Meg sucked in a breath as she beheld them. Quickly, she traded the brush for the charcoal and roughed in the outline of Mrs. Palmer at the moment her hand met Louis's. This one small interaction brought the spark of him to life, and it illuminated Mrs. Palmer too. By the time the socialite threaded her way back to the easel, Meg had sketched her image upon the canvas.

"I hope you don't mind." Meg watched Mrs. Palmer's eyes alight with recognition.

"Do you really think it an improvement, or are you trying to earn my affections?"

Heat rushed to Meg's face. She wasn't sure if Mrs. Palmer was teasing or if she really suspected Meg was manipulating her. She hid her right hand behind her skirt. "Truly, this is far better than I'd planned. This is an even truer context for Louis's portrait than just a relic in his hand with the destruction behind him. That was only the beginning. But your presence tells a story, don't you think? In a single moment, the rich and the poor connect, both equally representing the spirit of the rebuilding city. You are compassion. He is resilience. Both of you are Chicago." In the pause that followed, she wondered if she'd said too much.

Mrs. Palmer stood back from the easel and studied it, then looked at Louis and Lorenzo at their table, already chatting with another potential buyer. At length, she turned to Meg with tears glossing her eyes. "Sold," she said.

Meg blinked. "Pardon me?"

"My dear, I've already been to your shop. I saw the ad in the *Tribune* that you've reopened, and wanted to see if you were still interested in painting Jane Eyre and Agnes Grey for me. Your sister showed me the portrait you made of her, and I saw that your talent extends to translating from life. But this." She gestured toward the canvas. "This may be your finest work."

Meg was stunned. "This was intended to be practice."

"I want it. There is a new movement in the art world in France, barely begun. It's a softer technique, meant to portray an impression rather than copy the reality. Your painting reminds me of it very much. What I want to know is, can you produce more of the same?"

"A series of paintings in the same style," Meg confirmed. "Of everyday people in and about the city."

"Exactly."

Excitement took hold of Meg as she thought it through. "I could call it 'Spirit of Chicago.' It could showcase the courage and the potential of our city by featuring the people who will rebuild it. I wouldn't ignore the calamity but allow it to serve as a backdrop, a poignant contrast to hope. I'll show glimpses of beauty even though we are surrounded by ruins."

Mrs. Palmer agreed. "I've rented space in Mr. Jansen's gallery to auction some of the art I brought back from France as a fundraiser. Be ready in time, and I'll include your work as well. A percentage of your profits could be donated to the charity of your choice, and the rest will be yours to keep, to help with the cost of your own reconstruction." She laid her hand on Meg's shoulder. "Leave everything to me, and I'll see that your art gets the attention it deserves."

Chapter Twenty-Nine

Wednesday, November 29, 1871

It worked. It was through no power of Meg's, but it worked.

Between the conversations with Dr. Gilbert and the board, the legal letter from Jasper and his professor, the article Nate had threatened to write, and an untold number of prayers, something finally convinced the authorities to release Stephen from the asylum. If he proved a threat to anyone's safety, however, he'd be committed again, for good.

It had been one thing to sign forms this afternoon, and another to truly bring him home. This was the burden weighting Meg as she ushered her father into the shanty. The last time he'd returned after an extended absence, he'd never fully adjusted. After almost two months in an asylum, what new horrors had followed him here? The elation of his release quickly transfigured into worry.

Nate had accompanied her and Sylvie to the institution to retrieve their father but left them to continue their reunion with more privacy. "*This is a time best reserved for family alone,*" he'd whispered to her after she'd invited him in.

The brief tour of the two rooms finished, Sylvie took off her wraps, hanging them on the pegs along the front wall. "It's so good to have you home." Her voice was tentative, and she looked like she had when she was fifteen years old, welcoming Stephen back from war. Unsure. Hopeful. Cautious.

Meg felt the same. How had she devoted so much energy hoping and praying for and pursuing his release, and so little imagination to what it would look like to have him home? She had no idea how he would handle the confined space of the shanty in the middle of the burned district.

"Home," Stephen repeated, looking around the front room, then at the window, where dirt spotted the pane from last night's hard rain. Was that sarcasm in his voice, or just disappointment? He was thinner than when she last saw him, especially in his face, which was startlingly exposed without a beard.

"You're where you belong," Meg said, reassuring herself as well as him. "With us."

He looked at her with large grey eyes, his gaze moving to her hands. Lips straight, he nodded in acknowledgment.

She wanted him to take her hands in his, as Nate had done. She wanted him to touch her scars, to touch who she was now, and to say he loved her the same, or even more, perhaps, because now they both were marked, visibly or invisibly.

He did neither. He did nothing.

Meg's throat tightened. She reminded herself that he hadn't been comfortable with human touch for years. But for mercy's sake, if there were ever a day to take exception to his customary standoffishness, this would have been it.

Had that hateful Dr. Franklin been right? Was she expecting—if not demanding—more from her father than he was able to give?

This was not a reunion fit for fairy tales. It felt as stiff as the scar tissue on her palms.

Skirts swishing, Sylvie moved toward the stove, putting space between herself and Stephen the way she'd done so often before. Meg wondered if she felt ignored or insignificant.

"Coffee?" Sylvie called over her shoulder.

Stephen swung his attention to her. "I'll take some."

There were so many things Meg longed to ask. How had he been treated? Was he hungry or cold? Did they hurt him? Was he afraid? Did their letters help him at all? Whatever had transpired, could he recover from it, or had those weeks in the asylum added permanent layers of trauma atop the others he hadn't been able to shed? And Sylvie asked if he wanted coffee.

Meg's queries would have cut too quickly, too deep, too soon. It would have been a mistake to ask them, a selfish grasping to ease her own conscience. Instead, Sylvie had posed what might be the only question he could handle. Meg caught her sister's eye and nodded her approval.

With a sigh that sounded relieved, Stephen rubbed a hand over his jaw. "Smells good. What else have you got to eat?"

Meg set a plate of cold biscuits on the table along with a crock of butter and a jar of blackberry preserves. "We have chicken and gravy from last night too. I'll boil some potatoes to go with it."

Stephen slathered one biscuit after another with butter and preserves, until he'd eaten three in less than five minutes. Only then did he pause to look around the shanty. He licked his lips. "Did we have to pay for this?"

Meg detected disapproval in his tone and struggled to dismiss it. "No, this was built as part of a grant we received from the Relief and Aid Society, remember?"

He cut his gaze to hers. "You probably wrote that to me. I read your letters, but there is a lot I don't remember. The poetry, though. That I do recall. Thank you for bringing what you did."

With a satisfied smile, Sylvie poured a cup of coffee and placed it on the table before him. "Would you like to hear how business is going? Or would you rather . . . not?"

Wrapping his fingers around the earthenware mug, he sipped the coffee, brows plunging, as though even this was too great a question to consider.

"We can wait until another time to tell you about it," Sylvie offered. "Just know that it's going as well as it could right now."

"Good." Oliver bounded onto his lap, and he stroked the cat's fur, the lines of his face softening. The purring was audible from where Meg warmed the gravy on the stove.

She bit her tongue to keep from ruining the quiet he obviously preferred. But she wanted to report that five customers had already come and placed orders for books, including Anna Hoffman. She wanted to explain the evolution of her painting and about the new show she was going to do, sponsored by Bertha Palmer. She wanted to point to the portrait of Sylvie which now hung in the front room and ask him what he thought. If he'd noticed it, he hadn't given any indication. Instead, she added salt to the pot of potatoes and replaced the lid.

After pouring herself a cup of coffee, Meg sat with Sylvie and her father at the table while she waited for the potatoes to boil. "We've been invited to celebrate Thanksgiving tomorrow with Nate's stepsister Edith and her family. Jasper Davenport will be there too."

A shadow fell over their father's face. "Thanksgiving? I had no idea that was tomorrow. You want to spend it with Nate and Jasper?"

Meg's grip tightened on the mug's handle. "We want to spend it with you."

She was about to say she understood why he didn't want to go, and that she would stay home with him, when Sylvie shook her head.

Right. They had talked about this at length. Meg had to stop excusing her father at the slightest sign of his discomfort.

"We want to spend it with you," she said again, "but it would also be nice to accept the invitation, after everything all of them have done for us."

"They've become good friends," Sylvie added.

Stephen frowned. "As I recall, Jasper thought I killed his uncle."

"Only because of what the police said," Sylvie said gently. "And yet he still allowed us to live in the house for weeks. Not to mention, his letter outlining the law helped open the door that set you free."

Stephen looked up, surprise etched across his face. "No one told me that. I didn't know I was beholden to him."

Meg stretched her fingers backward from her palms. She wanted nothing more than to accommodate her father, but Sylvie was right. Such dependence wasn't healthy. "You do what you feel most comfortable with, Father. Sylvie and I will be sharing the Thanksgiving meal with our friends tomorrow. We'd love for you to join us, but the choice is yours."

Wordlessly, he turned his attention back to Oliver on his lap. The pot boiled over, and the water hissed as it hit the stove. Stephen startled violently, knocking his knee under the table, and the cat leapt away.

Her own pulse skipping at her father's reaction, Meg hurried to lift the lid and allow the steam to escape. She could hear him breathing too fast, too hard.

"It's all right," Sylvie told him quietly. "It's just the water. All is well."

But Meg wondered if it truly was.

Nate didn't like keeping secrets from Meg. But how could he tell her that something wasn't right with Otto Schneider's confession when it was that very confession that had cleared her father's name?

This was what troubled him as he took his leave from her reunion with Stephen. Almost without thinking, he followed Randolph Street toward the river. It had been a while since his shoes had been shined.

Martin Sullivan was bent over another customer's shoes when Nate arrived at the foot of the bridge. Fog hovered, plucking the color from the scene. The river looked cold and grey as it snaked between its banks. Fists stuffed into his trouser pockets, Nate's thoughts flowed in one direction too—back to Otto Schneider.

His confession had come too quickly, even before a lawyer had been assigned to him. Schneider had claimed the false witnesses lied to the police without any payment first. What kind of person risked prison on the mere hope of being paid for it later? It didn't add up. And Nate still didn't know how Otto Schneider knew to frame Stephen Townsend, of all people. The confession had said nothing about that. In fact, it said nothing about the false witnesses at all. Nate still hadn't learned their names.

So before he wrote the story, Nate shared his skepticism with his editor. "*You're not a detective,*" Medill had said. "*You're a reporter—at least for the moment. If you can't keep up with the pace of news in this city, find a different line of work.*" Nate wrote the article reporting the confession. That didn't mean he believed it.

Meg would be hurt to know Nate doubted Schneider's guilt for any reason. Today, while returning to the shanty from the asylum, Stephen had mentioned that he'd never met Otto Schneider. He wouldn't have known of him at all, had it not been for Hiram's stories. It only cast more doubt on Schneider's confession, which meant the real murderer could still be at large. But until Nate had the facts to back up his hunch, he'd keep his misgivings to himself.

Martin's customer paid and left, disappearing into the mist, and Nate took his place on the wooden chair. He propped one foot on the crate.

"It's been a while, hasn't it?" Martin asked good-naturedly.

"I'm overdue, that's for sure."

Martin's nose was red with cold as he wiped Nate's shoe. "Well, at least you'll look sharp for the holiday. Say, last time you were here, you were asking about Otto Schneider, weren't you? Did you see in the paper that he confessed to a murder?" Whistling, he shook his head.

"I did see that." Nate tucked his hands beneath his arms to keep them warm. "Did it surprise you?"

"Aye, it did. Drunkenness, sure. Petty theft, I believe it. But murder? I never thought he had it in him."

Nate hadn't come here for information, but neither would he interrupt Martin.

"You know what's really funny? I saw Martha, his wife, the other day with her three kids. They looked better than I'd seen them in years. New clothes for all of them, if I'm not mistaken. No patches, no short hems or sleeves, nothing." He grunted. "Christmas must have come early."

Nate stared into the fog above Martin's head. "Odd."

"That's what I thought. I told her she was looking well, and she colored a bit before saying something about a generous aunt in St. Louis." Shrugging, Martin worked his rag into a jar of polish.

"Well, if there were ever a time for an aunt to be generous, this would be it," Nate offered. Schneider might have been making very little income before, but now he brought in nothing. "Perhaps Martha was embarrassed that they need the help."

"True enough, sir. True enough." Martin nodded, then hummed Christmas carols to himself as he worked.

New clothes. An aunt in St. Louis? His own explanation notwithstanding, Nate had to see this for himself. His shoes shined and the service paid for, he wished Martin a happy Thanksgiving and took a cab to the barracks in the North Division, recalling the Schneiders' address from the police report.

The fog lifted, and the sky lowered and flattened like a dingy white sheet pulled taut. In the ruined neighborhood beneath it, four long, one-story buildings housed a thousand families. Chimneys towered sporadically among the burned-out blocks, ominous and lonely. As Nate neared Barracks Number Two, the sounds of those living within the thin walls seeped out to him. He knocked on the Schneiders' door.

It opened. "Can I help you?" A boy regarded him with guarded gaze, a soft pretzel in one hand. Heat radiated from the room, snapping and hissing as it toasted the moisture in the air. The smells accompanying the warmth were not those of poverty, but of preparation for a feast.

"I'm Nathaniel Pierce, *Chicago Tribune*. I was wondering if I could speak to your mother. This is the Schneider residence, isn't it?"

The boy opened the door wider, and Nate stepped through it. What the small space lacked in natural light was made up for with kerosene lamps, all of them lit. Odd, for a family he'd expected to economize.

"She's over there." The boy pointed to a woman with one arm up to the elbow inside a turkey. Sausage sizzled on the stove.

Doffing his hat, Nate approached her, introducing himself all over again.

"Well, I'm Martha Schneider, and you've already spoken to Frederick. You're from the paper, you say?" Her dark hair was streaked with grey, and lines splayed from appraising eyes. "What can you want? The article's already been printed."

A fair question. "I'm not here for an article, ma'am. I just wanted to see how you were getting along."

She frowned. "We're getting along as well as can be expected. As you see, I'm preparing for Thanksgiving. So if you're quite satisfied, Frederick will show you out."

He didn't blame her for being confused and distant. But he wasn't satisfied yet. "It smells divine in here. Are you cooking for a crowd tomorrow?"

A little girl scampered out of the other room. "Oh, ever so many!" she lisped through the gaps in her teeth. "As many neighbors as we can fit! Mama says we ought to share our blessings. And turkeys too. We have three of them this year, only Mama gave two away for other mamas to help cook."

"Hush, Mary!" Martha turned back to Nate. "She's a magpie, that one. There's no telling what she'll say."

He smiled at the girl while marveling at what she'd said. Three turkeys would be an extravagant expense for any middle-class family. For the Schneiders, it didn't compute. Nate bent on one knee to be on Mary's level, and she twirled for him.

"Look at my dress! It's special for Thanksgiving."

Nate was no expert in little girls' clothing, but all those ruffles looked fancy. The fabric, he could tell, was high quality.

"And you'll take it right off, young lady, and put it away for tomorrow." Martha withdrew her arm and slung turkey innards on a few layers of newspaper. "Tell your sister the same!"

Giggles trailed behind Mary as she scampered out of the room and relayed the message to her twin. Rolling his eyes, Frederick played jacks in the middle of the floor. The aid society outfitted the barracks with only mattresses, stoves, and crockery. But behind the boy was a matching sofa and chair, a pile of blankets spilling over the ottoman. A price tag was still tied to one wooden leg. This furniture was no donation.

None of this made sense. These people had been burned out of their home last month. They'd lost everything, just like Nate. Nate had a decent job and zero dependents, and even he could not afford what he saw here.

"I'm pleased to see you're doing so well," Nate said. "Considering."

Martha continued cleaning out the inside of the bird. "I still don't see that it's any business of yours, but yes, we're fine. Thanks to a generous aunt in Cincinnati."

"Cincinnati, you said?" Martin had said it was St. Louis. But then, he could have misremembered.

Frederick glanced up with something like worry in his eyes. Nate saw it in Martha's too. Why?

"You need to go now, Mr. Pierce," she said. "You can see I'm very busy."

"I'll show him out! I'll do it, let me!" Mary came tearing back through the room in a too-short sundress and bare feet.

Nate reseated his hat. "Thank you kindly, miss. Lead on." With a parting word to Martha and Frederick, he followed Mary the few yards to the door. When she opened it, he tipped his hat to her. "Your aunt must love you very much," he said quietly. "I'll bet you wish she could spend Thanksgiving with you."

She cocked her head and blinked. "We don't have an aunt."

Chapter Thirty

Thursday, November 30, 1871

Stephen wasn't in the mood for strangers. But then, he didn't want to eat cold bean soup alone in the shanty for the holiday either. He ought to be with his family, wherever they were.

It cost him, though. The commotion grated his nerves raw. At least the Novaks had the sense to time the meal for their sons' naptime, since they didn't have a governess to keep them quiet while the grownups ate. He couldn't handle all of this and children too.

The Novaks seemed pleasant enough, and he didn't mind Nate Pierce's company, but there was something about Jasper he didn't understand, and that worried him. Why had he taken such an active role to secure Stephen's release from the asylum?

Regardless, Stephen resolved to quietly enjoy turkey and cranberry relish, potatoes and gravy, while everyone else conversed around him. After asylum fare, he was happy to savor each bite in peace. There were actual textures here, and flavors that sang in his mouth. Edith passed him the fruitcake, and he took another slice.

Cutlery clinked on china as Meg's knife slipped from her grip to her plate, a buttered roll in her other hand. No one else seemed bothered by the clatter. "What other stories are you working on, Nate?" she asked. "Do you hear anything about the trial against Catherine O'Leary for causing the Great Fire?"

Nate's expression clouded. "Not yet. The inquiry started seven days ago, and still the press has nothing to report about the proceedings. We aren't allowed in the courtroom, but they've promised to give us the transcripts when it's over. In the meantime, the other papers are printing mere conjecture, and the public is left to form opinions based on nothing more than rumor and premature conclusions."

"From what I gather," Jasper said, "everyone has already decided Mrs. O'Leary and her cow are guilty."

"Which is why it's all the more important that I get my hands on those inquiry documents to report what really happened."

"That's the one." Frank raised his glass of water to Nate. "That's the story that will be your headliner. I can see it on the front page now."

Edith refilled his water glass. "Frank's right. It's about time you got some recognition at the *Tribune*. When Medill takes office as mayor, who will your new editor be?"

"I don't know." Nate wiped his mouth. "I heard one of the other editors will absorb the work until they find someone to take the job as city editor."

Stephen lost track of the conversation after that. Sylvie and Jasper exchanged a few words, but he couldn't make them out. He was too distracted by the sight of Meg trying to cut her turkey. Holding the fork with her left hand, she squeezed the knife between her fourth and fifth fingers and the palm of her right. The palsied thumb and first two fingers looked so awkward, like appendages destined to be in the way from now on. Meg managed to cut the meat, but it took her entire concentration. Then the knife slipped to the plate, and Stephen flinched.

Meg lifted her gaze to his and mouthed, "Sorry."

He nodded. It wasn't her fault. Every noise at the table was too loud for him. He felt more unsettled than he'd been a few days ago. In a strange way, he missed Hugh Brodie. He also missed Hiram, and that pang was sharper by far. The old man had always been kind to him, had made allowances for the way Stephen was, even when Hiram's brain faltered. Stephen hated that his last words to his closest friend had been harsh.

"More potatoes, Mr. Townsend?" Jasper asked. "You could finish these off."

"I'll do it."

Jasper passed the serving bowl around the table to reach him. When it got to Meg, she grasped it fine with her left hand but fumbled with her right. One side of the bowl dropped with a loud *thunk*, rattling the silverware.

"Meg!" The reprimand burst from Stephen before he could hold it back. He rubbed at the back of his neck. "Never mind," he mumbled. "It's fine." He could no more control his frayed nerves than she could control the bowl. He faulted himself, but not her.

From one of the back rooms, a baby's cry crescendoed into a siren's wail. Another followed. Pulse pounding at his temples, Stephen could bear no more. He left his napkin on his chair and marched out of the house, trying not to slam the door behind him.

He crumpled onto the front step. Cold seeped from the stone into his body, and he gulped the chilled air like water. At least a man could breathe out here. At least he could get some peace.

He lowered his head into his hands. Muffled sounds came from behind him of a mother consoling her child. He had humiliated his.

The peace that came with isolation was shallow and fleeting indeed. He wasn't crazy, he knew that much. He didn't belong in the asylum. He longed to fit back in with his family, but how could he, when he felt like he didn't fit his own skin?

"Oh, Lord," he prayed. "Can't we do better than this?"

Hinges creaked as the door behind him opened and closed. Frank Novak handed Stephen his coat. "Let's go for a walk."

Stephen rose and shrugged into the coat. Once they reached the sidewalk, he glanced at Frank beside him. "I understand you helped set a process in motion which resulted in my release. Are you wondering, now, if you were wrong?"

"Not at all. I'm wondering how you've been sleeping, though."

"Not well." It was an understatement. Stephen had slept better in the asylum than he had in his own home last night. Not that the shanty, where he slept on a pallet on the floor, felt like home.

A long line of trees stood sentry between the houses and the road. The last few leaves of autumn shivered, clinging to branches that reached toward a milk-blue sky.

Frank turned up his collar and hunched his shoulders toward his ears. "What kind of drugs were you on at the asylum? I'm a pharmacist, so I'm curious."

"If you're a pharmacist, wouldn't you already know?"

"Humor me."

The chill wrapped Stephen's throat, triggering the cough he'd never been rid of since the war. At last, it subsided. "Laudanum. Straight opiates," he said finally. "Enough to make an intelligent man unthinking, enough to make him drool and not much care." He shuddered at the memory. "Didn't mind it so much at the time—didn't have the strength of will. But I'll never go back to that again."

They walked over a mat of leaves sodden from last night's rain. "Opiates are a popular choice with doctors," Frank said. "But the amount you're describing is too much. Did the pharmacist at the asylum administer the doses?"

"Never saw a pharmacist. The attendants were the ones handing them out. I believe they were making their jobs easier by incapacitating those they could."

Frank's mustache pulled down at the corners. "I'd hate to think so. That's not the same as saying I don't believe you. If you were to take the proper amount, it might yet do you good. Dr. Gilbert would—"

"No." Stephen stopped him. "No more doctors, no more drugs."

Words and breath puffed in small clouds as they walked. "I can see how you'd feel that way, Mr. Townsend."

Stephen doubted it. They rounded a corner. Blackbirds pecking at a molding apple scattered when Stephen and Frank neared.

"Did they give you anything else at the asylum?" Frank asked. "Something to help you sleep?"

Burying his hands into his pockets, Stephen admitted they had. "A whiskey tincture. I took it, but won't go back to it now that I'm out. No liquor. No drugs."

"Ah." Frank nodded, the tips of his ears and nose pink from cold. "They must have used whiskey as the sedative's base. I'll bet they added bromide of potash as an anticonvulsant to help reduce shaking. Probably chloral hydrate too, as a hypnotic to help you sleep."

Stephen dismissed the fancy names. "Whatever it was, I won't have it again. Most of the inmates were addicted."

A pair of squirrels chased each other up a tree, chattering at each other the whole way. The sidewalk was littered with black walnuts that should have been cleared away. Stephen kicked them aside as he walked.

"I can appreciate that. I understand you've had a bad experience, but I do believe Dr. Gilbert could help you. You don't have to muscle your way through soldier's heart alone."

Stephen ducked his chin into his cloak collar, unmoved. No more doctors. No more drugs. No more drink.

This was new.

Meg, who had always wanted nothing more than for her father's welfare to improve, had made things worse for him. Sylvie, whose sympathy for him had worn to a thread years ago, had become the one to tell him she understood. He listened to her and seemed soothed to some degree. Meg was glad for that.

She just wasn't glad that her deformity-caused clumsiness had driven him away.

"I'm so sorry," she'd told Edith as Frank had gone after him.

"You've done nothing wrong," Edith said. "And neither has your father. He's doing the best he can." Sylvie voiced her agreement.

"He'll come back to you," Nate had added later. "Give him space. Give him time."

She invited Nate to join her for a stroll along the lakeshore later that afternoon, and he accepted. But first they went back to the shanty along with Stephen and Sylvie so Meg could change her shoes. While Nate stayed in the front room with her father, Meg followed her sister into the back room.

"I wish Jasper and I could go with you." Sylvie sighed. "But he said he needs to study."

Meg sat on the wooden chair and crossed one ankle on the opposite knee to reach the boot. "Exactly how much time would you like to spend with him, if you could?"

A half smile slanted on Sylvie's face. "As much as he can spare."

Meg's hands stilled on her laces as she watched her sister flush. "Do the two of you have an understanding? Is he courting you, Sylvie?"

"If he isn't, I hope he's very near it." Brown ringlets framed her blushing cheeks.

Meg considered this. And Stephen's inevitable reaction to it. He and Jasper had barely spoken to each other at the meal. "Is—is the timing quite right?" She pulled off her heeled boots and replaced them with shoes better suited to pebbly terrain.

"Is the timing right for you and Nate?" Sylvie's voice held an edge to it, but she helped Meg with her laces. Meg could do it herself, but it would take far longer.

"Nate hasn't said he's courting me."

"Yet he is. It's plain to see. And I'm happy for you, Meg, truly. Just, please, try to be the same for me?" With nimble fingers, she laced and tied the shoes and patted their toes when she was done. "All set."

Meg knew so little about Jasper. The few times she'd tried to question him, he hadn't exactly been forthcoming. Still, without his letter to the asylum, Stephen would still be locked up, and that spoke volumes to his character, she was sure. Unless he'd done it to earn Sylvie's affections.

Still ill at ease but unwilling to press the matter further, Meg thanked her and stood to leave. Spying a cardboard box in the corner of the room, she added, "You haven't taken Hiram's old clothes to the relief depot yet?"

"I meant to. But then I saw this." Sylvie spun and reached into the box, withdrawing Hiram's old uniform from the war. "Jasper doesn't want it, or it wouldn't be in the box. Since the historical society lost everything to the fire, I thought I could spiff this up and see if they'd like it. What do you think?" She handed the jacket to Meg.

Her fingers vaguely registered the scratch of wool. The buttons were in need of a shine, but the garment had aged well during the last ten years. "I think that's a grand idea."

She draped the uniform over the back of the chair and smoothed her fingertips along each section of fabric, checking for tears, stains, or spots where a mouse might have eaten through it.

Something crinkled in the trousers pocket. She pulled out an envelope addressed to Hiram. The return address was for Sarah Davenport in Indiana. Hiram's sister.

Meg flipped over the envelope. Scrawled in Hiram's hand, shakier than usual, were the words: *Update will. Appoint Townsends beneficiaries.*

Her heart lurched. Moving closer to the window to improve the light, she pulled out the letter and read.

Dear Hiram,

I know we have kept silent these many years. But I also know you would appreciate news of my grandson, your great-nephew, Jasper Davenport, whom I have raised as my own son since his parents passed away. You and he were close once, before our argument put an end to that. You wrote him many letters that I never did pass along to him, since you refused my request to cease contact. I was wrong not to let him read them. He would have liked hearing from you. I don't suppose you'll forgive me for a long while, if you ever do, but I ask it of you all the same.

As our president would say, Jasper gave the last full measure of his devotion to the cause. He died of typhoid fever in his army camp outside Petersburg, Virginia, in August. You should know . . .

Stunned, Meg looked at the date of the letter: October 18, 1864. *It can't be.* She turned the letter over to find his sister's signature, then flipped it again to reread the impossible words. *Jasper died.*

Shock jellied her knees. If Jasper was dead, then who was the man she had painted?

Sylvie frowned. "What is it? You look like you've seen a ghost."

Sylvie stared at the letter and envelope Meg had spread across their humble kitchen table.

"I knew it," Stephen mumbled. "I knew that man was up to something."

Sylvie glanced at Meg and Nate, silently begging them to contradict him. To say that Stephen was only being paranoid and suspicious again. Her throat dry, she poured herself a tumbler of water and left the pitcher on the table. The cold was bracing to her senses, reminding her that this was no dream.

"He lied to all of us," Meg agreed. "Poor Hiram! He didn't remember his nephew had died. It happened too close to the end of the war. That was when his memory began to grow unreliable."

Wind rattled the windows in the shanty, and the flames on the candles leaned away from the draft. "I—I don't understand how this could have happened," Sylvie stammered. All of them had been duped, but she was even more of a fool than the rest of them. She'd trusted him.

Oliver left the rug by the hearth and nudged Sylvie's skirt. She lifted him to her lap, sinking her shaking fingers into his soft fur.

Stephen looked up. "You said he found the will declaring him the beneficiary? What was the date on it?"

"It was dated 1869. I remember that it was after Mother's death," Meg replied.

"If Hiram updated his will after the real Jasper's death in 1864, what he showed you must have been a fake document," Stephen said.

"It looked real to me." Meg poured herself a glass of water too.

Nate folded his arms. "Forging it would not have been difficult for him. Assuming he really is a law student, he would have the template for the verbiage of a last will and testament."

Meg shook her head and stretched her fingers back from her palms. Her complexion looked sallow in the glare of the kerosene lamp. "But who is this man we call Jasper, really?"

The bench scraped the floor as Stephen stood. He paced the room, tapping at his thigh.

Sylvie watched him, her unease increasing with his. "Are you all right?"

His grey eyes shone. Halting, he clenched his fists, then uncurled them, resuming his stiff-jointed gait. "Whoever that man is, he isn't Jasper Davenport," Stephen growled. "He's a cunning deceiver, and dangerous."

Sylvie's hand went to the ache ballooning inside her. "Dangerous? No, surely not." That haunting song about the wayfaring stranger . . . that was him. He was a stranger, without mother, father, or any other relation. "We may not know who he is, but he isn't dangerous." He wanted to be a better man. For her.

"You don't know that," Meg whispered.

"And you don't know for sure that he is!" Oh, how desperate she sounded. Tears of shame and frustration rolled down her cheeks. "Wait." She sniffed, possessing herself. "Perhaps Hiram's sister was mistaken when she wrote of Jasper's death. She could have been misinformed."

Her father narrowed his eyes, and she felt his disapproval crawl over her skin. His nostrils flared, and a muscle flexed in his jaw.

"What power does that boy hold over you, that you should defend someone who has made fools of us all? Has he made promises to you, daughter, during those long weeks you shared a roof? Has he taken something—"

"No!" Groaning, she lowered her head to her hands, and Oliver fled her lap. "I assure you, he's been nothing but honorable."

"Honorable!" Stephen railed. "Will someone please explain to me the spell that man has cast over my youngest child?"

Meg raised her hands and patted the air in a gentling motion. "Easy, Father. None of us could have guessed anything like this."

"I could have. I knew there was something awry, some devilment afoot. Pure devilment." Stephen was slipping into a darker place.

"We can't answer the how and why," Nate said, "but we can discuss what we do next."

Sylvie folded her handkerchief in her lap. "We can ask him to explain it himself."

Stephen rounded on them, stomping over to the table and pointing a finger at Meg and Sylvie. "Under no circumstances, absolutely none, are either of you to be in that imposter's presence ever again. Whatever fancies you've been nursing about this boy, it's time you put them to a swift end."

Sylvie closed her eyes and saw Jasper's face. She saw his portrait hanging in the library. Then she saw him as he appeared in the carte de visite, still tucked inside the novel she'd borrowed from Hiram's library.

Her eyes popped open. "She was wrong!" she gasped. "Sarah Davenport was wrong, and I can prove it."

With a flurry, she swung her legs over the bench and hurried to the back room, where she found *Villette* and pulled the image from inside. Her heart pounded with relief and joy.

Hastening back to the kitchen, she slapped the card on the table. "Read the back. It's Jasper, identified by Hiram's own hand. He says it was taken in March of 1865. So he couldn't have died in 1864!"

Stephen's brows plunged as he studied the photograph. "What do you make of that?" He passed it to Nate, who looked at it with Meg.

"That's him," Meg confirmed. "I've spent hours studying the contours of his face. He's much thinner here, but the structure of his skull is the same, as is that scar. That's Jasper."

Nate took off his spectacles and closely examined the script on the backs of the envelope and the carte de visite. "The writing is the same too. So which version of Hiram do we believe? The one who tells himself to update his will, or the one who tells us the identity of his great-nephew is just as we thought?"

Sylvie clasped her cold hands together. "Photographs don't lie. That's the version we believe. Either Hiram's sister received a false report, or she deliberately lied to Hiram to make him believe Jasper was dead. They were in a feud, weren't they? Hiram had been writing to Jasper against his sister's wishes. This would have been a way for her to sever the relationship once and for all. He'd have no way of knowing if Jasper was really still alive."

"That . . . makes sense," Meg said slowly.

When no one else agreed aloud, Sylvie rushed to fill the silence. "It's the only explanation that solves this riddle."

Stephen shook his head. "I'm not ready to trust him so easily. Something isn't right about this. Why does Hiram date the photo so late in the war? Mine was taken as soon as I enlisted, and I left it with my family. Jasper told us he joined up in 1861."

A gust of wind sliced through a gap between the window and its frame. Nate pulled an old newspaper from his satchel, folded a page into a narrow strip, and wedged it into the crack.

"I wondered the same thing, Father," Sylvie said. "But maybe there wasn't a photography studio at the camp where he did his training. And his family was poor. I imagine he thought it a waste of money that could be better spent on other things. Maybe his grandmother Sarah begged for a likeness to remember him by, and he finally gave in. It's not all that difficult to imagine, is it? Just because his experience doesn't mirror yours, doesn't make it less valid."

Stephen rose and stood before her. "Do you trust him more than you trust your own father?"

For a moment, she faltered at his question. "No, Father. I trust you too."

"Then do not speak to him again. Do not spend time in his company. There is devilment afoot yet."

Chapter Thirty-One

Wednesday, December 6, 1871

The temperature hovered a few degrees above freezing, with no rain in sight, which was a blessed relief. Mrs. Palmer's Spirit of Chicago Art Show fundraiser was scheduled for the evening of Sunday, December 17, ten weeks to the day after the Great Fire. Days like today made the stress at home fade into the background as Meg willingly lost herself in her work.

Sunbeams broke through the clouds, a symbolic background of hope for a banker surveying the skeleton of his old building, which laborers were bringing down today. He'd worn a black suit, a top hat, and leaned on a cane, making him a stark figure. This time, she painted the subject from behind and placed him to one side so she could see what he saw. His posture in the presence of destruction captured the quality she was aiming for. He was unbowed, unbroken, even as construction crews knocked down the scorched arches and columns of his former bank.

They'd had to stay a safe distance away from the site, which was just as well, because Meg wanted to include as much of the scene on the canvas as possible. The banker stood a few yards in front of her, leaning on his cane. She could hear him reciting Longfellow's "A Psalm of Life."

"Let us, then, be up and doing,
With a heart for any fate;
Still achieving, still pursuing,
Learn to labor and to wait."

His voice warbled at first, but grew strong by the end. Victorious, even. It was beautiful. A smile spread over Meg's face as she painted in tones of ivory black, burnt umber, and burnt sienna the piece she would call *A Heart for Any Fate.*

The humidity coming off the lake deepened the cold in her fingers. She blew on them and kept working until it was time to pack up her supplies and fold her easel. Dusk was falling on the city ever earlier as they moved closer to winter solstice. But in less than three blocks, she would be home.

After pausing to tie her muffler more firmly about her neck, Meg adjusted her grip on the easel, canvas, and case that held her paint tubes, brushes, and palette. Twice last week, Louis Garibaldi had come with her when she painted, carrying her supplies even though she could manage on her own. The relic business was winding down, and she didn't mind tipping him for his help. She also gave him a copy of *The Adventures of Robin Hood*, and he gave her a melted blue marble in return.

With every step she took, her thoughts narrowed to her family. So much had changed since the fire. Some things hadn't.

In the week since Stephen had come home from the asylum, Meg felt a growing tension between her father and her sister, and at the heart of it was Jasper Davenport. Stephen had fixated upon him the way he had once fixated on patrolling the roof, watching for Rebel spies. He cast about outlandish theories to explain who Jasper was and how he had weaseled his way into Hiram's estate. Sylvie maintained Jasper was exactly who he said he was. She hadn't contacted him, but Meg could tell each passing day without him wore Sylvie a little thinner.

Stephen's traits of suspicion and paranoia were in full force, but he was trying to protect his daughters. After years of emotional detachment, and especially after what felt like his abandonment the night of the fire, Meg could appreciate his need to redeem himself in this area. But Sylvie—poor Sylvie. Meg thought at times she could hear her sister's heart breaking. Not only had their father forbidden her to see Jasper, but Jasper had done nothing to indicate he wanted to see her.

All Meg wanted was for her family to be together again, truly together. But here was a rift ever widening, and she balanced on a tightrope between them. *"What do I do?"* she had asked Nate the last time she'd seen him. *"I need to fix this. I don't know how."*

Nate had given her that rare sad smile of his. *"You can't please them both. Please God instead,"* he'd told her. *"If you don't know how, just ask Him."*

He had made it sound so easy. *Just ask.* She had. She did. But so far, the Almighty hadn't responded in a way that she could hear, and she could see no clear path forward. When she was home—which wasn't much, with all the painting she was doing outside—she tried to diffuse the charged atmosphere that had filled the shanty. But between her well-intentioned words and the occasional fumbling of an object with her hands, she only succeeded in irritating one family member or the other.

Her cheeks were numb with cold by the time she returned to the shanty. Wiping her feet on the rug, she set down her things, removed her boots, and hung up her cloak and hat.

At the table, Sylvie curled over a ledger. Stephen sat opposite, plying a needle to repair a book binding. A jar of glue sat on the table near a pair of scissors and a spool of thread. It was good to see her father working again, especially at something he'd once excelled at. Perhaps he could excel at it again.

"Good day?" Meg asked.

Sylvie's pencil hovered above the page. "Why do you always phrase it like that? It's like you're leading the witness. Why can't you just ask how my day was and brace yourself for the answer?"

A legal metaphor. She must be missing Jasper again. "So, not a good day." Meg moved her painting supplies to the back room and leaned the canvas against the wall before coming out again. "Do you want to tell me about it?"

Sylvie gave her a look that said she didn't.

"She won't listen to me." Stephen pulled the thread taut and dipped the needle back into the binding. "I've been explaining to her all day why she shouldn't trust Jasper, and she still isn't convinced."

"Surely not when customers have been here," Meg said.

"What customers?" Sylvie didn't look up from her accounting book.

The shanty was too small to contain the emotion exuded by both of them.

"Sylvie, I'll stay here in case anyone decides to come before closing time. Why don't you call on Anna Hoffman? She'd love to see you. Bring back something delicious, won't you?"

No sooner had Meg suggested it than Sylvie was closing her book and throwing her cloak around her shoulders. "Thank you," she said, and left.

Stephen shook his head. "She won't listen."

Meg put a kettle on to boil. "Maybe let the matter rest for a while, Father. She obviously doesn't want to hear about it anymore. In fact, it would be good for you to think about something else too. What's this book you're working on?"

"*Pilgrim's Progress.* A customer brought it in yesterday for repair. This edition is more than a hundred years old."

"That shows a lot of faith in you, that they would entrust such a volume to your care. I know you'll be an excellent steward of it until you return it to its owner."

His gaze met hers. He set the needle in the gutter of the book. "That's it. That's exactly how I feel about you and your sister. You don't belong to me, you belong to the One who created you. But I'm your steward, and it's my job to care for you and to repair whatever is broken. I've done miserably at it, and I'm trying to make up for lost time. If I come across too strong, it's only because I'm your father. I mean, I'm trying to be your father."

Meg wanted to cover his hand with hers but stopped herself in time. "You are. We'll never stop being your daughters."

Hope kindled and burst to full flame, warming her to the tips of her fingers and toes. He was getting better. He lacked finesse with his techniques, but his motivation and goals were there. Finally, he was coming home.

A short knock on the door preceded its budging open. "Hallo?" Karl Hoffman blustered inside, cheeks pink from cold. "Still open until five o'clock, ja?"

Meg assured him they were.

"*Gut*. My Anna and your Sylvie are visiting at our place. I'm in the way there. What do you say, Stephen, may I sit with you and read the paper? I'll not interrupt your work."

Stephen lifted his head, obviously surprised that Karl was seeking his company. "Sit!" He wiped a hand over his chin in an old habit that betrayed his discomfort.

Smiling, Meg caught her father's gaze and tilted her head toward Karl until Stephen blinked and said, "How are you, Karl? How is your wife?"

Nodding her approval, Meg took the kettle off the heat and poured the water into the coffeepot. The rich aroma of soaking ground beans immediately filled the room. Karl's amiable voice and rustling newspaper brought a refreshing cheer as he spoke of their bakery and customers.

"Now, Stephen," Karl continued, "there is nothing in this paper that interests me today. Full of advertisements and letters and not much else. I know I said I wouldn't interrupt you, but let me see what you've got there. *Pilgrim's Progress*? Never read it. Think I should?"

As the conversation unfolded, gratitude filled Meg. She didn't think Karl actually had an interest in *Pilgrim's Progress* so much as he had an interest in talking to Stephen about whatever interested him. It was an invitation to companionship, a declaration that Stephen's past was no obstacle. Coming from an immigrant who had often been shunned himself, the gesture was even more meaningful.

"Coffee?" she asked the men.

When both agreed, she carefully moved the old book out of the way before bringing the men their hot drinks.

That task complete, she poured a cup for herself and took it to the back room, where she sat on the mattress she and Sylvie shared. It had been no trouble to secure a second one for Stephen once she'd explained to the Relief and Aid Society that they needed it. They'd grown used to dragging them into the front room at night to be near the fire, and then back again in the morning. *"I've endured far worse conditions,"* Stephen had reminded them. A small reference to the asylum or Andersonville, or to any army camp, she supposed. But for him to bring it up, even in passing, felt like progress, and she celebrated it.

What was the rest of that Longfellow poem the banker had recited today? *"Still achieving, still pursuing, Learn to labor and to wait."* She had waited years for the kind of hope she felt for her father now. No matter what tomorrow held, she was thankful for today.

Setting her mug on the floor, she reached for the photograph of her father in his army uniform and studied it. He looked determined and perhaps a little afraid. Thirty-five when he'd enlisted, he had none of the eagerness displayed by the much younger recruits who had no wives or children. He hadn't gone to chase adventure or glory. He'd wrapped his meek personality in a uniform and done what he thought was right.

She took a sip of coffee and thought of Jasper's photograph. He'd been nineteen when it was taken. And yet he had no eagerness in his expression either, unless she misremembered. Curious now, she picked up Sylvie's copy of *Villette* and withdrew the photograph, laying it next to Stephen's. It was odd, she mused, how devoid of emotion the young man's face was. She shifted her gaze to her father's image again.

The backdrops used in the studios were exactly the same. Exactly.

Meg picked up her father's card and read the text printed vertically in the ivory border on the right side of the image: *Daniel F. Brandon, Photographer, Camp Douglas Studio*.

She picked up Jasper's card. The edges had been trimmed away so the lower half of the words had been cut off, making it impossible to read. But when she lined it up on top of Stephen's image, it was a perfect match.

Jasper had told Sylvie this year was his first visit to Chicago. But he'd had his photograph taken in Camp Douglas in 1865.

Why didn't he want them to know?

And why had Hiram never mentioned that his nephew had been there while he was serving there too?

Thursday, December 7, 1871

A cry pierced the night, jolting Stephen from an already worthless slumber.

Sylvie.

"The bridge is burning," she gasped in her sleep. "We can't cross it—"

He rolled off his mattress and knelt next to hers, hand on her shoulder to wake her. "Sylvie," he said quietly, then again, a little louder.

Meg roused at the noise. "Another nightmare?"

"Go back to sleep, Meg. I've got her."

She regarded him for a moment before rolling onto her side, facing the opposite wall, where the table and benches had been pushed to make room for them to sleep by the stove.

"Sylvie, wake up, darlin'," he tried again. "It's a dream. You're all right, I've got you."

Her nightmare was not reality, but it had been once. She was trapped in terror she'd known before. He wanted nothing more than to rescue her from it.

His own heart thundering, he slipped his arm beneath her shoulders and raised her up to sit. "It's all right, it's over." He gave her a little shake and felt by the jerk in her limbs that she'd finally awakened. He focused on calming his breathing, now that the crisis had passed.

"Father?" Two slender arms wrapped around him. Sylvie tucked her head beneath his chin. She was crying, silently sobbing against him. "It's been such a long time," she whispered, "since we did this."

Stephen frowned, trying to recall the last time he'd hugged her. He couldn't. "Do you miss it?"

She nodded, her hair catching in the stubble on his jaw. "So does Meg. A lot. She was the one who claimed your lap most often. She's always felt loved through touch."

A lump grew sharp in his throat as he recalled reading to Meg while Sylvie curled up with a book alone. Holding Meg's hand and waving to Sylvie as she headed to school without her sister. He swallowed. "And you? How do you feel loved?"

"Time."

He'd given more of that to his firstborn too. "Well, I'm all yours right now, if you'll still have me."

He was only half joking. Mindful not to bother Meg, he guided Sylvie to sit beside him on his own mattress and smoothed the hair back from her brow.

"I'll have you," she said quietly. It was a wonder.

Then, with a pang, Stephen thought of another man who had somehow claimed her heart. "You also want Jasper. Don't you?"

How could he make her see what he saw? She seemed blind to any misgiving. It was a reckless affection, a dangerous infatuation—he refused to call it love. For her own good, he needed to put a stop to it. He didn't trust that fake farther than he could throw him.

She sighed. "Let's not talk about him right now."

"Fair enough." Oliver climbed onto Stephen's lap and curled into a ball, purring. He stroked the battered animal's fur, weaving his fingers between its bald spots. "I'm sorry about the nightmares."

She leaned her head on his shoulder. "They don't feel like dreams. When I'm having them, I think they're real."

"I know," he said, and hoped she understood all that lay behind those two words. He knew what it was to be terrified, even when the threat was only in his mind. He knew what it was like to both dread sleep and long for it because insomnia was such a cruel master. Waking up in a sweat with a heartbeat that drilled right through his chest? Yes, he knew that too.

"I know you do," she whispered. "I wish you didn't. I wish neither of us did." She sat up straighter. Oliver climbed over her legs and wandered away.

They sat beside each other in the quiet, listening to Meg's breathing grow deep and steady. Outside, the wind moaned and reached its cold fingers through a crack in the wall. Stephen grabbed his army blanket off the floor and draped it over his daughter's back.

She spread it behind him to cover his too. "Did I wake you?"

"Not really."

"Oh no." Sylvie turned to face him. "Have you been sleeping poorly since you got back?"

He rubbed the heels of his hands against his eyes. "Sleep and I haven't been on the best of terms lately. What little I get is about as fitful as yours." He hated that it was worse now than when he'd been taking the whiskey tincture at the asylum.

"I'm so sorry." She yawned. "Did Frank have anything helpful to say to you on Thanksgiving?"

"He recommended I see Dr. Gilbert. I won't do it."

A few moments passed, and he hoped her delayed response meant she was growing drowsy. At length, she said, "I would go with you, if you wanted me to."

"I've had enough doctors, daughter. I told Frank, and I'll tell you. I'm through with the lot of them."

"All right. I suppose if you don't need a doctor, that means neither do I. We'll get better together, won't we?" With a pat to his knee, she said good night and crawled back into bed with Meg.

But long after she succumbed to slumber, Stephen still lay awake.

Friday, December 8, 1871

Energy coursing through his veins, Nate waltzed into the temporary *Tribune* building on Canal Street, his satchel heavy with paper. Eleven hundred pages, to be exact. At last, the court proceedings of the investigation into the cause of the fire had been released to the press. Nate had been first in line at the police headquarters to receive his copy. Now he was the first in the copy room.

The race was on. Whichever paper printed the news first would not only get the sales and bolster the paper's reputation, but it would establish public opinion on the topic of who to blame. Nate wanted to be first, but even more than that, he wanted to be accurate. To present the information in a way the people would understand.

Which meant that first, he needed to understand it himself.

He dropped the satchel on his desk with a *thunk* and followed the smell of coffee into the small room down the hall, grateful one of the secretaries had already brewed a pot. Taking a mug from the shelf, he poured the first of what would likely be many, many cups. Eleven hundred pages to analyze and synthesize would take all the focus he could muster. He could do this.

Burning his tongue, Nate gulped his coffee so he could walk without spilling it, then hurried back to his desk.

And there was Meg, her face bright from the early morning cold. "Thank goodness you're here," she breathed.

"I'm here, and I won't be going anywhere for quite some time." Nate set his cup on the desk and rolled up his sleeves. "The notes from the Catherine O'Leary trial are here."

Her gaze widened and fell on the satchel. "All of that?"

"All of that."

Her brow crimped. "Then I won't keep you. It's just that I found something I don't know what to do with. I didn't want to show Sylvie or Father, because I don't know what conclusions they'd draw. I don't know what to think, myself."

"Show me."

Unclasping her reticule, she withdrew two cartes de visite and laid them on his desk side by side. Jasper Davenport and Stephen Townsend. "Look at the backgrounds," she said.

They were identical.

"Now watch this." She overlaid Jasper's card on Stephen's and pointed to the printed edge. *Daniel F. Brandon, Photographer, Camp Douglas Studio*.

Nate took off his glasses. He picked up the cards, studying the words on both, sliding Jasper's card to the left, then back into position on top of Stephen's. "It's a match. It's plain to see he was at Camp Douglas."

She leaned across the desk toward him, and her rosewater scent lifted from her skin and hair. "He told Sylvie he'd never been to Chicago before this fall."

Unease trickled through Nate as he replaced the spectacles on his nose. "So what else is he lying about?"

"Exactly." There was a little too much curiosity and not enough fear behind that word.

He circled the desk to reach her, his hand enclosing her shoulder. The wool cloak was still cool from the outside air. "Listen. Your father was right when he told you and Sylvie to steer clear of Jasper. Whatever mystery this is, I don't want you mixed up in it." His attention drifted toward his bulging satchel. "I'll look into it as soon as I can. But I need to work on this article right now. Promise me you won't do anything about this while you wait. Don't say anything to anyone."

"I wouldn't," she said. "I won't. You're the only one I trust."

Nate released her, digesting the weight of that responsibility. "Leave the cards with me. Then carry on with your day as planned."

Sun slanted through the blinds, striping her cloak, her face, the hair spiraling down her back. "I will. You have a long day ahead of you, so I won't take more of your time." She snapped her reticule closed.

"I *want* you to have more of my time. I want to hear how your father is getting along, how the paintings are progressing, how business is going for the bookshop. I want to hear how *you* are."

She tilted her head, raising an eyebrow. "Perhaps over a slice of blackberry pie?"

Smiling, he took a step back from her. "I'd like that very much."

"Then we have something to look forward to, after all of that." She pointed to the work awaiting him.

His pulse quickened with the urgency. "I'd best get to it. Don't worry, I'll keep these safe." He squeezed her hand, and she slipped away.

The outline of her receding figure still in his mind, he tucked the photographs from Camp Douglas into the inside pocket of his satchel. *Daniel F. Brandon, Photographer.* The name was familiar. Nate had probably read it in the directory of burned-out businesses that had moved to new locations. If he could visit Brandon—

A different day. Right now, he had to focus. He pulled out the massive report on the O'Leary trial, covering nine days of questioning and fifty witnesses, and got to work.

An hour later, Nate leaned back in his chair and closed his eyes, rocking his head from one shoulder to the other, stretching his tightening muscles. After reading answers from so many witnesses, questions formed in the back of his mind for Otto Schneider.

"*People will say just about anything for money*," he'd said, referring to the false witnesses who blamed Stephen Townsend for the murder. But every instinct Nate had told him Otto had been paid off—at least, his family had been—to confess to Hiram's murder. *"I did what I had to do. For my family. Golden opportunity."*

It made sense. But he had no proof. This morning at the police station, he'd read Schneider's file one more time but gained no fresh insights. When he left with a copy of the O'Leary trial transcript, he'd also carried the nagging suspicion that Schneider had been set up to take the blame for Hiram's murder, just as Stephen had been. The difference was that Schneider was a willing participant in the scheme.

Part of him wanted to tell Meg. But until he could also tell her who Hiram's real murderer was, he saw no need to upset her. Between her father, Jasper, and the upcoming art show, she had enough to manage as it was. No, he decided. He wouldn't trouble her with this. At the moment, he ought not be distracted by the matter himself.

"Pierce."

Nate looked up to find Mr. Hollingbrook, his interim editor until a permanent replacement could be found. His clothes were rumpled, and Nate wondered if he'd slept here last night—if he'd slept at all. He'd taken on the city editor role in addition to remaining the editor over the national news.

"Good morning." Nate squinted at the sun that poured in behind his boss.

"Glad to see you've got an early start on this. I want the *Tribune* to be first to report these findings. Can you make that happen?" He straightened his suspenders over his shoulders.

"I'll waste no time, sir. But neither will I compromise quality for speed." Nate couldn't speak for what other papers would do, or how fast.

Hollingbrook nodded. "Your writing is clean and tight, and you don't bury the lead. All good things. But I also heard you tend to get 'bogged down,' I think was the phrase, with facts." A curious smile tugged the corner of his mouth.

Nate dropped his pencil and folded his arms. "I'm thorough. I ask a lot of questions. I double-check facts before I file my stories."

Mr. Hollingbrook appraised him, eyebrows drawn as if in thought. "Some would say that's the editor's job."

"Then I'm happy to lighten my editor's load." And Hollingbrook ought to be glad of it, with his increased responsibilities.

Chuckling, the editor thumped his fingers on the O'Leary transcript. "Then you best get back to it."

Nate couldn't agree more.

Chapter Thirty-Two

Saturday, December 9, 1871

Sylvie swept the shanty floor, shooing Oliver away when he attacked the broom. Not bothering to grab a cloak, she stepped outside, heartened by the tinkling of the little bell that hung on the door handle. She inhaled the bracing cold air and tossed the contents of the dust pan around the corner of the shanty so it wouldn't be immediately tracked in again. Hurrying back inside, she shut the door on the blustery weather and tucked strands of hair back into her braided chignon.

The bright curtains and rag rug she'd made with Anna lent a coziness to the meager place, and the smell of coffee was ever present as a welcome to anyone who might stop by. Karl and her father had fashioned two tall bookshelves that held a growing collection of old friends. Whichever titles did not sell she was happy to keep for herself.

With Stephen accompanying Meg as she painted on the North Side today, Sylvie was alone but not lonely. Helping herself to a piece of Anna's strudel, she returned to the table to indulge in one more chapter of *Villette*. But as this book was borrowed from Jasper, it only reminded her more keenly of his absence.

Hadn't he felt hers? At all? Had she only imagined that their moments alone together in his library a couple weeks ago had meant more than the words they'd said?

The bell jingled, the door unlatched, and Louis Garibaldi sauntered in. "The sign says open, so I opened it."

Sylvie laughed softly. "That's the idea." She cut him a slice of strudel and beckoned for him to join her.

Swiping his cap into his hand, he obliged. "This is good," he said, chewing. "Mama's going to have her baby any day now, so I'll be needed at home. You won't be seeing me for a while. But I wanted to tell Miss Meg that I finished the book she gave me, and I wondered if you have more stories like that. I've been reading to the little ones at home to keep them quiet for Mama, see."

"I do see." Sylvie went to the bookshelf and selected *Robinson Crusoe*. "This one has a shipwreck and adventure on a deserted island. Do you think they might like that?"

He said they would. "How much?" He took one last bite of his pastry, stood, then dug in his pocket, bringing out a handful of change.

Sylvie named an amount he could afford.

Replacing his cap, Louis dropped the coins in her hand and beamed as he took the book. "You'll tell Miss Meg I was here, won't you? Tell her I bought a book. She'll like that." He left with a bounce in his step.

Sylvie was clearing his plate from the table when the bell jingled again.

Stepping inside, Jasper doffed his hat and smiled, bringing the dimple to his cheek, and all thoughts of Louis and his family fled.

"Jasper! What a surprise to see you!"

He cringed, then turned to hang his hat on the peg beside the door. "Then I've neglected my friends for too long."

Friends. He'd lumped her in with her sister and father. "I'm sorry to say Meg and Father are out at present." Thank goodness they weren't due to return for a few hours. "But I can offer you strudel and coffee, since you're here. I don't suppose you need to purchase or order any books?"

"Of course! Isn't that why most customers come?"

So now he was just a customer. Sylvie pressed her lips together to trap a growing exasperation. Possessing herself, she smoothed a wrinkle from her skirt. "Why exactly are you here?"

He grew serious, all jesting fading away. "You all left in such a hurry on Thanksgiving. I wanted to see how things have been for you. Has your father adjusted to being home?"

"He's adjusting. We all are." She folded her hands in front of the belt at her waist. "That's why you came?" She longed for so much more, and yet she could hear herself pushing him away with her clipped tone and short words.

He studied her for a moment. "You're different, Sylvie. Something's wrong. I've been so busy with classes, and perhaps I should have called earlier, but I thought your family needed some time alone during your father's transition home. I hope that—other than that—I haven't done anything to offend you."

A short laugh escaped her. He hadn't done anything at all. And yet his presence stirred her in ways she wanted to deny. She ought to be done with it, with him, once and for all. She would stop pining for this wooden man, and her father would stop persuading her she ought to.

Lifting her chin, she resolved to do just that, for he caused her more angst than joy. "I borrowed this book from Hiram's library. I'll send it home with you now." She scooped up *Villette* and thought of his image nesting between its pages.

"Have you finished it yet?"

"I don't need to. I know how this story ends, and I actually hate it."

When he reached to take it from her, his hands lingered on hers. "Are you sure?"

She thrilled to his touch, to his question. Oh, the meaning she could assign to those three words. He could mend her heart or break it with so little effort, it scared her.

"Jasper, please," she whispered, folding her arms over her starched and pleated shirtwaist. "I'm sure I don't know what you mean."

"Don't you?" The dimple reappeared, and she turned away from it. "I'm sorry. I'm not a tease. I do want to see more of you, and

I'd supposed—perhaps wrongly—that our last conversation made my regard for you clear. It's just that my studies keep me very occupied."

"You want to see more of me as a friend?"

A charming pink stole over his features. "As more than that. If you agree."

Dare she believe him? Her heart lurched with a resounding *yes*, then plummeted. "My father would never allow it."

He frowned. "But why? What have I done?"

"Nothing." She bit her lip. Everything her father held against Jasper was based on misunderstanding, she was sure of it. She could ask him to clear it all up for her, thus clearing the path for their budding future together.

But did she really want to be the one to tell Jasper that his grandmother, the woman who raised him, had told Hiram he was dead in order to cut them off from each other? That could only bring him sorrow. And he'd already been through so much.

And the photograph. That was another question mark. For her, it was of no consequence that he'd had it taken a month before the war's end rather than when he signed up to serve. She had several good theories, but if she could resolve the matter definitively, perhaps Stephen would be satisfied.

"What aren't you telling me, Sylvie?" Jasper stepped closer, filling the space between them with his balsam scent.

She swallowed, glancing out the window to make sure no one else was coming. "There's a photograph in the book. That book." She nodded toward the novel he'd tucked under his arm. "Of you."

The color left his face. Going to the table, he set down the book and opened it, flipping the pages from front to back. Not finding it, he searched the pages again. Held the book upside down by its covers and shook it. Nothing.

He unwound the muffler from his neck and dropped it on the table, then unfastened the buttons of his cloak. "What photograph?"

"It must have fallen out in the back room. But it's a carte de visite of you in your Union army uniform. A studio picture. On the back, Hiram wrote the date it was taken. March 1865. It's a striking image, and I'm sure you'll want to hang on to it. Show your children and grandchildren someday."

"Perhaps." He scanned the front room, as though searching for the card. "Who else has seen it?"

She pinched her locket between her finger and thumb. "Just me and Meg, and Nate and my father. The only thing is, my father wonders why it was taken so late in the war. That is, what made you wait four years before having your picture made?"

There was only the slightest pause before he replied. "I wouldn't have had it made at all, but Uncle Hiram said he wanted to have my likeness." He shrugged. "So finally I gave in to please him. He was very patriotic, as you know. As proud of my service as he was of his own."

"Of course," she breathed. "That makes perfect sense. Give me a moment, and I'll go find it."

Bustling into the back room, she searched for the card, but to no avail. She didn't see her father's carte de visite either. Perhaps Stephen had taken them both when he left with Meg, unwilling to be without either one for some reason.

Irritated, she returned to the front room, the curtain falling closed behind her. "I didn't see it, but I'm sure as soon as Meg and my father come home, one of them will know where it is. We'll return it to you soon."

The corner of Jasper's lips curved up. "See that you do."

Snow flurries swirled into the room when he opened the door. As he left, he was no longer smiling.

Chapter Thirty-Three

Monday, December 11, 1871

Fog muffling her footsteps, Meg hurried to keep pace alongside Nate as they headed to Mr. Brandon's new photography studio. His eyes veined with red beneath the brim of his hat, Nate had come to get her before she'd had time to go out and buy a copy of his paper. Judging by the shadow on his jaw, he hadn't taken the time to shave this morning either.

She didn't think she appeared as ragged as he did, but she was undeniably exhausted from all the painting she'd been doing. The art show was a scant six days away. Her mind spun with all she must accomplish between now and then, but she locked that away for now.

"So?" She looped her hand through Nate's elbow. "Can you distill eleven hundred pages of notes into a single sentence for me? What's the verdict?"

His smile was weary. "Catherine O'Leary was found not guilty."

"Who then, or what, do we blame?"

"I spent hours upon hours carefully crafting the article to answer that very question. It pains me that you didn't read it." He pressed a hand to his heart in mock injury.

"I'll pick up a copy on the way home. But please don't keep me in suspense! Is the story at least on the front page?"

He shook his head. "The story is buried. The answer: they don't know."

She stopped and stared at him. "After all that?"

"After all that. A quote from their conclusion: 'whether it originated from a spark blown from a chimney on that windy night, or was set on fire by human agency, we are unable to determine.'"

Meg shook her head. The damp air slid under her collar and seeped through to her bones. "Let's hope we get more definitive answers from Mr. Brandon. You still have the photograph cards, I assume."

"Right here." He patted his chest. "Anyone miss them these last few days?"

"As a matter of fact, yes. Jasper came to the shanty on Saturday, and Sylvie tried to return the photograph to him, only to find it was gone. He told her he'd like to have it back."

He looked at her. "What did you tell her?"

"The truth. I told her I noticed something a little odd and brought it to you for your opinion, but you were busy on an important assignment. Honestly, if I'd known it would take you this long, I wouldn't have left them with you." She peered ahead, looking for landmarks she recognized along the street. The hovering mist rounded corners and softened edges.

"Ah, but if you hadn't left them in my care, Jasper's image would be with him now, and we would have lost our proof."

"Proof of what?"

"We'll find out shortly. Here we are."

Inside the photographer's studio, Meg wiped her feet on the rug and surveyed the dozens of sepia portraits covering the walls. Some had been tinted, making lips and cheeks artificially pink, their eyes a startling blue. Partitioned off by folding screens from the rest of the room, a portrait area was arranged with a chair and small covered table in front of a velvet curtain held aside with a tasseled cord. A pleated folding-box-style camera perched on a stand.

Mr. Brandon came out from the back room soon after the bell announced their arrival. His sleeves had been pushed above his elbows, and he quickly rolled them back down and fastened the cuffs at his wrists. A bright green and yellow parakeet chirped inside its cage as he passed it. Extending a hand to Nate, he used his other to smooth his brown hair.

"Greetings!" Mr. Brandon smiled. "What can I do for you today? I offer a full range of photographic services. We even do color tinting now."

"So I see." Meg stifled the urge to ask about that process. Instead, she introduced herself.

When Mr. Brandon offered his hand, she shook it with her left. It felt awkward, but this was how she'd decided to navigate this social custom—boldly and without apology.

"We were hoping you might be able to clear something up for us," she said. "I understand you were the photographer for Camp Douglas during the war."

He hooked his thumbs behind his suspenders. "That I was. Churned out many a portrait of Union enlistees, Union guards, and Confederate prisoners. What can I tell you?"

Nate produced the two images, then walked to the counter and set them on a green felt surface. "We see your stamp on the edge of this card." He pointed to Stephen's. "The other one has been trimmed, but it seems a match as well. Can you confirm this?"

Mr. Brandon slid Jasper's card over Stephen's. "You bet. I took both of those photographs, I'm sure."

Meg turned Jasper's image over. "Now look at the date. March 1865. We were told this young man enlisted in southern Indiana in early 1861. Do you have any idea why he would have his photo taken at Camp Douglas one month before the war's end?"

A cuckoo clock on the wall broke into the conversation, chiming nine times to mark the hour. Ignoring it, Mr. Brandon thrust out his lower lip in thought. "The only Union soldiers I was photographing at that time, other than the guards of the Invalid Corps, were Galvanized Yankees."

Nate's eyes flared behind his spectacles. The parakeet chirped and twittered.

When no explanation followed, Meg said, "I'm not familiar with that term."

"As early as 1862," the photographer began, "the U.S. government tried to alleviate the overcrowding of Union prison camps by offering the Confederate prisoners a way out if they took an oath of allegiance to the United States of America and promised not to fight the North anymore."

The fire crackled merrily nearby, rendering the damp air warm and almost suffocating. Meg unfastened the buttons of her cloak. "So prisoners could take the oath and be free? Just like that?"

"Not exactly just like that," Nate corrected. "They were sworn in as 'Galvanized Yankees'—a particular brand of Union soldier—and sent west to fight the Indians along with sorely stretched Union troops. They were released from prison only to be put back into service fighting for and alongside their former enemy. They were sent out west so they wouldn't have to fight their Southern comrades."

"And so they wouldn't be tempted to desert and put on their butternut greys again," Mr. Brandon added. "A small percentage of prisoners took the opportunity, but it came with quite a price. I can only imagine what sort of welcome they received from their families in Dixie after the war."

Meg searched her mind for a place to fit this information. Mr. Brandon was implying that Jasper had been a Confederate soldier first, a suggestion that didn't make sense. "Jasper Davenport told us he was a Union soldier from the first day he enlisted." If he hadn't said it in so many words, the implication had always been there. "He said his uncle, Hiram Sloane, requested that he have his photograph taken. Hiram was a prison guard at Camp Douglas."

Nate turned to her. "How do you know Hiram requested that?"

"Jasper told Sylvie on Saturday. She asked him about the date."

Mr. Brandon was nodding, his double chin flattening with each bob. "I remember Hiram Sloane. I was so sorry to read of his murder the night of the fire. May I ask what your interest is in him and this young fellow Jasper you're asking about?"

"Hiram was a dear friend of our family. His great-nephew, Jasper Davenport, has come back to Chicago and is the sole beneficiary of his estate." She did not add that her sister had fallen in love with him.

"Ah! I never knew they were related, Hiram and this young fellow." Mr. Brandon glanced at Jasper's image. "What a change in fortune for them both. Yes, Hiram insisted on paying for this photograph. It struck me as most unusual, a Union guard paying for the image of a Confederate prisoner. But if they were related, that changes things, doesn't it?"

She tapped his photo with her fingertip, a sliver of paint showing beneath her nail. "Forgive me, but what you're suggesting is difficult to swallow. I never would have guessed it based on this photograph."

Mr. Brandon chuckled, his gaze drifting for a moment to the parakeet dragging his beak across the bars of the birdcage for attention. "Photographs can be deceiving."

Exasperation needled her. Far too warm, she shrugged out of her cloak and folded it over her arm. "Explain."

"Well, now. You look at that image and see a Union soldier through and through. I see a Confederate prisoner who took the oath of allegiance, traded his rags for a uniform he despised, and sat for a portrait he didn't want right before he was shipped off to fight alongside soldiers he probably still considered his enemy. Look at his eyes. Does he look patriotic to Uncle Sam to you?"

A chill swept down her spine. She looked at Jasper's image again. She couldn't deny Mr. Brandon was right about his expression. Hadn't she noticed something off, something especially hard about it, even before she brought it to Nate?

"So that's the secret, then," she whispered. "Hiram's beloved nephew was fighting on the opposite side of the war. No wonder Jasper never wanted to talk about it."

Nate shifted his weight, spun his bowler in his hands. "Mr. Brandon, I understand you were burned out of your previous location. Did you happen to save any of your records?"

"Precious few. I don't have my ledger books from that time, but I do have a few other photographs from Camp Douglas, if you'd be interested. One is of a group of prisoners taking the oath."

"Yes, sir, I'd appreciate seeing that."

As Mr. Brandon left, Meg turned to Nate, resting one elbow on the counter. "It makes sense now, doesn't it? Jasper has never been open with us. He didn't want us to know he'd been to Chicago before because he didn't want to tell us it was only as an inmate at Camp Douglas." A pang of sympathy for Jasper broke through her shock at this discovery.

Nate studied the photo, the double cowlick on the back of his head splaying his hair into a little fin. "Something still doesn't fit. That letter from Sarah to Hiram . . ."

"Was a ruse," Meg finished. "She must have wanted to sever the tie between them once and for all. I imagine their family feud ran along patriotic lines. She must have been for the Confederacy, and Hiram was staunchly for the Union."

Nate lifted a hand. "But she said Jasper died in the army camp outside of Petersburg during the siege, the summer of 1864. *Outside* of Petersburg. It was the Union army camped outside the city during the siege."

"True, but Confederate troops built defenses outside the city too. Both armies were technically outside Petersburg." She summoned the exact words of the letter. "Perhaps more telling than his position was that Sarah also wrote, 'As our president would say, Jasper gave the last full measure of his devotion to the cause.' It was Lincoln who used that phrase about the last full measure of devotion in his Gettysburg Address. So if we believe Jasper was included in the pronoun *our*, he fought for the Union from the first."

Thoughts tumbling through her mind, she plucked the pencil from behind Nate's ear.

Reading her intention, he pulled paper from his satchel and slapped it on the counter. After stretching her hands, Meg made two columns with a line down the center of the page. At the top, she labeled one *Sarah says* and the other *Brandon says*. Into each, she scribbled the facts as they knew them, for once not caring that her left-handed script was inelegant.

Under the *Sarah says* heading, she wrote: *Jasper a Union soldier from the beginning. Died outside Petersburg, summer 1864.*

Beneath *Brandon says*, she wrote: *Jasper a Confederate soldier, prisoner at Camp Douglas, took the oath of allegiance to Union in March 1865, and then fought with the Union. Hiram paid for his portrait.*

"They can't both be true." Meg sighed. "The only thing they have in common is that Jasper was a soldier."

"And only one column is supported by actual proof." Nate pointed to Mr. Brandon's.

The photographer emerged from the back room, shaking his head. "It wasn't where I thought it would be. It must not have survived the fire after all."

Meg wasn't surprised. "Thank you for looking, just the same."

The parakeet chittering after her, she and Nate left with more questions than when they'd arrived, but at least she could return the photographs to their rightful owners. She had no reason to keep Jasper's from him anymore.

"Will you tell your family what you learned?" Nate asked her. "Even though it seems to contradict Sarah's letter?"

Meg unfolded the paper showing the columns of information. "You were right, Nate. The only true evidence we have says that Jasper was a Confederate prisoner of war. Father and Sylvie ought to know that. And Jasper shouldn't live with the burden of keeping it a secret."

Maybe now he would take off that mask he wore and be free to be himself.

Stephen's hand shook. He pinched the needle all the harder, determined not to let it stop him from repairing the binding on a customer's copy of *Paradise Lost*. It was so straightforward, this task. Match the needle's tip to the holes already scored in the pages, pull the thread through, and repeat. If he couldn't mend a book, how could he mend what really mattered in his life? If he couldn't bind the pages to the spine, how could he bind together what was left of his family?

Sitting back, he touched his chin, still not used to the smooth feel of his shaven skin. He would have let his beard grow back if Sylvie hadn't told him she liked seeing more of his face. More of him. It was the sort of thing Ruth had said early in their marriage, her gentle reminder he needed to shave.

Oliver climbed onto Stephen's lap. He scratched beneath the poor creature's chin, heart aching afresh at the sight of his singed-off whiskers. Gently, he stroked from the cat's head to his tail, feeling for his ribs. "I think he's hungry," he said.

"Is that what he's telling you?" Sylvie said without looking up. She was tying red and green plaid ribbons onto a spruce wreath to hang on the door. "Oliver Twist already had a meal this morning. He doesn't need more until this afternoon."

"Are you sure?" Stephen glanced at the pantry shelf, looking for something to offer him.

"Trust me." She lifted Oliver from his lap and, with a kiss between the cat's ears, deposited him into a little box she'd lined with flannel and set on the floor near the stove. "Don't let him distract you."

But he was already distracted by the effort of not speaking his mind about Fake Jasper. He didn't have a problem concentrating. His problem was that he was concentrating on the wrong thing. It would be a relief to let it go, but his thoughts seemed locked onto a one-way track with no destination in sight.

The bell jingled, and Meg and Nate came in, faces almost as pale as the mist that surrounded them. Stephen could see nothing out the windows, so dense was the fog today. It was as if the shanty were wrapped in a shroud. He shuddered at the idea, for he'd had more than one nightmare of being buried alive in a mass pit like the one he'd fed bodies to at Andersonville. He stomped his foot beneath the table, anchoring himself to the present so he wouldn't slip into the past.

Meg pulled the door closed and locked it before turning the sign in the window to *Closed*. Hanging her hat and cloak, she said, "We need to talk."

Stephen had a bad feeling about this.

Nate hung up his frock coat and bowler as well but left his muffler draped over his shoulders as he sat across from Stephen. "Sorry to interrupt." He nodded at *Paradise Lost*.

Stephen moved his project to the end of the table and covered the book and tools with a towel in case Oliver decided to take a stroll across the pages. "What's this all about?"

Waiting until Sylvie lowered herself to the bench beside Stephen, Meg took her place by Nate and sighed. "In a word: Jasper. We've just come from a visit with the photographer from the Camp Douglas studio."

Her voice ricocheted between Stephen's ears as she laid out two cartes de visite, his and Jasper's, and explained that they were taken by the same man in the same location. She unfolded a piece of foolscap and smoothed it out, turning it so two columns faced him and Sylvie.

His heart rate launched sky high. He heard Meg's voice, then Nate's, and Sylvie's higher-pitched surprise, but more than any of that, he heard the alarm inside his head. Layers of sound converged and diverged like a thousand clanging church bells.

"I knew it." He licked his dry lips. "I knew something wasn't right about him. Didn't I say that? Didn't I? He's a Rebel. I'd wager he's a Rebel spy, even now."

"The war is over, Father." Meg's tone was far too confident. She didn't understand.

"No, it isn't. Not for me. And probably not for him." He passed trembling fingers through his hair. It was short. So very short, because they'd shorn his head at the asylum. Scabs on his scalp caught beneath his fingernails. The sensation catapulted him back to Andersonville.

"He's not a spy, Father," Sylvie said with passion simmering just beneath the surface. "He's not even a Rebel anymore. This is why he never wanted to tell us who he really was. You're over-reacting."

No, he wasn't. The Rebels were here in Chicago. He'd always known it would come to this. It was why he'd patrolled the roof of his building for years.

"It's my job to protect you," he said. He'd left his girls defenseless for those long years of war. He'd never do that again. "I'll protect you from that Rebel, but you must cooperate with me and do exactly as I say."

Tears shone in Sylvie's brown eyes. "I don't want to be protected from him. Don't you see? I care for him!"

Her words were a blow. He clutched at his heart, then shoved back from the table and marched the length of the room, sixteen feet and back again, his hand slapping his thigh.

Meg spun around on the bench to face him, a strand of hair curling by her cheek. "Father, if we believe he's a Confederate veteran, then we also have to believe that he took the oath of allegiance to the United States years ago and fought as a Yankee too. We have to believe that Sarah Davenport was either mistaken or lying when she said he died, which means Jasper is who he says he is. He's Hiram's nephew. Hiram knew about his allegiances and loved him anyway. He left his entire fortune to him."

She looked so young, so naïve. In his mind's eye, he saw her wearing a pinafore and braids down her back. She was a child.

Inhaling deeply and slowly, Stephen attempted to steady his breath. He turned to Nate. "What do you say about all this?"

The reporter stood to look him straight in the eye. "It's rather a shock, isn't it? But it seems like there are still a few pieces missing to this riddle. And sometimes knowing part of the truth can distort the true picture a great deal."

"How's that?" Stephen struggled to remain rooted in one spot as Nate spoke to him. But the fire in his limbs wouldn't allow it. He broke into a pace again.

Nate grabbed the two ends of his muffler. "For instance, we knew the Great Fire began with a spark in Catherine O'Leary's barn. So we blamed her and her cow for starting the fire. Some even said it was deliberate. But the inquiry revealed she was in bed and could not be blamed. Unfortunately, the damage to her reputation and the reputation of Irish immigrants might be beyond repair. People love a scapegoat."

"I'm not talking about an Irish immigrant and a fire," Stephen growled. Sweat streamed from his temples down the sides of his face, and he mopped it with his cuff. "I'm talking about a Rebel and my daughters."

"Jasper is your scapegoat." Sylvie's voice was so quiet, Stephen almost missed her words.

He rounded on her, silently daring her to repeat them.

"You have to separate what happened to you from Jasper," Sylvie said. "You never met him before this fall. He never hurt you. And you weren't among those who hurt him. Make no mistake, Jasper suffered too. In ways you can understand better than the rest of us."

His chest was heaving. His pulse in a runaway gallop, he felt like he was about to come out of his skin.

"It's a surprise for all of us," Meg said gently. "But remember what you told us in one of your letters from early in the war? You said that at first, you considered all Southerners Rebels and assumed all of them were bad people. But then you admitted there were good men on the other side of war, even if they did things you didn't agree with. I think we owe it to Jasper not to assume too much. Let's judge him not on his past, but on what he does with his present and future. Wouldn't you agree?"

Stephen wasn't stupid. If the question had any finer point to it, it would have cut right through him. She was saying that if Stephen didn't want to be judged on his past—which he didn't—he ought not judge another man that way either.

"Take some time with this new information, Mr. Townsend." Nate pulled his muffler from around his collar. At least Stephen wasn't the only one who was overly warm. "It will take a while to grow accustomed to it, but I have faith that you will."

Faith. Stephen had that too. He firmly believed in a God who loved him, a God who had the power to heal. He had thought that if he prayed hard enough, tried hard enough, he would feel better than this, more in control. But what father, what Union prisoner of war veteran, could take news like this and not be upset?

He sank into a chair. *Lord, help me find my way through this*, he started to pray. But when he closed his eyes, he found himself back in Andersonville, trying desperately to scoop rainwater tainted by human waste into a tin cup so he would not die of thirst. A guard stood over him, casting all into shadow. He looked up and saw Jasper's face.

Stephen launched to his feet, shaking his head. That wasn't right. Jasper hadn't been there. But the fact that he'd seen that image so vividly scared him. For a fraction of a second, he wondered if he ought to have stayed in that institution, but another thought chased it away. He was home to protect his family. He was home for such a time as this. What would his too-trusting daughters do without him?

For the first time in months, his hand went instinctively to his hip. But his gun wasn't there. "Where's my gun?" he half shouted.

Suddenly Meg was at his side, her hands on his arm, but he shook her off. Nate was on his other side. Someone was crying. Sylvie. "Settle down now, there's no need for that," someone said.

"But where is it? A man ought to have a gun," Stephen insisted. "How else am I to defend you?"

Then all at once, he remembered. The fire had destroyed it. That Italian boy tried to sell it to him as a relic. Then the police showed it to him as proof that he'd shot Hiram.

Stephen had no gun anymore. There was an enemy in camp, he had his daughters to protect, and he had no gun. Panic sliced through his chest.

Chapter Thirty-Four

Tuesday, December 12, 1871

It had to be nearly midnight. But as Meg lay on the mattress, she could hear that her father's breathing still hadn't fallen into slumber's deep and rhythmic pattern. He lay awake, as she did, with only Sylvie truly at rest between them.

Rolling onto her side, Meg's gaze drifted to the bookshelf. Titles stamped in gold on the spines reflected the orange glow coming from the stove. She spied *Wuthering Heights*, and her thoughts flew to the woman who wrote it.

When Emily Brontë fell ill, her entire family knew she was dying but her. Or if she knew it, she denied it. She refused to rest or see a doctor or alter her daily routine in any way. Poor Charlotte and Anne had to watch her waste away until at last she agreed to call a doctor. But it was too late. She died that same day. She hadn't let her family help her.

Cold expanded from Meg's middle. Would this be Stephen's story too? He was unwell; she saw that now. She'd been naïve to think otherwise. Still he refused her entreaty to see Dr. Gilbert, and she was running out of ideas to help him on her own.

This was what swirled in her mind as she finally succumbed to a fitful sleep.

She awoke to chill air blasting her face. A thin wedge of moonlight slanted across the room, snowflakes dancing in its gleam.

The door was open. Stephen was gone.

With a start, she scrambled out of bed.

"What is it?" Sylvie jolted upright, then turned to their father's empty mattress. "Oh no."

Both sisters threw on their cloaks and shoes, grabbed their mufflers, and left the shanty, latching the door behind them.

The cold took Meg's breath away as she looked up and down the street. Chimneys from other shanties piped grey smoke into the sky, but there was no sign of her father.

"Where did he go?" Sylvie asked, her words small puffs of white in the dark.

"I don't know," Meg replied, "but I think I know why. What else can he be doing but patrolling again?" Only this time he lacked the advantage of a three-story roof from which to keep watch.

With a groan, Sylvie wrapped her muffler tighter around her neck, then pointed to footprints in the snow. They followed them until they disappeared.

Meg's heart drummed an alarm on her ribs.

She'd lost him. Again. He was no better off now than he'd been before the Great Fire. How could she have been so blindly optimistic to think that his coming home would make him well?

Tears stiffened on her lashes and glazed her cheeks. "I can't do it," she whispered to herself, to God, to Sylvie. "I can't take care of him." Wherever he was, she prayed God would protect him, guard his mind, and persuade him to come home.

Her feet carried her forward into the swirling snow. Bending her head to the wind, Sylvie kept pace beside her. They'd been heading toward Court House Square when the footprints disappeared. Meg led Sylvie across the street and made for the tallest building. What had looked like a ruin to her from a distance was the new construction of a work still in progress. Scaffolding made a dark grid beside it.

"That's where he would have gone," she said.

Sylvie looked up and covered her mouth.

"Come on." Meg's hair whipped about her face and neck as

she approached the building. "Father?" she called up. Snow floated down in giant feathery flakes.

A lone figure appeared in the open window of the unfinished third floor. "Meg? What are you doing here?" His cloak flapped open over his nightclothes.

"Sylvie's here too. Come down. You'll catch your death of cold up there. Let's go home."

They were right back where they'd started. She was calling out to a father beyond her reach.

"No, no, I can't come down. I need to keep watch."

Sylvie cupped her hands around her mouth. "You don't."

But he'd already marched away. The distance between them was unbearable.

"If anyone reports his behavior, will it be enough to send him back to the asylum for good?" Sylvie asked, voicing Meg's own concern. Was he displaying madness or simply an overdeveloped protective instinct?

"I'm going up." Meg expected her sister to argue.

"I'm going with you."

Bolstered by Sylvie's support, Meg pinched her nightdress in her right hand, lifted it above her ankles, and climbed the ladder of the scaffolding. Sylvie waited a few moments before climbing after her.

The rungs were cold enough that Meg could sense it even through the scar tissue of her left hand. At last on her father's level, she stepped onto the floor and felt the wind whistling all around her. Part of the wall was built, with holes for windows not yet set, but there was nothing but open sky above and on three sides of them. She helped Sylvie off the scaffolding.

They met her father in the middle of the floor.

"You don't need to be here. I've got this under control," he told them.

But he didn't. And neither did Meg. "This isn't working," she whispered, her nose and fingers tingling from the cold. She buttoned his cloak up to his collar.

"You're right," he said. "I'm not doing any good up here. If I see something suspicious, what can I do? Holler?" He shook his head. "It won't do. I need a gun. By heaven, tomorrow I'll buy one." The force in his words softened her knees.

What could he do—what would he do—with a gun? Maybe nothing. For years he'd patrolled the roof of their building, weapon in hand, but had never fired a shot. But that didn't mean he wouldn't pull the trigger in the future, especially now that he was even more convinced of Rebel spies in Chicago. They'd gotten him out of the asylum once. If he gave the slightest reason to be locked up again—and a menace to the public was reason enough—he'd be there the rest of his days.

"It's my right to have one," he was saying. "The Second Amendment says it's my right to defend myself and what's mine."

Sylvie steadied herself by gripping the lower edge of a window opening. "I don't think a gun is the answer." Ever so slightly, the brick she held moved, grinding on the brick beneath it.

Her eyes widened, and a shockwave of comprehension arced between her and Meg. In their haste to reach their father, they had climbed an unfinished building of brick construction. After all Nate had said about the mortar crumbling in the cold, after seeing a building topple over, Meg had placed herself and her sister at the top of one, and on a night when the wind blew strong.

Releasing the brick, Sylvie stepped away from the wall. "We should go."

"Yes," Meg agreed. "We need to leave now."

"I'm watching the city." Stephen was completely oblivious to the danger they were in. "Look how peaceful it looks, with the snow covering everything with a blanket of innocence and light. But it's what lies beneath that troubles me."

Meg's breath formed crystals on the inside of her muffler. She pushed it down beneath her chin. "I hear you. But let's talk down on the street. This building isn't stable."

Snow capped his short hair and caped his shoulders. He cocked his ear, eyes wide and shining as he scanned the blocks around them. "Do you hear that?"

She didn't. She didn't hear anything but the pounding of her own heart and Sylvie's breathing beside her.

A gust of wind billowed their nightgowns and sent three bricks from the top layer of the wall to the street below. The floor swayed.

Stephen jolted. "Someone's there."

"It was the wind knocking bricks off the wall." Meg's pulse rushed in her ears. "The mortar doesn't hold—the building isn't safe. It could topple any time, and all of us with it."

"Father." Sylvie's voice was small against the wind. "I'm scared. I'm really scared right now, and I need you to protect me, to protect us. That means we all need to go now, before we fall."

The wildness fled his eyes as he looked at her. Stepping across the gap that divided them, he took Sylvie's hand, then Meg's, scars and all. "I won't take you girls down with me," he said. "I never wanted that for you."

It felt like a small miracle to be touched by him, followed by another that compelled him to climb down the quivering scaffolding to the solid street below.

When they were half a block away, a great crash shook the earth and reverberated through Meg's being. She knew even before turning that the building they'd just left had fallen.

Sylvie gasped, her complexion pale as pearl. The horrified look she sent Meg said their escape had been far too narrow.

Stephen dropped to his knees in the snow, staring at the destruction.

Kneeling beside him, Meg placed a hand on his shoulder. "It's all right," she choked out, though it nearly hadn't been.

"By heaven, daughter. I think someone was trying to kill us."

Meg buried her face in her hands.

Wednesday, December 13, 1871

Exhaustion weighted Sylvie after last night's ordeal with her father. She had the nightmares and racing heart in common with him, but the similarities ended at the intense paranoia and suspicion that dogged him as much now as they ever had. He couldn't go on like this. None of them could. So after a tortured family conversation that morning, he'd agreed to consider seeing Dr. Gilbert next week, after Meg's art show was over. That wasn't much of a promise, but it was the best they could get from him.

In the meantime, he desperately needed to sleep. Perhaps with the shanty to himself right now, he could. Sylvie had other things to do.

She wondered if she ought to feel guilty for arranging a meeting with Jasper without her father's knowledge but quickly decided against it. The photograph belonged to Jasper, and she'd promised to return it to him. If she hadn't taken it out of his house to begin with, none of this would have happened.

But she had, so here she was, with Meg and Nate on the property of the burned-out Unity Church in the North Division, waiting to see if he would come. Meg had been here last week with Stephen and had painted Reverend Collyer in the church. But she needed to come back to finish the details of the building. As soon as Sylvie had learned of Meg's plan, she'd offered to join her and Nate and then sent a note to Jasper telling him when she'd be here. Stephen had a cold this morning anyway—little wonder, given last night—and was happy to stay home.

Sylvie wrapped her muffler around her neck more snugly and tied it under her chin. Wind scoured through what was left of the church, making eerie high-pitched moans and kicking up dust and dirt. Only the outer walls were left standing. There was no roof anymore and nothing inside, the debris having been cleared away. Seen from a distance, Meg had likened it to a line drawing, a mere charcoal sketch on a grey-toned background. She'd been right.

At least the temperature held above freezing, melting off last night's snow and allowing Meg's paints to stay malleable. The humidity in the air, though, soaked the cold right through Sylvie's layers.

Meg poked her head out from behind the canvas, brush in hand.

"Would the two of you move into the building, please? I want to add people in the sanctuary, re-creating that first Sunday after the fire. I need you to give perspective."

Sylvie's toes tingled inside her boots as she trudged inside the walls.

Nate pushed down his own muffler to speak. "How are you holding up, Sylvie?" His breath fogged the lower half of his spectacles.

She sent him a sideways glance. Unsure how to answer, she changed the subject to her father instead. "I keep thinking that it's a good thing Father's gun was destroyed in the fire and taken away from him," she said. "I hate to think of him patrolling like he did last night with a weapon. If he's viewed as a threat to anyone's safety, he'll return to the asylum forever. Despite our disagreements, that's not what I want."

"No. None of us want that." He lifted his head and gazed at the place where the church bell had been. Now there was just the outer wall of the bell tower rising above empty arches where doors and windows once were. "You do know he's not trying to make you miserable, right? He genuinely believes his job is to keep you safe from harm."

She nodded. "And he genuinely believes Jasper is dangerous. He's genuinely wrong."

A hansom cab rolled into view. Anticipation fluttering, she watched it draw near and slow to a halt. Jasper climbed down and had a word with the driver.

"What a coincidence," Nate murmured, raising an eyebrow at her.

In the edge of her vision, Sylvie saw Meg watching too. Meg hadn't been thrilled with this arrangement, but at least she agreed he deserved to have his photograph back. Meeting at the shanty was out of the question, and so was the idea of Sylvie meeting him at his house alone again.

"It will only take a minute," Sylvie told Nate. "Don't tell me you're uncomfortable with this."

"Not as long as I keep my eyes on the two of you."

She laughed. "There's nowhere to hide here, so that shouldn't be a problem."

A moment later, she was standing with Jasper in the church, several yards away from Nate. "I'm sorry it took so long to return this to you." She withdrew a small book of sonnets from her pocket that she'd used to keep the carte de visite flat. Opening to the middle, she withdrew the image and handed it back to its owner.

"Yes, curious. Why was that?" His nose and cheeks were reddened with cold. There was a guardedness about him. He probably thought she'd hate him if she knew who he really was.

Flustered, she tucked the book back in her pocket and resolved to be as honest as she could without hurting him. "I'll tell you. But please don't interrupt me, and don't jump to conclusions." As briefly as she could, she explained what Meg and Nate had learned at the photographer's studio. "I don't think any less of you, Jasper, for fighting for the South. It's important to me that you know that."

His silence grew uncomfortable.

"Are we wrong?" she asked. "About any of what I said?"

He blinked and looked away. "No. I did fight for the Confederacy. I was imprisoned in Uncle Hiram's camp, and he paid for the photograph, as I told you before. And then I became a Galvanized Yankee. You could have come to me with your questions, Sylvie. No need to ferret out the answers on your own."

"Would you have told us? Would you have shared all of that with me?"

The side of his mouth twitched up and back again. "Not all at once, if I could have helped it. But can you blame me? Chicago and I have a checkered history. You come from a very patriotic family, and your father . . . I can't imagine he took the news of my past very well."

Sylvie shifted and glanced at Nate, who was still watching her. "It was a shock to him. But he'll come around, I think, with time." At least, she hoped he would.

"Not any time soon, I wager. I'll stay away, out of respect for his wishes. And I'll ask you and your family to show me enough respect not to research me behind my back anymore. I'll save you the trouble and tell you outright. In case you were wondering, my family never had a single slave. Any other questions, all you need to do is ask." He tipped his hat to her.

She couldn't let him leave, not when she was finally getting to see behind his mask. "I'm asking you now," she said almost breathlessly. "Please talk to me. I want to know more of who you really are. Jasper—I saw your feet."

That stopped him. Something flashed across his face. "Frostbite. From being made to stand barefoot in snow and ice at Camp Douglas."

"How dreadful. I had no idea."

"Then you never climbed the observatory tower and watched the show. I'm glad."

"No, my mother never allowed such a thing." She was quiet a moment, waiting to see if she'd pushed too far. But since he wasn't walking away yet, she tried her luck again. "And that song about the wayfaring stranger—why did you react so strongly to it?"

He sighed, as if it took a great deal of patience to answer her. "That's a popular song down south. It brought me, and many a soldier, great comfort during the war and especially during our imprisonment. I was worried you'd guess I fought with the Confederacy by that song alone, and that you'd want nothing more to do with me."

With that small bit of honesty, the door to the true Jasper Davenport creaked open. She wanted to swing it wide but caught herself before she reached for him. She straightened her spine with the dignity that remained to her. "You needn't have worried on that score, Jasper."

The smile on his face was rueful. "Good day, Miss Townsend. I do wish you all the best."

He went, and the sun ducked behind a cloud.

Chapter Thirty-Five

Sunday, December 17, 1871

Meg closed her eyes and drew a deep breath. It didn't help.

Nothing was wrong between the two of them, Nate had said. He wasn't angry or offended by anything she'd said or done. She should have left it there and been satisfied. But she'd been so sensitive to the distance she feared was growing between them that she begged him to reveal whatever he was hiding. After learning Jasper's surprising past, she was through with secrets and half-truths.

Reluctantly, he'd told her. He doubted Otto Schneider had killed Hiram. He believed, but couldn't prove, that Otto had been paid to take the blame. *"I don't want you to worry,"* he'd added after telling her all his reasons. But what she heard was, *The killer is still at large, no one knows who he is, and the police aren't investigating.*

That was two days ago, and she'd carried that conversation with her ever since, along with a dread that wrapped and squeezed.

She hadn't been able to eat all day. Now that she was standing in Mr. Jansen's gallery moments before the Spirit of Chicago Art Show opened, she was glad of it. A hand pressed to her bodice, she smiled at Bertha Palmer and hoped her nerves were not as evident as they felt.

"You're ready for this," Mrs. Palmer told her with a smile. Gaslight sparkled on the diamonds in her hair and gleamed on the birch floor. Gilt frames hung at eye level on dark green papered walls. At the opposite end of the long room, a string quartet tuned their instruments and began playing, their music the perfect polish to make the evening shine.

If only Meg could concentrate on this, and not on a murderer still running free. With a silent prayer for help, she resolved to set aside her dismay and enjoy the evening. A month ago, she'd never have thought this possible.

"Maybe Father will come later," Sylvie said.

Maybe. But crowds rattled him, and the last thing Meg wanted was for him to be out of sorts tonight. At least at home he was comfortable. Still, the fact that he was missing this event stung, no matter how good the reason for it.

"Whether Stephen comes or not, you must believe he is proud of you. We all are." Anna Hoffman's voice refocused Meg's attention on what was before her, rather than what wasn't. Having come early to donate pies and pastries to the fundraiser, she beamed as she gestured toward Meg's work sharing wall space with several pieces Bertha had brought home from France.

Meg's gaze blurred as she took in the scenes she'd painted around the city, from Louis Garibaldi selling a relic to Bertha Palmer, to Reverend Collyer shepherding his congregation in his burned-out Unity Church. One painting showed Sylvie working at the aid distribution center, and another showed Anna Hoffman bringing pretzels and Berliners to German families in the ravaged North Division. And there was the banker, posture erect, wearing his best suit and reciting *"a heart for any fate"* as his old institution came tumbling down. A handful of smaller paintings were scattered between those five. Each one told its own story, but viewed together like this, they formed a tapestry of hope.

Sylvie grasped her hand. "Just think. You never wanted to paint from life before, and now look at the life you've captured."

Overcome with gratitude, Meg squeezed her sister's hand in return. "Ten weeks ago, every woman here lost nearly everything," she said quietly. "But look how far we've come. Look how far Chicago has come."

"Yes, dear." Mrs. Palmer nodded, taking a peek at the timepiece chained to her bodice. "Here we are, and more are soon to arrive. Are you prepared to meet them?"

While Meg and Mrs. Palmer discussed the silent bidding process, Sylvie and Anna receded to the edges of the room. From the adjacent reception area, smells of apple cider perfumed the air along with the evergreen boughs placed on the linen-covered table. Several footmen loaded silver trays with cups of cider to pass among the guests.

Not five minutes later, the first of them arrived in furs and jewels. Completely in her element, Mrs. Palmer ushered them toward Meg and introduced her in such glowing terms that Meg wasn't sure she could live up to them.

"See for yourself," Mrs. Palmer told her friends, sweeping an elegant arm toward the paintings. To Meg, she whispered, "Your turn."

Swallowing her nerves, Meg followed their gazes, noting where they lingered, and began telling them about the subject portrayed.

"But I heard you burned your hands," a gentleman said. "It must have been a rumor."

"It isn't," Meg said, and his gaze dropped to her scars. Weeks ago, she would have shrunk away from his curiosity. But she'd earned this night and the attention. All she felt was pride.

"Fascinating!" He turned to the paintings with new interest.

After that, Meg could hardly keep track of how many people she met. Helene Dressler and Kirstin Lindberg were among them, chatting with Sylvie for a long while after they admired her work. Jasper was conspicuously absent. She knew it was better that way.

When Nate arrived with Frank and Edith, Meg was talking with a couple from the Prairie Avenue district. She smiled and waved discreetly, then turned back to the woman who wanted to know more about the fate of Reverend Collyer's church. By the time the couple had moved on, Nate apparently had too.

Threading her way between guests, Meg was stopped a few

more times before she finally reached the Novaks and warmly thanked them for coming.

"We wouldn't miss it." Edith kissed her on the cheek.

"If she weren't already so fond of you, Meg, I'd say she's just as happy for a night away from the kids," Frank teased. Then his expression grew serious. "Nate told us what happened with your father this week. His urgency to get a gun, his patrolling in that building right before it collapsed? He really should see Dr. Gilbert."

"I know. He said he'd think about it. I'd love to schedule an appointment for this week."

"That would be wise."

"Now, if we can only get my father to agree." Meg looked around. "Didn't I see Nate with you?"

Edith accepted a cup of cider from a passing footman and sipped it. "He asked after your father. Then he disappeared."

"I think I know why." Frank nodded toward the door.

Nate and Stephen entered together. Nate found Meg and steered her father straight toward her. Frank clapped his brother-in-law on the back and shook her father's hand. Edith waved a footman over and passed a cup of cider to Stephen along with her greeting.

Tears gathered in Meg's throat. "I didn't expect to see you!"

Stephen glanced at Nate, then at her. "This is a big night for you. I said I would be here for you from now on, didn't I? Well, here I am."

"I can see that." She could also see by the hunted look in his eyes that it was costing him. He was exhausted as it was. "I appreciate it more than you know. Maybe you'd like to take a seat while you drink your cider. Be sure to get a slice of Anna's strudel too."

One of Frank's colleagues approached them, and Frank and Edith broke away to converse with him and his wife.

Stephen lowered his voice. "I'm not good at talking to strangers, daughter. Not unless they want to talk about books."

"You won't need to," she replied. "Just sit and look at the art. That's exactly the right thing to do."

Nodding, he went to one of the cushioned benches and lowered himself onto it.

"You look lovely," Nate said, "and so does your work. Enjoy yourself tonight."

She wanted to ask if he'd learned anything new about Otto since they'd spoken on Friday but then decided that could wait. "I will," she said. "I am."

"Good. I don't want to keep you from your guests, so I'll go sit with your father. If anyone tries to talk to him, they'll have to talk to me instead." He was protecting Stephen. He had his own family here with whom he could spend time, but instead he was attaching himself to her father.

She reached out and grabbed his free hand, pulling him back to her. "Thank you," she told him. "For coming and for convincing my father to come too."

"You're welcome." The way he smiled at her made her wish she could sit beside him too.

A cup balanced on his knee, Nate gladly put thoughts of Otto Schneider aside for the night and focused on Meg instead.

"It means a lot to Meg that you're here for this," he told Stephen. "It's good of you to come. I know it isn't easy for you, which makes it all the more meaningful."

Making no comment beyond a nod, Stephen sat ramrod straight on the bench, staring at Meg's paintings while he chewed the last of his strudel.

The Garibaldi brothers walked in, and Meg clasped their hands in warm welcome.

"That boy in the painting," Stephen said, squinting. "Who is that?"

A placard mounted beneath the frame gave general information, but Nate supposed Stephen wanted specifics. "That's Louis Garibaldi. He and his brother Lorenzo sold fire relics in the neighborhood until the weather turned too cold."

Stephen pulled at his collar, then stood. Taking two steps closer to the wall, he pointed at the canvas. "I've seen him before. Just didn't notice it until now."

Nate joined him. "Well, he's right over there, talking to Meg and Mrs. Palmer."

His brow folding, Stephen swiveled. "I know that boy. He took my gun. A man ought to have his gun, especially at a time like this." The cup of cider shook in his right hand, spilling a few drops over the side.

"Steady, Mr. Townsend." Nate took the cup from him and deposited it on a passing tray. "Tell me more," he prompted. "What happened?"

"The morning after the fire, that kid offered to sell me my Colt Army revolver that I lost the night of the fire. But I couldn't pay for it, and why should I have? It was mine. My initials were etched into the side."

"So he sold it to someone else?"

"He must have. The next time I saw it, the police officers said it was evidence in Hiram's murder. I want to know what Louis did with my gun after I saw it last."

Nate was intrigued as well. "Listen. There's a cloakroom just off the hallway where we can speak with a little more privacy. I'll bring him over, and you can talk to him there, but only if you promise to keep your voice down. Don't yell. Don't touch him. Can you do that, Mr. Townsend?"

Stephen's nostrils flared. "I'll try."

"Excellent. Go to the cloakroom. I'll be right there." Straightening his cravat, Nate ambled over to the Garibaldi brothers and inserted himself into their conversation with Meg, Edith, and Mrs. Palmer. After congratulating the boys on their new baby sister, Nate turned to Meg. "If you don't mind, I'd like to borrow Louis for a few minutes. We have a few questions about the relic business."

"That so? Then I ought to come too." Lorenzo squared his shoulders. "Louis is the loudmouth of the operation. I'm the brains."

"By all means." Nate smiled. "Right this way."

A forest of furs and frock coats lined the small space, dimming the sounds of conversation and music just outside it. Gaslight spilled from a single sconce, casting shadows beneath Stephen's eyes and cheekbones.

Lorenzo tipped his hat back on his head. "Interested in purchasing a relic, mister? We closed up shop for the season, but if you have a specific item in mind, I may be able to meet your need."

Stephen frowned at Louis. "You tried to sell me my old gun. The one with my initials on it. SJT."

Louis's eyes widened. "Surly Jaw T-bone?"

"Stephen James Townsend, you—" Stephen stopped himself and inhaled deeply. "You remember who I am."

"Gentlemen," Nate said. "This is Stephen Townsend. His daughters are Miss Meg and Miss Sylvie."

Eyebrows spiking, Lorenzo looked between his brother and Stephen. "Stephen Townsend is their pop?"

Louis kicked one shoe against the other. The top was peeling away from the sole. "I didn't know that. I didn't even know Miss Meg yet." His bravado began to falter.

"That's all right, Louis," Nate said. "We'd just like to know what you did with Mr. Townsend's gun after he told you he couldn't buy it back."

"That gun was important to me," Stephen added. "What happened to it is important."

Louis scratched the back of his head and straightened his cap. "Is it important to Miss Meg and Miss Sylvie?" Gaslight flickered in his large black eyes.

"It could be, yes," Nate told him.

Lorenzo pulled off his hat and wrung it.

"I sold it to someone else." Louis shrugged. "I made a pretty penny off it too. As soon as this other fellow showed an interest in it, I knew he could be had. So I set the price high. He set it even higher, so long as I did him one extra favor."

"What was that?" Nate asked.

"Didn't make much sense, but he told me to bury the gun somewhere, real shallow, and then tell the police I saw Townsend do it. I also had to show them where to find it."

"So you're false witness number one." Stephen stepped backward, his face darkening. But the slant of his shoulders made it seem like it was almost a relief to know. "You have no idea what you did."

"How was I supposed to know? I thought, how much trouble could a guy get in for burying his own ruined gun? The man offered me cash for it, and I took it. I got a family to look out for, after all."

Interesting. Otto Schneider said he hadn't paid the witnesses right away.

Nate bent on one knee to the boy's level. "Louis, do you have any idea who the other witness was? The one who said they actually saw Mr. Townsend shoot Hiram Sloane?"

Lorenzo clenched his jaw, then cleared his throat. "It doesn't matter anymore, does it? The charges were dropped. You're not going to put the witnesses in jail, are you?"

Straightening, Nate looked the young man in the eye. He knew something. Nate had one guess as to what it was. "Tell me, Lorenzo."

"I'm not talking on the record," he said. "If I sing, you have to promise not to put it in your paper. Leastwise, not the specifics. Not the names of the false witnesses. Bad for business, you know."

Nate did. "The only reason I want to find the witnesses is so they can identify the man who put you—that is, the witnesses—up to this. He's the real criminal. Witness names can remain confidential."

A frown rippled across Lorenzo's brow. Wearing fingerless gloves, he pushed his hair off his forehead. "Fine, I'll say it. That man who paid my brother off—I followed him and asked if he had any other work he needed done. All I had to do was say one little line, and I had enough money for—well, it was a lot more than he paid Louis. My brother didn't know I made that deal." He turned to Stephen. "But yeah, I told the police I saw you shoot Mr. Sloane."

Nate exhaled a long breath as he stole a glance at Stephen. It was the first confession he'd heard in a while that made any sense. "You all right, Mr. Townsend?"

Stephen rubbed his chin. "I will be once I know who was behind this scheme. If you don't know his name, do you recall what he looked like?"

Louis bit his lip and stuffed his hands in his pockets. "Not really. I see a lot of people every day."

"Did he know the gun belonged to Mr. Townsend before you found it?" Nate asked.

The boy looked up through the thick fringe of his lashes. "That's how I got such a high price for it. I told him it belonged to Stephen James Townsend. Now, if we're through, I think I'll have another slice of pie." He scuttled away.

"If you think of anything else, contact me." Nate handed Lorenzo his card as the young man followed his brother.

After a few minutes to allow Stephen to compose himself, they headed back into the gallery in time to see Daniel Brandon skip the cloakroom and reception area and bluster right into the main room.

"That's the Camp Douglas photographer," Nate told Stephen and hailed Mr. Brandon over. "This is Mr. Stephen Townsend. His photograph was one of the two we brought you. What brings you here tonight?"

After greeting Stephen, Mr. Brandon reached into his jacket and withdrew a file folder. "I found something after you and Miss Townsend left my studio, Mr. Pierce. You'll both want to see this, I'm sure. If I hadn't seen the notice about this show, I wouldn't have known where to find you. Now that I'm here, I'm eager to see what she thinks of this."

Nate's curiosity was piqued. "She's occupied at the moment. You could wait, but she's bound to be talking most of the night with whoever walks through that door."

"Then I'll show you." Brandon pulled a photograph from the folder. It was eight by ten inches, showing a group of about a dozen men with their right hands held aloft. "This is the last group of prisoners to take the oath of allegiance to the North. The last of the Galvanized Yankees to come out of Camp Douglas. See any familiar faces?"

Nate scanned the gaunt and haggard men. "That's Jasper, all right. Look, Mr. Townsend."

"So it is," Stephen said.

It wasn't exactly new information, but it did prove their theory that Jasper had been a Galvanized Yankee.

"No, it isn't," Mr. Brandon said in a low tone. "You keep calling this fellow Jasper. I couldn't place the name when you said it, but didn't think much of it since I photographed thousands of soldiers. But I can tell you now that this man's name isn't Jasper."

He flipped the photograph over. Affixed to the back was a typewritten caption with the date and names of the prisoners taking the oath.

Jasper's name wasn't among them.

Nate turned the photograph again, studying the faces. "But that's him. I'm sure of it."

"I agree it's the same man from the photo you brought in. But I'm telling you, Jasper is not his name." Mr. Brandon pointed to the back. "He's second from the left, front row. That man's name is George Skinner."

The air changed in the room. Stephen's countenance was thunderous, the atmosphere around him crackling.

"You're sure?" Nate whispered to the photographer. "Absolutely sure of this?"

"Absolutely sure."

"He's no relation." Stephen blinked over and over, slapping his thigh. "No relation to Hiram at all. He's a Rebel devil, plain and true. No relation."

"Wait." Nate squeezed Stephen's shoulder. "Slow down, Mr. Townsend. Steady. Remember the back of Jasper's carte de visite? Hiram wrote Jasper's name. He called it—" He frowned, recalling to mind the exact phrase. "The likeness of Jasper."

"So he did." Mr. Brandon's head bobbed. "I'm confident that what he meant was that George Skinner was the very likeness of his nephew. They looked alike. But they were two different people."

Stephen dropped onto a nearby bench. "All this time," he muttered, rocking back and forth, head in his hands. "All this time, all this time. The enemy in the camp. I need my gun."

"Easy, there. We'll sort it out." But dread filled Nate's belly with stones.

Looking up, he noticed several guests watching them. One of them was Louis. Nate crooked a finger at him, and the boy shuffled back over.

Nate showed him the photograph. "What do you see, Louis?"

The boy pulled up his trousers by the waist and leaned forward. "Why, that's him! The man who bought the gun! How'd you know?"

He was pointing to George Skinner.

Chapter Thirty-Six

Something was dreadfully wrong.

Nerves as tight as violin strings, Meg met Nate in the center of the gallery. Her father, Mr. Brandon, and Louis Garibaldi clustered around her.

"Tell me what's going on," Meg said.

Nate signaled to Sylvie to join them, then held Meg's hand. "We've learned some information that we need to take to the police."

Meg's mouth went dry. "Now?" What could be so urgent that it couldn't wait until tomorrow morning?

"I'm afraid so. Mr. Brandon and the Garibaldi brothers need to come with me to help explain it."

Patrons peppered the gallery, dividing Meg's attention between the show and what Nate was saying. "Care to explain it to me too?"

"We found the false—" Stephen began, but Nate put a hand on his arm.

Witnesses. They had found the false witnesses at last. Louis and Lorenzo wouldn't look at her. She didn't have to wonder why. A great sigh lifted and released her shoulders as she digested this. As disappointed as she was that her young friends had done such a thing, she was sure it had been for money, not out of malice.

"I promise to tell you everything after the show tonight," Nate said. "Your father will stay here with you while we run our errand."

He turned to Stephen. "Let me handle this, Mr. Townsend. It's better this way."

Meg pulled Nate into the hallway that led to the cloakroom. Sylvie followed, her cheeks flushed with more than heat. "Should we be alarmed?" Meg kept her voice low.

"It's Jasper, isn't it?" Sylvie asked breathlessly.

Nate took off his spectacles and dropped them into his jacket pocket. "I suppose I can't tell you to keep an eye on your father without telling you why. So yes, it's Jasper. He's not who he says he is, and now we have proof."

Meg's stays dug into her ribs as she inhaled. "But he admitted he was a Confederate soldier and then a Galvanized Yankee. He told Sylvie everything." She glanced at her sister.

"Not everything," Nate said. "Which is why we need to go to the police. You must keep your father in sight. Sylvie, can you do that? While Meg talks to potential buyers?"

"I can try, but—"

"It's imperative. If Frank and Edith are still here, you can ask them to help. Tell them why. Don't let him leave alone." His words were razors, whittling Meg's composure and scraping the charm from the evening. "Tell Brandon and the Garibaldis I'll be right with them. I saw Helene and Kirstin here—tell them not to go back to Jasper's tonight. They'll need to trust us on this. I don't have time to explain."

Sylvie paled. Swallowing, she swept away toward the sound of the string quartet and voices as light and tinkling as wind chimes.

Questions and conclusions exploded in Meg's mind, but she knew she only had time for one. "Do I need to tell you to be careful?" She still hadn't let go of his ink-stained hand.

Stepping deeper into a shadow, he pulled her closer. "As long as no one goes to see Jasper—or the man who claims to be Jasper—no. It's your father I'm most concerned about." His gaze left hers to scan the hallway before returning to her face. "I wish it wasn't tonight. I wish I hadn't just ruined your show for you."

Meg wished a great many things. She shook her head. "It's not your fault. Just be safe and come back."

He cupped her face in his hands and smiled. "Haven't you noticed? When it comes to you, I can't stay away."

Sylvie had never aspired to be an actress. She had no fondness for feeling one thing and expressing another.

But tonight, as she smiled at Chicago's elite and agreed with them about her sister's talent, her heart wrung itself out over the two men she cared about most in the world. Thank goodness Frank, Edith, and Anna had all agreed to help make sure Stephen didn't leave. It would take all four of them, she supposed, to keep her father from doing something he'd regret. Did he even realize how much people cared about him? Here were three friends he hadn't had before the fire, and that wasn't even counting Nate and Karl. All of them were Sylvie's friends now too.

And who did Jasper have?

No one.

He could have had Sylvie, though. She would have joined her life with his willingly if he hadn't shut her out. What could Nate have possibly discovered about his past that they needed to go to the police about? Every minute of not knowing seemed like an hour.

"Excuse me, Miss Sylvia Townsend?"

She turned to find a red-haired woman of middling years wearing a beaded and bustled silk gown. "Yes?"

"Mrs. Palmer told me to speak with you about scheduling an appointment with your sister. I'd like to commission a painting."

Sylvie smiled and opened the appointment book she carried. "Certainly."

This was the fourth patron Meg had gained tonight. Between that and the silent bids collecting in a box for the paintings on display, the ledger book was sure to prove the evening a success.

The ledger book didn't account for Sylvie's breaking heart.

Her gaze filtered over the room again as soon as she finished making the appointment. Meg was deep in conversation with Bertha Palmer and another patron about the painting techniques emerging in France. Not seeing the Novaks or her father, Sylvie wandered toward Anna Hoffman in the reception area instead.

This late in the evening, the baker looked weary but happy. Sylvie suspected that with her early mornings, she wasn't used to staying out this late. Karl was most likely in bed by now, and Anna really ought to be as well.

"Thank you for all you've done for this event, Anna." Sylvie wrapped her arm around Anna's soft shoulders and squeezed. "Why don't you head home?"

Anna's smile pushed seams into her cheeks. But, looking beyond Sylvie, her smile slipped. "My dear, isn't your vater with you?"

"I thought he was with Frank and Edith." Sylvie looked behind her.

"Oh no." Anna cringed. "I forgot to tell you. They asked me to let you know that they had to go home to their babies. You were busy with a gentleman, writing in that book of yours, and they didn't want to interrupt." Her face twisted with worry. "I kept Stephen with me after that until I needed to use the toilet. I sent him over to you and watched him cross the room in your direction before I went. . . ."

"I'll find him," Sylvie assured her, but Anna's concern had become her own. After bidding the woman good-bye, Sylvie wove through footmen and patrons, urgency building. She looked in the hallway, cloakroom, reception area, and gallery, her pulse crescendoing along with the music still coming from the string quartet.

He was gone.

For a man who had spent two years fantasizing about escaping from a prison camp, slipping away from an art show had been easy.

His breath clouding in front of his face, Stephen bounded up the front steps of his old friend's home and pounded the brass knocker on the door. This was Hiram's house. No one else's. There had to be a reckoning with the man inside, and as the police had proven worthless, Stephen would be the one to do it.

He banged on the door again, this time with the side of his fist. A light came on above his head.

The door opened. "Mr. Townsend?" How young Jasper looked, how sharply hewn. He was wily, this one.

But so was Stephen. "I'd like to come in."

"Please do." Jasper—no, George Skinner—stepped back to allow him entrance.

Stephen hadn't been here since the day he first met this young man, which was also the last day he'd seen his friend alive. Coincidence? No. "Can you guess what's on my mind?"

Skinner's mouth pressed as flat and thin as the white scar lining his brow. "I reckon I can. Come, we'll visit in the parlor."

Stephen followed him into the room but remained standing. "I don't much feel like sitting." Or visiting, for that matter. What he felt like doing, he couldn't do, on account of not having his gun.

He glanced at the untidy tea service on a table and recalled that the maid and housekeeper had been at Meg's art show. All the better that they were still gone. This confrontation was for George Skinner alone.

A kerosene lamp flickered next to the teapot. When Skinner noticed Stephen staring at it, he said, "Habit. I keep forgetting the gaslights work again." He pushed his girlish locks off his brow and folded his arms. "If you're here about Sylvie, I'll tell you right now that we've done nothing dishonorable."

"Sylvie?" This was disorienting. "What about her? What have you done?"

Skinner frowned. "As I said: nothing. She returned my photograph to me, but Meg and Nate were also present, and they can tell you everything that transpired. I accepted what was mine and returned what was yours. That is, I told her we would honor your wishes and not see each other again."

Stephen's limbs told him to pace and slap, to move, to give vent to the energy tumbling through him. But he stood his ground. "I'll bet you were glad to have that photograph back. George."

The boy-man blanched. "What did you say?"

"I said I know you're not Jasper Davenport." Stephen straightened and threw back his shoulders. He was a soldier again and ready for the fight. "Your name is George Skinner, you were a prisoner under Hiram at Camp Douglas, and you came back to take revenge. You took his life, you took his estate, you almost took my daughter. But the jig is up."

"Be reasonable, Mr. Townsend," Skinner said, but he steadied himself with a hand to a chair. "You're at odds with yourself. Again."

Oh no, he wasn't. "Not this time."

"If it's your word against mine, who do you think the police will believe?" Skinner said. "You may have been cleared of the murder charges, but you're still unstable. Folks know it. Besides, all I have to do is say you tried to harm me, and you'll be locked up for the rest of your days. Is that what you want? Is that what your girls want for you? Do you want them to live in the shadow of your insanity for the rest of their lives too?"

Stephen paused, but only for a moment. This was a battle of the mind, but wasn't he a veteran of those too? Skinner was striking where Stephen was most vulnerable. But Stephen refused to yield. "What I want," he said, "is justice."

"You are suspicious and paranoid because of your soldier's heart. Perhaps we were mistaken when we had you released. You ought to be under a doctor's care."

"You mean I ought to be locked away and discredited so you can get away with murder. Hiram was my friend. You killed my friend, and it wasn't even a time of war." The faces of all of Stephen's lost comrades paraded through his mind. They'd been killed in battle, or died of starvation, or of epidemics no doctors could stop. But Hiram had been murdered. Shot in the back, Meg had said. "Coward."

Stephen launched his fist into Skinner's nose.

Skinner's head snapped back, but he rallied, punching Stephen square in the jaw. Tasting blood and fury, Stephen returned a blow to Skinner's gut. Doubling over, Skinner caught himself on the parlor table, sending the tea service and lamp smashing and skidding across the floor. He lunged forward and boxed Stephen's cheekbone so hard that the light flickered.

Stephen shook his head and stumbled away, then leaned on his knees to catch his breath, feeling every one of his forty-five years. "If anyone's going to be locked up, it's going to be you," he said.

When he looked up, George was training a Colt Army revolver on Stephen's chest. "No, Mr. Townsend. I don't think it will."

A crack rent the air, and the parlor filled with smoke.

A second later, Stephen blinked at the plaster rosettes on the ceiling. Distantly, he realized he was lying on the floor, bleeding from his thigh.

Across the room, a small flame leapt from a puddle of oil surrounded by broken glass.

Chapter Thirty-Seven

Nearly breathless with suspense, Sylvie paid the cab driver and dashed through the gate—left open, she presumed by her father—between the stone lions, and up the steps. Just as she reached Jasper's front door, a gunshot sounded inside the house.

She thought she was going to be sick. She imagined Jasper bleeding out on a rug, her father standing over him. But the blood was on her hands too, for she'd been charged with watching over Stephen.

Stomach in a vise, she beat on the door, then tried to open it only to find it locked. Bunching her skirts into her fists, she ran back down the steps, over a boxwood hedge, and around the side of the house, where she saw light seeping from the window.

She gasped when she looked inside. Jasper was pointing a gun at her father, who lay motionless.

Had she lost him already?

Fear was the force that moved her. Fear, and regret, and love for the only father she had.

A large stone urn stood beneath the window, empty of flowers for the winter. After climbing onto it, Sylvie opened the window and tumbled inside, knocking over a pedestaled fern. It sprawled on the floor in a scattering of dirt and broken pottery.

"Sylvie!" Jasper made no move to help her. His gun was still trained on her father.

"What have you done? What did you do?" She ran to Stephen and knelt at his side. One look at his leg, and she peeled back the hem of her skirt, tearing strips from her petticoat.

"Daughter," Stephen said, "his name is Skinner."

She jerked her attention to the man with the gun.

Sweat trickled down Jasper's temples, and blood smeared from his nose. "Sylvie, it's not what you think."

"I think you shot my father!" she shouted. "He was unarmed!" With all the strength she had, she ripped fabric and wove it beneath his leg, binding the wound.

"So was Hiram," Stephen whispered.

Three words, small and soft as gunpowder. They exploded in Sylvie's mind.

"What does he mean?" she said.

Cold night air brought a dampness to the room. A fire popped and snapped.

"I can explain," Jasper said desperately. "If I'd wanted to kill your father, I'd have shot him in the chest. You'll understand me once I explain."

She tied the petticoat tourniquet as tightly as she could. "I have no idea who you are." Her voice was strangely controlled, but inside she was flying apart. "Tell me your name. Tell me everything."

He wiped the back of one hand across the blood leaking from his nose. "My name is George Skinner."

She couldn't look at him. She looked at her father instead, cradling his head on her lap.

"I was right," Stephen rasped. "Right all along. Beware an enemy in the camp."

George's laugh was short and dark. "But I didn't have to be *your* enemy, Mr. Townsend. And, Sylvie, I'm certainly not yours. I was a Confederate prisoner at Camp Douglas. What we suffered there, you cannot begin to conceive. I told you I lost my toes to frostbite, but I didn't tell you men lost their fingers too. One of my friends lost all ten of his. He had only clubs for hands. We took turns feeding him, trying to keep his body and soul together. But he stopped eating so he would die."

Sylvie stroked the side of her father's face, feeling the stubble beneath her fingertips. She saw the scabs still on his scalp. But she was listening to every word.

"I can't bear to tell you the torturous games the prison guards played with us. Hiram was one of my guards. He wasn't one of the worst. He inflicted no physical pain, but he did take everything that mattered to us. He took all of it."

"The gold?" she asked, her head still bowed over her father. Outside air swirled with the warmth of the fire, mottling her skin with an odd mixture of cold and hot.

"Mine. That coin you found was mine, and many more pieces besides. Never mind how I came by it, but it belonged to me, and he stole it. It was my future. Without it, I had nothing. He knew that, and he took it anyway."

Tears clotted her throat. "I can't believe he would do that."

"You held the proof yourself."

Sylvie lifted her head and gasped. The fire she had thought was in the hearth was instead a wild thing, loose in the room. It had crawled up the wall and was chewing the doorframe that led to the hall. Chunks of flaming molding fell to the floor. Smoke billowed out through the open window. They had to leave. They had to leave now.

"The fire," she said, her tongue already feeling thick. "The room is on fire. We have to go."

Stephen pushed himself up to sit.

George came closer, aiming the gun at her. "Not yet. My story's not through."

Her chest heaved, her stays an oppressive constraint. "Don't be a fool, Ja—"

"George," he corrected her. "You might as well say it."

"George. The fire. I can't—we can't—" Her thoughts jumbled in her mind. She squeezed her eyes shut, and it was October 8 again. She was in the art studio in the apartment, pulling Meg away from the fire. Stephen was gone. Meg was burned. They had to run for their lives without him.

"Sylvie." Her father grasped a fold of her skirt. "We'll get out of here together."

Each breath sliced so sharply, she almost couldn't think. Bewildered, she looked at the blood seeping through his bandage. "Can you walk?"

"Help me stand."

George glanced at the fire, then back at them. He stepped closer, too close, much too close.

Leaving her father on the floor, Sylvie stood between them. "Let us go. We have to leave, all three of us."

"And let you run to the police? Just listen to me, and I don't think you'll want to. You love me, Sylvie, I know you do. You owe it to me to listen."

Sweat bloomed beneath her arms and across her back and chest. She looked at the gun. "Then speak."

"I never meant to hurt you. And I never meant to hurt Hiram either." The fire lit one side of his face, casting the other in dark shadow. "It's true I was a Galvanized Yankee, though it meant betraying the sacrifices my fellow Confederates had made. When the war was over, I went home, only to find that my brothers had died in battle, and my parents told me I was no son of theirs. They were so ashamed of me for turning Yankee that they told everyone I was dead. They preferred to believe it too."

Sylvie's gaze shifted to the fire creeping across the floor. It lapped at the settee, and the upholstery began to blacken. "What happened next?"

"There wasn't enough work at home, so eventually I reenlisted. After one three-year term, I wanted another way of life, but I'd managed to save only a pittance on my army pay. If I'd had that gold Hiram stole from me, I could have set myself on a new path. So I returned to Chicago to take as much as I could from him."

Smoke swirled along the ceiling, smudging the plaster with soot. There were no flying firebrands or fiery whirlwinds here, and yet through strength of memory Sylvie could feel sparks piercing her clothes and skin. She rubbed her arms and patted her hair to extinguish them. She felt herself slipping and turned to Stephen.

His presence grounded her to the present. He was here. This wasn't October 8.

"Hurry," Sylvie begged. "We need to go."

But George was completely ignoring the fire. "Before I could take anything from Hiram, he saw me on the street and welcomed me in as his long-lost nephew. I recalled him saying in Camp Douglas how much I looked like him. His mind had grown stuck in the past, and I decided to play along. He would give me far more than I could ever take." He edged a little farther away from the fire. "I could have played the part forever."

"Then why did you kill him?" Stephen ground out between his teeth.

"I never intended to. I found him wandering outside the night of the fire on my way home from the library. He had a moment of lucidity and realized I wasn't his nephew. When he threatened to go to the police, I couldn't let him. I couldn't let my life fall apart all over again. I have a future now, don't you see? An education that will lead to a solid job. A house, a home fit for a wife."

Sylvie bristled, the hair rising on her arms. He was a murderer. He had confessed it. The man she'd fallen in love with had killed her father's best friend. Behind her, Stephen groaned.

On the other side of the room, table legs burned away, and the tabletop crashed to the floor. When George's attention jerked that way, Sylvie lunged for the gun, wresting it from his sweat-slicked grip. She turned it on him with a trembling hand.

"Daughter." The voice behind her sounded far away. "Give me that weapon."

But she held it on George with both hands.

He backed up a pace. "You'll never do it, sweetheart. You wouldn't shoot the man you love."

Shaking, sweating, Sylvie gritted her teeth. "The man I love doesn't exist."

As soon as someone told Meg they'd seen Sylvie dash off without taking her cloak and hat, she knew why her sister had left. She only wished Sylvie hadn't gone alone. With a quick apology to Mrs. Palmer, Meg left the sparkling gallery to chase her sister, who could only be chasing their father. And there was only one place they would have gone.

The parlor in Hiram's house was glowing when Meg arrived.

No. Not glowing. Burning.

This couldn't be happening.

Finding the front door locked, and the side door too, she ran to the side of the house and climbed onto a stone urn to see through the open window. At first, all she saw was the fire on the opposite side of the room, blocking the door to the hall. Then her heart skipped a beat. In the middle of the parlor, Sylvie trained a gun on Jasper. They stood unmoving, a living tableau about to be burned. Her father, she couldn't see.

Heat from the flames took the chill off the outside air. Meg shed her cloak and hat, dropping them to the frosted ground. Inside, Sylvie was shaking her head. Was she looking at Jasper or at Meg?

"You're in shock," Jasper was saying. His back was to the window. "You're upset—you're not thinking straight. Put the gun down, nice and slow."

"You murdered Hiram," Sylvie said loudly enough for Meg to hear. "You shot my father. Why do you think I would trust you enough to put this gun back in your hands?"

Breath stalled in Meg's lungs. The revelation hung like something dark and uncaged in the room.

"Because you love me," Jasper said. "You forgive me because you love me. And I love you, Sylvie. Give me the gun, and we'll work this out. I never would have shot your father if he hadn't attacked me first. I had to defend myself."

"Don't listen to him, daughter!"

Relief jolted through Meg at her father's voice. She'd heard enough. Stephen was incapacitated, and Sylvie would never pull the trigger.

Every fiber in her being told Meg to run from the fire. Her hands tingled with apprehension, as if they had memory of their own and fears separate from the rest of her brain.

But this fire was not big enough to consume a third of the city. It was not even big enough to have alarmed the neighbors or night watchman yet. She would not run from this, but into it.

Bending, Meg wrapped her skirts around her left wrist and carefully climbed inside the parlor, the noise of her movement covered by the crackling fire. Instantly, sweat covered her.

Sylvie kept Jasper talking. "And what will become of us? What future could there possibly be for you and me after this?"

Meg couldn't hear his response and didn't care to. He'd murdered Hiram, shot her father, and was manipulating her sister. She felt a rush of courage born of fear and anger. She knew what she had to do.

Silently, she reached into the alcove next to the window for the marble bust of Robert Burns, her right hand struggling to find a good purchase. It felt awkward in her grip and far heavier than the sum of its pounds, and the muscles in her arms trembled. Her palms were slick, the fused fingers of her right hand maddeningly in the way. Smoke choked the air and her lungs as she moved away from the wall.

Sylvie was faltering, the gun shaking, lowering.

Jasper had taken a step closer. "Enough negotiating." He lashed out and grasped the revolver's barrel, twisting it while Sylvie held fast.

It happened in less than an instant. But in that flash of time, past, present, and future melted together in Meg's mind. She saw Stephen as a wounded soldier, a prisoner, and as her father, wounded still. She saw Hiram in his nightclothes, shot in the back. She saw her sister longing for romance, falling for Jasper, and being shot by him, just as he'd shot Stephen.

Meg hoisted the bust above her head and brought it cracking down on Jasper's.

He collapsed, insensible, and she dropped her weapon beside

him. Flames strutted across the floor, glowing orange in the vacant eyes of the poet Hiram loved.

Sylvie looked from Jasper to Meg, her expression twisted with relief and sorrow. Then, shaking her head as though to clear it, she stuffed the gun into her pocket and said, "Let's go."

The fire blocked the hall. While Sylvie pulled Jasper toward the window, Meg went to her father and helped him stand. He coughed the smoke from his lungs as she supported him.

"This will hurt," she told him.

His face was flint, his mouth a seam.

Sylvie went out the window first, waiting to help guide Stephen's dangling legs to the stone urn below. He stumbled, Sylvie broke his fall, and Meg came tumbling out after them. Together, they took Stephen across the road.

Before Meg and Sylvie could turn to go back for Jasper, horses thundered up the street, pulling a fire engine. It stopped in front of the house, and two firemen bounded out of it.

"Is anyone else in the house?" one of them shouted.

"Yes, one man!" Sylvie replied, handing Stephen to the care of a third fireman. "First room on the left, but you need to go through the window." Her voice thinned as she pointed the way.

"Meg!"

She spun toward the familiar voice just as Nate swept her into his arms, holding her so close that she felt his heartbeat against hers. He buried his hands in her hair, his face in her neck, before leaning back to look at her. "You weren't at the gallery or at home, so I knew something must be wrong. Are you hurt?"

Overcome, she could only shake her head. Behind him, the firemen emerged, carrying Jasper like a sack of flour over their shoulders.

Nate kissed the top of Meg's head, then her forehead, her nose, her freckled cheeks. Then he lifted her chin and kissed her lips, so lightly she barely felt it. It was soft and undemanding, an affirmation more than anything else. *You are here*, *you are safe*, it seemed to say to her. The kiss that followed said, *You are mine.*

Her response told him she agreed.

Chapter Thirty-Eight

Monday, December 18, 1871

Outside the small window of the shanty, dawn warmed the sky from grey to pink, then to winter's washed-out blue. Meg added more kindling to the stove and poured a second cup of coffee for Sylvie and for herself. Stephen slept on the mattress on the floor, his wound having been treated last night.

Meg sat beside her sister at the table. Their calm was only surface deep, a thin shell over what lay beneath it, the way ice covered a lake. With a word, they would both fall through it to the memories gathered below.

Curls of fragrant steam rose from her coffee, misting Meg's face. "You couldn't have known," she murmured. "You were so brave. I'm so proud of you." She still marveled that her sister had pointed a revolver at the man she loved.

Tears rolled down Sylvie's cheek. "I still can't believe it. I don't think I can ever trust my heart again, Meg. If he had asked me yesterday morning to marry him, I would have said yes."

Meg disguised a shudder. "But you would have waited until Father granted his blessing. You wouldn't have eloped." Her tone lifted at the end, turning the statement into a question she was almost afraid to ask.

The fire's crackling filled the room when Sylvie didn't respond. Instead, she merely closed her eyes and drank. Her hands cupped the mug as she set it down. "What a horrible life for George Skinner. I don't justify the murder, but everything that happened to him, the things he saw and suffered . . . I wish I didn't feel sympathy for him, but I do."

Meg wrapped her arm around Sylvie's shoulders. "So do I, in a way. But his consequences aren't ours to decide."

"Do you believe a person can change?" Sylvie's whisper was tenuous, a gossamer thread stretching between hope and dread.

"I do. Of course I do." Meg angled to glance at Stephen, then bent and pulled a blanket over his shoulders. "We can change for the worse and we can change for the better with God's help. Even trying to change is an improvement. Father is a living example of this."

"Because we didn't give up on him." Sylvie rubbed the bridge of her nose. "George wanted to be a better man. He told me so. Perhaps . . ." The conviction in her voice gave way as her sentence went unfinished.

"Sylvie, you have to let him go." Meg gentled her voice but knew there was no gentling the sentiment. "You loved the idea of him, the idea of love. You couldn't have loved George Skinner because you didn't know him."

Sniffing, Sylvie stared into her coffee. "I loved a phantom, then. And my heart still breaks for someone I never actually had." She drew in a sharp breath and shook her head. "I will never do that again."

"You'll never love what isn't real, you mean?"

She shrugged. "Never love a man I cannot trust. And I don't know how I can possibly trust a man—"

A knock prevented her from finishing. With a flick of her wrist, Sylvie dismissed what she was about to say, though Meg could guess it easily enough. It was a conversation that needed time and space to unfurl.

With a squeeze to Sylvie's shoulder, Meg whispered, "To be continued." Then she smoothed her hair before opening the door.

"I came as soon as I could." Dr. Gilbert stood outside the shanty with his medical bag, cheeks rosy above his mustache. "May I see the patient?"

Gratitude washed over Meg as she closed the door behind the doctor and hung his cloak and hat. Stephen stirred at the cold air and noise, squinting toward the light. He sat up in slow, stiff movements.

His joints creaking, Dr. Gilbert lowered himself to the floor beside the mattress. "Good morning, my good man." He reintroduced himself, since the last time they'd met was moments before Stephen's arrest in the church. "I hear you had an eventful night."

Stephen told him he had.

"I'm here to see after your continued care, if that's all right with you."

"You come here for that? I don't have to come see you?"

Dr. Gilbert smiled. "Though the ball missed arteries and bone, I still don't suppose you're in much of a condition to travel, do you?"

A sigh heaved Stephen's shoulders. "No, I don't suppose I am." He shoved his fingers through hair that had grown back more grey than brown. "You know I have soldier's heart, I take it?"

Meg receded to the table and held her breath. Oliver ambled out from the back bedroom, sniffed the doctor's trouser cuffs, and hopped onto Sylvie's lap.

"I'm aware." Dr. Gilbert nodded slowly. "I'm also aware of the overdoses of medicine they gave you at the asylum. Did you know, Mr. Townsend, that one of the powders they use in the whiskey tincture can cause hallucinations in some patients? Cannabis. It can be helpful for some, but not for others, and it all depends on dosage."

Stephen's eyes rounded. "The medicine made me worse?"

"It's possible. But there are some medicines that really do help."

"God can help me get better without your drugs. I'll pray harder. I'll do better, I know I can."

Dr. Gilbert pinched the end of his waxed mustache. "I, too, believe God can help you. I've no doubt God played a role in sparing you last night, the way the ball took the least damaging path it could through your leg. But He also helped you by using a surgeon to stitch up your flesh. You didn't pray that your skin would close over the holes on its own, did you?"

Stephen frowned, but Meg could tell he was considering the logic.

"If you were dying of thirst and prayed for life, wouldn't you take a glass of water offered to you and call it the answer to prayer? I'm offering you a glass of water, Mr. Townsend. In this case, it may not fully heal you, but it very likely will improve your condition. And we'll still know it's an answer to prayer."

Stephen met Meg's gaze, then Sylvie's.

"Please, Father," Meg whispered. "Please try it."

"Water, you say?" he asked the doctor. "Because I won't take whiskey."

When Dr. Gilbert nodded to Meg, she poured water into a tumbler and set it on the bench near him. He opened his bag and withdrew two vials. "I'll add some of this one right now, to help calm your racing heart and steady your nerves. Take it daily, in the morning. At night, take this one to help you sleep. Your body needs solid sleep more than you'd imagine." He named the dosages for each as he tapped powder into the glass. "Will you do it?"

Stephen agreed, and drank the dose with a grimace.

"Good. Then I'll come check on you in a week." Closing his leather bag, Dr. Gilbert sat on the bench. "There's one more thing I'd prescribe for you, Mr. Townsend. Friendship with another veteran, someone who can relate to where you've been and how far you've come."

"Asa Jones remembers you," Meg reminded him. "He'd love to see you again, I'm sure."

"Asa?" Stephen rubbed his whiskered chin. "Asa Jones. I recollect him."

"Go see him, Mr. Townsend, as soon as you're comfortably able. Doctor's orders." Dr. Gilbert bade them all good-bye and left.

Meg turned to Sylvie, tears in her eyes. "You were right," she whispered. "I should have taken him to a doctor years ago. I thought with time and love he would get better on his own. I thought I could take care of him."

"You didn't know Dr. Gilbert years ago," Sylvie offered. "All you knew were doctors like Dr. Franklin. And Father isn't cured yet."

But there was a glimmer of hope, real and within reach, and Meg grasped at it.

She sank to the floor beside Stephen. "Forgive me, Father. I didn't know how to help you. We lost so much time."

Stephen shook his head. "Nothing you could have said would have compelled me to see a doctor on my own. Look what it took for me to see one now."

"You will do as Dr. Gilbert instructs, won't you?" Sylvie asked, hand motionless on Oliver's back. "You'll take these medicines and give them a fair trial? The powders and the friendship of other veterans?"

Their father closed his eyes. The hollows around them looked bruised and sunken from his chronic lack of sleep. But when he opened them, he didn't blink as he said, "I promise to try."

"Thank you." Meg kissed his cheek, resolving not to make unreasonable demands of him. Almost as quickly, she realized her touch might not have been welcome. "Oh, I'm sorry. Did that bother you?"

The corners of his eyes crinkled. "I'll try to get used to it."

Another knock on the door drew Sylvie to answer it.

"Special delivery." Nate strode into the room, unshaven. Meg stood, her spirit lifting with his presence. He dropped the *Tribune* on the table before taking off his hat and cloak. Splashed across the front page was the headline: *Local Man Frames Two for Murder He Committed*.

Sylvie looked away, then quietly refocused on her coffee.

"Let me see that, son." Stephen reached for it, and Nate promptly supplied the paper.

"Does it say—did you find out—how George managed to involve the Schneiders?" Meg asked.

"Will you never read my articles for yourself?" Nate winked and touched her back, then settled his hand in the hollow of her waist. A look passed between them that was so small, Meg doubted anyone else noticed. But to her, it was confirmation that last night had really happened. All of it. Even after the smoke had cleared, the crisis past, Nate still wanted her, and she wanted nothing more than to belong to him.

"Actually, not every detail is in the story," he confessed. "For instance, I didn't name Louis and Lorenzo, or say that George's interest in Otto Schneider began with Hiram's stories. When you and I kept hunting for clues to the murder, he decided to deflect attention and wrote the threatening note to Hiram we found."

"I wondered how George hadn't already found that himself," Meg said.

"Right. It turns out that he had done his own research and learned Otto Schneider was one of the prisoners released from jail the night of the fire. He figured that we needed a little nudge to look into Otto as a suspect again."

"It was perfect." Meg slipped her arm around Nate's solid waist and waited for Stephen to object. He didn't. "George knew the police would already be looking for Otto."

Stephen grunted his assent. "I'll bet he staged the break-in at Hiram's house, didn't he?"

"He did," Nate confirmed. "As soon as the police had Otto Schneider in custody, George went straight to the jail and made him a deal he couldn't refuse. In return for his false confession, George promised to take care of his family financially. Hiram's wealth certainly made it possible."

Meg glanced at her sister. "If Sylvie hadn't found George's photograph, he would have gotten away with everything."

"No," Sylvie said, looking up for the first time. "George's story didn't begin to unravel until you took the photo to Mr. Brandon. What happened to the real Jasper Davenport?"

Nate hooked his thumb into his trouser pocket. "I suspect that what his grandmother said in the letter was true. I wrote a letter to the department of the army, asking for military records of Jasper

Davenport's service and death. It will take weeks to hear back, but I expect we'll get our confirmation. I also suspect the will is a fake. It will take a few days to verify that, but either way, assuming there is no living Jasper Davenport, the house will go to public auction." He looked at Stephen. "I'm sorry, Mr. Townsend. If the original will had been found, I know it likely would have named you the beneficiary."

Meg's father looked up. "I wouldn't want it," he said. "I wouldn't want to be rich because my friend was murdered. I'll take my own lot, come what may."

"Is that all?" Sylvie asked Nate, nodding toward the paper. "Can we set this behind us now? Please?" Her voice sounded as if it had been scraped from the bottom of a well.

Meg moved away from Nate, closing the gap between her and her sister. "Yes," she told her. "Absolutely, we can."

Sunday, December 24, 1871

Sylvie couldn't imagine feeling any more alone than she felt right now.

Which was ironic, since she shared the Novaks' cozy home with Meg, their father, Nate, Frank, and Edith. After the evening church service, Edith fed them all dinner, then tucked Henry and Tommy into bed before coming back to the parlor, which was crowded with a spruce tree strung with popcorn and dried cranberries.

Everyone was paired off. Tommy and Henry in their bedroom. Frank and Edith on one sofa, Meg and Nate on the other. Sylvie and Stephen sat in armchairs that flanked a tea table. This was how it would be now, she supposed. She'd always considered Meg and Stephen a pair, but now that Meg was becoming part of Nate's family, Sylvie had assumed the role of the caregiving daughter. She loved her father more than ever. But this was a sharp swerve from the path she'd dreamed of.

Sipping a cup of mulled cider, Edith nestled against Frank. "Harriet so wanted to be here. She especially wanted to meet you, Meg—

and you too, Sylvie—but teaching doesn't leave much room in the budget for travel."

Nate stretched his arm possessively behind Meg as she asked how Harriet was getting on in Iowa.

"I suppose there's no word from Andrew," Nate said in a break in their conversation. When Edith sighed, he nodded. "I figured you'd have told me if you'd heard anything. Not every story wraps up the way I want it to."

"Ah, but the story isn't over yet." Meg looked from Nate to Sylvie. "We never know what the next chapter holds. God is working and things are happening even when it's not written on the page right in front of us."

Sylvie knew what Meg was trying to do. For the past week, her sister had dropped gentle yet persistent remarks in the same hopeful vein. *"You won't always feel the way you feel right now. Tomorrow will be better. You will find someone else, someone worthy of you."* But that last line rang a bit hollow, coming from a woman who had already found a man who cherished her.

Sylvie made herself drink her cider, though she couldn't taste a thing. She didn't want this seed of bitterness to take root in her heart. It was not Meg's fault that Jasper—George—

Even thinking about him brought a pang to her chest. Sylvie quickly shut the door on his image in her mind. Instead, she swiveled toward her father, checking to see if he was silently tapping his leg in agitation. He wasn't. Even so, two small nicks on his jaw betrayed that he'd cut himself shaving with an unsteady hand before church.

"Are you all right?" she asked. His bandaged wound was healing well, but the strain of traveling here—his first time out of the shanty since last Sunday—might have taxed him more than he admitted. "Are you tired?"

His grey eyes appraised hers, flashing in the candlelight from the Advent wreath on the table between them. "Are you?"

She was exhausted. A few days ago she had secured two extra blankets from the ladies at the First Congregational Church and secretly taken them to the jail for George. Fickle organ, the human heart. She despised what he had done and made no excuse for murder. Yet knowing what he had suffered as a prisoner in Chicago, she couldn't bear the thought of him being cold. She wanted to deliver the blankets herself, to see him one last time. She didn't want their last moment together to be when she'd held a gun on him, fire lapping toward them.

He wouldn't see her. Sylvie had left the blankets with the guards and returned home.

"I'll be fine," she said at last and prayed it would be true. Larger miracles had happened, after all. She had survived the Great Fire of Chicago. Her father was seeing a doctor.

Sylvie lifted her gaze to the handmade angel perched atop the tree. *Fear not,* it seemed to say. *Immanuel, God is with us.* Yes, God was with them, with Sylvie, even now. If George Skinner called upon Him, He would be with him too. This was logical, this made sense. She only had to train her heart to listen to her mind. If George truly wanted to change, to become a better man, God would help with that.

Not her.

Meg watched Sylvie and their father with a wary eye. Neither seemed to be in a celebratory mood, and she couldn't blame them. She was so glad they'd both chosen to come, though, for she couldn't stand the idea of them staying at the shanty alone tonight. Last Christmas Eve, they'd been with Hiram in his home. Those memories fluttered through Meg's mind, chased away by more recent events. The art show had been a week ago. The art show and the dreadful confrontation with George Skinner.

But this was Christmas. She resolved to set aside last week and enjoy the bounty that was here and now. Frank and Edith's home brimmed over with what mattered most: faith, family, and friends. Reverend Collyer's sermon from just after the fire scrolled through Meg's mind once more. *"We will thank God as soon as we can."*

Today she could, and she did. These last few months were not what she would have chosen, but she was far richer now than she was before she'd lost nearly everything to the flames.

The fire crackled merrily behind its grate, warming the parlor enough for Meg to feel drowsy. She leaned against Nate, breathing in his sandalwood scent along with that of the cider and spruce. While Edith tried to draw Sylvie into conversation, Nate spoke to his brother-in-law.

Frank smoothed his thumb and index finger over his mustache. "How does it feel not to be a reporter anymore?"

Meg turned to Nate, alarmed. "What's this?"

Color crept above Nate's starched white collar. "I was going to tell you."

"Well, I'm all ears." But she imagined her smile was a thin veneer to her confusion. Had he lost his job? Was he trying not to ruin Christmas with bad news? But that didn't make sense either, after his front-page story on Monday.

"Frank!" Edith swatted her husband's arm. "You shouldn't have said anything! He was going to tell her when the time was right!"

A nervous laugh tripped over Meg's lips. "No time like the present."

Nate stood and offered her his hand. "Let's go for a walk." He turned to Sylvie and Stephen. "We won't be long, and then if you're ready, I can take you all home."

Frank clapped Nate on the back as Meg rose. "Sorry, pal. I thought you'd told her." Behind him, Edith just shook her head.

None of this set Meg's mind at ease. She'd had enough of secrets to last a lifetime. She hadn't expected this from Nate, especially not now.

Outside, snow fell in a fine white powder around them, and their breath glittered in puffs of vanishing crystals. Meg folded her arms.

"I was going to tell you," Nate began.

"You already said that." She looked up at him. "Did you lose your job? Did you lose it because of my family and Hiram and George?"

"In a manner of speaking, but don't worry. I can explain." For a man with years of experience writing the news, he was having a terrible time finding words fast enough.

"'Don't worry'?" Her voice caught. Worry was the only thing she felt right now.

"When Edith, Harriet, and Andrew left to start their own lives, I felt relieved. I yearned for independence." He straightened his hat on his head, and his gloves came away dusted with snow. "I didn't want that kind of burden again."

"You didn't?" Meg's steps slowed to a halt. "Or you don't?"

Snow melted into little droplets on his spectacles. He took them off and tucked them into his pocket. Then he held Meg's shoulders, as though to keep the distance between them from growing any larger. She didn't pull away.

"What I'm trying to say is that I didn't plan to be responsible for anyone again for a very long time, if ever. I figured I'd paid my dues, that I'd already raised my family and had no need for another. But you've changed my mind, Meg. Loving you is no burden at all." He swallowed, his eyes bright and glossy from the cold. "Surely you already knew that I love you."

Something untwisted inside Meg. Hearing those words from Nate filled a part of her that had been untended and barren. Her mother had said she loved Meg. Before the war, so had her father. But here was something different. Love by choice, freely given, not bound by duty or obligation. Love despite her imperfections.

A smile slowly curved her lips. "I love you too, Nate. More than I can say."

He slid his hands down her arms, and she gave him her bare hands. All she had to do was tilt her chin, and she could kiss the melted snowflakes from his lips. But she checked the impulse. "What about your job?"

"I was coming to that. My job as a reporter would not have supported you well. The hours were lousy, and so was the pay. But I've been promoted. Hollingbrook put in a recommendation. I'm the City Editor now."

"Why, that's wonderful! Why didn't you tell me before?"

"Because I wanted to wait until I had this."

Releasing her, Nate pulled off his gloves, dropped them at his feet, and bent one knee in the snow. Gaslight from the lamppost lit the flakes swirling around him. When he drew a small box from his pocket and opened it to reveal an amethyst and gold ring inside, Meg's heart grew wings.

"I love you, Meg Townsend. And I want to go on loving you, if you'll have me, as long as we both shall live. If there is any burden, we'll share it together. I want to raise a family again, my own family—*our* family. Will you marry me?"

Warm tears mingled with the snow dusting her cheeks. As soon as Nate saw them, he was on his feet again, looking worried. She flung her arms around him and kissed away any doubt he might have had.

"Yes," she whispered, shielded in his embrace while the storm danced and spun around them. "Haven't you noticed? I already belong to you."

Epilogue

Chicago
June 1872

Outside the new Corner Books & More, Chicago pulsed with the noise and activity of reconstruction. Inside the bookshop, however, Sylvie Townsend steadily rebuilt herself. Today she moved comfortably between customers, shelves, and cash register, while Stephen worked in the back on a new binding for an old book. She smiled as she thought of his work. She had the same binding as ever. It was the spirit inside that had been sewn back together, one painful stitch at a time. By God's grace, she was more resilient, she'd found, than she'd realized.

"I've made up my mind. I want this one."

Sylvie looked up to find Lucy Marsdale, one of her younger patrons, hugging a book.

A quick scan of the store showed several other customers browsing the shop, but for now, none waited at the counter to check out. "And which one is this?" Sylvie was happy to share Lucy's enthusiasm.

The young woman turned the book to display the cover. "I hear it's terribly romantic." She was sixteen years old. Romance was her chief interest.

Sylvie stifled a sigh when she saw it was *Jane Eyre*. "It was my favorite at your age too."

A ridge formed between Lucy's clear blue eyes. "You don't like it anymore? Why not?"

Taking a moment to choose her words, Sylvie smoothed the front of her periwinkle bodice and brushed invisible cat hair from the horizontal draping on her skirt. "I still believe it's one of the greatest works of literature ever written. It has not just romance, but moral depth as well. In fact, I'd love to discuss it once you finish. But may I recommend another volume as well?"

Beckoning Lucy to follow, Sylvie rounded one bookshelf and crossed to the end of another, footsteps dimmed by the carpet runners in the aisles.

"Don't mind Oliver Twist." She chuckled, stepping over the cat's outstretched body as he lay in a swath of late afternoon sun. "Here we are. *Villette*, also by Charlotte Brontë." She handed a copy to Lucy. "Not as popular as *Jane Eyre*, but it should be. Plus, the heroine shares your name."

She didn't tell her young customer that Sylvie hadn't learned to love it—particularly the ending—until a few months ago. But she understood now. She understood that marriage to one's first love was not the only way to end a story. That fulfilling work was another path to happiness.

Lucy took the novel and opened to the first chapter, beaming when she found her name in the character of Lucy Snowe. "I'll take it. I'll take both of them. I'm sure Grandmother won't mind." She waved to Mrs. Marsdale, and the dignified older woman glided in a rustle of brown bustled silk to meet them at the counter.

While Sylvie rang up the purchase, Mrs. Marsdale gestured to the front corner window. "Your display is lovely, dear, but I miss seeing your sister at her easel with her paints. I so enjoyed watching her work."

Sylvie missed Meg too, in more ways than one. But that corner spot had grown too confining for the artist she'd become. A few of her character portraits hung on the walls, but most of the new bookshelves went all the way to the ceiling. "She's broadened her horizons. She paints from life now, Mrs. Marsdale. You can still watch her work. You'll just have to find her first, somewhere in the city."

Mrs. Marsdale laughed as she paid for the purchase. "I think I'll find her at her next art show instead. Thank you!"

The bell jingled above the door as she and Lucy left, two books the richer.

While other patrons continued browsing, Sylvie sat on the stool behind the counter and updated her inventory list. Business was good. It was steady. A plan had been adopted for a new public library to be established, but it wouldn't open until January, so she wouldn't fret about how that might affect her shop yet. There were debts to pay for the cost of construction, but Sylvie was convinced she had the most loyal customers in the city. Rent from the new third-floor tenants, who'd moved in two months ago, helped too. Sylvie wasn't worried—at least, not very much.

A gust of warm, humid air flounced through the shop as the door opened again. One day June would again bring the fragrance of roses and lilacs. But this year, the wind carried only the scents of hot bricks and fresh mortar. Meg swept in on such an industrious-smelling breeze, blond curls tumbling over the shoulders of her white cotton tabby dress. She let her folded easel slide from beneath one arm, and set down the case containing canvas, brushes, and paints.

"There you are, Mrs. Pierce. Don't forget, your rent is due at the end of this week," Sylvie teased.

Meg laughed. "You're a harsh mistress, sister. Never a break, is there?" Tucking her art supplies behind a shelf, she came to the counter, her freckled cheeks flushed.

Sylvie arched an eyebrow, amused. "As if you need one." From what she knew, Nate's job at the *Tribune* was secure, and Meg was so busy on commissioned paintings that she was rarely in the bookshop anymore. "How was work today?"

Removing her straw hat, Meg used it to fan herself. "Excellent.

My next show is scheduled at the gallery for the first week of October, right before the first anniversary of the fire. That's plenty of time for me to work on a collection of paintings based on the Great Rebuilding."

"I'm sure time will go by quickly."

"I'm sure it will." Sobering, Meg lowered her hat to the counter and fingered the green ribbon above its brim. "But there's something else. You know Hiram's house and all the property inside went to auction last week."

A stillness settled over Sylvie. She surveyed the shop to be sure she wasn't neglecting any customers. One gentleman sat in an armchair, reading, and another was conversing with Stephen. "The estate went to a new bank president, I believe. I suppose he and his family have moved in by now?"

"In the process. I received a letter from him today. He found the painting I did of George Skinner and has no use for it. He learned I was the artist and asked if I wanted it back, or if I knew anyone else who would want it."

The portrait burst upon Sylvie's mind. "No." The word slipped out like a sigh. "No. I don't think you do."

"Of course not. I wouldn't have mentioned it, but you did ask about it once." Meg seemed to study her.

"That was a long time ago." Weeks. Months. Ages.

"It was. I'm sorry, Sylvie. In case I never said it before, I'm so sorry for what you've been through. Not everyone would have come back from that the way you have." Meg stretched her fingers away from her palms. "Thank you for what you've done with the store, and with Father."

Sylvie started to shake her head, but Meg touched her wrist to stop her.

"I mean it. I'm so grateful for how you've managed everything. If you're more tired than you're letting on, or if you ever need to vent any frustrations, I hope you'll come to me. In fact, come for any reason. My being married doesn't change that we're sisters."

"Thank goodness for that." Sylvie squeezed her hand, warmed

by what Meg had said more than she had time to express. "You're welcome, and yes, I will come to you." She flicked a glance at a waiting customer. "But for now, could you ask if the new owner plans to keep the portrait of Hiram with the house? If not, I know Father would want it."

Meg agreed and went upstairs.

At the end of the afternoon, Sylvie hung the *Closed* sign and locked the door to the outside world. After reckoning the accounts and exchanging a word with her father, she climbed the stairs to their apartment.

Her room was her own again. The yellow-and-white curtains Anna had sewn for their shanty now graced her windows, and a quilt made of the same cheery shades covered the whitewashed iron bed. On her nightstand, her father's framed carte de visite sat beside her mother's coverless copy of *Little Women*. Sylvie smiled as words from the character Marmee seemed to lift from between the pages: "*Work is a blessed solace.*" Yes, it was. She was blessed that she loved what she did.

Sitting on the edge of the mattress, Sylvie removed her shoes and let them drop to the thick rag rug. Her own face—or a younger, simpler version of it—stared back at her from the canvas leaning against the opposite wall.

It was special as the first portrait Meg painted after the fire that wasn't of herself. This was a marker of Meg's journey, an early milestone to prove how far she'd come. But it was more than that. For Sylvie, it was a portrait of her own naïveté, for that was what she looked like when she'd thought she loved George.

She looked happy. She looked deceived.

Sylvie never wanted to be that way again.

Jasper Davenport, Nate had learned from the army, had died at the time and place his grandmother Sarah had said. George Skinner had been convicted of murder and was in prison, where he would spend the best years of a man's life. In her mind, Sylvie had turned him over to God's care. She would trust His will for her life too.

Rising, she drew a sheet over the painting to protect it from dust blowing through the window, and headed to the kitchen to prepare dinner for two.

After dinner with Sylvie, Stephen stood on the roof of his building alone. Twilight colored the clouds unfurling like a banner low in the sky. But it was the city below that concerned him.

Thousands upon thousands of men had rushed in from the east for this Great Rebuilding. Heaven knew who they all were, if all were legitimate. It made Stephen uneasy, this constant churning of bricks and dust and humanity. None of Dr. Gilbert's powders had succeeded in curing his wariness. He'd been right to be suspicious of George Skinner, hadn't he?

Stephen rubbed the back of his neck. His nocturnal vigils wouldn't make much difference now, he figured. There were night watchmen and police, all younger men than he, and stronger too. Besides, sleep was a precious gift he wasn't willing to forfeit. So he kept his lookouts to evening hours, before dark. If he was honest, as much as he disliked the hordes of strangers in his city, there was something satisfying in seeing the progress day after day. It was a wonder how quickly buildings could rise from ashes. The *Tribune* reported a million bricks were laid each day.

Slowly, he walked toward the other end of the building, well away from all the edges. Prairie winds whipped around him, flapping his shirt. A warning pulsed in his thigh. Resigned to the lingering weakness from his bullet wound, he sat in the chair Nate had carried up for him weeks ago. Clay pots of red flowers squatted near it, thanks to Meg. At first he'd questioned her effort to fancy up a rooftop, but he didn't mind the bees, butterflies, and sometimes birds who caught sight and came to visit.

The neighborhood was quieting after another long day of labor, but echoes and voices still carried. Crickets joined them. Stephen pulled a dinner roll from his pocket and tore it to pieces, scattering the crumbs. A sparrow fluttered nearby and landed on the roof, tilting its head at Stephen before pecking up the crumbs he'd tossed. Stephen watched it and then another bird who joined it for the feast. They flew away too soon. They'd be back.

A deep breath filled his chest, triggering a round of coughing. At least his heart didn't race nearly as much as it did, and he thanked God and Dr. Gilbert for that. But sometimes his hand still shook. Sometimes fear or anger grew unreasonable. He had to remind himself to display affection for his daughters and often forgot altogether. Sometimes he still saw his friends who'd died in camp, battle, or Andersonville, either in daydreams or night dreams.

Now he saw Hiram too, another casualty of war. This one troubled him most of all, because Stephen could have prevented it, if only he'd figured out earlier what George Skinner was up to. But he'd trodden that road in his mind so often by now that the ruts were deep as trenches. And it didn't bring Hiram back.

A tear ran hot down his face. He let it fall, along with the ones that came after. Stephen had made his peace with seeing his friends in his mind or in dreams, preferred it, even, if the alternative was forgetting them. His comrades, and memories of them, weren't something to be cured of. They were to be respected and honored.

At least, that was what his son-in-law said, and Stephen agreed. He'd gone to the Soldiers' Home to talk to other veterans, like the doctor suggested, but it didn't help any. The men there were even more stuck in the past than he was, and living insularly and idle like that had made them hard to relate to. None of them had survived Andersonville either.

He missed the friends he'd had.

But he'd been working with Nate on a project to bring them back with the printed word. He woke early and made the coffee before Sylvie stirred. After feeding Oliver and spending time in the Bible, memories spilled through his pen. It was a strange thing. Years he never meant to mention again before he met Nate Pierce, he now committed to paper. He'd kept them corked up for so long, the released pressure brought a relief he hadn't expected. His pages were scattered and disordered, but Nate sorted them into something that was coherent, asking questions when blanks needed to be filled in. One day his story would be fully told—beyond what the tiny columns of a newspaper could hold—and in so doing, he'd tell the stories of his friends. The notion satisfied him.

Stephen would never be the man he'd been before the war. But he didn't think that was what God had in mind anyway.

He leaned back in the chair, lifting his gaze to the heavens. Glory spread across the sky in royal shades of crimson and purple, so beautiful it stung.

Was the world a broken place? It was. Despite his improvements, would some degree of soldier's heart be a thorn in his flesh to the end of his days? He reckoned so. But wasn't there still a Light the darkness could not destroy? Didn't God still love Stephen Townsend and have a plan for his good, and a plan for the good of his family?

He did.

As soon as Meg opened the door to the roof, her father was up out of his chair, spinning toward her.

"Meg? What are you doing up here?" His tone was surprised but not dismayed. She only hoped she hadn't rattled his heart. He'd gained a healthy amount of weight since his release from the asylum, but he still seemed frail.

Crickets creaked. "I thought—I was hoping you'd let me paint you." She stepped over the threshold, and Nate followed her, carrying the easel and canvas. "Please?"

Blinking, her father smoothed his grey-threaded hair into place. "You want to paint me? Why?"

She approached him, her skirt billowing behind her. "I'll sketch you tonight. Painting will come later. But yes, I want to capture you looking out like a sentinel over a new Chicago." He would think she'd lost her wits if she used the word *beautiful* to describe this scene.

A year ago, she would have agreed with him. They were surrounded by buildings in various stages of completion. Streets were virtually impassable. Hoists and derricks stabbed at the sky, ready to lift masses of bricks and stone. It was disordered, chaotic. Dangerous.

Tomorrow there would be another trade union burial for more laborers accidentally killed on the job. Walls made in haste still toppled. Derricks—narrow cranes—made the work go faster, but too often dropped their cargo. Tomorrow a thousand bricklayers would set aside their work and parade the coffins to their graves. Meg would be there to paint that too, for no depiction of the Great Rebuilding would be complete without recognizing those who died in the process.

But today she saw progress, not just in the floor-by-floor reconstruction, but in her father, who'd been restored to her more than she'd thought possible mere months ago. Stephen was not patrolling in the dark with a gun, but watching the world around him without panic. And she, with hands forever marked by the fire, would somehow transpose this wonder to canvas.

Her mother's words echoed somewhere deep inside her. *"There is beauty in the imperfect too. You are a God who uses broken vessels. You are not afraid of human limitations or scars."* She'd been right.

Stephen looked at Nate, who waited for his response to set up the easel. "I suppose it's all right. If you think it would help your show."

"I do." Gratitude—to her father, to God—expanded inside Meg, not just for this small concession, but for the uncounted steps, small and large, they'd all taken to reach this point. "Thank you."

Nate set the easel and canvas in the spot she requested, then came to stand beside her father. His chestnut hair ruffled in the breeze. "I can see why you like it up here." After that, his low voice was heard only by Stephen before the wind snatched his words away. Whatever he said put her father at ease, and that was all that mattered.

She and Nate wouldn't always live in the apartment above Stephen and Sylvie. Soon enough they would move into a home set apart, with room to grow a family. But for now, the arrangement suited them. She had no wish to skim over the present with expectations for the future. If time were a tangible thing, she would hold this moment like a pearl in her hands, cherishing it for the treasure it was.

This was why she painted now. Not to escape into her imagination and create harmony she didn't feel in life. But to preserve reality that ought never to be forgotten.

Charcoal in hand, Meg adjusted the pressure in her grip to match the lines she wanted to draw and set to work. After more than six months of practice, she rarely dropped her charcoal or brush anymore. The mechanics of working with her scar tissue figured out, she'd learned to paint with her mind, not with her hands, as Michelangelo had said.

Clouds thinned and stretched apart, allowing the sun to make her final caress before bending her head to the night. Windows dazzled, bricks turned a rosy gold, and steel winked from below. Years webbed at the corners of Stephen's eyes as he stood gripping the back of the chair. Sleeves rolled to his elbows, Nate stood near enough to talk to him, but not so near that he blocked Meg's view. Light gilded them both before fading into softer, velvet tones.

A firefly landed on the top of her canvas, throbbing yellow before flitting away. Soon the dusky sky blinked with tiny glowing insects. Sunset lingered, and Meg lingered with it, sketching as much as she could before calling it a day.

Her father circled around to face the canvas and smiled. "Tomorrow you'll add the colors?"

"I will," she told him. "We'll make a start of it, anyway."

He nodded. "Well, good night, then." He didn't open his arms for an embrace or offer his cheek for a daughter's kiss. But he did leave the roof of his own accord, before dark, and this was beautiful too.

Nate looped his arms around Meg's waist. After the day at work he'd described over dinner, she'd thought he was exhausted. But the fresh spark in his expression suggested otherwise. They'd been married for two months, and she was still learning to read the lights and shades in his eyes, the tilts of his lips. Every line and curve in his handsome face was a language she intended to master. But more than that, she would spend a lifetime as a student of her husband's heart and mind, and never grow weary of it.

"What do you think?" he asked. "Are you ready to go in for the night too? Or do you prefer a romantic serenade of mosquitoes as they have us for dinner?"

She laughed. "As tempting as that sounds, I think we're done here."

"Almost." He enveloped her in his arms, wrapping her in comfort and belonging while the cool of evening deepened.

Linking her fingers behind his waist, Meg rested against his chest and watched the sun set over the city she loved. One might mistake the reconstruction for ruins, for in the shadows, they looked remarkably the same. She knew better.

Nate kissed the top of her head. "It's getting dark," he whispered.

But light would come again.

Author's Note

While the Townsend family and Nate Pierce's family are fictional characters, many details in this novel are true to history.

- The fire did begin in the O'Leary barn on DeKoven Street. Other details of the fire's progression and firefighter and citizen response to it, as represented in the novel, follow what history tells us. Readers who want a detailed accounting of the Great Fire will find it in *Chicago and the Great Conflagration*, written by Elias Colbert and Everett Chamberlin in 1872, and in the impressive website GreatChicagoFire.org.
- Catherine O'Leary and her cow were first blamed for starting the fire by reporter Michael Ahern of the *Chicago Republican*, an accusation that was repeated all over the city. In 1893, Ahern finally admitted he made up the story.
- Precise figures are impossible to determine, but the estimate is that more than 300 people died in the fire. More than 17,000 buildings were destroyed, leaving 100,000 people homeless. The property damage was $192,000,000, which would be $3,692,307,692 by today's standards.

- The Chicago Fire was not the only one taking place at the time. The Peshtigo Fire swept through northeast Wisconsin on the same date (October 8, 1871), destroying 1.2 million acres and taking at least 1,200 lives, and other fires burned in Michigan at Holland, Manistee, and Port Huron.
- The newssheet Stephen picks up dated October 9, 1871, was the actual newssheet put out by the *Chicago Evening Journal*.
- The *Tribune* did run personal notices for people to be able to find each other after the fire. The examples used in the novel are taken from actual notices.
- The Board of Police and Fire Commissioners found Catherine O'Leary not guilty at the conclusion of their 1871 investigation, but public opinion was not swayed. In 1997, the Chicago City Council passed a resolution formally exonerating her—and her cow—of all guilt.
- The Sherman House hotel did exist opposite Court House Square, but Corner Books & More and Hoffman's Bakery are fictional.
- The Chicago Relief and Aid Society distributed millions of dollars' worth of donations, provided vaccinations, and provided shelter houses (referred to as shanty houses in the novel) and barracks for one thousand families in the North Division, all of which were outfitted with the items mentioned in the book. For more on how Chicago dealt with the magnitude of need, see *Smoldering City: Chicagoans and the Great Fire 1871–1874* by Karen Sawislak.
- Historical characters who really lived during that timeframe include: Fire Chief Marshal Williams; James Hildreth, who blew up some residences to create a firebreak; Joseph Medill, City Editor of the *Chicago Tribune* who was elected mayor; Bertha Honoré Palmer, philanthropist and wife of Potter Palmer; Philip Sheridan, the Civil

War general who established martial law with his troops; Thomas Grosvenor, the attorney who was shot and killed by student Theodore Treat for breaking curfew; Daniel F. Brandon, Camp Douglas photographer.

- All the anecdotes about the Brontë family are true. The Charlotte Brontë quotes come from *The Life of Charlotte Bronte* by Elizabeth Gaskell.
- Some of the interior details of the fictional Hiram Sloane's house were inspired by interior details of the Driehaus Museum, which you can visit at 40 East Erie Street in Chicago.
- Hiram Sloane's Prairie Avenue neighborhood was a real location. You can visit the Prairie Avenue Historic District in the 1800 and 1900 blocks of South Prairie Avenue.
- Camp Douglas was founded as a training center for Union troops in 1861 in the present-day Bronzeville area of Chicago and served as a permanent Confederate prison camp from 1863 to 1865. Though built for 6,000 prisoners, at its peak it held 12,000. By the end of the Civil War, 26,000 men had been imprisoned there. More than 4,000 died in the camp (17 percent of the inmates).
- Most Galvanized Yankees, Confederate prisoners of war who obtained release by enlisting with the Union army, came from camps in Illinois (Rock Island, Camp Douglas, Alton, and Camp Morton); Columbus, Ohio; and Point Lookout, Maryland. They were mustered out in November 1866.
- Stephen Townsend's memories of Andersonville include experiences that really happened there, including the conflict between the Raiders and the Regulators. On June 29 and July 1, 1864, with permission from Confederate authorities, the Regulators hunted and arrested at least seventy-five Raiders, who were then held outside the stockade. After a court-martial found many guilty, the six

most notorious Raiders were hanged. Like Camp Douglas, Andersonville held twice its intended capacity. In all, 13,000 men, 28 percent of the prison population, perished there.

- The Cook County Insane Asylum became notorious for its treatment of inmates. In fact, it wasn't until Mrs. Helen S. Shedd led a reform movement that the asylum was made to stop its wholesale drugging of the patients.
- The file that Nate Pierce read in Dr. Franklin's office contained real, historical anecdotes of veterans with soldier's heart. Readers who want more information on soldier's heart and PTSD in Civil War veterans ought to consult *Shook Over Hell: Post-Traumatic Stress, Vietnam, and the Civil War* by Eric T. Dean Jr. Stephen Townsend's symptoms and signs in the novel are based on real experiences detailed in Dean's book.
- The benefit concert is an event I invented for the story, but Turner Hall did host events like it. The song lyrics quoted were from actual songs written and performed in honor of the Great Fire.
- The French style of painting Bertha Palmer refers to in the novel would come to be known as Impressionism. In the early 1870s, the trend was only just beginning to take shape.
- The library mentioned in the epilogue is the Chicago Public Library. It was established in 1872, and opened in January 1873, largely based on an 8,000-volume donation of books from Great Britain, sent as a mark of sympathy after the fire.
- The Great Rebuilding was an amazing time of growth for Chicago, but more lives were lost during the reconstruction than in the fire itself.
- The name of this series of novels, THE WINDY CITY SAGA, comes from Chicago's nickname as the Windy

City. The origins of this moniker aren't entirely clear, but most agree it refers to the boastful "hot air" claims made by politicians and city boosters, particularly while competing with other cities to host the World's Fair in 1893.

Acknowledgments

As always, I owe a debt of gratitude to many people who have had a hand in the creation of this novel.

To my editors Dave Long and Jessica Barnes, for believing this story was worth investing in, and for helping shape it into something worth reading.

To my agent, Tim Beals of Credo Communications, for his continued support and enthusiasm.

To Kevin Doerksen, owner of Wild Onion Walks in Chicago, for giving me a personalized tour of Chicago during my research visit, for staying in touch afterward and responding to all my follow-up questions, and for reading the novel in advance with a lookout for any historical inaccuracies. (If I've made mistakes in this regard, the blame is mine alone.) *Psst*, readers! Next time you're in Chicago, look up Wild Onion Walks! Kevin is a phenomenal tour guide.

To Lesley Martin, reference librarian at the Chicago History Museum Research Center, for supplying the materials I requested both in person during my visit and through continued correspondence afterward.

To Ken Hall, professor of art at the University of Northern Iowa, for spending hours with me talking about oil painting techniques, creativity, and how a burn injury might affect an artist's psyche and methods.

To Dr. Neil McMahon, for answering my many questions about burn injuries and the recovery process.

To Dr. Dave Beach, mental health director at VetGR in Grand Rapids, Michigan, who lent his expertise working with veterans with combat trauma as I was shaping the character of Stephen Townsend and his spiritual and emotional arcs.

To all the people who prayed for this story and for me as I was writing and editing, and especially Susie Finkbeiner, whose daily encouragement bolstered my spirit.

To my husband, Rob, and children, Elsa and Ethan, for all the grace and patience you display during the multiple deadlines associated with each book.

Last and most important, thank you, Lord, for being a God who uses broken vessels, and for not being limited by that which limits us.

Dear reader, thank you for devoting your time and energy to this story. I pray that God has used it to inspire you in some way, and shine some hope into whatever fire or ashes you may be experiencing in your own life.

Let's stay in touch. Connect with me at www.jocelyngreen.com.

Discussion Questions

1. The history of the Great Fire of Chicago and the Great Rebuilding contains countless stories of human resilience. What is something you experienced that you never would have chosen, but from which you came through stronger?
2. Nate Pierce is convinced that a story that tells only one side is dangerous. When have you seen half-truths cause harm, either in your own life, someone else's, or on a larger scale with the news?
3. Even aside from owning a bookshop, the printed word plays a role in each member of the Townsend family. How did literature influence Stephen? How did it influence Sylvie's perspective? How did Meg relate to Charlotte Brontë?
4. Stephen replayed his past in his mind for years. Is there an experience in your past that still affects you today?
5. How have books influenced you and your own worldview? Are there particular titles of fiction or nonfiction that have played a prominent role?
6. In Chapter Sixteen, Meg learns a secret Sylvie kept from her regarding Hiram Sloane's will, and feels betrayed.

Are there any legitimate reasons to keep secrets from your loved ones? If so, what would those circumstances be?

7. When Meg was relearning how to draw and paint with her left hand, she compared her attempts with what she'd been able to do before she was wounded. She struggled to give herself grace during the process. When do you struggle to give yourself grace?
8. Ruth Townsend cleaned to the point of obsession during and after the war, since it was the only thing she felt she had control over. What other ways do people tend to cope when they feel life is spinning out of their control? What are some healthy methods of responding to stress?
9. In Chapter Twenty-Seven, Stephen quotes from Shakespeare, "Make not your thoughts your prison." How do you think a person can be imprisoned or limited by their own thoughts? How can one break free of that?
10. After the Great Fire of Chicago, from a distance, reconstruction might have been mistaken for ruins. When a person is reconstructing his or her own life after trauma, how might the progress of rebuilding be mistaken for something else?

Jocelyn Green inspires faith and courage as the award-winning and bestselling author of numerous fiction and nonfiction books, including *The Mark of the King*, *Wedded to War*, and *The 5 Love Languages Military Edition*, which she coauthored with bestselling author Dr. Gary Chapman. Her books have garnered starred reviews from *Booklist* and *Publishers Weekly* and have been honored with the Christy Award, the gold medal from the Military Writers Society of America, and the Golden Scroll Award from the Advanced Writers & Speakers Association. She graduated from Taylor University in Upland, Indiana, with a BA in English, concentration in writing. Jocelyn lives with her husband, Rob, and two children in Cedar Falls, Iowa. Visit her at www.jocelyngreen.com.

Sign Up for Jocelyn's Newsletter!

Keep up to date with Jocelyn's news on book releases and events by signing up for her email list at jocelyngreen.com.

More from Jocelyn Green

With a Mohawk mother and a French father in 1759 Montreal, Catherine Duval finds it easiest to remain neutral among warring sides. But when her British ex-fiancé, Samuel, is taken prisoner by her father, he claims to have information that could end the war. At last, she must choose whom to fight for. Is she willing to commit treason for the greater good?

Between Two Shores

You May Also Like . . .

All of England thinks Phillip Camden a monster for the deaths of his squadron. As Nurse Arabelle Denler watches him every day, though, she sees something far different: a hurting man desperate for mercy. But when an old acquaintance shows up and seems set on using him in a plot that has the codebreakers of Room 40 in a frenzy, new affections are put to the test.

On Wings of Devotion by Roseanna M. White
THE CODEBREAKERS #2
roseannamwhite.com

After the rival McLean clan guns down his cousin, Colman Harpe chooses peace over seeking revenge with his family. But when he hears God tell him to preach to the McLeans, he attempts to run away—and fails, leaving him sick and suffering in their territory. He soon learns that appearances can be deceiving and the face of evil doesn't look like he expected.

When Silence Sings by Sarah Loudin Thomas
sarahloudinthomas.com

Gray Delacroix has dedicated his life to building a successful global spice empire, but it has come at a cost. Tasked with gaining access to the private Delacroix plant collection, Smithsonian botanist Annabelle Larkin unwittingly steps into a web of dangerous political intrigue and will be forced to choose between her heart and her loyalty to her country.

The Spice King by Elizabeth Camden
HOPE AND GLORY #1
elizabethcamden.com

BETHANY HOUSE